DRAGONFALL

THE DRAGON SCALES TRILOGY: BOOK ONE

L. R. LAM

DAW BOOKS

NEW YORK

Jacket design and illustration by Micaela Alcaino
Interior design by Fine Design
Map by Deven Rue
DAW Book Collectors No. 1939

DAW Books
An imprint of Astra Publishing House
dawbooks.com
DAW Books and its logo are registered trademarks of Astra Publishing House

Printed in the United States of America

Library of Congress Cataloging-in-Publication Data
Names: Lam, Laura, 1988- author.
Title: Dragonfall / L.R. Lam.
Description: First edition. | New York : DAW Books, 2023. | Series: The dragon scales trilogy ; book one
Identifiers: LCCN 2023000743 (print) | LCCN 2023000744 (ebook) | ISBN 9780756418410 (hardcover) | ISBN 9780756418427 (ebook)
Subjects: LCGFT: Fantasy fiction. | Novels.
Classification: LCC PS3612.A543285 D73 2023 (print) | LCC PS3612.A543285 (ebook) | DDC 813/.6--dc23/eng/20230113
LC record available at https://lccn.loc.gov/2023000743
LC ebook record available at https://lccn.loc.gov/2023000744

First edition: May 2023
10 9 8 7 6 5 4 3 2 1

For Robin Hobb and all the other fantasy authors whose books I gobbled up. Thank you for creating worlds that felt like home. I hope this world does the same for someone else.

TABLE OF CONTENTS

PART 1: COLLISION

1. Everen: The Fall   1

2. Arcady: Do Not Fear These Bones   7

3. Everen: The New Old World   16

4. Arcady: Loc & Key   24

5. Sorin: The Merchant's Scion   29

6. Everen: A Land of Fog   35

7. Arcady: The Silver Setting   44

8. Everen: The Dragon's Heart   53

9. Arcady: The Last Golden   62

10. Everen: The Kiss of a Knife   70

PART 2: CONNECTION

11. Arcady: The Stranger   77

12. Everen: The Prince & the Thief   84

13. Arcady: The Feast of Storms   94

14. Sorin: The Siren   100

15. Everen: Lockpick   115

16. Arcady: The Red Coat   123

17. Everen: Larkin & Wren   130

18. Arcady: The Rules of the Game   140

19. Everen: The Stories We Tell Ourselves   149

20. Cassia: The Silver Pool   160

PART 3: COHESION

21. Arcady: Cinders   169

22. Everen: The Cote   178

23. Arcady: Partitions   190

24. Sorin: The Captain   199

25. Arcady: The Question   206

26. Sorin: The Wolf   211

27. Everen: The House of Ikari Dwell   219

28. Arcady: Widow Girazin's   225

29. Sorin: The Auction   235

30. Everen: The Tower   238

PART 4: CONVICTION

31. Arcady: Blood, Feather, Bone   245

32. Everen: Entangled   254

33. Cassia: Hold Fast   259

34. Sorin: Beliefs   261

35. *Arcady: Lay Down Your Weapons*   266

36. *Everen: Half-Remembered Dreams*   278

37. *Arcady: The Barrow Hill*   283

38. *Cassia: A Veiled Storm*   294

39. *Everen: Golden Bonds*   296

40. *Sorin: Cold Metal*   298

41. *Arcady: The Monster*   301

42. *Sorin: Gods in Flame*   305

43. *Everen: Starfire*   308

44. *Arcady: Promises Broken*   313

45. *Arcady: Promises Kept*   318

46. *Sorin: Utterances*   325

47. *Magnes: Relic of the Past*   328

48. *Everen: Left in the Dark*   331

◇◇◇◇◇◇◇◇◇◇

Herein lies first-hand accounts from the dragon Everen Emberclaw and the human Arcady Dalca during the events of the Dragon Scales Prophecies. I have re-created additional perspectives via scrying and telepathy. In some instances, I have asked for added input from those still living or willing. Braiding a narrative is not so different from setting down a vision sent by starfire and fate. Many do not understand how strange it can be to dip a claw into someone's life for a spell. To feel as they feel, to dream as they dream.

There is a trick to emerging from it all, scrysilver falling from fangs and the taste of lightning on the tongue. It is difficult to pour oneself back into one's own bones. To wonder if, each time, we might come back changed. All Seers learn this, to their sorrow.

I digress.

Pray humor me for taking the liberty of filling in some gaps, but I wished to create a complete and thorough account of this tumultuous period. The official reports are so very dry. A copy of these volumes is stored herewith in the archives for as long as they remain standing. Let us hope it will be a long time yet before fate reaches the tail and begins again at the head.

—THE TWELFTH ARCHIVIST OF VERE CELENE

PART 1: COLLISION

Pray to the five gods:

Kalsh, the blue dragon of the sea, who shifts luck, fortune, and form like waves.

Piater, the strong god, metallic gray, who moves that which is heavy as stone.

Zama, god of clarity, indigo-black, with power over wind, storm, and the magic best left forgotten.

Jari, the green god of new growth and healing, who knits the world back together.

Aura, the dragon red as blood and full of might, who burns it down again.

1. EVEREN: THE FALL

I will share how I fell. But first, I must tell you what it is like to fly. Let me try, though it is still another thing I should have shared before it was too late. Most humans will never experience flight. Though I pity the creatures for many things, it is perhaps that most of all.

Imagine running with all the speed your four legs can muster. Launch from the top of a cliff with a last push of talons into solid earth. There is nothing but the deep dip in the belly. The angling of your head toward gray-green water. The rocks grow close, impossibly fast. Wind whistles along your scales, ruffling the feathers at your wing and crest.

There is a trick to drawing the eddies of your magic tight, holding it close as you sense the thermals as sure as the currents of the waters below. You will know the perfect time to spread your wings with a—

Snap.

Your chest muscles strain, but have faith the thermal will catch you. With a stroke of your wings, you can draw yourself, steady and sure, up into the sky. From above, any world seems so much smaller and larger at the same time.

I remember other dragons circling the bone-pale cliffs, beginning their hunts. Their wings catching the fading glow of the sun. Purple, blue, green, gray. Some as red as my own scales. They all hoped to come back with full claws.

(As I write this, I can imagine flying back to the pryde of Vere Celene to share my cuts with my mother and sister before claiming my own portion. Fire and stars, but I did not know how much I would miss it. Gliding over those white cliffs, the scent of sea salt and sulfur on the air and in my lungs. I can almost taste the fatty, oily meat, the blubber against my tongue. Forgive me; I have been so hungry for so long.)

On another cusp of evening, I would have joined them, flying over acidic seas in the hopes of a successful hunt. If I had plucked another thread of fate, perhaps that was what I did.

But that night, I did not seek anything made of blood and sinew. I searched for something far more elusive.

I hunted a prophecy.

I was the last male dragon, born to know the past, the future, the gossamer of fate that spread in all directions like a dew-caught spiderweb. Prophesied to be a great Seer who would save our kind from ruination. My whole life, the weight of that expectation had been so heavy, it was a wonder I could fly at all.

And yet, the prophecies passed without even a tugging of the web. Each scrying pool showed me only my reflection. I was a failure, and I could not bear it.

I was meant to be more than this.

I worked my wings harder, passing over the edge of the island's peninsula. A few centuries ago, an ancestor had used precious magic to carve the earth into the shape of a dragon—the effort killed her.

She was magnificent, the Lady of Vere Celene. Her earthen muzzle snarled at the setting sun, her sharp teeth blunted by centuries of harsh weather. Her eyes were the entrances to the inner caves. The gentle swell of her skull led to shoulders topped with scorched grass. Her wings were tucked tight against her body, the tips tall enough to provide protection from the worst of the sun. The main bathing pool rested between her shoulder blades, and dragons of flesh and bone would sprawl in the shade after bathing and scrubbing their scales with sand.

We are not meant to see the writings about ourselves, not since the last male dragon was driven mad by them. Prophecies are kept locked away. Only Miligrist, the old Seer and Archivist, has access to all. My sister helped her, and would one day be Archivist, Seer, and Queen.

So, earlier that evening, I had finally stolen the key and searched for secrets. It had been too tempting, knowing my whole life might be written within.

Prophecies can take many forms. Some are careful rhymes, their somber rhythm lending them an extra air of portent. Others are only strange fragments, cryptic even to the Seer who wrote them down. Still more are as ephemeral as the dreams and visions that birthed them. It is nowhere near an exact art. And yet, dragons still strive to untwist fate.

One of the first writings I found was almost delightfully straightforward and meant to come to pass that very night. Surely fate—that cruel, fickle mistress—had passed it right to me, like fat prey on an open plain.

And so I made the best and worst decision of my life. I had to know if it was another broken promise from the future.

I chanted the stolen prophecy in my mind as my wings brought me closer to the horizon.

On the Night of Locked Tombs,
when the last male dragon has come of age,
the Lady of Vere Celene points the way.
A Veiled storm and a golden chime
will guide him to the fading light of home.

I glanced behind me.

Red wings caught the flames of sunset.

—*Everen*, my sister called, her flying desperate. She must have followed as soon as she'd realized what I'd done.

—*Leave me be, Cassia.*

I flew faster, my eyes desperately searching the dimming horizon. But there was no Veiled storm, no golden chime, whatever that meant. Only the ever-present gray of volcanic smoke.

—*Everen!* Cassia called again. *You cannot do this.*

—*If the prophecy is dead as the others, then you have nothing to fear*, I challenged.

—*I have everything to fear! You do not know what you risk.*

—*Do you?*

—*I know better than to meddle in this.*

—*Perhaps fate should have told you to keep a better eye on your key, then, sister mine.* I was giddy with the potential spread before me.

She roared her indignation. I ignored her.

There.

I felt it before I saw it. A whisper of magic in the air, like the sharp scent of rain just before it breaks. A rushing hiss of the wind. A Veiled storm.

Rips in the Veil between worlds were common enough, but most were only small enough for magic and visions to sneak through, guided by the pools. This one was large.

Large enough for a dragon.

I chanced another glance behind me. My sister's scales glinted as she glided onto a thermal, bringing her closer. Did no part of her want to see how this might pass?

—*Your way has not worked, Cassia, so let us try mine.* My shoulders burned with every movement of my wings.

—*Everen,* she pleaded. *We might lose you.*

—*And you would be the only one to mourn.*

—*That is not true.*

I had been the golden son. The hope of all dragons. But the opposite of hope is despair. For with every year that passed, this world became hotter, and dragons grew hungrier. I was meant to see how to save us. Every time they looked at me, they saw their own demise reflected. It all confined, like skin that would not shed.

Cassia keened in frustration, circling wide, wary of the storm's pull. She would never be brave enough, fool enough, to try to follow me through.

—*I love you, Cassia,* I said. *But if I am to be a master of fate, then I will take it.*

And with that, I dove.

The rip in the Veil grew closer. A slice of darkest, starless night.

Something within me caught—a thorn ripping at tender flesh.

I fell toward the schism with all the grace of a wounded bird. My body shifted and changed, wings flapping uselessly as magic rippled along my hide. The wind whipped over my melting flesh. My body shrank, curling into itself, my bones shortening, my muscles weakening. Red, scaled hide smoothed to a pebbled near-white. My muzzle pulled back, teeth dulled but for my smaller fangs, talons shifted to blunted digits.

I had just enough thought left to deeply, deeply regret what I had done before the pain chased all away in agonizing waves. I opened my mouth to roar, but instead I screamed. A high, pitiful sound.

The darkness cupped me in its palm, clenching into a fist, taking my old world with it.

◇◇◇◇◇◇◇◇◇

I was in a bruised, liminal space. Lightning moved in impossible directions, too bright against the deep purple and blue. Wind roared. Raindrops hung suspended, as if frozen in time.

For a moment, I worried I had died and was waiting for my mother and sister to sing my soul onto whatever came next.

(Would they, still? After what I have done?)

The keening of the tempest grew louder. Time broke. I could have been there for a span of seconds or a handful of days. Somewhere, in the black, I felt more than saw something move, sinuous and impossibly large. It paid me no mind, as if I were nothing but another raindrop. I had never felt so small, so insignificant. I almost swore I heard whispers, and far off, a deeper sound, like a dragon's roar. Panicked, I tried to pull myself back from the darkness's wake, to resist the current. The edges of myself began to blur.

In the darkness, I sensed a pinprick of gold. A ray of sun through storm clouds. A distorted echo of a scream turned into a high-pitched ringing, and the gold drifted away, like a feather on the wind. I needed it. That I knew. If I wanted to live, I needed to make my way to that little speck of gold.

A Veiled storm and a golden chime will guide him to the fading light of home.

With all my effort, I forced myself away from the pull. When I broke free, I swam or flew through the storm. Did I even have a body in that place? I imagined one, and it was so. My wings pulsed, displacing the floating drops of water. The wind had fallen. The ringing rose again to some high, haunting cry. The tiniest part of my soul reached out and answered—

◇◇◇◇◇◇◇◇◇

And I fell, hard, onto stone.

I gasped through new crests of pain, gaping like a fish out of water. For a moment, I could only try to fill my lungs.

Soon, the cold settled into my marrow. Vere Celene was always hot, the air thick and humid. Even in the depths of the caves, the coolness was never chilled.

I forced myself upright. I was unbalanced. With dawning horror, I realized I was still in my diminished preterit form. One of my wings had been wrenched by the fall. My left shoulder throbbed. My weakened body shivered.

It took time to settle into a preterit. We took this shape when we did work too delicate for talons. Many saw it as an abomination, a distorted echo of what we hated most. Several in Vere Celene had never transformed at all.

I'd helped my sister and Miligrist enough in the parts of the archives I was allowed in that some deep corner of my brain couldn't help but catalogue details. My nostrils flared with the scents of stagnant water and stale air, ancient stone, and back notes of decay. To my right was a faint pulsing of gold. I twisted my head and was hit, full force, with newer smells. The bitterness of a recently spent flame, the stink of magic, and something undeniably alive.

My eyes adjusted to the near darkness, taking in the sprawled hump on stone. I crawled forward on all fours, not yet trusting myself on two. My lips drew back from barely pointed teeth, my hiss echoing through the darkness.

I knew what I would see. Some ancestral part of me recognized the scent. The creatures that had hollowed us out, nearly destroyed us, and banished us to a dying world. A flame of hatred sparked bright in my chest, my hands clenching to fists.

It was a human. The first I had ever seen in the flesh. I reached out, one fingertip hovering above its cheek. When I think back to that moment, it, too, seems suspended in time.

For that human was, of course, you. And this is our story, Arcady.

2. ARCADY: DO NOT FEAR THESE BONES

There were only three times in my life I had prayed to the five gods with every part of my being. The first two times, no one listened. On the Night of Locked Tombs, I should have known the dragon gods would never give one cold shit for the likes of me.

The full moon rose above the City of Vatra, bright as a coin, as I belatedly honored the last promise I'd made my maire.

I wove through silent streets, clad in my nicked priest robes, all embroidered with bronze scales. The Citadel, the seat of the Lochian government and the home to the University of Vatra, loomed above me. I'd seen this confection of pointy spires every day these last nine years, but I'd never dared climb the hill. Not with the life sentence I had hanging round my neck.

I took the steep path, carved through the rocks, rather than the gentle slope for the carts and litters. Winter-night jasmine bloomed, and I crushed the petals as I passed with shaking fingers. My paire had liked that scent.

I wouldn't be going into the Citadel. I was going behind, beneath, to steal something that shouldn't exist.

Hours earlier, a gaggle of students would have gone into these catacombs for the Night of Locked Tombs. A rite of passage, to strike fear into any little arsewipes tempted to rebel.

By that age, I'd already lost pretty much everything I'd known not once but twice. I'd been twelve when I'd slunk back to Vatra, broken and alone. And now I was about to be confronted with all those memories I'd buried deep.

To distract myself, I imagined the students jostling each other as they formed an untidy queue to the openings of the caves, wrangled by a harried priest.

"D'you think one of them will pop out of a tomb?" one might ask in a scandalized whisper.

"Don't be daft," the friend would reply. "They all died hundreds of years ago."

"The Plaguebringer didn't," the third might whisper, and they would hush, aflutter with nerves.

I reached the gatehouse, pulling my dragon mask over my face. The horns, black and polished ebony and edged with gilt, curled over my ears. The golden scales glittered at my cheeks.

The nodding-off acolyte on duty startled awake as I entered.

"Wings keep you," I said, trying for the educated tones of a priest and holding up my hand, fingers splayed wide to the five gods. It only shook a little. "I have come to pray, to seek clarity during the Spirit Moon."

The acolyte blinked sleep from Their eyes. They were probably a few years younger than me and a few years older than the students who had just traipsed through these caves. Sixteen, maybe. An easy job for an acolyte, as long as They weren't afraid of the dark and the bones.

"Dragons welcome you," They said, passing me a torch. Anyone who visited the caves had to leave their seal at the door, but they didn't ask it of priests (or supposed priests). While the Citadel had posted guards just after the Plaguebringer had been interred, they had grown lax in the years since. There was magical security, of course, but it had been lightened so the children could touch the tops of the tombs and be suitably scared.

No one had ever stolen from the Locked Tombs. There was nothing in there but the hated dead. Who would be foolhardy enough to risk such wrath from the gods?

Only yours truly.

I nodded my thanks, grateful They didn't seem to wonder why a priest would carry a small rucksack into the caves. The dark maw of the opening gaped before me. Nothing for it.

I'm not afraid. There's nothing to fear but old bones and nightmares.

I stepped inside.

The air grew colder with every echoing step. The light of my lone torch could never hope to reach the ceiling. Above me came the chirping and rustling of thousands of bat wings. The air reeked of bat shit and damp.

I reached the first cluster of tombs. Many of them were carved from the large stalagmites growing out of the cavern floor in simple, oblong coffins, the flat tops wet with dripping water.

The priest would have made Their charges pause as They told the story of each of the pariahs of Locmyria. I ran a hand along the carved letters on the nearest lid. All these villains, their deeds deemed so evil that their bodies couldn't be burned. After all, their tainted smoke could never be allowed to rise toward the firmament.

The younger members of the Marricks—that band of thieves I'd once run with—had come here when they were twelve, since they'd grown up in Vatra. Brev, Aby, Driscoll, Joana, and Lightfinger said that at one point all the torches were doused, to show the children what pitch black was truly like. Even the darkest places usually had a sliver of moonlight through the curtains or shutters, or the faint flame of a lamp in the next room. But in pitch black, closing or opening your eyes is one and the same. I felt a pang somewhere behind my ribs at the thought of Lightfinger in particular. Their wide grin, the little gap between their front teeth.

I ran my hand along another coffin lid, reading the inscriptions by torchlight. Here lay Laen the Ignited, the last Monarch of Locmyria. The Mad Monarch who starved Their subjects and sent so many off to an endless war with Jask to the south. Some say the Ignited demanded a sacrifice a day, bathing in young blood to keep Themselves immortal. They lived to nearly three hundred. Even the richest nobles who could afford to go to healers every week usually conked out at one hundred and fifty. Turned out Laen the Ignited proved mortal enough when the axe sliced through Their neck twenty-seven years ago.

With the Monarch's death came the Schism. Locmyria cleaved right down the middle like a pig corpse in the abattoir. Royalist sympathizers to the east claimed two chancelleries and called them Myria, with Laen's cousin propped up on the throne. To the west, Loc installed a Consul of three Chancellors. They melted down monarch coins and replaced them with suls: one side still had the same old dragon in flight, but the other had the three prongs of the council instead of Laen the Ignited's profile.

Already, a mini stalagmite had formed on Laen's tomb. The limestone was rich enough with nutrients that they grew faster here than in many other caves. One day, in the not-too-distant future, it would be tall enough to kiss the stalactite above.

I edged forward along the path, tentative. Some buried down in these caves had simply played a bad hand against power and lost.

The newest tomb was deep in the cave. The limestone was still pale, the inscriptions crisp and unoiled by curious fingertips. Few would be brave enough to touch this coffin. There were no bats this far in, and all was silent.

My heart hammered in my chest. The hand that held the torch shook. Fear and fury were fist-fighting, and I hated that fear was better at the uppercuts.

Mouth dry, I placed the torch in the small holder next to the tomb. I banished the simpler spells of stay-backs, cantrips, and linger-nots, feeling the answering pulse in the stone around my neck. I placed my palms on the lid of the tomb of Barrow Eremia.

The Plaguebringer.

The most hated person in Loc and the larger world of the Lumet.

The Plaguebringer had once been the Consul's most trusted advisor. A genius who had invented new spells and ways of doing magic. Yet they said the Plaguebringer's experimental magic became so corrupted that it rotted him from the inside. That his evil spread, jumping from one seal to the next, killing a fifth of the population. That's the story, in any case. The first Strike of the plague hit eleven years back, when I was nine, and then the second hit only three years later. We mourned the fallen, but the threat of a third wave hung over us like an executioner's axe. Maybe it would fall. Maybe it would not. We were tense about it, just the same.

I cast another couple of spells, muttering the words in the Old Tongue, but there were no obvious locks on the lid itself.

I steadied my breath and, grunting, pushed hard. The heavy lid barely budged. I went to wipe the nervous sweat from my forehead with the back of my hand but forgot the mask in the way. I ripped it from my head and let it clatter to the ground. Rummaging in my rucksack, I took out my iron crowbar.

Levering it against the lid, I braced my feet against the ground. On the next try, my groan was loud in the dark. Again, no luck.

Lightning strike me. I'd have to use more magic. Blue Kalsh was my chosen god, so shapeshifting was what came easiest. But my paire had been blessed by Piater, and he had taught me the basics. I was well out of practice. For years, I'd done as little magic as possible except for my shapeshifting.

The small, cylindrical amulet around my neck grew hotter still, flaring silver instead of blue as I pushed again with both body and magic. There was a hiss as the seal of the tomb broke, along with the faint ripple of magic and a gut-churning stench.

I stumbled back, heaving, drawing the robe up over my nose. I leaned against the cave wall, not yet ready to face what was inside. The foul smell made my eyes water. I was half-afraid I'd hear the clatter of bones, the howl of something unholy, but beyond my panting and the hiss of the torch, there was only the silence of the dead.

My heartbeat eventually slowed, magic settling back into my skin. I reached into another pocket of my rucksack and took out a sweetsphere—the honey and seed confections kept on hand by all magic users for emergencies. Cramming it into my mouth, I chewed greedily, holding my nose against the smell of the cave and trying not to gag.

When the honey had steadied me, I forced my gaze into the depths of the tomb, illuminated by the flickering torch.

The Plaguebringer was now nothing more than wet bones and sodden scraps of cloth. I swallowed back more bile. The former advisor had been tortured, exposed overnight in front of the Citadel for all to see, and then buried alive. No one had heard last words. No one had said the rites. The Traitor of the Lumet had been all alone.

I blinked quickly and moved the torch closer, searching for what I needed.

The seal and its metal setting had fallen through the rib cage to rest against the puddle of muck covering the spine.

I couldn't help it: I whimpered. At least there was no one to hear.

"I do not fear these bones," I said aloud, over and over, as if I could speak it into truth as I put on my gloves. "I do not fear these bones."

I reached into the stone coffin and yelped when my hand brushed against a rib. My fingers scrabbled through the muck and clasped the seal, dragging it out.

With a spare bit of cloth, I wiped it clean as I could with the aid of the flask of alcohol I'd brought, still struggling with my rising gorge. I took a long pull from the flask before tucking it away and bringing my prize closer to the torch's light.

The metal seal setting was stamped with seashells. I followed a familiar whorl with my fingertip. I popped the carved seal out and held it in my palm.

These bits of stone help funnel and enhance magic. Before the Strike, and even after the Schism, only the noble drakines or wealthy merchants had them. Yet after the plague burned through the country like kindling, Loc needed magic to help rebuild. For the last eleven years, a priest whispered the blessing to every new citizen of Loc and gave them a seal carved with their name and the stars of their birth. Most were blessed within three days, unless they lived somewhere well rural.

No one could give away or steal another's amulet; most magic could be traced back to its owner. Even if most people didn't have much power, a seal was still an indelible, unshakable piece of identity. They were pretty enough, I supposed, for dragonstone looked like opalescent quartz. No one save the Order of the Dragons knew where the stone came from, or how to create the seals and tie them to their owners.

Like everyone else, I'd worn my own seal every day since I was a babe, but unlike most everyone else, I hated it. I was a pariah by association, for while I wore it, I had no chance at a proper life.

This was the secret that no one knew, not even the priesthood or the Consul, or they'd *never* have left it down here: the Plaguebringer's seal was different. My maire hadn't dared tell me until she was dying, blood bubbling along her lips, her breath hot against my cheek.

"Even death can't stop its song," she had said, her teeth stained pink. "You have to take it. He would want you to."

I couldn't help looking into the coffin again, though I knew it'd be better for my future sleep if I didn't.

The flames lit the grinning skull, throwing it into sharp relief. It was easy enough to imagine the flesh that had once laid over those bones. Older, with smile lines around the eyes, looking at me as he crouched down and held out a hand to a wyvern.

"Come on," the one who would be named Plaguebringer had said on that long-ago sunny afternoon, dangling a bit of gristly meat my paire had saved from dinner. We had been in the courtyard of our old, grand house just below the Citadel, with its warm yellow stone and trellises of green plants. The fountain in the center had sent out a fine mist to protect us from the worst of the summer heat.

The little wyvern had considered the outstretched palm and then hissed, darting out and biting a finger, drawing tiny beads of red blood. I'd raised my arm to swat at the winged lizard, but a hand had caught my wrist.

"Don't be mad at the creature for biting any more than you'd be mad at a river for flowing or a tree for losing its leaves come autumn," he had said. "It's the way of these things." By the end of that last, warm summer in the capital when I was six years old, the wyvern had perched on my shoulder as I did my chores.

We had fled that house not long after, when the neighbors set it aflame, hoping we were still inside.

I could *never* believe that a person that kind could release such an evil upon the world. I refused to. He was not wicked. Never had been. I'd do whatever it took to prove it.

I swore I could almost feel my grandsire, my taie, there in the cave. Another presence just behind the veil of the living and the dead.

"Taie?" I asked.

The flame flickered and I sucked in a breath. But there was nothing more.

"I'll spend this life well," I told his bones. "I'll get the truth out. I promise. The world will remember you as Barrow Eremia once again." Not the Traitor of the Lumet. Not the Plaguebringer.

That ember of hatred I'd nursed for those who had destroyed my life had often been the only thing keeping me going these past few years. The Consul had used my taie as a scapegoat. My parents had thought so, too. He was an easy person to pin all the world's ills on. He'd been a villein, a peasant who had dared rise through the ranks too far, too fast. But it was only in the last year I'd realized there might be a chance to help find out what truly happened. To actually set things to rights.

Even after the pieces fell into place, I still almost hadn't come. Too afraid my maire had been wrong and there was no chance to take a new life after all. Sometimes, it was better to leave your hopes as dreams, because then they could never disappoint.

Most of all, I'd delayed because I didn't want to face what my taie had become.

"I do not fear these bones," I whispered thickly.

With another spark of magic, I dragged the lid of the coffin, sealing him back inside with a sob I was grateful no one could hear. I wished I had enough power to set the bones aflame. To let the smoke curl through the cave, eventually finding its way out to the night, to the sky and the heavens.

I took my old seal from around my neck. Thanks to the carvings on this little bit of stone, I hadn't been able to go to school, or apply for an apprenticeship or traditional job. For any path on the straight and narrow, I'd have to roll my seal in ink along vellum or parchment or clay, signing my contract with magic. If anyone chanced a look at my records, I would be revealed as the supposedly dead grandchild of Barrow Eremia. A ghost who should not exist.

I'd been thieving in Vatra for nearly a decade. But a year ago, after my life yet again went pear-shaped, I'd struck out on my own. Searching for closure, I'd headed back up to the mountains and broken into the locked-up cabin where once upon a time I'd hidden with my family. People thought the building was cursed. No one had broken in. After a systematic search, I had found my maire's old notebook. Dusty, stained, but whole.

I'd read it over and over the past six months, until the cheap binding had nearly given way. She'd done her research well. The instructions for a spell that must have built on an initial bit of magic from my taie. The new engravings I must imagine belonged to someone around my age who had died in the first Strike. A child from a noble but unremarkable line that had been all but wiped out by the plague. Even had the same first name, since it was common enough. But this Arcady was noble enough to present themselves at court without inviting too much gossip. It was all there. Knowledge from my taie, refined by my maire.

I stood in front of the Plaguebringer's tomb, my old life in one hand and my chance of a new one in the other. I whispered the words my maire had written, trying not to trip over the unfamiliar pronunciation of the Old Tongue.

> *Kjetim-lei ak ar-dźakain,*
> *lei-turei, iév-turo.*
> *Ar-réal vanok vaugain*
> *śajak val jain reno.*
> *Dźo eje loj el-dźakain*
> *fanas arfan lo.*

I wasn't sure if I was pronouncing them correctly, nor had any idea what they meant. All I could do was close my eyes and try. Usually, spells were just the odd word in the Old Tongue—only masters up at the university would know full phrases. But my taie had been brilliant. He'd been able to see what others couldn't. In magic, and in life. It was what made him so dangerous to the Consul.

I felt the magic leaving my old seal, traveling along my arm, across my chest, and down the other, power sizzling through my veins.

I imagined the carvings and spoke my new name: "Arcady Dalca." I said the stars of the night of a dead person's birth. With this, I would become a drakine who was afraid of nothing and no one. A damn sight braver than Arcady Eremia.

The magic of my new seal flared gold as the sun, throwing the cave into stark relief. Above me, an unseen wind roared. I raised my arm to my head, squinting. Somehow, the world itself *opened*.

I screamed at the storm raging above me, harsh and fierce and angry. My hair lashed against my forehead. Not even the person in the world most blessed by Zama, the weather god, would be able to create such a thing. The raging wind hurt my ears, smarted my watering eyes. I was drawn to the swirling dark, stark against the gold. Part of me wanted to cower, but another wished to reach up and touch it. Raindrops fell on my face. Some were ice, others almost burned. I should have been afraid, and yet, I wasn't. There was something familiar about it. Almost comforting. Like that moment as you drift off, caught between the real world and the dream.

I swayed, my magic nearly spent. As the spell burned away the last of who I used to be, another scream tore its way from my throat.

As I slumped to the ground, my vision darkening, I swore I saw the shadows of wings.

3. EVEREN: THE NEW OLD WORLD

I pressed myself into a crevice, my naked back flush against stone. I had tucked my wings away with effort.

I was beginning to suspect I was not dead. Or that the prophecy had not been, either. That did not mean I had the faintest idea what to do next. My mind spun, struggling to understand what had happened.

The creature was still slumped over, a heap of fabric and dark hair. I had been taught, in no uncertain terms, that a human was an enemy. Something dangerous.

Eventually, you roused yourself, wincing. You seemed young, from what I could tell of humans. More than a hatchling, newly adult. A similar maturity to me, though it had taken me a while longer to reach the same stage.

The thing in your hand still pulsed blue, but the gold had vanished. You put it and another that did not glow on a chain about your neck. They hung against your sternum. The blue faded. Your hands shook.

My gaze sharpened. Hundreds of years ago, humans created seals to house our magic, stealing our power and banishing us into the world of Vere Celene. In a cruel twist of fate, the centuries passed, and humans, with their shorter lives, had forgotten what they had done. The ignorant little fools worshipped dragons as gods, with no idea how much their "gods" despised them.

I had seen sketches of humans, but never been confronted with the real specimen. Your skin was a pale golden brown, black hair tied back in a short plait. It had come half undone, curls loose about your face.

You were vulnerable as you patted about blindly for a fallen torch, scattering a few loose pebbles. The sound of your breathing was loud. I caught your scent.

It would have been easy to kill you, especially if I had still been in my dragon form. A simple swipe of talons. A snap of teeth. Soft flesh would part, blood welling red.

You found the torch and lit it, throwing you into further relief. Eyes wide, pupils blown, blue irises nearly lost in the black. Your lips pulled back from your blunt teeth. You panted like an injured animal caught in a trap. When your head turned in my direction, I thought you saw me. That we were locked, eye to eye.

A chime sounded, somewhere far away. My mind suffused with gold. There was the same yearning to fall into it, to let go.

And the hunger bloomed.

I pressed my palms against the stone. My stomach hollowed against my spine. I wanted to eat. I wanted to devour.

Your arms crossed over your stomach as you doubled in pain.

With a deep chill, I knew: it was not *my* hunger.

Still, I craved. I wanted to dart across the distance between us, to sink my fangs into your neck, even as the thought repelled me. Something about you was *not prey*.

You moaned, and I nearly did the same. All of you hungered. All thoughts yearned for satiation. You would eat anything if it was set before you. Anything.

I could smell food in the small bag next to you. Even as I wanted the nourishment for myself, I mentally nudged you toward it, instinctively, not sure what I was doing.

Your hand snatched out. You ripped open the sack and ate. And ate. And ate.

Most of it did not smell familiar, and most of it was not meat. Yet it still tempted me. My own hunger flared, but I waited. I watched. You crunched, chewed, swallowed. Crunched, chewed, swallowed. Ripped some type of dried meat with your teeth. Bit down into something soft and sweet, the juice running over your lips, down your chin. I wanted it all.

When the food was gone, you slumped against the carved stone edifice behind you. You stared blankly in my direction again. I was used to draconic body language and could not read your expression, but I sensed something determined about the set of your chin.

"Hello?" you called in Locmyrian. "Is anyone there?" It was strange to hear it rather than read it in the archives, and it took a moment for me to piece together the words.

I said nothing.

"Taie?" I did not recognize the term.

You sniffed, rubbing at your eyes with the back of your hand.

Eventually, you rose and gathered your things. Holding the torch aloft, you gave a last look at the stone formation before taking the path back to the entrance of the cave.

I did not know what to do.

You were responsible for whatever had just happened, as much as I was. Yet you did not seem to know what you had done. Still, you had to be powerful beyond imagining to break through the very fabric of the world. Powerful enough to spawn a prophecy.

You had left something behind. I picked up a carved bit of wood and gold, with two holes for the eyes. Curved horns. The priests wore them, I thought, but I did not know the word in Locmyrian. I put it on, and, strangely, it helped me feel more like myself.

I followed the path, silently as I dared. You had already left the cave. I smelled bat guano and musk. At the mouth of the cave, I caught the scent of a second human, but it too had fled.

Outside, the night sky was clear. I gazed up, stunned by the sheer number of stars despite the wisps of clouds. The constellations I knew were often hidden by volcanic smoke. This was a different sky.

I crept closer to the edge of the rock ledge in front of the cave. A human city spread below me, speckled with lights. The ocean caressed the line of the shore, stretching off to the horizon that pinked with dawn. How much time had I lost within the storm?

The city itself grew from the surrounding forest like the pale, yellow mushrooms that flourished in our caves. Thin bridges twined across some of the higher buildings. Even in darkness, I could tell everything was so green. The very air smelled of it, damp and free of smoke and sulfur. It was a world alive.

The shock of what had happened was slowly fading. Once I had seen the prophecy, I had rashly leapt into the sky without another thought. There had been no time to second guess, no time to hesitate. Beneath those foreign stars, I started to shake.

Dragons had been trying to pierce the Veil for centuries. No one, as far as we knew, had ever managed. I twisted, staring up at the Citadel lit from within. I was in Vatra, the capital of Loc in the world of the Lumet. The human world.

Our true home.

And here I was, now with proof that the predictions about me had not been overwritten before I had even hatched. By this act, perhaps I had forced the thread of fate back onto its true path. I was heady with the thought. Maybe I would be the one to save dragonkind after all.

My head whipped to the left. In my awe, I had lost you. I followed your scent until I found a discarded piece of fabric hidden beneath a bush. Yours. The garment was not so different from the robes we would wear in our preterit forms, though the weave was finer. I pulled it on, my weaker body warming.

I closed my eyes, questing, but I sensed nothing. Maybe the faintest of hums. You had slipped from my grasp. Fear slithered its way down my spine. Had you known what you had done after all? Did you, little human, have your own plan?

I needed the space and quiet to think. To cast aside this too-small form and take my true shape. On the outskirts of the sprawl of buildings, I spied a dark swath of forest.

I picked my way down the path toward the city, still unsteady on two legs. All I saw, I committed to memory. The layout of the gates and battlements. The configuration of the buildings. The stench of stagnant, refuse-filled water in containers dotted along the streets—in case of fire was my guess. Several types of four-legged creatures roamed the streets, rummaging for food. Dawn began its pale, rosy path, the sky shifting every few minutes. Here orange, there yellow, finally transforming to a pale blue. The stars winked out.

Near the bottom of the hill, I spied another human. I pulled up my hood. This one was tall, and likely female, judging by the mammary glands (strange things). It had a basket full of some sort of food that smelled delicious.

The human said something to me, but it had spoken too quickly. I had studied various human tongues so I could help Cassia record scrying visions or read old manuscripts, but I was not fully fluent in Locmyrian, especially spoken.

Yet when the human grew close enough to see beneath my hood, it gave a shout and dropped its basket, making some sort of supplication and babbling away.

The human splayed its hand across its chest and looked up at the sky. Ah. Yes. It was praying. They seemed fond of that sort of thing.

I knew what it must have seen: pale, pebbled skin, pointed ears, eyes that were far too green, the pupils vertical slits. Combined with the dragon robes and the carved horns rising from my skull . . . I fought down something like laughter. I must have indeed looked divine.

"Food?" I asked inelegantly, pointing at the basket. That gave the human a glimpse of my fangs, which did not help matters.

The human bowed its head, mouth slack as it pushed the basket closer, gazing up at me. Expectant. Reverent.

"Secret," I said, struggling with the words, my accent unlike anything the human would have heard before. I pointed at the sky, to underscore my point.

The human nodded emphatically.

Word of a dragon god would probably be around the entire city by midmorning. Humans loved to gossip even more than they liked to lie. They were often one and the same.

"Blessings," I managed, reaching down to touch the top of its head, and the human burst into tears.

I left it crying in the dirt.

◇◇◇◇◇◇◇◇◇

Once out of sight, I pulled the hood of the robe up to keep my face in shadow. Hopefully no other human would fall to its knees, insensate at the sight of someone so holy walking among them. I snorted.

Though we had been spying on the human world for centuries, it was piecemeal. There were so many things we did not know. Or things we did not understand. I was one, they were many. Like ants on a corpse, they could overwhelm me if they chose.

I made quick work of the food in the basket. It was my first time eating something other than meat, greens, tubers, or nuts.

The outside of the food was firmer, and darker than the pale innards. It was soft, half air, almost sweet. I was sad when it was gone.

—*Bread*, I could almost hear my sister's exasperated voice in my head. *It is only the most common human foodstuff there is, and you cannot remember its name, featherheart?*

I grimaced, guilt roiling in my stomach. Did Cassia know I had made it through? Was she even now hunched over the scrying pool, trying to trace my magical signature and find me among all these humans and their stolen power? Or did she think me dead?

I continued my way through the city. Vatra made me uneasy. It was clearly meant for far more humans. Some of the buildings had broken glass in their windows. Vines choked the walls, and a few humans hung out clothing to dry like strange, empty hides. The streets were quiet.

Most humans ignored me, but others watched me as I passed, sizing me up as though I were potential prey. I kept clenching my hands. I had no idea how well I could fight in my preterit form; I had never needed to try.

I reached the outer rim of the city. Acrid smoke rose from the fires, along with the scents of charred meat, the distant stench of offal, blood, and too many animals in too-close quarters. A large, thick wall of stone rose before me, flanked by two humans clad in interlocking scales of metal, holding long, pointed sticks. *Guards*, my mind belatedly filled in the gaps in Locmyrian. *Armor. Spears.*

I nodded at them, and they inclined their heads at me, a supposed priest. No threat.

As soon as I reached the trees of the forest, I exhaled, the tension within me easing. I walked until my preterit feet, soft and new, began to bleed. The trees were tall and straight, many of them with a white bark, their branches bare, the tips of the branches fading from brown to a near-purple. Others were not dissimilar to ones we had, but they were lusher than any I had ever seen. I stopped at a stream to drink cold, clear water. I walked more. My hips and knees ached. In Vere Celene, I had only shifted into preterit to go down into the archives. I did not have the knack of moving so far on two legs. I sensed a few pockets of humans long before I saw them. They were easy enough to avoid.

Eventually, I found a clearing with a still pond and a shallow cave sheltered by a rocky overhang.

I took off my robe and put it in the basket, resting the piece of wood on top. A mask. I had finally remembered the word. I held my arms wide, closing my eyes, willing my preterit form to fall away and let myself become a dragon once more.

My wings unfurled easily enough, coming back into being. They were constructed like bat wings, though with feathers along the top. The early morning light dappled through the membranes. The one I had fallen on was sore. I could barely extend it.

Nothing else.

I ran my hands over my chest and stomach, confused. I concentrated, trying to grasp my magic. I almost caught it, and then it slithered away, locked away somewhere I could not access.

Horror thrummed through me.

Up until that point, I had been confused, afraid, overwhelmed, but I had not panicked since landing in that cave. Not even when I had lost your scent.

But realizing I was trapped in my small, soft, useless preterit form? That. That tore down all my defenses.

I tried to transform until I was almost dizzy.

I fell to my knees at the side of the pond. Taking a deep breath, I leaned over the still water.

—*Cassia?* I called, softly. First in my mind, and then aloud. I hoped to see her, even if her red crest would be raised in frustration, head tilted to the side. I felt untethered without her.

Yet there was only my preterit face in the warped reflection of the pond. Hair, more feathered in texture than a human's, copper red. As a dragon or preterit, I was not cold-blooded, but there was still something reptilian about me in this form. My nostrils flared.

I used another spark of my magic to experiment with shifting the texture of my skin and rounding my pupils and the tips of my ears. It was slow work, but eventually, though my face was still angular and my eyes wide-set, I looked human enough. I stared at that false version of my face before letting it bleed away.

I tucked myself under the rocky overhang, wrapping myself back in the robe that still smelled faintly of you. The prophecy had mentioned a golden chime, and there, in the woods, I began to suspect what it meant.

Once, nearly all dragons had been bonded to a human, though plenty of humans had never bonded to a dragon. We had been a partnership, one we thought was based on mutual respect, or even love. We had learned the cost of that trust. We had loved humans to our ruin.

A bond was an ancient magic, and much of the knowledge had been lost to us. Had that been what had drawn me across? If I was correct, did it mean I was now shackled to you like some common beast? I snarled.

No human and dragon had been bonded for nearly eight hundred years, as far as we knew. Not since we had been betrayed and banished. For centuries, our magic had been depleted, though in my lifetime it had recovered. We were not what we once were, but we were still fearsome.

As the sun kept rising in the sky, I knew: all I needed to do was find you again. Fate would tell me what to do next.

4. ARCADY: LOC & KEY

On the way home, I kept touching the two lives hanging around my neck, side by side.

It'd felt awful to leave my taie behind, even if I was selfishly grateful to escape the cave of bones. Was the storm some sort of vision from too much magic use? There'd been no sign of it when I woke up, but my skin had crawled and I'd felt watched.

Out under the sky, I wanted to dance down the streets. I'd bloody done it. All I needed to present myself at court and university was a barrel full of coins and the manner of a member of the noble families—as a drakine.

Once I had enough, I could be living at the top of that hill in the heart of Lochian power, sharing the halls with the mighty. I would come face to face with those who had buried my taie down there in the dark, and once I had proof, I'd make them pay. Somewhere on that hill, there would be records of the sham trial. Someone would have messed up. I'd find it, and then I'd live the life my parents had always wanted for me. My maire had talked about her years at university with a far-eyed wistfulness. My paire had always wished he could have gone—he'd had the magic for it, but not the coin. He'd instead been a lifelong independent scholar, as best he could with limited access to texts. My parents had both loved the pursuit of knowledge. I wanted access to a life that didn't revolve around thieving.

I was tired of having to steal every little crumb.

I took the familiar twists and turns to the seedier end of the merchant district by the docks on the south side of the city. The markets were already setting up shop in the grand square in front of the harbor. Fishers had brought in their catches, and the mongers laid them out on melting, pink-stained ice. Others set up wheels of pungent cheeses or hung drying cuts of meat.

I spent a coin to buy a cinnamon bun from a bakery I passed, my hurried feast in the cave already wearing off. This was the most magic I'd used in months, maybe years, and my reserves were nearly empty. My magic felt different, too, now funneled through my taie's seal, like it had changed . . . flavor. I couldn't think of another way to explain it. I chewed on what had happened, cinnamon spice on my tongue, my fingers growing sticky with sugar syrup.

Two blocks from home, I passed a Struck beggar holding out their hands for coins. I averted my gaze from their black-veined palms. They twisted toward me. So many had died during the plague, but those who rose from their sickbeds and survived were never the same, and they were forever marked by the experience.

The beggar watched me as I passed, their eyes dark beneath the white tufts of their eyebrows. Bruised black marks radiated from their eyes and fell down their cheeks like tears. Beggars were not rare in Vatra, but a Struck one was. The marked mostly lived outside of the city and towns, clustering together in hamlets that had been abandoned during the first wave of the Strike.

The first rule of magic was that it required energy. And if you did not give it enough energy, in the form of food or internal reserves, then it would find a way to sate it. With food. Or flesh. Or blood. This was a risk to everyone, but many believed the Struck had a higher chance of turning Starveling. It was the worst fate imaginable.

Beneath those rags, the beggar's seal would be nothing but inert marble, any chance of magic confiscated. It was a punishment. A Struck could not sign documentation with their seal. Could not own property. They were largely locked out of society. I'd always felt a kinship with them, in more ways than one. I tossed the beggar a copper, refusing to meet their gaze as they thanked me.

Many of the cramped storefronts were still boarded up even years after the second Strike, their owners long vanished or dead. No family or apprentices left to carry on the trade. Knowledge and skill were more casualties of the Strikes.

I stopped at the Loc & Key, the swinging, fading sign proclaiming it the best locksmith in Vatra. With a quick glance around me to make sure the street was empty and that no one lurked at the windows above, I swung up one of the boards and unlocked the door.

Old sheets were strewn haphazardly on the floorboards, to hide the trail through the dust. I'd hung up black curtains over the windows so no one would peer inside. But there was a gap, and a few stubborn streaks of early morning light landed on the counters, hitting the hundreds of forgotten keys and padlocks displayed on the back wall. There was an ancient fireplace, empty display cabinets. Several carved wooden pillars. Dust motes danced in the air, and like every damn time I entered the shop, I sneezed.

Ducking below the counter, I opened the trapdoor and slithered down through the cellar and up into the back room.

I threw my rucksack on my coveted chaise longue. Getting that through the streets and the back window unobserved had been a feat in itself. But when I'd seen it at the Last Golden—the shop run by the fence for my stolen goods, Kelwyn—I'd forced him sell to it to me at a discount. I ran my fingers through my hair and let the tension bleed out of me.

The lock shop was the first place I'd truly let myself think of as home in a long time. Though, ultimately, this would be as temporary as all the other places I'd lived. Everything I touched had a way of turning to shit.

After working with the Marricks had imploded, I'd decided it was easier to work on my own and rely only on myself. That way I couldn't be disappointed or heartbroken. That way I wouldn't end up dead from pissing someone off a little too much.

I'd chosen Loc & Key because one wall in the back had rows and rows of miniature safes. People had hidden all their little treasures with someone they could trust. Most had been emptied by their owners at the start of the Strike, but when I'd finally cracked the main safe and opened each and every one, I'd found a jeweled necklace or a small stack of copper or silver suls in a few of them. I'd added them all to my collection.

I'd kept a cut of my findings when I'd stolen with the Marricks, but it was only over the last year I'd started amassing proper coin. I checked my safe, as I did every time I came home. There it was. A tidy pile of gold, silver, and copper, and even one sole wraithwright coin, made of coveted green-blue star metal and worth fifty gold. Most of the poor in this city would never even come close to one of these. I touched it for luck in my usual ritual, placed my old seal and my maire's notebook next to the rest of my treasure, and locked it all away.

Yet despite stealing more than I ever had before, I still only had a few months' tuition. Room and board would cost just as much again, plus the costs of robes, tunics, hose, good boots, slippers. Fighting leathers, a practice sword, a bow and arrows, hunting green and russet, hammered bronze headbands, and a ring or two for flash. Face paints, schoolbooks, and enough to be able to cover sundry expenses like drinking at taverns with classmates.

I thought I'd have more by now, but life was sarding expensive. I'd had to do enough to the Loc & Key to make it livable. The Marricks no longer covered my food, and the materials for con jobs could be pricy.

I was running out of time. A student had to apply to university by age twenty-two. It was an arbitrary rule, a holdover from ushering even the nobles into the military during wars with Jask. While Arcady Dalca was a year younger than me, that still didn't leave me long. At this rate, I wouldn't make it. I needed at least a year of total costs—ideally two. Even if I continued stealing at university, I'd have to slow down—less time, and more chance of being caught. The university rarely offered scholarships, and I was afraid to apply in case they looked too closely at my background.

Going through the priesthood might have been an option if I was younger, but by the time I was back in Vatra, I was too old. Most joined under the age of six. Now and again people turned to the cloth later, but with it too came more scrutiny. I was also quite sure I'd be terrible at pretending to be pious, and I would look absolutely awful bald. Becoming a drakine was my best option.

I needed a frankly *silly* amount of coin.

I paced the short length of my lock shop. It was cluttered and gloriously, wonderfully mine. At least as long as no one discovered I was squatting.

I had my beautiful green brocade chaise longue. The battered desk in the corner had already been here when I claimed this space. The magnifying glass I used to check over my pilfered jewels lay on top of an untidy stack of parchment. My bed was a nest of pillows and blankets, tucked away in another corner behind a wooden dressing screen so the dawn light wouldn't wake me. Near the fireplace were my copper tub and a giant mirror hidden by a second screen. I'd hung a few scarves for some color along with the paintings from my brief but intense botany obsession. Blue crystals on string winked from the iron-barred window, casting ever-shifting shapes along the floorboards and threadbare rug during the day. I had candle stubs strewn about, for when I studied at night, and of course, every space I could spare, I had books.

Books I'd stolen from classrooms after hours. Books I'd stolen from drakine libraries, plucking one or two tomes from a shelf the same way I'd take a jewel or two from a safe, before slipping my way out of a cracked window and up onto the roof slates. Secondhand, crumbling books I'd bought from marketplaces, and every now and again, the new volumes I'd splurge on from the bookstores on Binder Street. Some I'd stolen before I left the Marricks, but once I'd settled into the lock shop, I'd taken as many as I could get my hands on. There wasn't much rhyme or reason to where I stored them, but I knew where everything was. They were on subjects I thought I'd need at university, things I'd missed because I'd never been to a traditional school, or simply topics that intrigued me.

For if there was one thing I'd learned in my life, it was that knowledge was power. Knowledge was escape. Books were thresholds, and you could cross them and leave yourself behind, or use what you found inside to transform into someone else. Each book I read was another brick in constructing Arcady Dalca.

I had been coming up with a plan to amass plenty of coin, looking at it from all angles like a puzzle box in my quieter moments. But no matter which slant, it all came back to the same thing: it was something I couldn't do alone. I sighed, setting it aside to wrangle with another day.

I was too tired to risk more magic, and I'd never been fire-touched by Aura, so I lit the hearth with a flint and steel. The kettle heated over the flames until it whistled, and I made myself a cup of spiced black tea. It steamed beside me as I opened the book I'd been reading on the last Lochian-Jaskian skirmish before the first Strike. I scribbled some notes on cheap parchment, but I kept staring into the flames, rolling the seal I'd stolen from my grandparent's bones between my fingertips.

What was that storm? Why had it appeared, and why had it disappeared? Was this little piece of dragonstone around my neck now truly mine? At least, no matter what, I now had a little piece of my taie. Everything else had been lost in the flames.

I had no answers and no way of finding them. I gave up on reading. Sleep was something I normally had to chase, and when I caught the slippery snake, I could rarely keep it. But that day I slowly, surely slid down the chaise longue until I was horizontal, my tea growing cold beside me.

As I often did, I dreamed of dragons.

5. SORIN: THE MERCHANT'S SCION

The house smelled of money: sweet perfume and incense, orange soap, and wood polish.

Sorin climbed the ivy trellises to one of the top-floor windows, banishing the wards with whispered spells. She held her breath, ears straining for any noise. The grand manor was silent save for the ticking of the clock in the hall. Vines created green curtains, but inside was another small forest—plants in solid brass pots, green tendrils twining around lamp chains. A prayer altar was dark at the end of the hallway. No fresh ash.

She exhaled shakily. She'd had to sneak past near a dozen guards and find the window with the least number of wards. Yet her job was only beginning.

The lush carpets dampened her footsteps as she crept into the bedroom to the left. The room was as lavish as the rest of the house. Nothing but furniture made from the finest woods from the Emerald Jungle. A wardrobe that was probably filled with nothing but velvets, furs, and fine fabrics. Her footsteps were muffled by the thick carpet. Karys lay beneath a silk canopy, Their mouth open as They sighed in Their sleep, short hair dark against the pale pillow. They had a small scar by Their eye—perhaps a result of one too many brawls after a night in Their cups. They shifted, settling deeper into the bed. She stared down at the sleeping form of her target: the merchant Tintari Fall's youngest heir. Though her lip curled with contempt, it was easiest to think of a target in the honorific pronoun. More distance. That and, perhaps, deep down, Sorin thought everyone was above her, no matter Their station in society.

The Fall family was one of the richest merchants in the city, but They still were not one of the original thirty drakine families. From her research, she knew her target Karys Fall had grown up wealthy as sin, but without the responsibility of Their older sibling. They'd made countless mistakes that Their paire erased with purses of coin. But after Their latest mistake, no amount of coin would save Them.

Sorin listened again, but there was only the sound of Karys's breathing.

This was the moment. This, right here, was when she'd find out if she had what it took to kill.

She swallowed and drew out an unmarked glass bottle from an inner pocket. Her hands were steady, despite the fast fluttering of her heartbeat at her throat. Sorin tipped a few drops of poison into the glass of water at Karys's bedside. She had her instructions. Magnes had told her widow's sleep was a useful tool when subtlety was required. The death had to look natural.

She'd already delayed too long. Her fingers crept to her seal and she let loose a spark of green power, drawing the saliva from Karys's mouth until Their body became horribly, desperately parched. She was Jari-touched. Her magic was meant for healing, but she only used it to hurt.

There. It was done. She should leave. Slip out of this house like a shadow and make her way up the rest of the hill to the Citadel. But this was what she'd been working for, training for, for years. This was her proving herself worthy. She would not be a coward. She would bear witness. And so she crouched in the dark corner of the room, dragonstone clenched in her fist.

The silence broke when Karys gasped through a dry, cracked mouth and reached for the water at Their bedside like a traveler in the middle of the Blackstone Desert finding an oasis. All too soon, the glass was empty, and They had unwittingly drunk Their death.

Sorin blinked rapidly, fingernails digging into her damp palms.

Within a few heartbeats, Karys's muscles stiffened. They tried to call for help with a swollen tongue. Their hands opened and closed, opened and closed, grasping at air.

Sorin forced herself to draw closer to the bed. Karys's eyes snapped to hers, the whites already bloodshot. Sorin knew what They saw: a muscular figure in dark, form-fitting clothes. Black eyes, hair shaved short as a priest's. Skin as warm golden brown as plenty of Lochians, but the sandy blond hue to her hair and freckles across her cheeks marked her as part-Jaskian. Blasphemy lurking in her own blood for all to see. She forced herself to focus on what this dying person had done. Why They couldn't live to see the dawn.

Sorin leaned over Them, saying nothing.

Karys's seal flared a deep, dark purple, but Their weather magic was weak. Sorin could only catch the barest scent of petrichor in the room. The fog outside was no thicker than before, but faint rain lashed the panes of glass.

"Pray," Sorin signed in Trade. "The Dragons may yet take you under Their wing."

Karys made a horrible choking noise, Their breath rattling. Their lips moved. Sorin drifted closer.

"I don't . . . want to die," Karys managed. "Please—I'll do—"

Sorin leaned back, watching Karys's eyes bulge and then go blank. Their seal returned to neutral opalescence.

As the life fled from Karys's eyes, she reached for a sense of peace. She imagined reporting to Magnes. Telling Him she had done all He'd asked and more. He would place His hand upon her head and bless her, telling her the Gods would be pleased. She let that imagined warmth assuage any emptiness, any guilt.

She took Karys's seal from the setting between Their breasts with leather-clad fingers. She bowed her head, whispering the prayers.

What happened next was not up to her. Karys's body would burn on the pyre, and the gods would decide whether They would ascend.

Sorin clicked the seal back into place and arranged the bedclothes, then rinsed out the empty glass in the sink and refilled it, setting it by the bed. Whoever examined the body would likely determine Karys Fall had died of an apoplexy in Their sleep.

One last time, Sorin stared down at what she had done. She smelled the orange oil. Listened to the ticking of the clock in the hallway, the drizzling of the subsiding rain as the rest of the household slumbered, unaware of what They would wake up to find.

When the last of the rain had sputtered out, Sorin tiptoed back along the carpeted floor, climbing out the window and down the ivy.

The sky was lightening with the promised dawn. She would have to be quick.

As she hurried down the path toward the city, Sorin's wyvern circled overhead, silent as a shadow. She lifted her arm and Jaculus dove with a soft cry, landing on her shoulder.

"Hello, little protector," Sorin said as the wyvern rubbed his scaly head against her cheek. She reached into a pocket and gave him a piece of jerky, and he hummed as he ate. Stomach contented, he slithered along her shoulders, curling his neck around hers to rest his head in the hollow of her throat,

draping his black-green feathered wings on either side of her right collarbone. A living necklace. Clever as a crow, and fiercely protective. She'd found
him as a hatchling on an ignored outcropping of the Citadel, the only survi-
vor in a nest full of broken shells and dried albumen. Weak, starving, but still
strong enough to hiss at her. She'd brought him back to her room in secret
and raised him until he was old enough to join the Rookery. Magnes had
almost forbidden her to keep him—to the outside world, Sorin needed to
present herself as nothing special. An invisible acolyte no one noticed or
suspected could ever be so important to the Order of the Dragons.

Eventually, Magnes had relented. Perhaps He realized that Sorin needed
something to cherish, to love. A wyvern, at least, could spill no secrets. She
wasn't the only acolyte to have her own, though most of the Rookery was
filled with creatures that belonged to court drakines, or university students,
or the ones the Falconer trained for the races or sent as messengers.

Sorin ghosted through the empty streets of Vatra, the cityscape blurred
gray with fog. The sky was just lightening as she scaled the outer wall of the
city, evading the guards with ease.

She reached the outer edges of the woods, rummaging in her bag, putting on her plain black mask and pulling up her hood.

A drakine was waiting, shifting foot to foot, nervous. They were short
and had a craven chin. Even this early, They'd taken care to oil and curl
Their hair. The scent offended her. Sar Saunder Bane was from one of the
oldest families, though Their fortunes had not fared well the last score of
years.

The drakine blanched when They saw her, reaching for the knife at
Their belt. Jaculus settled on a nearby branch and watched it all with black
eyes.

Sorin shook her head once. A warning.

The drakine swallowed, taking her in.

"Karys?" the drakine whispered.

Another shake of the head.

The drakine sobbed, once, as if They couldn't keep it back. A hand still
gripped the hilt of the knife.

Sorin held out her hand, palm up.

"Please," Saunder begged. "I had no choice."

She only flicked her fingers twice. Beckoning. She drew her other hand from her pocket, and the trident knife flashed in the morning light. Three blades, to represent the past, the present, and the future that the Order took along with a life. Designed in a way to do the most damage with the least amount of blood. Unlike Karys, she was allowed to give this drakine a choice.

Sorin had no need to speak. Sar Saunder Bane knew exactly what she wanted, and exactly what would happen if They did not obey.

The drakine's hand shook as They fumbled with Their pocket. With a gulp, They placed the relic on her open palm. A tip of a horn, polished smooth, a sapphire attached to the broken bottom. Hundreds of years old, a piece of a literal god, that should never leave Loc's shores. Sorin felt the power emanating from it, like a whisper of a seal.

Sorin's hand closed into a fist, and she spirited it into a pocket. She let the trident knife fall, but it dangled from the tie around her wrist.

"You know what happens if you tell a soul," Sorin signed in Trade. "Do not squander this mercy."

It was only Their noble blood that saved Them from the same fate as Karys Fall. They were not the first drakine to attempt to sell a dragon relic. They would not be the last. So far, anyone who had such a warning from the Order of the Dragons as this did not try again.

Sar Saunder Bane nodded, eyes wide, watery, and unblinking. Without being told twice, They fled, their robes flapping behind Them.

There, in the darkness of the forest, Sorin reached again for what she thought she would feel after her first successful mission. A glimmer of peace. A sense of righteousness.

Nothing.

But Magnes would be pleased. She took the relic out, turning it this way and that. She bent over it in prayer. Her first major test, and she had not failed Him.

Jaculus fluttered and perched on her shoulder again. She stroked the smooth scales along his neck, retracing her steps home to the upper crevices of the cliff just below the Citadel. She paused, resting her forehead against the cool stone, before pressing her palm against the entrance to the secret door and darting inside.

No one saw Sorin re-enter the priest's quarters or heard her open the door to her cell. Jaculus hopped to his perch and preened before tucking his head under his wing. She sat on her bed and waited until morning, her palms resting over her seal. Head bowed. Eyes closed.

Any doubt was nothing more than her own failure. She prayed and she refused to weep.

6. EVEREN: A LAND OF FOG

While the first night in this new world had been clear, the next day dawned gray and ephemeral as a dream. Frost blanched the edge of the pond, the tips of the evergreen trees. By midmorning, much of the fog burned away, leaving a film of mist and a frigid damp only tolerable with my stolen robe and scant echoes of magic.

I stayed in the forest.

I knew cold and hunger would soon drive me back to the city with its smells, its press of humans and their stolen magic. I needed to find you, to make sense of what had happened, but I did not know where to begin. The forest was strange, but at least wild enough to feel something like home.

When the sun was higher, I peered into the still pond, searching for Cassia. Even my mother or the old Seer, Miligrist, would have been a welcome sight. No matter how long I stared, the ice-rimmed surface only showed my preterit form and the pale clouds above.

I punched the water, but all it did was leave me cold and wet, my knuckles scraped by stone.

Perhaps my sisters and the others could not reach through the Veil. Or perhaps I had been abandoned and this was my punishment. All their careful machinations and plans and I had gone and burned them to ash.

That prophecy had seemed a flagrant call to arms. Last night, I had been so certain that this had put me on the right path. But were the decisions I made helping or hurting? Was I, as ever, too proud to admit my faults?

One of my wings was still painful from my crash to the cave floor, so I kept them tucked out of existence. They would heal with time, but meanwhile I could not fly. I had lost my scales and most of my fire. I had lost myself.

That first day, I grew more used to this preterit body. Until walking no longer seemed such a foreign way to move. Until I could run, dodging the roots of the undergrowth without tripping, weaving through the trees with ease. Some were nothing but sticks, others still thick with dark green needles.

Dead ferns furled at their bases, brown and dew-dropped. Damp mulch squelched underfoot. I practiced until I would be able to fight if I had to. At least a preterit form was still stronger and faster than a human's.

By evening, the fog rolled in again, thick enough I could barely see two wing-lengths in front of me. A few nocturnal creatures rustled, but otherwise all was still. The heavy silence lulled me into fractured dreams.

I was on a hard bed of silver, like a scrying pool turned solid. My cheek was against the cold metal. I tried to twist, but I was tied down with glowing ropes of gold. I struggled, but they only grew tighter, cutting into my flesh. Above me, the frozen storm between worlds raged. Somewhere, I heard the roars and chitters of unseen creatures. My bones were so cold I worried they'd shatter, though the skin beneath the bonds burned. Eventually, I raised my head enough to see another flat, shallow bowl of silver. I could just make out a figure, curled on one side. Dark hair obscured the face, but I knew it was you. I screamed and the wind snatched it from my throat. The storm clouds grew thicker, hiding you from view.

I awoke, reaching after the details, but they blew away like petals on the wind. A vision, or merely a dream? Formless dread still clung to me.

That morning, I learned to hunt.

I set my sights on gray-brown animals with long ears that looked big and fat enough to be worth a meal. I caught the first with little more than blind luck—the creature was already injured—and made quick work of it. The meat was stringy, with less fat than I had hoped. I cooked it on a fire, for my preterit form did not appreciate raw food. When I did drift off, it was the same dream again. Silver beneath me and gold around my throat. A bound human just out of reach. Urgency pulsed through me.

The next morning, I caught another animal by following the scent and throwing a stone to flush it out and snatch it. Another near thing. I skinned the animal and charred it on the open flame. I closed my eyes and the storm flashed behind my lids as I slept. The sense that I had to find you only grew stronger. I awoke, gasping.

On the third day, I had delayed enough. I bathed in the pool, and the water was so frigid I had to spend another spark of my diminished magic to warm me. I shapeshifted my features to as close to human as I could, grateful that it did not take too much effort to maintain. The robe was grubby, but I shrugged it on and made my way back to the city of my enemies.

Dream or fate, I finally heeded its call.

◇◇◇◇◇◇◇◇◇

The morning haze dampened the sounds of Vatra. The guards watched those streaming through the city gates, but did not bother a priest.

I closed my eyes, reaching for that golden light. The link was not severed, I sensed that much, but the labyrinth of the city was too large, too sprawling. It was like trying to track a singular leaf blowing on a wind in a gale.

The larger paths between buildings were called streets, and the smaller ones that sprouted like the ribs of a fish were alleys or wynds. In Vere Celene, we followed the natural curves of the land, but humans preferred to raze all to the ground and build again. The river through the city had been diverted, shored up with square stones so it ran straight, as if to prove even water itself could be tamed. The current flowed blue-brown and sluggish.

Humans called to each other, announcing their wares or trying to lure customers into their shops. Young children ran wild through the streets, many barefoot and dirt-stained. A few waved at me as they passed, asking for blessings. I raised my hand in their direction, which seemed to please them. They ran off, leaving only the sound of their laughter behind.

A flutter of wings caught my attention, and my mouth fell open at the sight of small flying lizards the size of birds of prey. Someone bumped into me and swore, but I paid it no mind. Wyverns. They had died out in Vere Celene long ago. But here—here they had thrived. The sounds of their calls and the sight of them perching on the eaves of buildings reminded me of my home in miniature.

I swallowed and carried on, squinting at the signs of various shops. I knew a chandlery was for little wax lights, a spicemonger contained the ground aromatic leaves and seeds humans added to their food for taste. An apothecary had to do with healing. I wandered too close to the smithies, and the clang of metal hammered against metal hurt my ears. I shuffled away and eventually paused in front of a bakery, my mouth watering.

The human behind the door looked me up and down. This one was older, with gray hair on its face and the lower half of its head.

"Wandering priest?" it called, poking its head from the shop.

I nodded, cautiously.

The human disappeared and came back a moment later with a few pieces of bread and a round piece of copper. It gave them to me, somewhat begrudgingly.

"My thanks," I said, trying to soften my accent. Speaking aloud was a challenge. Dragons often spoke mind to mind, even in preterit form. The human showed its teeth, which I had to remind myself was *not* a sign of aggression, and I made myself return the gesture before shuffling from the shop.

I tried to savor the food. The bread had a flavor that tickled along my tongue, the white studded with something dark purple and chewy.

Bells gonged at regular intervals to tell the time. Why humans could not simply look at the sky, I did not know. We dragons used bells only for music.

Over the course of the morning, a few others came up and gave me more of the little copper rounds. Coins. Clearly a common practice for wandering priests. I knew currency could be exchanged for goods, but I had no true metric for their value.

There is some measure of truth to the notion that dragons hoard treasure. We are drawn to beautiful things; however, we are communal with basic possessions and amenities. Even as the seas emptied, we did our best to ensure that no one in Vere Celene went too hungry. Humans were the ones prone to hoarding.

My accidental disguise had proven apt, but I worried about the attention. My accent was distinctive. How long before I acted decidedly un-priestlike, and people began to suspect I was not what I claimed to be? Or I came across a true priest who recognized me for the fraud I was?

I stole some clothing hanging on a line between two buildings, and I ducked into an alley to change. It took me a time to figure out what bit of my body went where, but eventually I was covered. The fabric strained at my shoulders and the clothing on my legs seemed shorter than on other humans. My feet were still bare, but I found a pair of shoes left on the threshold of a door. They pinched.

In my new disguise, fewer people gave me lingering looks, and I enjoyed the relative anonymity. The golden thread in my mind would hum, but quiet as soon as I reached for it. Yet it told me you were still in the city. The anxiety grew, roiling in my gut, but for now, I needed a way to gain more of those copper coins so I could purchase food. I considered more stealing, but work seemed a safer option.

I headed to the water, figuring a foreigner would be less remarkable there. Ships creaked, bobbing in the sea harbor, like a subtly shifting forest. So this was how humans crossed oceans, trusting wood to hold together through storms and high waves.

The stench was appalling: seaweed festering in the sun, rotten fish, or spoiled food. Human sweat. The sharp, volcanic scent of tar and pitch.

Bodies moved about with purpose, loading and unloading wares from the bellies of the ships. I watched for a time and approached a group that seemed to have fewer hands than the rest.

"Looking for work," I said to the human in charge. It gave me a cursory gaze from head to foot. I was too thin for a preterit, but still muscled for a human.

"We're always short a few hands," it grunted. "Five coppers day rate."

That was easier than I expected, but I supposed even a few years after the humans' plague, workers were in short supply. I nodded, having no idea if that was fair, but set to the tasks. The others spoke little except to order me about. I fought the urge to curl my lips and bare my teeth. Taking commands from humans. I swallowed back bile and worked without complaint.

We unloaded crates of a sharp-smelling yellow fruit. As the day grew warmer, some of the workers took off their shirts. Their skin ranged from about as pale as mine to a dark, deep brown. The ones with mammary glands seemed to bind or support them with fabric, but the ones without did not. They had vestigial nipples, which I found amusing. While even in preterit our physiology was overall not dissimilar to humans', I dutifully brushed a pale human with the back of my hand so I would be able to re-create these details later, along with the knotted scar all humans had where the umbilical cord had been cut at birth.

It was strange, as one raised among only females, to find myself among a roughly dimorphic society. What did it mean to be male in this land? To not be the only one? What was masculine, or feminine? They did not act notably different to my eyes. Gender was a language I had not learned to speak.

Though it was warm enough to sweat, I kept my shirt on, knowing my lack of a seal would brand me foreigner even more than my accent. The laborers spoke among themselves, calling out jests or teasing another for working slowly. We finished unloading the yellow fruit and started on orange ones. When the leader told us to take a break, we each plucked fruit from a pile. I imitated the others, tearing away the peel and eating the sweet, sharp flesh within. I took a swig of water from another human's jug, with thanks.

As the afternoon lengthened, my muscles screamed with the effort and repetitive motion, but I almost enjoyed it. My only task was moving a crate or box from the dark insides of a ship to the docks, where the merchants carted it away, and then doing it all over again. The sweat drove out all thoughts and worries.

At one point, I paused in my work. The gold rang louder, my mind thrumming. My skin prickled, like I was being watched.

You were nearby.

My neck craned as I took in passing faces. I saw no flash of dark hair, that sharp chin I remembered from the cave, or the blazing dark-blue eyes. Still. You might be wearing a false face, but you were here. I focused on a cluster of passing humans. A flash of yellow hair. There? I could not be sure.

The glow began to fade. One of the workers clipped me across the back of the head and told me to get back to work. I hesitated, tense, ready to run after you. But I can be honest here, as you will never read this: I was afraid.

And so, bending my back for another box of fruit, I gave myself excuses. I needed to learn more about this world. I did not know if you were planning to kill me first. I had to be ready.

When the sun kissed the horizon, the ship's belly was empty. My new clothes were damp from exertion. One of the other workers slung an arm around my shoulders and patted me on the back, which I took as a sign of camaraderie. The leader gave me my five coppers and asked if I would return the next day. I nodded.

I had eaten nothing but bread and fruit, and I swayed with hunger. Immediately, I spent one of my coins at a stall that was about to close. I clutched a clay bowl of some type of once-warm stew and a small loaf of hard bread layered with something sharp and tangy. It came with a mug of beer, which tasted awful. Dragons drank no alcohol, and I understood why. It was clearly low-grade poison.

After scarfing the food, I searched the city, trying to keep my mind open to the hum of gold. I tried not to think of my dream, how the bond had choked as the storm buffeted me. Perhaps the glow grew brighter, or perhaps it was only my imagination. After a few hours, I gave up, berating myself for not chasing after you when I had the chance. What would Cassia have said?

Defeated, I headed back to the forest. Still, I felt a glow of triumph. For a full day, I had passed as human. It was exhausting.

In the clearing, I lit a fire for warmth and washed the worst of the sweat from my body and my new clothing, drying them with a spark of magic and putting them back on.

The pond kept drawing my eye. I knelt by the edge and leaned forward to the dark, smooth surface.

"Cassia," I said aloud, and then in my mind. —*Cassia.*

The wind rustled through the air. Somewhere, a night bird called.

I stayed there, calling my sister's name, as the moon rose higher and lightened the night mist to silver. I imagined the Veil, tiny pinpricks opening like reverse stars. Dark against gray. I envisaged the upturned head of the Lady of Vere Celene, and the caves she held deep within her. Down in the depths were the pools of molten scrysilver warmed by the center of the world. Perhaps, even now, my sister was bent over the smooth surface. Searching for me as I reached for her. I pictured her draconic face. The shape of her head, the way her crest half-rose when she was concentrating. The little clicks she made in the back of her long throat when she was interested in something. The lashing of her tail when she was frustrated. All the little details that made her my sister. My nest mate. The only other hatchling in our clutch that had broken through her shell.

—*Everen.* A whisper in my mind.

I opened my eyes, and my sister stared back at me.

As dragons and preterit, we looked largely alike, save she was smaller and her crest brighter, closer to crimson than copper. Her face was narrower, but her eyes were just as green. I drank in the sight of her.

—*Everen,* came her voice, faint through the Veil, distorted as though underwater. *I found you. You survived.* Her eyes brightened to emerald.

I resisted the urge to dip my fingers through the water, as if I could reach her through the surface. —*What has happened since I left?*

—*Near chaos,* she admitted.

—*Oh, does it turn out they care for the last male dragon after all? I asked. I suppose that is sweet.*

—*They've always cared for you.*

I gave a strange, human noise of derision. —*They cared what I represented. What is the verdict? Do they think I have saved or doomed us?*

Cassia tossed her head. —*Miligrist is going through the writings. With Mother.*

I shivered at the thought of our mother let loose within the archives.

I knew what they feared. Ammil, the former last male dragon, had been driven mad by constant visions. It was why they had taken such a cautious approach with me. So that I, too, would not be taunted by the future and burn my own bones to nothing to escape them, taking much of the library with me. Hundreds of years later, we were still reeling from the damage and picking through the burned fragments left behind. Miligrist, the old Dragon Seer, rarely saw anything new these days, and my visions had not materialized. Cassia could only see the present, not the past or future.

I supposed I could not blame the Queen of Vere Celene for being cautious. The unspoken hung over every interaction with my mother: she kept herself from loving me too much, so that she would not hesitate to destroy me if she thought I was dangerous enough.

Her eyes sharpened. —*You must open the Veil by the Feast of Flowers.*

I scrambled to remember that human holy day. That was the mid-spring festival, where they had a celebration to Jari, the green dragon. Two passes of the human moon from now, give or take.

—*Why?* I asked.

—*It is another night, like the Night of Locked Tombs, when the barrier to the human world grows thinner.*

I hesitated. —*I–I cannot. I am largely without my magic and trapped in my preterit form.* The admission shamed me.

After a day of parsing human faces, Cassia's draconic features were harder to read. Once, I would have sworn I knew her better than myself. Since she had delved further into the archives and worked more closely with Miligrist, she had turned colder, calculating. I had to remember that she would be the one to rule Vere Celene one day. The first Dragon Seer Queen. I would have to answer to her.

—*Have you realized why?* she asked instead, without surprise.

—*Cassia,* I said, dread tingling through my hands. *What do you know?*

She said nothing, waiting for me to admit what she must have already read in those dark caves.

—*What drew me through* . . . I hesitated, then forged ahead. *I have bonded with a human.* .

My sister's mouth opened, revealing curved fangs. She made no sound, but her eyes were knowing.

—*Did you intend this to happen?* I demanded.

—*I tried to stop you, if you recall, brother mine. But you have set us on this path, and now you must follow it. Do you yet dream of the storm?*

There was a ringing in my ears. My fingertips dug into the damp mud at the edge of the pond. —*Yes. There are golden threads tied around me like bonds. I am on a bed of silver, like a mirror. I am in the storm with someone else.*

—*The one you bonded to.* My sister was serene, the very image of a Seer. A shiver ran down my spine. When I was younger, I thought Miligrist knew everything. That each and every one of my sins was written so plainly, she would catch me in all of them. Yet, with so many potential futures, there were few ways for Miligrist and Cassia to know which were most likely to come to pass. It was a relief and a terror to realize they were often in the dark as well. To them, I had been nothing but a shooting star: the promise of change, a brief brightness that flared out, burned, fell.

Until I had fallen *through.*

A ripple disturbed the smooth pond. Cassia grew more ephemeral. The gaps in the Veil were closing over, and I could do nothing to make the vision stay. We would not have long, and I did not know how easy it would be to reach her again.

—*Find the human,* Cassia said. *I will research more. This was a path we thought long gone, but it has returned thanks to your* . . . *impulsivity. Listen well: you must find the human before the Feast of Flowers.*

Cassia's gaze went distant, and her cadence changed. She drifted away like mist. —*"What has been torn asunder shall be mended, two halves of a larger whole. The dragon scales will be upended, set aflame as if made of coal."*

She was reciting a prophecy. The words, of course, meant nothing to me.

—*There is a fork in the path,* my sister said. *Either you succeed, and you give us our world. Or you doom us all, Everen.*

7. ARCADY: THE SILVER SETTING

The next day, I stole.

To be fair, I stole most days, so this wasn't unusual. I'd go to a market and pinch something from a vendor I knew overcharged, or dip a hand into a pocket that looked heavy enough to spare a coin or two. I had various schemes that required a longer lead time or crafting an identity to gain someone's trust. It always boiled down to the same thing: find a weak point, lean in hard. Watch it give or break.

I'd wake up grumpy, my dreams unsettled. I wore one of my nicer houppelandes, in the Myrian fashion, which I'd sewn myself from a dark brown cambric, along with the surcoat of dark blue. I slipped on fresh white gloves and draped a forget-me-not-blue hood over newly blond curls. I'd given myself a sweet, heart-shaped face and roses in my cheeks. Nonthreatening, entirely by design. Patting my seal on its chain beneath my clothes, I set off to the nicest part of the merchant district.

I was in such a disgustingly good mood, I hummed as I made my way to Lacewing Temple, just off Lace Street. The Citadel hunkered overhead, our constant guard.

I sidled in just as service began, sitting in a pew near the back. The standard five stained-glass windows, each dedicated to a god, dominated the wall behind the eaves. Blue Kalsh, violet Zama, green Jari, gray Piater, and red Aura. All of them surrounded by glass flames, the light falling through the windows to paint the congregation in a riot of color.

Icons for the saints were peppered around the church, framed in gold. Kalsh's Saint Ini, of Luck, held Their usual cup of blood. Saint Wyndyn, Jari's saint of Faith, wore a claw around Their neck. Piater's Saint Dolard, for the Lost or the Wandering, wore a thin circlet of scales. Saint Etter, Zama's patron of Clarity, was clad in dragon-hide leather, and Aura's Saint Bryni, of Righteous Anger, wore a necklace of bone.

The Head Priest of Lacewing walked sedately on the red-lined path between the pews, dressed in Their dragon-scaled robe and gold-limned, swinging a burner of sweet incense that made me want to cough. Above Them was the crowning glory of the Lacewing Cathedral: a dragon god's skull. The Five were the ones who had created us, but evidently They'd had many avatars, creating a body and leaving it behind once They had bestowed divine blessings, or whatever it is They supposedly did. The skull was gilded, painted, only missing a few fangs. The white of bone was long yellowed. I eyed the teeth covetously. Just one would be worth a decent number of wraithwright suls if anyone were brave enough to try to sell it on the black market. But a church was not the only place to find a relic. Most drakines had them too—gifts from Monarchs in generations past. The grand temple was drafty, and I tucked my skirts tighter around myself.

At the nave, the priest turned toward Their congregation. Rows of leaf dragon idols were stacked neatly to the side of the grand altar, waiting for the end of service.

It started with the singing, which was always my favorite part. It went downhill from there. Our collective hymns rose to the stone eaves. My eyes darted around those dressed in furs and velvets, seeing who had a bracelet with an easy clasp, or a brooch I could pluck from the rich fabric. Who might have deep pockets that would clink with silver and gold instead of copper. No one would be fool enough to walk around with wraithwright.

My eyes snagged on my true target: Sar Ikari Dwell. A rich merchant who did a lot of business in Jask, newly returned to Loc. They were once from a drakine family but after the Schism grew poor enough they lost the title. Dwell had since built up a shipping empire. They were probably richer than half of this congregation combined. They were a strange blend—not-quite-noble and merchant. Useful to both worlds but accepted by neither. Even so, they were not my ultimate mark, but a useful stepping stone to what I truly wanted.

I never thought of drakines or merchants in the honorific pronoun, though I hadn't managed to shake the habit for the clergy, the gods, and those I actually respected, like university professors. My paire would have despaired at that, but I clung to my little rebellion, all the same.

My eyes snagged again on the dragon skull. Many holy relics had gone missing from drakine families over the years. After the Schism, the new Chancellors gouged drakines with taxes to "prove" they were making things better for the common people. Plenty of villeins left the drakine estates and headed to Vatra or Derktin for better wages. Merchants were also allowed to have more of a say in government, which further eroded drakines' power. As the costs added up, a relic of a tooth might disappear, or a few scales. A vertebra. Though it was illegal and blasphemous to sell them, people pretended not to notice if a cabinet of curiosities was just a little emptier at the next dinner party. Merchants and guilders were often the ones snapping them up, wanting to prove that they could be as fine and fancy as any drakine.

If I could get my sticky hands on a suitably valuable relic, all my money problems would be solved in one fell swoop. There was a healthy black market for them, and Ikari Dwell was the person who could help me get one.

There was a secret auction happening in the not-too-distant future at Widow Ulla Girazin's estate in Redwing Valley. The Girazin family had once been one of the richest drakine families, but, like many, the widow, too, had fallen on harder times. Rumor had it that Girazin was finally parting with a few of their treasured relics for discerning non-noble buyers, including some pieces that had been hidden away for centuries. There was one in particular I was desperate to steal. And rich-as-the-gods Ikari Dwell would be able to walk right through the front door.

After the last, ringing note, we sat, and the sermon droned on with all the usual messages—avoid temptation and darkness. Look after your magic as an act of worship to the gods. A reminder that though the gods are benevolent, They do not suffer those who slander Them. Once we leave our mortal coil, we would rise up to join Them and fly through endless rays of sunlight forevermore. And so on and so forth. I wondered if I could get away with taking a nap until it was all done. Finally, we chanted the last, collective prayer.

After the service ended, merchants and their families waited their turn to burn a leaf idol at the altar, whispering a prayer and pressing a splayed hand to their hearts. I joined in for appearance's sake, though I made no wishes. The leaf caught the flame, burning to black ash.

The congregation spilled into the courtyard like coins upended from a stone vase. Fur-lined hoods were pulled up against the chilly morning. Wyverns skittered along the columns or flew overhead, letting out their sharp cries and flapping feathered wings.

A few of the merchants held up leather-braced wrists, and their wyverns landed on their arms, flashing tiny fangs as they ate delicacies from their palms. Many wyverns in the city ferried letters or were kept as pets or racers, like hawks. The rest were feral, holy little pests. But all of them, wild or tame, knew holy day was the best time to have a good feed.

It was time to strike.

I said my greetings, dimpling at those who were friendly, and moved through the crowd, placing my gloved hand on an arm, tucking a bracelet I'd eyed earlier up my billowing sleeves. My hand ghosted into pockets. I palmed a pocket timepiece—a score. They were a Jaskian invention, and we had few horologists this side of the water.

People let their guards down outside a temple, not expecting someone would be so bold as to steal near a house of the gods.

When my pockets were heavy, I edged over to Ikari Dwell. They were handsome enough—tall, dark hair, but rather lacking in lips, which made them look severe. They were droning on to a drakine couple about the cost of salmon in Jask and how it was a good time to invest. The couple looked like they wanted nothing more than to flee. Dwell had a lazy way of speaking, a sonorous voice, and seemed very fond of speaking *at* someone without ever a pause to listen.

Their guard, a dour, bullish type, lurked nearby. Some of the richer merchants liked to have them, partly as actual protection, but also to signal they were powerful, important, and rather rich.

I crept forward, easing off one of my gloves. But just as I came within touching distance, the guard's eyes snapped to me. Fuck.

I gave the guard a vapid smile and continued on. I tried to subtly circle back around to them, but Dwell was already making their way to the carriage.

Well. There went that part of the plan. I bit down another curse.

With a resolute sigh, I wove through the crowds of people I'd just stolen from. Did I feel guilt?

Not a jot.

At least it wasn't a total failure. I counted my take in satisfaction. I swung back home and added my stash to the lockbox in the back room. The pocket watch, two gold bracelets, one garnet and one beryl with small diamonds, a mourning silver brooch with a jet stone and rubies. Almost anyone rich enough wore the red stone, for rubies were meant to protect from plague, just as diamonds supposedly protected from poison. More superstition.

It was a decent haul, but still not enough. Never enough.

For that, I needed something more. I needed that relic.

I comforted myself with a cup of tea and some toast with butter and jam.

My work for the day was not yet done. Next, I had to see if my new seal had truly taken. I rebuilt the shapeshifted features I'd used that morning and headed back out.

My lock shop wasn't far from the jewelry district—just on the other side of the harbor. I lifted my heavy skirts above a puddle. I rarely wore dresses or robes, far preferring the freedom of breeches or hose. Scaling a building in skirts was a bloody nightmare.

I loved the excitement and slight danger of the harbor. For the years of the Strike, it had been eerie, the borders closed and only the bare minimum of cargo coming through. Now, it was heaving. Sailors swarmed the ships like termites, checking the rigging and the sails, performing what repairs they needed before they set off again.

Streams of workers hoisted bags and crates of goods, merchants buying them for a few coins to sell them for a few more. This was the gateway into and out of Loc. If you had the money and the adventurous spirit, you could buy a ticket to anywhere you liked. The horizon was yours.

Like any magic user, I was always hungry. For power, for knowledge, for new and shiny things.

At one point, a few years ago, I had considered running—the problem was where. They didn't have seals in Myria, just dragonstone wands, so I would have to craft a fake and keep my real seal hidden, which was a risk. The Glass Isles were mostly for the traveling Traders who wintered in Opal, or criminals and pirates who had claimed the smaller islands on the outskirts. Neither Traders nor pirates took kindly to outsiders. I'd never set foot in Jask, which was too bloody cold and far too obsessed with rigid ideas about sex and gender. They wouldn't know what to make of me.

But one day. After I'd cleared my taie's name. After I'd gotten my education, like my parents always wanted. Then I'd have all the opportunities I could desire. Using this new name, this new life, I'd set sail on the finest ship in this harbor and take a leisurely tour of the known world. And maybe I'd never, ever come back.

A street away, my stomach clenched with sudden nausea, and I stumbled to the side of the street. A few people I jostled hissed curses at me. I panted, leaning against the stone wall of a shop, and felt magic ripple across my skin. My hands went to my face, tracing the too-familiar shape of a nose and cheekbones. It was like going from fully clothed to naked. I was exposed.

I had never lost a form by accident. I prided myself on my control over Kalsh's magic. This was more shapeshifting than I had done for quite some time, but I'd always been in control. Control was vital.

I staggered toward the window of the nearest shop—an apothecary. Sure enough, there was my normal face in the reflection, wide-eyed with dismay. Whispering the spell in the Old Tongue, I tried drawing the illusion again, with its pale curls and pert mouth. It held, but it felt like it could rub off like face paint. Hunger already gnawed at my belly. I rummaged in my pocket and unwrapped a sweetsphere.

My hand went to the seal beneath my clothing. Was it that my magic didn't funnel through it as easily? Would I have to re-learn how to use it? The thought chilled me more than the winter morning. That would set me back sure as my lack of coin.

I banished the illusion and squared my shoulders, striding back onto the road. Fine. I'd simply have to use my true face to test my first official outing as Sar Arcady Dalca, minor drakine, future student at Vatran University. I shoved away my unease with equal determination.

The shop's bell tinkled as I opened the door. "Welcome," the shopkeeper said with a flash of teeth. They were middle-aged, though their brown hair showed no streaks of gray. "Are you seeking anything in particular?"

"A seal setting," I said with a nervous swallow.

"You've come to the right place then," they said with the bland pleasantness of most shopkeepers. They led me to a glass-topped counter. "Have you grown tired of your old one? We offer credit exchange."

I shook my head. "No need."

The shopkeeper nodded with that same affableness. "I'll leave you to browse."

The settings were nicely made. They could be in a variety of metals, magic-treated so they were safe for skin and wouldn't rust or oxidize. They had to be touched up every few years or so.

It didn't take me long to make my choice: a simple, triangular setting with a few geometric designs stamped into the metal. The seal would be set into the middle of an open shell that snapped closed, for Kalsh.

"Kalsh is a lucky god," my paire had said when I'd first accidentally shapeshifted into him when I was eight. He'd called my maire, and I'd touched her cheek and turned into a miniature version of her, too. I'd burst into tears, overwhelmed. They had held and rocked me, feeding me stewed apples until I'd quieted.

I was forgetting little things about them. The sound of their voices, the exact shade of their eyes. I'd whisper their names every night before I fell asleep: my maire: Jyosi Eremia. My paire: Thand Eremia, who had chosen the surname when my parents bonded. Even now, I could turn into them and see their faces in the mirror the way they'd been when I'd last touched them. I never have. It's too sad to wear the bodies of ghosts.

I took my new seal from around my neck and popped it into the setting, admiring the effect. The dragonstone glimmered like the inside of a nacre shell. I pressed the metal to my chest, point down, over my clothing. I glanced at the tag, and the price made me blanch. Nothing for it.

"A fine choice," the jeweler said as I came to the counter. I was sure they said it no matter what the customer selected.

I fought the urge to shift from foot to foot. "I was wondering if I could sign a note of credit and pay in installments?"

The jeweler cast a discerning eye over my good clothes, the stolen emerald on my finger. I raised my chin, haughty as any highborn.

Their eyebrows rose as they smiled. "Most certainly, dear Sar."

They thought me either drakine or as minted as one. The jeweler brought out a sheaf of creamy vellum. With a fresh-cut quill, they dipped the point into the ink and began writing the spell. "How many payments?"

I calculated. "Eight, please. One a fortnight."

"Direct from the bank?"

Like I had an account. Though I suppose I'd have to open one soon enough. "I'll pay with coin."

If they thought that strange, they said nothing. The jeweler's head bent over their work. They finished with a flourish. "For your perusal, and it's still ten percent today."

I dug out the suls and passed them over, then cast an eye over the contract. Straightforward, no hidden loopholes. Satisfied, I nodded. The jeweler poured ink into a shallow dish and gestured for me to continue. I pressed my seal into the liquid, holding it by the sides, and then rolled it carefully at the bottom of the vellum. There they were: the stars and symbols of Arcady Dalca. My seal flared blue, burning away the remnants of the ink on the dragonstone.

The vendor took out their seal and did the same. There were the stars of their birth, and the name written in the curving beautiful script of the Old Tongue. Ildred Ayne.

"Is all in agreement?" Ildred asked.

I nodded, nerves fluttering through me.

"*Naustje*," Ildred said, one fingertip resting on their seal.

The spell was tied with records in the Citadel. A careful, clever tracker. Within a minute, I'd know if I would need to sprint down the streets and come up with a whole new plan for my life.

I held my breath until the jeweler's own seal, proudly displayed in the gap of their shirt, flared silver.

The deed was done. If I reneged on my loan, the jeweler would be able to track down my seal and make me pay in either coin or pain. I restrained a triumphant wriggle. I had successfully become Arcady Dalca, and the Citadel was none the wiser.

How had my maire and taie done it?

"Wonderful doing business with you," the shopkeeper said, holding out their gloved hand. I pressed my palm against theirs.

The jeweler wrapped up my purchase. I made my way back home for tea and the honeyplum cakes I'd pinched from the market the other day. I looked over my sketched map of the Girazin manor from when I'd snuck in as a wine deliverer a few weeks ago. I tapped my fingertips on the room where I suspected the auction would be held, but my attention wouldn't hold.

I had several problems.

One: my magic was acting strangely, so I'd have to investigate and make sure it funneled properly through my taie's seal.

Two: no matter which way I looked at it, there was no way to do this job alone. I'd known it all along, deep down. I needed *at least* two more, plus someone to sell it for me after.

Three: the only thieves I knew who could help me pull it off would happily wear my guts for garters. Yet again, I thought of Lightfinger with a pang. They'd been my closest friend in the Marricks. Probably the only person I'd ever trusted once I came back to this cursed city. They would have helped me, no questions asked. Perhaps I was only meant to have a confidante like that once. But they were long gone, as dead as everyone else I'd loved.

My eyes stung. I rubbed at them with a napkin hard enough I briefly saw stars. I sniffed, clearing my throat.

Four, and the more immediate: I needed someone I could trust to help fit the seal setting. No illusions would make it through the pain of fixing the metal to my skin, and whoever did it would see the truth of me. I couldn't do it myself, not with my lack of Jari magic and my seal behaving strangely.

I knew who could help me with the last point, at least. Solving any of my problems meant swallowing a bucket of pride, and the last giving up a secret.

But one person would do it for the right price.

8. EVEREN: THE DRAGON'S HEART

The next ten days grew increasingly unpleasant.

My preterit muscles were so sore I could barely move after my first day at the docks. But I went back, day after day. For the docks were an insight to the wider world of the Lumet. I unloaded fish from further up the Lochian coast. Wide planks of wood from Jaskian forests to the south. Spices from the other side of Myria. Casks of an alcohol called rum from the Glass Isles, the winter home of Traders. Those same traveling Traders often came to purchase certain goods directly from ships to make their way to other cities throughout the known world.

As I worked, I listened. Locmyrian was related to Celenian but twisted and shifted. Many terms were unfamiliar—particularly slang—but I was learning the cadence, like a refrain of music. I matched the sounds to words I had read on parchment or vellum. With work, my speech no longer sounded so foreign when they fell from my tongue.

One of the most useful discoveries was just how little humans used their stolen magic. Piater's magic, as they called the ability to move objects with the mind, would have made short work of the heavier loads from the holds. Yet instead, they used their muscles or the leverage of simple machines. I tucked that observation away with all the others.

The human voices grated as they laughed or joked. They thought me quiet and surly, though I cared not at all for these insignificant creatures and their opinions. When my kind returned, they would all bow to us. If they survived.

All I knew was that days were slipping past, the Feast of Flowers that much sooner, and I had nothing.

As soon as I was finished with the day's work, I hunted you. I must have walked down nearly every street and wynd of Vatra over those nights, from the nicest to the poorest parts of town. Sometimes I was sure I sensed a hum of gold, only for it to disappear.

Who are you? I asked the dark. *Where are you?*

When exhaustion overtook me, I flew back to the cave in the woods, grateful for the cover of thick, winter fog. Sometimes, I risked a fire for warmth. More often, I simply curled up in those old priest robes and found no rest as the nightmare of the storm plagued me again and again. At dawn, bleary-eyed, I did it all again. Feeling no closer. It was a form of low-grade torture. I grew wan, my mind sluggish from lack of sleep.

I tried to scry Cassia, but the pond remained still and half-frozen.

On the sixth night, a group of humans followed me through the street as I searched for you. Strong, burly types who thought me easy prey. I was so exhausted, they nearly snuck up on me. But before they grew too close, I struck.

I kicked one into the stone wall of the alleyway, winding it. I used a hand to bend back the wrist of the next until it cried out and I punched it in the jaw with the other. The third turned tail and fled. The last was a braver soul, running at me head on with a snarl and nearly managing a cut. I will admit I played with that human. Its pride would not let it quit, and it was beyond easy to block its attempted hits. I jumped backward over one of its groaning companions and circled, ready to strike again. Humans moved so slowly. They were such vulnerable things. I found myself laughing. I had missed the thrill of the hunt. And least this was doing *something*.

I darted forward and pinned it against the wall, taking its knife for myself I grinned and let my illusion fall away. After so many days pretending, it was a rush to watch the human's eyes widen at my fangs. This one thought me no god. I tasted its fear, and I let myself savor it.

The human whimpered and pissed itself, the stench of urine sharp. I reared back and hit its head against the wall, hard enough to daze it. By the time it staggered upright, I was already on the roof above. The human checked its injured brethren and helped one to its feet. The would-be thieves limped off. They were lucky I did not do more.

I tested the edge of the knife. The next morning, I spent a few of my pennies for a sheath for my belt before starting my work down at the docks. I felt better with the extra sharpness.

I quit when I had enough coin to keep me fed for a few sennights and spend my days searching for you too. From dawn until the deep of night, I hunted. The tenth night, as I walked down a street full of inebriated humans, a voice yelled in my direction.

One of the dockworkers was waving at me from outside a tavern. Gellid,

I remembered it was called. I almost did not recognize it, freshly washed and clad in a finer shirt. I slowed.

"Come on, Surly. Stay for a drink!" Gellid said, clapping me on the back and tugging me inside. "Let's see if we can loosen you up."

I protested, but somehow found myself holding a mug of beer I had no desire to drink. There were too many bodies in too close a space, and it was loud, and I hated it. I would stay for this one drink, and then I would leave. The ceiling was low, the walls dark wood, tables sticky with old beer. The air reeked of humans, alcohol, grease, and smoke from the fire.

A musician strummed a stringed instrument in the corner, with lyrics largely about mating, or attempting to mate, or the trouble that arose after mating.

Dragons loved music, but I was not sure I could call the ribald, simple songs that followed any great works. I listened, and somehow the mug in my hand emptied, and Gellid handed me another. The second went down easier, as did the third and the fourth. I no longer minded the taste, and when someone called out for a repeat of the song "The Prick in the Haystack," I found myself joining in the chorus.

Yet I was all too aware that everyone around me wore those cursed seals around their necks. I could smell their stolen magic and it made my skin itch. I drank more of the not-so-foul beer to distract myself.

Gellid threw an arm around my shoulder and took me out into the street.

"Good night," I said thickly, trying to pull away and shocking myself with a hiccup.

"The night is young!" Gellid said. "You ain't got anyone warm to go home to, do you?"

The human dragged me along. I could have pulled away at any point, but there was a heat in my stomach from the beer, and perhaps I was tired enough of being alone that even a human seemed company. I had no faith that another night of searching would yield any results.

Gellid made its way down the cobbled street, warbling the rude song from the tavern. I am ashamed to admit I might have joined in, and soon we came to a place called the Dragon's Heart, its painted sign swinging in the night breeze.

It was nicer inside than the last tavern. Flowers in vases were set up high where a drunkard could not accidentally knock them down, and paintings of barely clad humans graced the walls. The clientele seemed to consist mostly of merchants. Some wore feathers in a buttonhole, behind their ears, or pinned to their hair.

Gellid was counting the coins in its palm. "Just about," it muttered. "Just about."

I staggered into an empty chair, and determinedly turned down another small glass of something that smelled acrid. Gellid shrugged and emptied the glass. Winced, like the liquid caused pain.

"That one there has been eyeing you since we came in," Gellid said, nodding its chin at a human with hair that rippled like black seaweed. It wore clothing much like mine but of nicer fabric and belted very tightly about the waist. "Reckon they'll give you a discount if you ask nice. Do you like the look of them?"

"Perfectly acceptable," I said expansively.

Gellid laughed, patted me on the back, and closed one eye at me in an exaggerated fashion. It wove through the press of people, leaning close and whispering something in the ear of the human in question. The one with dark hair looked at me before gliding through the crush of people. It wore black powder about its eyes. It reached out a gloved hand.

"Come along," it said.

Gellid grinned from across the room, one gold tooth nestled among the slightly yellowed smile, and gestured that I should go.

I rose, only a little unsteadily, and followed it to a door at the back. We climbed the stairs and entered a room on the right.

"That will be twelve coppers," the human said, voice soft.

"For what?" I asked.

"Whatever you like, love." Confused, but drunk enough that the answer made sense, I fished for my pouch and counted out the coins. It did not occur to me that I was handing over a significant portion of my worldly wealth. The coppers disappeared somewhere, and the human came closer. It murmured a couple of words under its breath and a flash of magic flared from its seal. I startled, lips pulling back from my teeth.

It held up a palm placatingly, like I was some spooked animal. "Don't worry, it's only a spell against disease, plus a shapeshifter protection that lasts for a few hours," it said, and pulled the glove from its hand. A bare finger grazed my cheek. "See? You can't become me, and I can't become you."

I had a flash of alarm. Could a human even imitate a preterit form? The thought of a human reaching for an illusion and unexpectedly sprouting feathers and scales amused me, and I stifled a laugh.

A ghost of fingertips along my jaw and down my neck. I blinked, and the human was closer. It rose onto its toes, and lips pressed to mine. A body flush against me, soft and pliant. Hands danced down my back, across my hipbone, lower—

I stepped back. "Wait—I—" The foreign words tangled in my mouth.

The human paused and pulled away, the space between its eyebrows puckering. "Your friend said you needed a helping hand, though they put it a little more colorfully than that. The cost is actually fifteen coppers—they gave me three."

I sucked in a breath, wondering how my mouth could feel so dry when I had drunk so much liquid.

"If I don't suit, there are others downstairs. We cater to all tastes, here. Do you prefer a crook over a cranny? If so, it's no matter. I think Pavic is free." This utterly mystified me. I felt like I was thinking in slow motion.

The human drew near again, but I stiffened.

A line appeared between the human's forehead. "Is this not done where you are from?"

"Is what—Oh. *Oh.*" I felt stupid. We had a couple of dragons who offered such services when someone needed release or comfort. Not for money, but for other favors. "Never with a—" I paused. *Human,* I had almost said. ". . . person." There had been other dragons roughly my age who had been curious about a male dragon. I had satisfied that curiosity well enough, I would like to think.

The human's eyebrows rose, and it gave something like a pleased hum. "Now that is surprising, pretty thing like you. I suppose you're young enough yet." The human tilted its head. Its eyes were a warm brown. "Well. Do you *want* to?"

I stifled a recoil. Yet I refused to dwell on how nice the closeness had been before my mind had caught up to my preterit body. How beneath my hands, a human had felt no different than a preterit. "No." A heartbeat. "Thank you."

The human let out a laugh. "So polite. No need to be embarrassed, love. Sometimes the mood passes. It's no matter."

The human pushed its hair back from its face. "If you go down now, your friend will likely be confused. If they haven't already gone off to a room with one of our other fine beauties." It gave me a sly smile.

I lifted and lowered my shoulders, a gesture I had learned. "Not a friend."

"Well, you paid your coin, and I'm not giving it back. I don't fancy fishing for someone else tonight. I'm tired. So if you want to rest here awhile, you're welcome." The human was being . . . nice. Since I'd shucked the priest robes, humans had either barked orders at me, disinterestedly given me whatever I purchased, or tried to stab me. Gellid had wanted a companion on its night of debauchery, nothing more. But this human was smiling at me.

I glanced around. A small fire in the grate warmed the room. The bed took up most of the space, the covers of a shiny green material. The walls were a paler green. There was also a soft blue chair, a table with fruit in a bowl, another small table with a mirror on it and a low stool. A painting on the wall showed someone half-undressed, and I realized with a start it was a depiction of the human in front of me.

It was a good sight more comfortable than a cold, damp clearing in a forest.

"All right," I said, cautiously.

The human passed me a glass of water, and I drank it greedily as I sank into the chair. The human perched on the stool and took the jewels from its ears. "I'm Mirel." It flashed a hand signal at me.

I had gleaned these gestures had something to do with politeness. My confusion had made the other dockworkers laugh, but I had been too proud to ask.

Mirel caught my bemusement. "You're foreign, but surely you can't be that new to our shores?"

I gave a careful shrug.

"Where from?"

"Beyond the Glass Isles." Technically true.

"A handsome foreigner. What fun. Pity you don't fancy a tumble." Mirel made the gesture again. "It's to let you know to think of me as she or her. A sign of friendliness, or informality."

The skin between my eyes puckered. "But . . ." I trailed off, gesturing vaguely.

Mirel laughed. "We don't ignore the differences of body shape, but it'd be more than a little rude to call me a woman afore I told you I was one, and it'd be the same for me to assume you're a man. You'd usually be right, but it's polite enough to check. Some feel between, or outside of male and female, man or woman." She stretched her arms over her head, arching back in the chair. I followed the way her body moved beneath the clothing.

"We use neutral with strangers. And if they're above you in status, like a drakine, the clergy, or a gaffer, then you would use an emphasis." She demonstrated. "You'd capitalize it in writing, too—it's called the honorific. You can do that for specific genders once you know 'em, too, but it's considered a little stuffy."

I had not done that to the superior at the docks, but in retrospect, the others had. Small wonder it had been a bit gruff with me.

Mirel continued. "You'd use neutral for children until they choose, whenever that might be." She walked me through the signals: he, she, they, any. The movements came from Trade. I had learned that most understood at least the basics, so sign language was a common tongue throughout the Lumet, especially when haggling at markets.

I clumsily signed "he" at Mirel. I did not share my name.

She nodded and started brushing her hair as I mulled her words. "If I had said 'she'?" I asked.

"Then I'd adjust." She shrugged. "People know the truth of themselves, sure enough. Quite a few of us can use blue or green magic to shift or alter ourselves, you know. Haven't you noticed, pet? All people care about here in Loc is *power*." She made a little flame appear above her open palm and clenched it into a fist. "Less the form that houses it."

I had learned more in five minutes than Cassia had through hours of scrying.

"Hm," I said.

Mirel leaned toward me, eyes crinkled with mirth. "You're getting it a right sight faster than the Jaskians. Had a few come my way, after borders opened again. They're all married to this idea that the shape of your body is what you are and all you can ever be. Be modest but cover up your body in a cut of clothing and wear your hair in a way that announces the shape of your genitals." She snorted. "They didn't like it one bit when I pointed that out. Guess since down south they aren't keen on magic, physical strength is all that's left."

She sighed and, as she began to plait her hair, her robe fell open to reveal a long expanse of light brown leg. "Is it more like Jask where you're from, then?"

"Raised among women. Only women."

Mirel's eyebrows rose. "Well, that's one I haven't heard before. Sounds fun. How do they grow their numbers, then?" She eyed me speculatively.

I hesitated. No way to answer that honestly—that a parent laid an egg that resulted in a miniature version of themselves. Because of rising temperatures in a dying world, all eggs hatched female. Save me, who had crawled out of my shell inexplicably male three hundred years after the last.

"They manage," I said at last.

Mirel rolled her neck, her fingertips working at the muscles of her shoulders, her eyes fluttering shut. She was too trusting. I could snap her neck in a second. I knew my mother would have done it without hesitation, just as she would have killed my attackers the other night. She would never deign to work alongside humans. Once she came through the Veil, she would lay waste to every human in her path. I wondered if it would be kinder, to end Mirel's life, and spare her what would happen when my kin arrived. They would char this city to ash.

And yet I stayed still and silent as Mirel wiped the paint from her face with a damp cloth. She looked younger without it. The room was so warm, but it was no longer spinning as the effects of the beer worked their way from my system.

Mirel kept up an idle stream of chatter, telling me about the brothel, how it was owned by the workers, each paying a portion of the running costs and keeping the rest.

"This is . . . what you want to do?" I asked, curious.

She gave me a slanted look. When she found little sign of judgment, she relented. "Sometimes it's fine. Sometimes it's a chore. Rarely, it's downright awful. Like most of the sirens here, I probably won't do it overlong. There'll always be someone happy enough to take over the room."

"Sirens?" I asked, remembering it was a term for a mythological creature.

"Has more than one meaning, love."

Mirel sat on the edge of the bed. When I peeled my eyes open, she was taking me in. I think if I had gone to her and dipped my head, she would have willingly taught me a little more of what it might mean to be human.

I shook the heaviness from my limbs. "I should go." I was wasting time. This was not why I was here.

Mirel's mouth curled. "If you like. I've my coin either way." She climbed underneath her covers, wrapping them around her like a cocoon and sighing deeply.

I made for the door, but a few steps away, I gasped.

The pain was so great, I barely registered falling to my knees. It radiated through my chest, spreading through my fingertips. I groaned, clutching at my chest. The agony was nearly as strong as the night I had arrived. Like someone was trying to claw out my heart with sharp talons. Every breath only dug them in deeper. I clamped down on a scream as sweat broke out along my human skin.

Mirel sat up, eyes wide. "Are you hurt?"

I could hardly hear her over the chimes in my mind. My breath heaved in and out as the pain pulsed and pulsed. I ripped open my cheap shirt and stared down at a sheen of blood.

"My gods," Mirel said, but she was not looking at my chest. Her eyes had snagged on my face, her mouth hung open. From the itching at my back, I knew my humanoid form had fallen away. Miligrist said that trouble loved to come in threes. For the third time, I revealed myself as preterit.

Mirel pushed herself back against the wall as I staggered to my feet and toward the window. I opened it to cold, thick fog. The bond was blazing a bright gold, pointing the way to you like a beacon. Were you in trouble, or were you attacking me before I could do the same? Either way: it was time.

I let my wings emerge, ripping the remnants of my bloodstained shirt to tatters. They spanned nearly the width of the room. Mirel gasped, eyes pools of black, jumping from the bed and pressing herself into a corner.

"What are you?" she asked, her hand at her throat.

I had been honest enough so far. "A dragon."

With that, I jumped from the window and into the dark to find you.

9. ARCADY: THE LAST GOLDEN

It took me over a sennight to work up the courage to go to Kelwyn's.

I kept putting it off, hoping I'd somehow find a way to slot my problems into neat, tidy stacks. Unfortunately, problems left alone had a way of growing tentacles and toppling over. The bastards.

The rain-slicked cobblestones gleamed yellow as lamplighters sparked the lanterns with snaps of their fingers, a whispered word, and a bit of Aura's red magic.

I raised my hood to keep the drizzle off my neck. I'd felt off the last few days. My muscles ached, though I had no fever. My sleep was worse than ever, and I often woke in the middle of the night, sketching fading images until my mind slowed down enough to let me fall back asleep. My dream last night had been more a memory: sweat-drenched sheets, the stench of illness in a shuttered room, and red paint splashed on the blue door of a little cottage in the shadow of the peaks of the Fangs.

I'd spent the week conducting experiments with my new seal, which was not proving promising. I could barely light a fire, and none of my shapeshifts lasted longer than a candlemark or two. My magic had returned to the taste of bracken and salt, but sometimes I caught an undercurrent of smoke. I kept holding my taie's seal and my old one, looking at them side by side and wondering if the cost of taking a name was worth sacrificing most of my magic. Was this temporary, or permanent? If I tried my mother's spell again, would I even be able to shift it back?

I tried to tamp down the panic. At least I'd hopefully squish one squirming problem into shape that night.

As usual, I went to Kelwyn's shop long after closing, weaving through streets that hummed with muted music and murmurs from the inside of taverns. Lights glimmered in the windows of the tenements above, but more than two stories up all was lost in the fog. Nights like this were perfect for breaking and entering, but otherwise made me nervous. Footsteps didn't echo. Shadows remained hidden.

I paused in front of the Last Golden: Kelwyn's unassuming but tidy antiques and pawnshop. The blue paint outside might have faded in the sun, but it remained unchipped. The hand-lettered sign in black and gilt was recently refreshed. I stole down the narrow alley between the buildings to the cramped stone courtyard behind it. Even with my blunted magic, it was easy enough to slip past Kelwyn's security wards. A quick shimmy up the drainpipe, and I was on his small roof terrace. I crouched outside a window on the first floor and peered through the bars.

Kelwyn hunched over his desk, examining a gemstone through a small microscope fastened to his eye. His silver-streaked brown hair curled over his ears, and he wore the tattered tunic he always changed into once he closed the doors to the shop. As he put down the gemstone and glass and stretched his neck, I had a moment of double vision, remembering how he'd looked when we'd first met eight years ago. A little less lined, a little less gray.

Kelwyn had been the one to set it all in motion, really. I'd returned to Vatra as a traumatized, scrawny twelve-year-old with nothing but the clothes on my back and a talent for attracting trouble. I'd botched a pickpocketing job and the mark chased me halfway down the street. I'd climbed a drainpipe to escape and I was panting, belly-down on the roof, when I realized I wasn't alone.

Kelwyn was smoking a rolled cigarette and flicking the ash into a nearby flowerpot. It'd been right outside the apartment above the Last Golden.

"You've got promise, but your technique is piss poor," he'd said mildly. "You'll be dead or in jail by month's end if you don't learn how to pick a pocket at least half as good as you climb." He had a country accent softened by years in the city.

I'd glared up at him, dirt-streaked and defiant. "Teach me, then."

He had a dimple in one cheek when he smirked. "Imperious little imp, aren't you? Fine. Stand."

He gave me a lesson for the length of three cigarettes and almost certainly saved my life. He'd shooed me off, and probably thought nothing of it. Less a kindness than a way to pass the time while he smoked. But the smell of smokemint always reminded me of the day on that rooftop.

I got better. Much better. Before long, I had a pile of stolen things I didn't know how to sell. I returned to the Last Golden, lingering out of sight, noting how many shifty people came in and out at odd hours. They weren't buying antiques, of that I'd been certain.

One night, I'd followed Kelwyn to the Night Market and slipped a small purse with a cabochon and a note in his pocket:

Sell this for me. See you in a sennight. —The Imperious Imp

I showed up on the promised night and, sure enough, he'd sold the jewel. I took my money—he definitely short-changed me, the cad—and wandered off again. At the time, I was squatting in an apartment with a red-paint-splashed door, empty since the first Strike. I slept on the floor, for who knew who had died in that bed.

I came back with more jewels. I took away more coins.

Then one day, Larkin was at the Last Golden, waiting with Kelwyn. And that was that. I joined the Marricks.

I shook off the memory and knocked on the window.

Kelwyn startled. "Gods damn you, Arc, how many times have I told you to ring the bell downstairs after hours! And make an appointment!"

"Where's the fun in that?" I asked through the glass. "I'm keeping you sharp. Come on, lemme in. Need a favor."

Kelwyn sighed and undid the latch, letting me climb inside.

"How's trade?" I asked.

"Bogdi tried to sell me glass yesterday," Kelwyn said with a roll of the eyes. "Nearly broke the arsehole's nose."

"Might be good for them. They've broken it twice already and they're always moaning about how they can't breathe out of it."

Kelwyn barked a laugh, then gave me one of his too-sharp looks. "You've been quiet these last few weeks. Where've you been?"

"Around." I collapsed onto a plush chair next to the fire, hooking a leg over one of the arms.

"Ah, of course, the mysterious land of Around where you reign like a Monarch of Locmyria," he replied with a courtier's rolling wave and bow. "Does Your Highness have anything for me to sell?"

"My full title is Monarch Arcady, Conqueror of Around, thank you very much." Reaching into my pocket, I passed him the jewelry and pocket watch I'd stolen from the temple. "Here. See how much you can get for this."

"How hot are they?" he said, examining the garnet bracelet critically.

"Nicked from Lacewing Temple almost two weeks ago."

"Stealing in a temple is going to damn your soul."

"Technically, I stole from *outside* of the temple. And I hardly have a soul to damn."

"Hah, hah." Kelwyn rolled his eyes but slipped my spoils into his safe.

"That's not the favor, of course," I said, pouring myself a generous measure from his decanter of rum. "That's your job." I fluttered my eyelashes at him.

Kelwyn gave me his best woe-betide-me face as he snatched the bottle back. "Ask away, then."

I wanted a lot more rum. "I need a seal setting fitted."

He frowned at my chest. "You don't have one already?" At the terse shake of my head, he added: "You know I'm no healer."

"You have some green magic," I said. "Fixed up enough scrapes for me in my time. I can't go to a normal healer for this."

"Why not?"

I chewed the inside of my cheek. I'd rarely been to a healer. My parents had had decent enough Jari magic, so they'd looked after me when I was young, and when I'd come back to Vatra, I hadn't dared. I taught myself enough to get by. I'd only gone to one once, when I was eleven, to change a few aspects of how I would go through puberty, but even that was a few months before my parents died.

I swirled the last few drops of rum in my glass, the amber liquid catching the firelight, and reluctantly gave Kelwyn another morsel of truth. "Any legitimate healer would report me."

"Report you . . . ?"

"I need your word," I said. "That you won't tell a soul. You could have sold me out to Larkin half a dozen times or more over the last turn of the seasons, but you haven't, so I trust you more than most."

"I suppose I should be honored," he said, but his eyes glittered. If there was one thing Kelwyn liked more than treasure, it was secrets. After all, secrets could be changed for coin easy as jewels.

"All right," he relented. "I'll even seal sign for it, if you like."

He said it lightly, like it was nothing, but I hid my surprise. If he broke his vow, it'd be painful, and he'd be in my debt.

"Your word is bond enough," I said, reaching into my bag and passing him my still-wrapped purchase from the jeweler's.

A curt nod, and he went to wash and sterilize his hands and the setting while I steeled my nerves. It wasn't complicated, but it wouldn't be pleasant.

When he returned, he held the metal in his palms, taking in the design. "Suits you," was all he said. "Ready?"

I swallowed and pulled my shirt over my head.

I couldn't look at him. I knew what he would see.

The darkness against my skin clustered above my heart in an angry tangle, spidering out in all directions. Marks like blue-black lightning danced across my bare chest and torso, growing lighter and disappearing just below my collarbone. They snaked down my upper arms and disappeared by my elbow, and though he couldn't see it, they were mirrored on my thighs. A map that declared only one destination.

I was not as Struck as some. But I was still one of them.

"Gods above," Kelwyn breathed, taking it all in, including the oval scar at my shoulder. I fought the urge to hunch and forced myself to sit tall.

I hated my marks and all they represented. Sometimes, I'd even shapeshift when I took a bath alone in the lock shop. They were a reminder of all I had lost, and how close I'd hovered at death's door. My new seal hung on its chain, nestled where the setting would rest.

"If you're caught doing magic . . ." Kelwyn started.

"I have it under control."

"Do you?" he asked, and I forced myself to meet his eyes. His gaze searched my face.

"I do." I kept my tone firm. "Have you ever suspected me at risk of turning Starveling? If I fuel myself properly, I'm as safe to use magic as you are. I thought you knew better than to fall for propaganda."

I was stretching the truth a little. There was some proof that the Struck could turn Starveling quicker, but it wasn't by much. But it was easier for the Citadel to point at the danger of the marked to distract from how poorly they had handled the Strikes. They were the reason it had spread so far: they had refused to acknowledge it as a problem until it was too late. They had left the harbors open too long. Because of them, the plague had even spread to Jask and Myria. It was harder to die without a seal, but thousands still did.

The Struck were a constant reminder of a time the Consul wanted us to forget. Anyone could turn Struck—from the drakine class down to the lowliest peasant. But the rich had hidden in their grand houses, and that made all the difference.

Kelwyn's head bowed over the setting. He could still back out. It was why I hadn't let him seal sign for it. He didn't know what he'd be promising.

"If I'm caught, this will only be one of my many problems, Kel," I pressed. "I know what I'm risking. So, I'm asking again: will you help me?"

He swallowed, inching closer. "Did the Marricks know?"

I shook my head, throat closing. "No one. Not Wren. Not Larkin. None of the younger ones. Not even Lightfinger."

His eyes went soft at the mention of my long-gone friend. Kelwyn was the one I'd come to after it had all gone to shit with the Marricks, after all. He'd been the one to give me space to lick my wounds.

"You kept it from the whole group for eight years?"

"You may have noticed I'm proper sneaky." I was aiming for lightness, but it fell short.

Kelwyn reached out one finger, nearly touching the seal on its chain against my sternum. "Won't this say what you are just as much as your skin? How have you avoided the marble?"

"It's not on my record, so my dragonstone was never confiscated." He'd had enough of my secrets tonight. Like many, Kelwyn spat when he heard the Plaguebringer's name. His hatred ran deep. Deeper than most. I'd never pressed why. Yet I knew, with a certainty, that if he ever learned my true last name was Eremia, no matter how he might care for me and the pretty jewels I brought him, he'd deliver my sorry arse to the Council himself. The eyewatering bounty he might get for his trouble would just be the sugar dusting on the cake.

"You're playing with fire, Arcady," he whispered. "And you're not blessed by Aura."

"I'm not burned yet."

He was silent for so long I thought he'd pass me the setting and turn his back on me. My mind began scrambling for alternate plans.

His hands moved, and he took a cloth he'd brought from the bathroom and washed my skin. He pressed the setting against my chest, measuring the fit.

"I'm taking thirty percent of your Lacewing haul."

"Fine." Relief swept through me. "Thank you," I whispered.

"Pass me a saltsphere," he said, nodding to a covered basket on the side table. I found them sour and bitter, but Kelwyn loved the seed and nut snacks speckled with sea salt and rosemary or other herbs. I popped one in his mouth, and he chewed. When he opened his mouth like a bird, I gave him a second.

I took my seal off the chain and slid it into the setting.

"You ready?" he asked. "This'll sting."

I exhaled. "Nothing for it. Don't hesitate."

Kelwyn closed his eyes and his mouth moved as he whispered the spell. The seal at his own chest sparked green, glowing from within. He pressed the metal against my chest, and after a push of resistance, it began to sink into my skin. Blood welled and trickled down my chest in red rivulets. Pain pulsed with every heartbeat. My hands gripped the side of my chair.

The pain knocked loose something within me.

The gold from the cave suffused my vision and rang in my ears. Kelwyn's apartment disappeared.

A room in shades of green. A fire in the grate, the warmth of it on my cheek. Hands clawing at my chest. Someone looking at me in fear, stumbling back. I staggered to my feet, warmth at my back.

I gasped, like I was trying to breathe through smoke. My lungs burned.

"Arc?" Kelwyn was saying. "You all right?"

"I'm fine," I lied. My stomach dipped like I was falling. I tried to move, but Kelwyn's hand was heavy on my shoulder.

"Not finished," he muttered. He bent close, eyebrows furrowed as he concentrated. His seal still shone green, magic dancing over my skin. The air smelled of rich, loamy earth and new-growth green. Slowly, so slowly, my skin knit together. He leaned back. "There."

I stared down at the silver setting. It seemed to grow straight from my flesh, like it had always been a part of me, half-covering the dark knot over my heart.

Kelwyn took a damp cloth and wiped away the blood. I tried not to hiss. He smeared a stinging ointment on the inflamed skin around the metal. Green Jari magic sped up the natural process, but it'd still be a few days until it was no longer tender.

When he finished, Kelwyn washed his hands and ate another saltsphere. He disappeared into the kitchen and came back with a tray of pastries and two mugs of strong, sweet tea. He must have brewed them before and left them covered. He touched each of them to heat them up a little more, his seal flaring his usual red orange. He bit into a lemon tart with relish.

"Eat," he instructed.

My stomach was still fluttering, but I took a tart. I hadn't technically used magic—or had I? Had that room merely been a pain-filled waking dream?

"Thank you, Kel," I said, gulping my tea and biting into the sour-sweetness of lemon curd. It puckered my mouth, and I washed it down with more tea. "I owe you one."

He pressed the tub of salve into my hands and gave me a nod. "Be careful, Arc."

"Always."

He went back to his desk, picking up the glass and peering at another bit of shine, as if I'd never interrupted him at all.

I took the apartment stairs. My chest was too sore to climb, and as I walked down the street, I cupped my hands loosely over my new setting, as if that would somehow protect me from the pain. My feet knew the way home. The taverns had shut, and all was quiet. Half of the street lanterns had sputtered out, and the few that remained barely penetrated the gray gloom. I strained my ears, once again cursing my Strike-blighted hearing. It didn't impact my day-to-day life overmuch, but I relied more than I'd like on lipreading in places with a lot of background noise. But when thieving, missing a minor noise could be the difference between life or death.

Though I was distracted by the pain, at least instincts honed by years of near misses hadn't left me. The hair rose on the back of my neck.

I was being followed.

10. EVEREN: THE KISS OF A KNIFE

I thanked the stars for the thick fog as I flew through the streets of Vatra.

My chest still stung as if it had been branded like livestock. I spared no thought for any humans who might see me from the windows of their small homes. I followed that connection between us like it was the strongest thermal off the ocean.

I chastised myself with every flap of the wings. I should have tried harder, these past ten days, instead of fraternizing with humans and letting my guard down. Little better than a feather-brained hatchling.

I knew one thing: you were my weakness. We were bonded, linked. And that could not stand.

With a turn, I glided over the rooftops and landed on an angled, shingled roof. Down below, I sensed more than saw you through the gray.

I followed you from above, tucking my wings away. You were moving slowly, so I raced ahead, to the end of the building block, and started climbing down the wall, my fingers finding the small divots in the stone with ease. Not so different from climbing the cliffs of Vere Celene, save for a lack of talons.

You stopped, your outline a black shadow, coat pulled tight about your slim form.

After a moment, you continued. Your head shifted side to side, the sound of footsteps muffled in the mist. I could smell your fear, and the iron tang of your blood.

You passed beneath me and I dropped down silently, drawing my stolen knife and my human illusion.

I made to grab you, but you danced back faster than I had expected. A knife of your own flashed in your hand. Belatedly, I found your aim to be true. My right forearm stung, the cut shallow. Blood blotted the frayed sleeve.

You stiffened and stifled a hiss, but you pushed me against the stone wall with surprising strength, knocking my blade from my hand. Metal clattered on stone. There was that familiar face from the caves, from my dreams, inches from mine and twisted with anger. There were the three marks above the wings of your eyebrows. This close, I could count the faint speckles on your nose. The blue of your irises looked black in this light. Your lips were pressed white in anger. The knife was at my neck, the point kissing my jugular. Your coat had fallen open, the laces of your shirt loose enough I spied the pristine white of a bandage. The cut on my forearm pulsed.

I could have grabbed your wrist. Ground the bones together until you lost your grip on the knife. It was not a matter of whether I could kill you.

It was knowing, with a horrible certainty, that I could not.

"Wait," I said, swallowing, the sharp metal nicking my skin. You flinched.

Your right hand pressed harder against my shoulder. You were sinister handed. A mirror to me. "I'm not in a particularly forgiving mood tonight." Your voice was deeper and raspier than I thought it would be.

I drew my lips from my teeth, thwarted by the failed hunt. I wanted to howl a curse to those hidden stars above us.

Your eyes narrowed, the three dots above your eyebrows shifting, lining up like a constellation.

"Did the Marricks send you?" The knife moved a little closer.

"No," I ground out. The name was unfamiliar.

"I could gut you like a fish right here and now, and no one would ever know it was me." You kept your voice soft, almost thoughtful, but undercut with anger. "Guard patrols are few and far between. A body is found in Vatran river or the docks once a week, and no one works too hard to discover who might have helped them meet their end."

The way the hand holding the knife shook belied your words. For all your bravado, you had never taken a life. I was sure of it.

"You do not kill," I managed, my accent thick even if the words were correct. "Though I know you steal from tombs."

Your eyes widened. I took advantage. My hand shot up and gripped your left forearm. You hissed in pain as I squeezed the injury, and the knife dropped from your hand. In an instant, our positions had reversed. You were the one pinned against the wall, glaring up at me, false bravado leaving your eyes. Both our weapons gleamed on the stones from the lantern light above.

My hand was darkened with your blood. It felt so cold it almost burned. I twisted my palm, wiping the blood onto your collar, but my skin still stung. My body was pressed against you, your ribs moving against mine.

"Wait," I said again.

You tried to wriggle free, without success, and one of your hands went up and grabbed my wrist, attempting to wrestle it away.

Your touch sparked. I was drowning in freezing, liquid sunlight. The taste of salt water flooded my mouth, burning my throat and lungs. Magic drained from my body, seeping into yours. I was an instant away from losing my human form. My wings ached to break back into existence.

I tore my arm free and stumbled back, gasping.

You stared in awe and fear at your glowing palm. Gold threaded with the barest blue and red, pulsing like a beating heart.

"What in the five gods?" you asked, voice hushed. The chime was back, echoing around us in a song only we could hear. Your lips had fallen open, pupils shrunk to pinpricks, features limned in gold. The sound faded along with the light, the darkness of the night closing back in.

"Your gods have nothing to do with this," I whispered. Though I wondered if, in another world, in a dusty room of the archives, some prophecy wrote of this. If old Miligrist had seen this in the depths of molten silver. A year ago, a century ago. If I was back on the path that had been written for me, or I was on one all my own.

"What did you do to me?" you asked.

My breath hissed against my throat. I feared I would empty the contents of my stomach on the stones. My eye caught on the knives, just a few steps away.

"The Night of Locked Tombs," I said. "There was a storm."

"No." A dark curl of hair was stuck to your damp cheek. "No."

I leaned heavily against the wall, my vision flickering. I was barely able to stand. You had stolen some of my magic. Humans always stole. They took, they took, they took.

—*Didn't you just try to steal your future, featherheart?* imaginary Cassia taunted. *Do not be angry at what you found when you went looking.*

"If I die, you die," I managed as I slid down the wall, using all the magic I had left to cement my illusion and hoping it would hold. Your face hovered above me, floating in and out of focus. I caught the sheen of the two blades in your hand.

I wondered if you would take my words for a threat and kill me anyway. Maybe it would be easier if this finished before it began. A dragon's throat slit by a human. I laughed, weakly. All my mother's plans and machinations, for nothing. All Miligrist's visions, for naught. Perhaps this was the wrong fork in the path.

I felt hands beneath my arms, hauling me up. You let out an impressive stream of curses.

Somehow, I found the strength to put one foot in front of the other, at least for a few more steps. Then darkness closed in, and I knew no more.

PART 2: CONNECTION

What has been torn asunder shall be mended,
two halves of a larger whole.
The dragon scales will be upended,
set aflame as if made of coal.

To slip unseen, through the Veil between, find:
the light and the dark.
Fire and water.
For one is chosen,
And the other cursed.

—Seer Miligrist, Vere Celene Year 718, Fourth Month

11. ARCADY: THE STRANGER

"This is daft," I muttered, grunting with effort.

I dragged the stranger's unconscious body behind me, grateful it wasn't far to the Loc & Key. I was strong, but I had to risk a bit of Piater's magic to help me.

I was well aware it was remarkably ill advised to take someone who had just tried to kill me into my own home. Far easier to slit their throat and be done with it. And, there I was, yet again doing something foolish.

They'd seen me in the caves. What else did they know?

My chest stung from Kelwyn's ministrations, and my exertions weren't helping. The metal pulled against my tender skin, and the new scab had already broken. Blood trickled down my torso. My arm stung from a knife cut from the fight.

I heaved the inert body over the threshold with difficulty, letting go of them long enough to grab some ropes from the shelves below the counter I used for extra storage. With more grunting, I managed to prop the stranger against one of the pillars, thanking my stars for the week I'd been bored out of my mind during a rainstorm and learned all my knots. I cast a couple of stay-put charms, risking still more magic.

Darting into the back room, I plucked a stolen temple candle from my supplies. Yes, that was likely damning my soul again, but priests make the best candles. I grabbed an apple and a sweetsphere for good measure. I half-expected the stranger to have somehow spirited their way from the bonds, but they were still against the pillar, head slumped to one side.

I lit the candle with a match and crouched in front of the stranger, chewing the sweetsphere and studying them in the faint light. Red hair, bright as a copper coin, had fallen across their eyes. It was just long enough to curl, and uneven. Their brows were a shade darker, closer to auburn, and black eyelashes lay above cheekbones like cut glass. Their skin was the shade of pale sand, their body tall and lean, but clearly strong. The back of their dark shirt was shredded, but the front was largely intact. Pretty masculine in appearance, and also just plain *pretty*.

They'd also drunk half a barrel of beer, by the smell of them.

I went to the small water closet at the back of the shop and filled a cup from the sink. I dipped my fingers and splattered droplets on the stranger's face. Eventually, they groaned. One eye opened, showing an iris of startling green. A drop of water fell from a lash.

At first their gaze was hazy, but their eyes sharpened when they focused on me. They lunged, but the ropes held fast. I was just out of leg's reach, resting my elbows on my knees and idly peeling the apple with the stolen knife. As if I didn't have a care in the world and invited people who tried to kill me into my home all the time. Casual, like.

I gestured at them with the blade. "Talk."

The stranger shifted their shoulders, testing the restraints again. I had studied my knots well. Their jaw was set. Anger or frustration? A lick of the lips. A glance at the locks on the wall, the marred dust on the floorboards.

"And say what?" Their accent was unlike anything I'd ever heard, almost musical in its cadence. They didn't seem remotely drunk.

"You accused me of stealing something." Never give away more information than the other supplied. Larkin had taught me that. I ate a curl of apple peel, the sweetness fizzing along my tongue.

The stranger hesitated, testing the bonds again, this time with magic.

"They're charmed, too," I said. "Don't bother." The spells wouldn't last long, but they didn't need to know that.

They took me in, green irises bouncing as they searched my face. The eyelids narrowed, and I reeled. Anger, definitely anger. "The storm brought me." Each word clipped. They offered nothing more. A standoff.

My knife paused. I'd suspected the strange, magical storm had been a result of the spell, though there had been no mention of it in my maire's journal. There was certainly nothing about drawing through a stranger who'd hold a knife to my throat and glare at me like they wanted to skin me alive. A little forewarning might have been nice. I forced myself to resume peeling.

"You stole me from my home," the stranger said. Their eye teeth were white and sharp, nearly pointed.

"Why do you think it was me?" I asked, playing for time. I usually had a plan, but the pain, the attack, having someone in my home—I had no idea how to play this.

"I see—I saw you among the bones."

My mouth went dry. I had felt watched that night, but I'd put it down to fear, the dark, the aftereffects of magic. I fought the urge to lick my lips. It'd give away my nerves.

They shifted. I realized, with a start, that parts of their shirt were black with blood, though not enough they were in danger of fainting.

"Why did you attack me?" I kept my tone carefully neutral. The peeled apple was pale and naked. I bit into it with a satisfying crunch.

"You harmed me first."

"What?" I asked, mouth full. "I haven't even *seen* you before tonight." *I'd certainly remember that face*, the too-interested corner of my mind added, unhelpfully. I squashed it down.

The stranger cocked their head, studying me so intensely I almost wondered if I'd said the second part aloud. "Open my shirt," they commanded.

I nearly choked on the apple before swallowing painfully. "Come again?"

"Open my shirt." Each word was so crisp it almost crackled. Still. A little disdain had bled into the anger. As if I was something stuck to the bottom of their shoe. They expected me to obey.

I hesitated, imagining them rearing back to headbutt my face and break my nose.

They raised their chin in a challenge.

I set aside the half-eaten apple and tucked the knife into the small of my back. Up close, I spied a spot of blood at the corner of their mouth. They smelled of stale beer, woodsmoke, spice, and sour sweat. I tore the buttons in one quick movement. The shirt was ruined anyway.

I froze.

There, on the muscled planes of hairless skin, was a bruised and bloody triangular scab. The exact size and shape of my own new seal setting. My fingers hovered over the skin. Heat rose from the stranger in waves as though they were fevered.

"No," I whispered.

The stranger's gaze drifted to my forearm. In horror, I ripped away the remnants of their shirt, the sleeves pooling at their bound wrists. The right forearm. I pulled up the sleeve of my left. The same angle and depth, but mirror images. Both wounds still slowly wept blood.

"Fuck no," I added, for good measure. The stranger said nothing. They'd clearly already made the connection back on the street. They didn't look any happier about it, at least.

I took the knife from the small of my back. The stranger stiffened, but relaxed when I put the knife to my own arm, right above the first cut. I dragged the metal against my skin, creating another red line. I hissed, both from the pain and from the matching wound that appeared on the stranger's forearm where it pressed against the pillar. If they felt the pain, they did not show it.

There was a ringing in my ears. *Do not faint,* I told myself. *You are not the fainting type.*

"Yes," the stranger said, voice rumbling deep within that bleeding chest. "If I die, you die. That night—connected us. I know not how." Their lip curled, as if the thought disgusted them.

The feeling is mutual, pal.

My eyes dragged back to the triangle of blood. The top of their stomach was rippled with muscle. I glanced away.

I thought of that golden glow on the cobbles. The way, over the last few weeks, my head would turn now and then, as if I'd heard someone call my name just out of earshot. Part of me had been waiting for someone to answer. Here it was.

"A magic connection," I said, as my stomach curled with certainty. And the only thing that could do that was mind magic—Zama's magic—which had been forbidden for years. No one was allowed to teach it, and anyone blessed by the indigo god could only do weather-work. If you were caught using mind magic, you were dead. No warnings. No second chances. My body shook, and I bunched my hands into fists. Panic was clamoring at the edges, but I would not let it win.

"Yes. Your power . . . it is different? Since that night?" they asked.

I battled the knot in my throat. "No," I lied, still trying to keep things together. *Mind. Magic.* "You did this. I don't know what your ploy is, but you need to stop it. Undo it. *Now.*"

"Did you call magic on the Night of Locked Tombs, or did you not?"

I said nothing. Their nostrils flared.

"Do you think I *want* this?" Fury dripped through their every word. They struggled against their bonds again, and I hissed and looked at my wrists. Rope burns appeared, red welts rising against the skin. We both stared at them.

"I would *never* want this," they said, almost hissing the last word. I saw it: a little gap in the disdain. A glimmer of fear as deep as mine. I felt it, somewhere along that thin golden bond.

I rocked back on my heels, uneasy. "Right. We agree that this is terrible. What now?"

"I propose a . . . ." another pause as they searched for the word. "Peace. We find a way to break the bond."

"A truce? And then you'll leave me alone?" I demanded.

"Truce." Candlelight played over their features. "You will no longer be my problem."

Rude. But I turned over their words.

The stranger shifted, restless. "My fingers are numb."

I narrowed my eyes. "I know my knots. They're fine." Would my fingers go numb if theirs did? The stranger tugged against the ropes, and I hissed at the answering burn at my wrist. "Stop that."

"Let me go. I give you . . . my word. That I will not harm you on this night." The tone was so resentful I almost believed them.

I snorted.

"My kind take our word very serious." A pause. "Seriously." They seemed annoyed whenever they misspoke.

I pressed my lips together. I saw no obvious signs of lying, but they could be a good actor. I tapped my teeth together while I thought it through, the sound loud in the quiet shop. I felt like I was faced with one of those large felines from Myria I'd once seen when a Trader carnival passed through town. That creature had looked at its owners with that same restrained fury, the same waiting watchfulness.

I was not stupid enough to turn my back.

"Sorry, no," I said. "Tonight, you stay right there. In the morning, if you haven't worked your way from your bonds and run, *then* I'll think about a truce."

They lunged at their bonds again. "I could burn these ropes to cinders if I wished."

"That's good rope, not easily flammable. Though I could always fetch some metal chains, make it that much harder for you."

They glared at me. If they could burn the rope, it wouldn't be quick. They'd likely used too much magic earlier. The thought caught at me.

"Do you need food?" I asked. "Are you in danger?"

The stranger cocked their head at my sudden urgency. Another tug at the bonds, a groan of frustration. "No."

Part of me wondered if I should force feed them, to be safe. But their eyes were clear, and their expression was angry, not hungry. In the aftereffects of the fight, I was exhausted. My nerves were fraying badly. I wanted to retreat and fall apart in private.

"I don't feel safe enough to let you go," I said. "If you get yourself free, I won't be able to stop you. My offer remains: if you're still here in the morning, and you haven't killed me, then we can try to figure this out."

I was all out of plays. This was all I could offer.

The stranger heaved in a deep breath, nostrils flaring. They hit the back of their head lightly against the pillar. "I seem to have little choice."

We glared at each other some more, for good measure.

"If you get free and need food to keep yourself safe, there is some below the counter," I said, too sweetly.

With that, I blew out the candle, leaving them in darkness.

I slammed the trapdoor shut behind me, securing my charms and my three locks. Made sure the window was well-barred. I ate a whole bag of candied orange peel and ginger to recover, my teeth aching from the sugar.

I changed from my bloodstained clothing, checking my seal setting in the mirror. It was bleeding again. I smeared an unguent on it. I should have tended to the stranger's wounds too, but they'd survive the night. I brushed my teeth, pulled on my sleep shirt, and slid into my nest of bedding.

Though I kept my knife beneath my pillow, it still took me hours to fall asleep. I read my maire's notebook from cover to cover again. My mind kept spinning over all that'd happened. Was it a trick? Were we truly connected? I strained my ears for signs of the stranger leaving the shop, but either they hadn't, or my ears couldn't catch it. The rope burns at my wrists stung occasionally.

This was impossible magic. And yet here it was, undeniably real.

When my mind spun itself out, I stared at my palm, tracing the lines in the moonlight. For a moment earlier that evening, it had glowed, like a small sun surrounded by blue and red lightning. It had been beautiful.

Just before I slipped off to sleep, I caught the scent of dust, the tang of metal, and the waxen smoke of a spent candle.

12. EVEREN: THE PRINCE & THE THIEF

It took me half the damned night to get out of my bonds. When they finally burned away, I hissed in triumph, working the feeling back into my fingers.

I peered out of the curtains to the dark street, debating whether to leave. I did not have enough magic to transform again, so going back to the clearing in the woods would take hours. And I had given my word.

Instead, I prowled the shop as quietly as I dared, taking in every detail. Below the counter some goods were stored. Rope, folded cloth. Preserved food, as you had said—dried sticks of meat and fruit. Fresh apples. I ate a bit of everything, for my evening meal had been long ago. While using magic made dragons hungry, it was not a danger to us in the same way it was for humans, because magic was an innate part of us. Not something stolen.

Another door proved to be a commode. It had what I needed: a small looking glass.

While scrying was normally done through still pools of water, silver-backed mirrors could also provide windows into the opposite world. Over the last century or so, it had become affordable for many humans to have them—an unexpected boon to us. Few humans even had the magic to recognize we were there, staring in on the intricacies of their short lives.

Starting when I had seen fourteen scorching Vere Celenian summers, I had been invited down to the prophecy pools every few nights to watch Miligrist in her trances, Cassia scribbling in a corner in preterit form. Each time, I had been awed, watching the old Seer tap into the power of starfire, dipping into a space where time no longer held its bonds over the matrices of the worlds.

Miligrist had nearly pressed her nose to the molten pool, scales dull with age, eyes milky with cataracts the healers could no longer shrink. One day, perhaps soon, the depths would show that her time was finished. She would fly off to the horizon and never return, like other dragons have before her.

I had itched to slither over the rocks and stare down into the depths my-

self. But when it had finally been my turn, there had been no spark of starfire. Nothing.

My human face stared back at me in the mirror, and it was a relief to let
it fall away, like a snake must feel after sloughing its skin. I imagined those
small rents in the Veil, trying to draw through pinpricks of the storm.

—*Cassia*, I sent. *Sister.*

I reached out with my dampened power, imagining crossing the Veil,
through the storm. Pretended I was flying over the upturned Lady of Vere
Celene, landing on the back of her neck before twining my way down
through the dark caves. I felt a flare of someone else's power, like talons
grabbing mine.

I opened my eyes, and my sister stared back at me.

She was in preterit, and I caught the shadows of tomes and scrolls behind
her. She was in the archives, using one of the mirrors. Nearly my twin in this
form, too. My female mirror image.

—*I felt you*, she said. *But it was a near thing. You must be careful when you reach
out if you do not want the others to know. Think only of me.*

—*I am new at this*, I admitted, grudgingly. *But I shall try.* Even among the
Seers, scrying was an inexact science or magic at best. Mostly, it was latching
onto an emotion, a yearning, and hoping starfire would show you what you
needed. For Cassia, it had always been one-way observation because there
had never been a dragon on the other side. We were both discovering how
to communicate from our respective worlds. Resting my hands on the cool
surface of the sink, I leaned closer to the mirror.

—*Have you found your human?* Cassia asked.

—*Not* my *human. But yes. This evening I almost killed it.*

Cassia winced. —*I am glad you did not.*

I clutched the edge of the sink. —*What have you discovered, sister mine?*

Cassia tilted her head to the side. —*I believe you have half-bonded. Your
bodies are intertwined as your souls have not finished the connection.*

My stoniness must have immediately given me away, for my sister's eyes
grew brighter. Another kernel of a prophecy proved true, I gathered.

Something like pride bloomed within me, but it was tinged by forebod-
ing. I had watched my dreams turn to ash before. Reverence turned to in-
difference. I wanted to believe I had moved fate back on its proper path, but
I feared it just as much.

—*And what does that mean? I asked. To be half-bonded?*

The mage light illuminated the shelves behind Cassia. Our treasure of remaining knowledge, so carefully guarded.

—*There is little on the nature of bonds, much less incomplete ones*, she admitted. *Much was destroyed in the fire. I found a few fractured pieces. Journals with veiled, offhand references . . .* She drifted off.

—*And?* I tried to hide my impatience.

She sighed, her eyes half-lidding. —*Dragons and humans did not remain in this state for long. Historically, they bonded young. Children raised together to foster the connection.*

I made a derisive noise.

—*It makes sense*, she said. *Children are usually more open unless they have been given cause to be guarded.*

We both looked away from each other, the specter of our mother hovering between us. Cassia cleared her throat, delicately. Her head tilted and the mage lights hit her cheekbones.

—*And so how do I free myself?* I asked.

—*As far as I can tell, you cannot. Both of your magics are fueling it. This is why you cannot turn back to a dragon. Your little human's power is also likely diminished. It is a protective measure to ensure a connection is completed, or if they are unworthy of it, both perish.*

I recoiled, stifling a snarl. Her last words echoed between us. Despair knotted itself through my stomach.

—*What am I meant to do, Cassia?* I asked.

She tilted her head in the other direction, giving me another slow, lidded blink. —*Isn't it obvious? You must complete the bond.*

This time I could not contain the hiss.

—*Once you have, you will have access not only to your own magic and form again, but perhaps also the human's. They stole our magic, long ago—the reverse may also prove true. This human is powerful, to have been able to draw you through in the first place.* She moved closer to the mirror, nostrils flaring. *You, in turn, should be able to use it to tear open the Veil. A symmetry to what happened, long ago.*

Much of what we knew came from Miligrist, the only dragon still alive who remembered being banished to Vere Celene. She told us a group of riders had grown jealous of dragons' magic—the bond granted humans a much longer life, but while dragons could take a humanoid form, the opposite never proved true. The humans believed dragons must be lying, keeping some of their magic separate. The Betrayal followed, and dragons had been trapped in Vere Celene in the centuries since—at least, until I had broken through.

—*How do I complete the bond?* I asked.

Cassia's eyes were unblinking, the vertical pupils wide. —*Make the human trust you. There was mention of a ritual in some of the writings to help cement the bond, but I'm almost certain it is symbolic. It is the trust itself you need.*

Every muscle in my preterit form stiffened. —*This human trusts no one.* That was clear enough from one interaction. You had left me tied up like an animal, and I suspected the only reason you had not left me on the street was your own survival instinct.

—*Do not be deterred,* my sister encouraged. *It is simply another hunt.*

I focused on a crack in the plaster on the wall. —*So, I bond with a human, gain access to its magic, open the Veil. Jubilation and celebration forever more.* Save for the humans.

Cassia steepled her hands, pressing them against her lips. —*There is only one more step to take.* She dragged her fingertips down, tucking them beneath her chin. *You would have access to most of the human's magic, but not all of it. And I do not think it would be enough. The human could always turn against you and take it back.*

I thought of how the human's touch had hurt and how I had felt my magic leave me. I had not told my sister that part.

—*There is a way to keep it. All of it.*

She saw me put it together as the glass blurred.

—*Yes,* she said, as she faded from view. *Make your little human love you. Do what you must. And then kill it.* Her gaze was unblinking. *Bring us home, Everen. Give us our world.*

◇◇◇◇◇◇◇◇◇

You emerged from the trapdoor holding your knife.

I had never gone to sleep, instead mulling over my sister's words all night and nursing a growing, pounding headache.

Your eyes flicked to the singed rope, neatly curled, the rags of my shirt stacked on top, then back to me. You took me in, lingering on the wound at my chest. I wore my human face. I had washed the blood from my—our?—injury, but it was already fading. Preterits healed faster than humans. It was another sign of our strength and their weakness.

I wondered what the wound looked like on you.

Every line of you radiated hostility tinged with wariness.

"I have not killed you," I said. "I have not run." I gave a pointed look at the knife.

We stared at each other in an uneasy silence that only two who had nearly killed each other could muster. You were making a concerted effort not to glance at my torso, whether from squeamishness or prudishness, I could not be sure. You were dressed much the same as you had been the night before: dark shirt, loose trousers tucked into boots, and a long coat. No paint or jewels like many Lochians seemed to favor. The shadows beneath your eyes hinted at broken sleep. You had something tucked under your arm.

With a grimace, you threw down the knife between us. The point hit the floorboards and it quivered.

"Here," you said, roughly, setting the bundle down well away from the knife. "Medicine for your wound. Some basic toiletries. A new shirt." Your tone was tight. You clearly did not want me here, but you could not risk making me leave. I doubted I looked any friendlier. I had just found out I was tethered to a human that could steal my magic with a touch. A human I had to convince to trust me so I could kill it. You.

"Thank you," I said, bending to gather up the bag.

You gestured with your chin to the washroom.

I did not want to turn my back to you when there was still a knife within throwing distance. I had no doubt you had at least three other knives hidden on you.

In the water closet, I splashed my face but kept out of sight of the mirror as best I could. I needed no stray thoughts dragging Cassia back to me or drawing another dragon's attention. After tending to myself, I drank deeply from the tap before facing you once again.

"Now what?" you asked, running your hand through your hair, mussing the curls.

I spread my hands wide.

Your jaw tightened. "Well. I don't have any food in, and I'm not doing this on an empty stomach. Let's go." Spinning on your heel, you opened the door to the shop, checking the street was empty before looking back. "Are you coming?"

Once I slid past you, you locked the door, the key disappearing into a pocket.

The fog had thinned by midmorning. Your home was on a quiet street, but soon we were surrounded by humans. I stared at the soft curls at the nape of your neck. You were slighter than I'd realized that first night in the caves. The scent you wore reminded me of the sea—salt undercut with sweetness. Your features were delicate enough, but your jawline was strong and your chest was as flat as mine. You struck me as somewhere right in the middle of masculine and feminine, from what I understood of the concepts. You were tall for a female but average for a male. When you glanced at me, your expression was cool, revealing nothing.

We were circling, searching for a vulnerable part to strike.

We stopped at a small restaurant called Emme's. You chose one of the outside tables tucked back into the corner with a good view of the street. I passed you some of my few remaining coins from my old clothes to my new pockets, not knowing if it was too little or too much. You took them without comment, which made me suspect the latter.

You went up to order, and soon, a human brought a carafe of a bitter drink called coffee and a pot of milk made from nuts. I followed your lead and took a sip.

"The beans are imported from Myria so it's pricey, but I almost died yesterday, so I figure I deserve it." Your tone was acidic as the taste of the coffee, but you drank your cup with obvious relish, watching the people as they passed on the street.

"As soon as the food arrives, I am asking you to explain everything," you warned. "But you can start with your name."

I swallowed. I had spent the night trying to think up some believable lie, but there was simply too much about this world I did not know. I skirted as close to the truth as I could. "My name is Everen." I held up my hands and signed "he."

You smirked and added more sugar to your coffee.

"Arcady," you said, taking another long sip. After a long pause, you signed "any." I was momentarily grateful for Mirel's impromptu lesson. Had it only been last night?

We focused on the coffee, but the silence grew brittle until a human finally brought two earthen plates laden with food. Bits of charred meat in different shapes, cooked eggs, which I'd had once before from a cart by the docks—dragons eat them raw, shell and all—and a small bowl of something you called barley porridge, scattered with spices and fruit. I poked experimentally at the egg and watched the yellow break onto the plate. Fascinating.

You closed your eyes and pressed your hands over the seal hidden beneath your shirt. With a few whispered words I didn't catch, a thin film of magic washed over the table.

"No one will be able to hear us properly for the next quarter candlemark." Dragons had a similar spell, but it functioned differently. You leaned your forearms on the table. "So speak. How in the gods' names do we fix this?"

"If I knew, would I not tell you, Arcady?" I tried out your name on my tongue. The click of the 'c' at the back of my throat. The tongue kissing the roof of my mouth for the 'd.' Your gaze flicked to mine. The blue of your irises had the smallest flecks of green.

I took a few more bites of my food. Many of the textures and flavors I'd tried in Loc were different from anything I'd had before. The barley porridge almost popped along my tongue.

"Where did you come from?" You took your own large bite.

"Beyond the Glass Isles."

You stared. "There is nothing beyond the Glass Isles."

"So you are told." I took another bite.

"How were you in the cave?"

"You drew me through the storm. My land, then yours. I fell."

"With magic."

I pointed at you with my utensil. "From *you*." I leaned closer. "What spell did you use?"

You shook your head. "No, this is a one-way interrogation." You narrowed your eyes. "I still don't believe it. Any of this. You're up to something."

You were a perceptive little human, I would give you that. We stared each other down, the space between us crackling.

You inhaled deeply, your nostrils flaring. "What life did I steal you from?"

I stabbed at another piece of food and took my time chewing. Delaying was annoying you, and that gave me a modicum of power. I controlled the flow of information.

I tilted my head. "My mother is Queen."

You had just taken another sip of coffee and you nearly choked. I felt the answering tickle in my throat.

"You expect me to swallow that you're a sarding prince, too?"

I shrugged, as if I did not care if you believed me. While I had just told you a partial truth, I leaned forward for the lie. "I fell with *nothing*. Knowing no one. You have taken me from everything I know."

I was the one who had gone searching. I had not fallen. I had *jumped*.

Still, you were chastised. You drummed your fingers on the table, focusing elsewhere. The last of the mist had cleared, pale sunlight catching on the shine of your hair.

"So you wish to go home," you said.

I was so homesick I was heartsick. "Yes," I whispered. "But not sure if I can." If I ripped open the Veil, dragons would stream through to the human world. Vere Celene would be abandoned. I hadn't, until that moment, realized I might never see the Lady snarl at the sea again.

You caught my sadness. You opened your mouth, paused, lapsed back into silence. "Well. We'll just have to find our way out of this mess and send you back where you came from. Wherever that may be."

"Perhaps. But the way will not be easy."

You gazed toward the street, not seeing it. "There must be something in the university library or official Citadel archive about magical bonds, but anything relating to mind magic would be heavily censored or long destroyed. Zama's magic is beyond forbidden."

I shrugged. "I know not." My language still did not flow as well as I wanted it to. "Have heard of magical bonds like this but they are . . . very old. The last one broke many years ago." *When your people tried to destroy mine.* "You can access this library?"

"Not any time soon." You stared hard at the crumbs on your plate, a line appearing between your brows. "And it's impossible to sneak into. I've looked into it."

I lifted an eyebrow. "Ah. You are a criminal."

It fit. Why you lived in an abandoned shop. Why you did not wish to tell me a thing about yourself. The careful way you took in everything.

"Not all of us are born royalty," you said. "I bet your pacifier was made of gold and jewels." Your mouth twisted. "Sometimes, people have to steal what others deny them."

Your tone raised my hackles, but were you wrong? There was treasure, deep in the Vere Celene caves. Some carried with us long ago in haste as the world's walls closed around us. After, we had pried pearls from their shells, or tapped the veins of metal deep in the earth. In our preterit forms, we had crafted them into beautiful things, solely for the sake of beauty.

Our archive was diminished after the fire, but still housed unimaginable treasures. In some ways, we were rich by your standards. But we were poor in food. In clean air. In a world that was not trying to kill us. In losing this land that had once been ours.

That hum of magic that had drawn me to you, across the barrier of worlds, still vibrated between us. Even now, I was drawn, observing every detail with far more scrutiny than I had bothered giving any other human so far. The shape of your jaw. The line of your neck, the pulse flickering beneath the skin.

"And are you any good at it?" I asked. "Stealing?"

A smirk. "Extremely. You'd never see me coming."

I could not help giving a dismissive scoff. Like a paltry human could sneak up on me. Not even you.

You gave an offended noise of your own. "I'll prove it."

"Ah, yes? How?"

You took a copper coin from your pocket. I had not seen one of its kind before. The edges were hexagonal and there was a hole in the center.

"This is a Myrian crown," you said. "Put it in one of your pockets, and by the end of the day, I'll have stolen it back." You covered your eyes with your hands for good measure.

I gave a slow smile as I put it in my right trouser pocket. Dragons love a good wager.

"And what do you usually steal?" I asked when you lowered your hands.

Your smirk was still intact. "Whatever shiny bauble catches my eye.

Whatever seems lovely, and above all, expensive." Your voice almost caressed the last word.

Of course, a dragon understood the nature of hoarding, though we did not often take what was not freely given. But you might also trade what you stole for power.

A dragon understood that, too.

13. ARCADY: THE FEAST OF STORMS

After breaking our fast, we strolled along the cobbled streets. I was acutely aware of my new "friend" Everen at my side, taking in the city with those hard green eyes. He still acted as though everything he saw was beneath him, especially me.

I didn't want to go back to the Loc & Key with the new stranger at my side. I wanted to observe him, out and about, to decide if he was telling me the truth or just a nicely spun fairy tale.

Perhaps he was a prince. I wouldn't be surprised if he had been waited on hand and foot. His every wish granted. Probably didn't even salt his own eggs. You could see it in his bearing, even in the cheap, borrowed clothes. If he was right, my maire's spell had somehow called forth a godsdamned member of foreign royalty. But something deep in my bones knew it was the truth, or partly. It sounded outlandish because he was an outlander.

We passed through Blackwell Market, and he lingered longest at the weapons stalls, taking in all the swords, the bows, the maces, pausing at a long line of daggers. My fingers inched toward my own knife at my belt.

"Every handle is shaped like a dragon," he said, seemingly derisive at their lack of creativity.

"Guess most people want a god to watch over them to make sure they don't get stuck with the sharp end," I said.

"Are you planning to give me my knife back?" he asked, running a fingertip along a blade. It made me nervous.

"No. It was an awful knife, anyway. Basically made of tin. Come on."

Morning had lengthened toward noon, though it was still cool. Above us, birds and wyverns circled lazily, calling out to each other. Everen watched them, and I thought I caught a crack in his hard shell. A hint of wistfulness. The crowds grew thicker on the streets.

"Damn. I forgot this was today."

"What was?"

"The parade."

He echoed the word at me. This was going to get old, quickly. "Surely you have them where you're from. Stars, they probably throw them in your honor." It was easy enough to imagine him in finery, waving at the crowd beneath him, a crown resting on his head. "Lots of pomp, great displays of might and power. Entirely too many ribbons."

At his blank look, I sighed. Not only was I stuck with a man whose life was tied to mine, but I'd have to play schoolteacher, to boot. "Last month was the Spirit Moon, which is the darkest and coldest part of the year. This moon and the next belong to Zama, god of weather, and everyone gives offerings to avoid storms wrecking the ships or flooding the lowlands or what have you. It's called the Feast of Storms. Won't be as grand as the proper spring or harvest celebrations—"

"Like the Feast of Flowers?" he interrupted.

"Er, yes, that is the mid-spring one," I said. "But it's still a nice enough spectacle, if you like that sort of thing."

His silence was wary. I crooked my fingers. "Come on, we can't cross it anyway, so you might as well learn a thing or two." And I'd watch him in turn. Was he truly as ignorant as he was claiming? He still spoke our language, even if he was sometimes hesitant. What else did he know?

The streets were clogged with crowds of people gathering alongside the Royal Thoroughfare that ran from the base of the Citadel down to High Ash, the largest cathedral in the city proper. Music floated on the air. Horns, flutes, and drums I felt in my ribcage.

We paused in front of a temple. Everen looked distinctly uncomfortable in the press of people. Wherever he was from, it was sparsely populated. I tucked that bit of knowledge away. I could barely see over the crowd, so I hopped onto a column plinth. Even though Everen was tall, he soon climbed up, sitting close enough I could feel the heat of his thigh near my hip.

"Not long," I said. "Weather's too nice for the Feast of Storms, really. Last year it was pissing it down—I was soaked to the bone. Added to the atmosphere, though."

"You come to these?"

"A few. Great day to steal. Everyone's distracted by all the fluttering and prancing." It was also a chance to see those who lived up on that hill come down to the masses—university professors, administrators, merchant and guilders, minor drakines. One of the few opportunities to gather information, and I needed every little nugget I could get.

Vendors sold mulled ciders, wines, or rum with honey and cinnamon, the scent of their spices warming the air. Children sat on their parents' shoulders, waving ribbons in the reds, blues, and golds of Loc. Plenty of people had painted their faces in swaths of blues, purple, or black, bisected with jagged white bolts of lightning. It was an old ritual, but I wondered how many realized it made them look reverse Struck.

I glanced away from a particularly happy family, pushing away the sickness of jealousy and grief in my gut.

The expectation of the crowd heightened as the music grew louder.

"What are those?" Everen asked, craning his neck.

I squinted. "You can see the floats already? Your eyes are keen. They're decorated carts, drawn forward by horses or Piater's magic for a full display of Lochian might." My words were bitter as hemlock, and Everen glanced askance at me. I had been alone too long; it was making me sloppy—I was giving away more than I should. *Be a fortress*, I chided myself. Letting in anyone was a mistake. I heard my parents' voices, my taie's laugh, and saw Lightfinger's gap-toothed smile, but I pushed them all away. They were gone. Nothing lasted forever.

The parade began with the guards in their interlocking scale armor. Black horses in five rows of five. Most guards rested their swords against their right shoulders, others brandished fluttering flags with Loc's heraldry. The sound of horns and flutes grew louder. Horses tossed their heads.

The first float moved sedately in the horses' wake, fluttering with cloth and ribbon in dark, stormy colors. A stylized tree carved from lightning-singed wood had small crystals hanging off its bare branches like frozen rain to catch the winter sunlight. A masked and robed priest stood in front, the copper-scaled embroidery on Their robes glimmering as They raised Their hands.

A storm bloomed above Their heads, twining through the branches of the tree. Bruised clouds, flashes of miniature lightning. It reminded me of the storm in the caves on the Night of Locked Tombs, and I fought the urge to shiver. Thunder boomed, startling the crowd even though they were expecting it. Next to me, Everen stiffened. A child started to cry even as others laughed in delight.

Behind the float marched more priests in Their horned masks, hands clasped as if in prayer to the gods above. Two priests perched at the top of the second float, one using magic to levitate a small, false moon over Their head. The other created dark clouds to cast the moon half in shadow. The float was followed by another contingent of soldiers on foot. Everen watched it all with sharp eyes. Was he distracted enough for me to steal my copper crown back? As if he sensed my gaze, his head turned toward mine.

"These next ones are the merchant Guild," I said, pointing. "Here are the jewelers." These guilders sparkled with metal, jewels floating above their heads like crowns thanks to Piater's gray magic. As ever, merchants and drakines received no honorific pronoun from me.

"The masons. Stoneworkers," I said as the next came into view, nodding toward the guilders with carved stone dragons hovering above their upturned palms.

"The next?" Everen asked.

"Agriculture." At his blank stare: "Farmers, growing food and such." He nodded, filing away the word in Locmyrian. The guilders had green vines twining about their arms, flower crowns in perfect bloom atop their heads. On and on they came. The shipwrights on floats that looked like ships, of course, twisting water into various shapes. The blacksmiths showcased a dragon made of red-hot iron. After that came a float from the hospital, but there was no real way to demonstrate healing someone without hurting them over and over, which would be grim, and so they kept to waving ribbons or growing a few flowers. So many businesses represented: textiles like wool and silk. Furriers, leather, and iron workers. Truth be told, I always found this part of the parade the dullest. There's only so much spectacle you can take in at one time before your eyes glaze over.

"Your people like to separate into different . . . levels," Everen said.

"We're all about our silos," I agreed, readily enough. "Stay in your place, don't aim much higher." I sliced my eyes at him. "Your people probably do too, it's just easier to ignore when you're at the top."

He had no rebuttal to that.

Even if he wasn't from here, he still represented all I was fighting against. The Consul was little more than a monarchy under another name. How fairly did his mother treat their people? Not very, I'd wager.

"Oh, here's the delegation from the university," I said, pointing.

"Strange hats," was all he said, and I laughed, despite myself. I supposed they were. The professors were in Their full regalia—sumptuous dark purple robes embroidered with alchemical symbols and conical caps. They each displayed something about the subject They taught. One slowly transmuted lead into gold. Another made a rose bloom, wither, and bloom again. Others echoed the storms and weather phenomena on the other floats with Their own twists. Still more twined thin metal wires into fantastical shapes.

On the lower level, students in dark blue robes waved clusters of ribbons. I had long decided if I did manage to get into the university, I was going to ride on the float at least once. To celebrate that I, the Plaguebringer's grandchild, was hiding right in their midst. If anyone ever found out, they'd be terrified I knew Barrow Eremia's corrupted magic—they would be right, on some level. I knew one spell that my taie had begun and my maire had finished.

The sounds of the crowds rose as we came to the grand finale. The reason I went to nearly every one of these gaudy things.

"The Chancellors," I said, knowing it came out in a hiss. Four figures on their thrones. Three with dark purple robes embroidered with gold, silver, and copper stylized dragons at their breasts. Wraithwright masks shimmered over their faces. Even if they were only plated, it was an extravagant expense. The Head Priest wore Their golden-horned mask, head swiveling back and forth as They took in the crowd's upturned palms. Slowly, the Head Priest stood and walked to the front of the float. The back of the robe was stitched with large, feathered wings. Like many of the magicians on the other floats, They conjured another miniature storm between Their gloved hands.

"One of those masks could feed an orphanage for a decade, at least." I leaned closer to Everen, almost whispering in his ear. My fingers itched to reach into his pocket and take back my crown. Not yet.

Before the Schism, Locmyria had had five chancelleries. Now Loc had three—Stormfell, Redwing, and Swiftsea, where we currently were. Myria had the other two—Greenscale and Blackstone.

I listed the Chancellors' names like they were curses: Ketrel of Stormfell, Carym of Redwing, and Yrsa of Swiftsea. They had been in power since the Schism. These were the people who had buried my taie alive.

There were rumors that the Chancellors in the parades were actually paid actors, to reduce the chance of assassination. I wouldn't be surprised, but I funneled my hate at those three masked figures all the same.

The Chancellors took turns sending shafts of sunlight to the storm, scattering the clouds until the spectacle began anew. The amount of magic they were displaying always made my head spin. The Chancellors were three of the most skilled thaumaturges in the country, which was how they'd grasped the power in the first place, along with plenty of cunning and scheming. The crowd cheered as the water vapors caught the faint sunlight and cast rainbows. It was a message: *we are still powerful, and we are still in charge.*

"Why do all of this?" Everen asked.

"Reminding us that the cold days are ending, and warmth and sun is on the way."

A troupe of dancers and acrobats closed off the parade, flipping and twirling, dressed in parti-colored clothing. A few played small flutes that trilled like birds. The parade continued along the thoroughfare, leaving behind a few ribbons that had worked their way free of the floats. The crowd broke the barriers, spilling into a street party, the music growing louder.

"They'll be here until curfew," I said. "Then they scatter back to their homes, most blazing drunk. We do like an excuse to get plastered in the name of the gods." Especially when people still remembered those years when there was no laughter, no celebrations.

Some of the crowd filed into the temple behind us, and I caught the scent of incense and burned leaves as worshippers prayed. Everen watched the believers leave, expression unreadable. I knew this person not at all.

"What higher power do your people believe in?" I asked.

The question caught him off guard. He paused, formulating the words. "We worship the fire in the sun and stars. It can show us the way—the past, the present, and the future."

"Huh," I said, folding it away to think about later, or see if there were any references in one of my books. The fire of stars. A land beyond the horizon. I shivered. "Sorry, but I don't believe in fate. I think you have to make your own luck."

Everen gave me a strange look. "I thought so too, once. Now, I am less sure."

Something about his words chilled me. I hopped off the plinth, dusting my palms. "Well. There you have it, your first taste of Lochians spending far too much coin and magic to show off for our gods and remind us lowlifes not to think too highly of ourselves. The powerful will always be above us, and we'll be scrabbling for the scraps below them." I sent a scornful look up to the Citadel, glowing like a flame lit behind a shell even in daylight.

Quick as a snake, a hand closed just above my wristbone.

Fuck. I'd gotten the coin from his pocket and was just taking it out. He wasn't touching my bare skin—my shirtsleeve was a barrier, but I still felt the heat of his palm. I tried not to gape, twisting to look up at him. His eyes were half-lidded in triumph.

"You lost the wager," he said, voice low.

The heel of my palm burned hot against his hip bone. Everen's grip tightened on my lower arm.

He'd caught me.

He stared down at me, eyes green fire. He released me before reaching into his pocket and flicking the Myrian crown above him. I caught it in one hand.

I rubbed my wrist, even though he hadn't hurt me. I'd been cocky when I'd made the bet this morning. I'd wanted to show off. Now I looked the dupe.

The crowds moved around us. A puppet show had set up in the square, and people had crowded around the makeshift stage, waiting for the performance to start.

I pressed my lips together. A very, *very* reckless idea was coming to me, and I didn't like how easily one part was melding to the next. A plan that involved a beautiful pile of wraithwright at the end of it. I'd still have to swallow my pride and ask help from a certain criminal group who wanted me dead. But in this stranger, I would have an ally, whether he wished it or no. His reflexes were fast. He was light on his feet. He could climb. He couldn't physically hurt me, at least not while we were ensnared like this, so he was less likely to double-cross me. I hesitated. He was also a liability, and it would mean having to teach him a lot. For this to work, he'd have to listen to me. I wasn't even sure he'd want to be taught.

"Your Highness," I said with forced casualness, passing the Myrian coin back to him. "Have you ever considered becoming a thief?"

He turned the coin over in his hands. For a second, I was certain he'd say no. And then he smiled.

14. SORIN: THE SIREN

S orin's kneecaps ached from hours of prayer.

The altars of all five gods were clogged with the ashen remnants of leaf idols. She'd prayed for the lost souls of the city below. She'd prayed for clarity. But mostly, she'd prayed for Magnes's safe return.

The morning after her mission, she'd left her coded missive in the wooden puzzle box on her desk before going down to the amphitheater for weapons practice. Even as a quiet, bookish acolyte, she went regularly, so no one had cause to wonder why an acolyte who had taken a Vow of Silence and spent days in study and prayer was so broad across the shoulders.

When she'd returned, the note was gone, but Magnes had been missing from the high table in the Great Hall. He'd been called away to the Nalore Monastery in the north. Sorin had known what that meant—that Magnes would have several stops at the leyline along the way. Protecting the world from the rips of the Veil.

Her tongue stayed glued to the roof of her mouth. No one save Magnes had heard her voice for the last six years. The Vow was voluntary, but she had taken it willingly. The gesture was somewhat symbolic—she could, after all, still communicate in Trade or writing—but she'd wanted to emphasize to Him that His secrets were safe with her.

She'd long thought of the Vow as her strength. Recently, it had begun to chafe. After so long without a voice, the thought of breaking it pained her. What if she had nothing much to say?

Her incense had burned to ash. Her prayers had run their course. She blew out the candles and rose from the hard floor, wincing as her knees protested. She stretched, letting the blood flow back to her hands and feet.

The chapel was less ornate than the main cathedral, with its stained glass, its golden ceiling, its organ that almost shook the rafters with its music, but she preferred it. The chapel was her favorite part of the Citadel—all who came were quiet, respectful. Here, she felt at peace.

Sorin left and crossed the courtyard, people milling along the cobbles or lingering near the fountain. She entered the hall, steering clear of the high table with its thick brocade tablecloth reserved only for the highest ranks. The Chancellors themselves rarely showed, preferring to keep to Their private wing. She spun between servants hurrying steaming dishes to drakines and visiting Stewards until she reached the long trestle table on the wall nearest the kitchens.

Sorin filled her plate and headed back down the hall, the tables growing lower in rank: first professors, some members of the clergy and others not. Drakines, both those who lived at court and those from elsewhere in Loc. Visiting knights, who were usually the third or fourth offspring from drakine families. Then administrators, treasurers, healers, and other Citadel officials. Bards, jesters, dancers, court artists, and poets. Servants ate in a separate hall, long after the rest were finished.

Half of the hall was devoted to students, most laughing and joking with Their friends. Others propped books behind Their plates, frantically studying for tests the next morning as They ate.

It was a careful dance, where all knew Their place. Hundreds of people lived on the top of this hill, and many rarely went down to the city proper at all.

Sorin sat at the end of the long table of acolytes. She was never sure if they were considered above or below the students in status. Around her, the priests were as jovial as the students, but Sorin kept her head bowed over her food. They had the baked egg cups stuffed with vegetables she liked best.

Gazes had a way of passing over Sorin. She'd spent years perfecting the art of being invisible while never leaving one's sight. The only thing remotely remarkable about her was her silence and her obvious Jaskian blood, but after years, this no longer even provoked mild curiosity. She spent her days toiling as a scribe or helping in the gardens. When the other areas of the Citadel were short-handed, she stepped in: assisting the Healers in the infirmary, or proctoring tests for the professors at the university. No one would ever suspect her of anything more.

Sorin rolled her shoulders and finished her food, taking a sip of well-watered wine. She stood, briefly catching the eye of Gemiean. Once, she'd run through these halls together with the other acolytes, laughing, until the servants chastised Them. Even after six years of her ignoring Them, sometimes her old friends would smile hopefully at her. Sorin might nod her head, but she always turned away.

She'd heard the whispers—that she was so serious, like she had the weight of the world on her shoulders. Just because she couldn't speak didn't mean she couldn't hear.

Sorin wrapped a few pieces of meat in a napkin for Jaculus and made her way toward her rooms. Habit made her glance at the Head Table, and she froze. Magnes was talking to Sar Anted Selly, reaching for the carafe of wine. His gaze swept the room and landed on Sorin, not even for the length of a blink. He turned back to the drakine next to Him.

Her breath caught in her throat.

She hurried through the corridors of the Citadel. The mage lights glowed against the sandstone. The Jari-touched flowers in every alcove showed not even a hint of wilting. The servants she passed bobbed her a bow, and she lifted her hand in blessing.

She was always surrounded by people.

She was always apart.

Her window was open to the crisp night air. Jaculus was out hunting. Even though it was early, she changed for bed. She lay, flat-backed, her fingers crossed over her stomach, waiting for Magnes's call. Jaculus came in a few hours later and forewent his usual perch to curl up warm at her side, his scaled head resting on her forearm.

She waited.

She'd just drifted off when red light woke her. The candle by her bed hovered, the flame burning crimson. Sorin was instantly aware, pulling her robe around herself as her heart quickened. She plucked the wax taper out of midair and put it into a holder, making her way to the corner farthest from the door. It was earlier than when Magnes usually called her, she'd guess not yet midnight. The red light flickered against the walls.

Without looking, she pressed one of the stones at knee height. The hidden door opened and she slipped behind the wall. In the alcove tucked in the secret corridor, she hid her stash of poisons, her disguises, her black robes, her trident knife. All the things a priest had no business having, where no cleaner could accidentally stumble upon them.

She knew the route blindfolded by now. Straight, left, left, down the stairs, right. Neatly, she avoided the tripwires and magical cantrips threaded through the passages for added security. She had never seen anyone else in this labyrinth, though sometimes she noted broken cobwebs, or boot prints in the dust. She wondered about these other emissaries, these secret spies for Magnes. His Eyes. If she ever passed them in the rectories or the halls.

Sometimes, when she had no other business, she wove through the passageways simply for her own curiosity. Magnes must know she did it, but He had not forbidden it. Sorin would look through the eye holes in paintings in the Great Hall or eavesdrop in cabinet rooms. She'd watch lectures unseen in the university. The only place where the wards were strong enough she hadn't risked undoing them was the Chancellors' wing or Magnes's private quarters.

Anything she saw in those wanderings behind the walls, she committed to memory. Snippets that seemed important enough she might pass onto Magnes. Yet, mostly, she watched for herself. Friends teasing each other. Professors gossiping in the lounge. Two people practicing a dance in an abandoned classroom, laughing when They trod on one another's toes, pulling close for a kiss. A parent wiping food from a snot-nosed child. Glimpses of other lives.

Sorin pressed another hidden catch and slipped into one of the many private study rooms in the university library. It was magically shielded, ostensibly for those practicing unstable spells under the guidance of a tutor, but it suited Magnes's purposes just as well. No one could listen in without tripping the wards and charms. And no one would expect to find the Head Priest in a room for students or professors.

Sorin set the candle on the table and stood still as a statue in that dark, wood-paneled room, waiting for her master.

Sometimes, Magnes called her once a fortnight. Sometimes, once a moon. Every time the crimson candle hovered by her bed, she came to this room. For Magnes was the hand. She was the knife.

Her heart tripped with excitement at seeing Him, but something like fear flickered at the back of her mind, a darker shadow cast by the crimson flame. Would Magnes be pleased with how she'd handled her first mission, or had she disappointed Him? He could be mercurial in his affections—sometimes warm and proud, other times taciturn and cool. Peace had eluded Sorin, these past ten days. She kept dreaming about raindrops against a window.

The air changed when Magnes entered; the scent of His magic was like stormwater and the burn of ozone. The door slid shut behind Him. Sorin inclined her head.

There was a gravitas to everything Magnes did—each movement considered, every word weighed, turned over like a sweet in His mouth. Sorin studied the High Priest from beneath her eyelashes. A buzzing energy pulsed through Him, beyond His magic, and Sorin felt it echoed in the tips of her fingers. Where had He gone? What had He discovered?

"My child," Magnes said, placing His gloved hand on Sorin's pate. Warmth spread through Sorin's stomach, chasing away some of the twisted doubt. She leaned into the glow. He was here. All was well.

"Your All-Holy Eminence," Sorin signed in Trade.

Magnes took His seat at the table, Sorin flowing into the opposite one. The red flame of the candle danced along the High Priest's bald pate. He had pale skin, and His eyebrows were nearly invisible, lashes light, irises a warm golden brown. Though a different shade, those eyes reminded her of Jaculus—sharp and missing nothing. The lines to either side of His mouth were deep. His age was impossible to guess—Sorin knew He couldn't be younger than His forties but He looked anywhere from that to His early sixties. Like others of high ranking, He likely visited the Healers regularly, magic chasing away the aches and slowing the effects of time on His body. He was largely unchanged from her memory of Him in childhood. She suspected He would grow old all at once, transforming from vital to withered and stooped overnight.

Sorin folded her palms together. The red light almost erased the freckles on the backs of her hands. She could almost pretend they were not there, along with her sandy hair. When she was young, she had wondered if her birth parents had loved each other, or if it had been a cruel encounter. Yet she no longer cared why she'd been left one morning on the cold, stone steps of the Citadel as the weak sun rose. What use was daydreaming of it when she would never know the truth?

Magnes had been the one to find her tiny, swaddled form and take her into the kitchen for warm goat milk. He had located the wet nurse. And so Sorin had grown up a ward of the Order.

Sorin had heard that as a babe she had never been silent, shaking her tiny fists as she screamed her constant anger up to the firmament. There had been no other fosterlings Sorin's age within the Order's heart in the Citadel, and she had trotted around at Magnes's heels like a puppy. Of course, she had idolized the one who was closest to the dragon gods, the one who had saved her. She had always been His.

She'd played with other children—the gets of academics and servants, mainly—but they found her odd. A small adult more than a child. It was easier to seek company with the priests. Easier to become one. And, later, easier to say nothing at all.

As she grew older, Magnes increased His distance, at least in public. When no one was around, He still sometimes brought her barley sweets. She'd rationed them carefully, trying to make them last. She'd been so upset when ants had found her stash once when she was seven.

The first time Magnes had called her in secret, Sorin had been nine. She had come into this very room, and He had asked her for a favor. She had been assigned to pour the wine at a function. He asked her to report back what a drakine, Sar Belric Idilwild, said to Sar Festin Mordend. She had parroted the conversation to Him as well as she could. Not verbatim, as the dinner had gone on for hours, but evidently well enough that He saw her promise, and her lessons had begun in earnest.

"You have been away," Sorin ventured, her finger movements hesitant. He hadn't called her after her report. He'd appeared at the Feast of Storms, and then He was gone. She'd dangled, worried she'd failed Him after a decade of training.

"There was a larger rip."

Magnes stretched His neck, trying and failing to hide His exhaustion. "Near Inveld. It was larger than it was last moon, and my Eye couldn't handle it on their own. I reached it just in time."

Inveld was at least three hours' ride north, on the other side of the Royal forest. "And the tear is mended?" she signed.

"For now. Though it's like trying to stitch a bleeding wound with spider's silk. I'm not sure how long it will hold." He rubbed at His temples. "I do my best to predict, but . . ."

Sorin was not sure what arcane mathematics Magnes used to project the rips in the Veil. She knew they most often appeared along the leylines that surrounded the Fangs like a star. It was a small, strange mountain range, jutting up from surrounding woodlands like its namesake, far smaller than the Spine that bisected Loc from Myria. Nalore Monastery was nestled at its center. The rips appeared most often at night during certain phases of the moon. Most were in Loc, with a few trailing off into Myria. They never appeared in Jask, which was lucky, as elsewise Magnes would have lost His battle long ago in a war that no one knew He fought, save the Chancellors and Their most trusted advisors.

Few realized that since the Strikes, the very fabric of the world had frayed. If they didn't guard the Veil . . . something would break through. Magnes referred to them as wraiths—slips of darkness that poisoned plants or sickened nearby animals. If they were stopped quickly, killed with the power in reclaimed relics, the area recovered. Otherwise, they remained blights on the land. There were whispers that the land was cursed, or that the land owners had angered the gods.

So far, the Eyes had held them back. So far.

"Teach me, so I may go in your stead." Sorin leaned forward, her signs fluid. "You are needed here." It was not the first time she had asked. It would not be the last.

If anyone on those lonely roads realized who Magnes was . . . there were Starveling camps in the mountains. Bandits who would find the Head Priest a boon of a bounty. Never mind that He was working himself to the bone to save them all. She yearned to help Him.

"You've so little faith in my ability to protect myself, my child?" He asked with the ghost of a smile, smoothing a hand along her head again, the leather gloves warmed by the skin of His hands. She fought the urge to lean into it, like a cat.

His power was drawn to Him, like iron filings to a magnet, but His place was here in the Citadel.

"Patience, Sorin, but fear not. Chaos has been pushed back a little longer."

Sorin's stomach fluttered. Magnes had first told her of the Veil after she'd taken the Vow at thirteen. Magnes said the Plaguebringer had caused the first rip in the Veil, letting loose the Strike. The Plaguebringer was long dead, and supposedly his darkness with it, but who knew what damage that place *between* could still bring?

Sorin had seen the aftereffects, just once. Magnes had ridden back to the

Citadel in the deep of night with one of His injured Eyes. Sorin had watched through the gaps in the Infirmary once she'd heard whispers of a stranger with odd injuries. They had put Them in one of the private rooms.

The Eye had deep gashes that already looked putrefied, though They had only been injured a day before. She'd seen the wriggling of maggots. The ranting chilled her more. They spoke of swirls and gyres, of this world being nothing but a pale echo. They were desperate to return. "I'm needed!" They kept screaming, to anyone who would listen. "I'm needed!"

Stare too deeply into the chaos between our world and the gods' realm, and a mind turned to mush. The Eye had died the next day and was burned with only basic ceremony and rituals. No one had attended.

Magnes had lost at least a dozen Eyes this way over the last handspan of years. They were lured in, tempted. A test where They were found wanting. Sorin often wondered what happened to Their souls after. Did They rise to the firmament by the grace of the gods? Were They whisked away into the storm, or sunk deep into the earth where no light could ever touch Them again?

The gods were meant to watch from afar with a benevolent or vengeful eye. The divine had woven order from disorder and left the world to Their followers, but chaos always spread its tendrils, desperate to destroy what had been built.

"And the relics from Karys?" Sorin asked.

A shake of the head. "Completely consumed."

Sorin mourned the loss of the glimmer of scales.

"There is something more," Magnes said, tucking His leather-clad hands into His sleeves. "Rumored sightings of a god." His lip almost curled.

Sorin's breath caught. People often claimed dragons appeared to Them. Portents in dreams. Waking visions. For some, the rumors renewed Their faith—They might walk through temple doors They had avoided for months. But the trade in false or true relics would also rise, with the hope They would bring blessings or protection.

"You give them credence." Her hand stayed flat at the end; a statement, not a question.

Magnes's eyes were inscrutable. "Normally, I would not. How many sightings of gods have we heard about over the years? A creature of dark wings and fire-bright eyes flying far out to sea. Dragons swimming in lakes or hidden in caves, guarding treasure." His mouth quirked before He spread His hands.

"But my source heard of a baker spreading tales of a draconic being near the Cave of Locked Tombs on the Night of the Spirit Moon." A long, slow blink. "The baker was convinced they were telling the truth. Yet my source said they were also acting . . . odd. Curiously blank. Like someone who had been brushed by a gap in the Veil. I sent others to investigate. The caves were thick with spent magic, yet the rip in the Veil had closed of its own accord. A rip I had not calculated. It did not follow the pattern."

Fear iced Sorin's insides.

Magnes steepled His gloved hands, pressing the index fingers against His lips. "It was enough I said any rumors of further sightings must come straight to me."

Sorin inclined her head, waiting.

"A few nights later," He continued, "a group of thieves sought treatment from the Healers near High Ash." Magnes stared at the red flame. "They claimed the mark they'd targeted moved impossibly fast. The worst injured gave the description of glowing green eyes and strange features. They were . . . as vague as the baker."

A god, or something sinister? True sightings, or simply two people happening to make up the same story? Wordlessly, she glanced at Magnes, urging Him to continue.

"Two instances could be mere coincidence, yes," He said, as if gleaning her thoughts. "Of course, there was a third." Magnes rose, holding out a gloved hand. "Come, my child."

Sorin tried not to gape at the outstretched arm. Any training had always taken place in this room. The closest to an exception had been loaning her an armful of scrolls or old books to hide in the corridor next to her room and study under the cover of darkness. Even teaching and sparring had happened here, building on foundations honed on the training grounds.

If she passed Magnes in the hallways, she would incline her head with a gesture of respect, as all the other acolytes did. No more, no less.

Magnes rose and strode from the room, extinguishing the red flame with a clench of His fist at the threshold. He waited for her.

As He knew she would, Sorin followed.

◇◇◇◇◇◇◇◇◇◇

Magnes led her to an abandoned drakine's house halfway down the hill. She and Magnes were both clad in standard priest robes and horned masks. Some nobles had lost Their heads in the Schism and been so disgraced that few wished to risk misfortune by taking those drakines' old homes. Others had perished in the Strike. And so grandness grew to ruin.

This one had belonged to the Ketch family, Sorin believed. After fifty years of abandonment, the roof was losing some of its scale-shaped slates and slowly collapsing. Water had dripped in during storms, painting the ornate wallpaper with darker brushstrokes. Curtains were moldering and moth-eaten. Leaves and dirt lay scattered along the parquet or marble floors, the bulk of the furniture broken. Any valuables had been rescinded by Loc to fatten its coffers after the brief but bloody war. The rest had been picked over by thieves who didn't mind chancing a bit of bad luck or a guard this close to the Citadel. Soon, the Chancellors would raze it to the ground, and a new rich merchant would build something even grander in its place.

Magnes climbed the sagging stairs, leading Sorin down the corridor. Moon and starlight streamed through the long-broken windows. He opened the door.

The person within looked up, startled. Pale skin, dark hair. They wore an overgown of silk, neckline low enough to reveal the seal setting peeking from between Their breasts. The chemise underneath was thin as gossamer. Around Their shoulders lay a cloak of deep ochre, lined with rabbit fur. Purple jewels made of paste glimmered at Their throat and the lobes of Their ears, matching the paint on Their eyelids. Their eyes darted between Magnes and Sorin.

"Thank you for agreeing to speak with us," Magnes said, a bland smile on His lips.

"I'm not sure I had much choice in the matter." They shifted.

Magnes's smile widened imperceptibly. "What is your name, my child?" They hesitated.

"I could always read your seal, if you'd rather," He said, almost gently.

They stiffened. "Mirel Denevin."

"You are a siren at the Dragon's Heart, correct?" He asked as if He did not already know.

"Yes." There was no hint of shame in the one word, but more than a little defiance.

Magnes nodded. "Tell us what you saw the night before last. Leave nothing out." His tone was soothing, a priest who would listen and forgive your sins. Some of the tension leaked from Mirel's shoulders.

"I was working. Seemed a normal enough night. A dockworker asked me to look after their friend and paid part of the fee. I took my mark to my room." They continued, telling of a person drunk and confused, a little shy. Said the mark asked questions about Loc, and claimed to have just arrived from somewhere far away. Mirel barely paid any attention to Sorin, as if she were another piece of broken furniture. Sorin stepped back into deeper shadows.

Magnes came closer, taking off His right glove and pressing His bared fingertips beneath the siren's chin. "You said they scared you. That they became something you could not explain. I want you to imagine it in your mind as clearly as you can. Go back to that night."

Mirel stared up into Magnes's eyes, lips parting. Their features became blanker, pupils widening. Fear, but something else. Longing? Sorin's curiosity caught.

The air grew thicker with the scent of rain and the promise of lightning. Mirel's seal began to glow as purple as Their false jewels. An echoing glow came from the seal beneath Magnes's robes.

Wisps appeared in front of Magnes and Mirel, and Sorin fought the urge to stumble back into the wall as they coalesced into shapes. A blurred image of a room. A person emerged: red hair, pale skin, green eyes. Tall, muscled but not bulky. Dressed in cheap clothing. As Sorin watched, the memory of the person fell to Their knees, clutching at Their chest. Their shirt had ripped open, showing a smear of scarlet blood.

"Are you hurt?" came the echoed memory of Mirel's voice. It sounded deeper, for They heard it from within Their own skull.

Heaving breaths, huffs of pain. The person looked up, and Sorin suppressed a gasp of her own.

Green eyes as bright as a seal when someone used Jari magic. Pupils slitted rather than round. The figure's features had sharpened, losing Their human cast. The skin texture was pebbled, almost scaled. They drew back pale lips to reveal pointed canines. They looked feral. Entirely inhuman.

The creature rose, and, with a crack like a tree split by lightning, wings emerged, spanning nearly the length of the room. Feathers the colors of flames ranged from deepest red tinged with blue to almost yellow. Beneath, she caught the delicate membranes stretched between the wing bones. Each one glimmered with magic. Even within the transparent echo of a memory, they were incredible. Sorin stayed silent, but only just. Her eyes stung.

The image blurred as Mirel lost concentration. They slumped against Magnes, breathing hard, seal still glowing violet. They slid to the ground, Their fingertips scrabbling for purchase on the splintered floorboards. Their gaze grew wild, features hollowing. Faint marks spread across Their skin like the dark purple of a bruise, eyes deepening to black until no whites showed.

With a scream, Mirel rushed toward Sorin, Their mouth a gaping maw. Sorin brought up the knife, but before she could use it, Magnes dragged the siren back. Mirel screamed wildly, all fingernails and teeth.

Magnes pinned Them to the ground and tilted a vial into Their mouth from His gloved hand. Sorin smelled honey, strong spices, nuts and some type of fruit. Mirel drank like a babe suckling from the teat. Like an animal. Like a starved thing.

A Starveling.

Sorin had never seen one so close. Anyone could fall afoul of magic— from the highest drakine to the lowest villein. Mirel had expended too much power channeling Magnes's spell, and Their body was demanding the price. Sorin's hand gripped the hilt of her blade. If Magnes had not dragged Mirel back from the brink, Sorin's knife would have struck true. She hadn't been in any actual danger. She knew this. Her heartbeat would not listen.

Mirel was sprawled flat on the ground, lips wet and sticky with honey. As Sorin watched, the faint markings retreated until Mirel's skin was unblemished once more. Their irises returned to brown, though the whites were bloodshot.

They sat up, pushing Their hair back from Their face with shaking hands. Tears streamed down Their cheeks.

"My child," Magnes said, fingertips again at Mirel's chin.

They met Magnes's gaze, trembling.

"You will not remember coming here this evening. You remained asleep in your bed. Yes?" Magnes's voice was smooth water, rushing over Mirel in waves.

"Yes," they echoed.

"You will not remember meeting the red-haired stranger two nights ago. Yes?"

"Yes."

"You will not remember speaking to anyone about this stranger. If anyone asks, you will change the subject. Yes?"

"Yes."

"You will not use magic for the next three moons, not even for the smallest spell. Yes?"

"Yes." Each affirmative was distant, distracted, as if Mirel was already off dreaming.

"Good, my child. You have done well." Magnes kissed Mirel on the forehead. Their eyes fluttered, and They lost consciousness. The Head Priest turned Their head to the side and drew the cloak tighter around Their sleeping form.

Magnes nodded to the siren. "Take them back to the Dragon's Heart," He said. "Let no one see you. I'll ensure someone keeps an eye on them over the next few days and nights."

Sorin stood in the middle of that moldering room as her world tilted entirely. The Head Priest of the Order of the Dragon knew the forbidden magic of the indigo god.

"What . . . ?" she started, but her hands failed her. She let them hang heavy at her side.

Magnes drifted closer, and for an awful moment, she wondered if He would put His fingertips underneath her chin and make her forget, too. A sneaking thought, quickly buried before it could take hold: had He done it before? But no, she only ever remembered Him touching her while wearing gloves.

He could have made you forget that, too, came a traitorous corner of her mind.

"We both know that to do the utmost good, you must sometimes dance with evil," Magnes said.

She had recently learned that all too well. She had the memory of Karys Fall's eyes going blank to remind her every night. "You . . ." Sorin's hands paused and she gestured to Mirel with her chin. "You're letting Them go? Seal intact?" The law dictated that anyone who turned Starveling, regardless of damage, had their seal replaced with marble.

The corner of Magnes's mouth quirked, perhaps at her using the honorific even for a siren. "It was I who pushed them to it in the first place, so it would be cruel to take their seal for that." Magnes crouched in front of Sorin. The reversal of the usual pose between them was beyond strange. She had always looked up to Him, yet He rested His hand on her knee, pinning her in place. "This is one less secret between us, my child. An offering of trust. Do I have yours?"

Sorin sucked in a breath, ducking her head. "Always. I am the knife," she signed.

"Good." He patted her knee.

Sorin's heart unfurled with the warmth of His approval. She closed her eyes, keeping the image of the being with wings crisp and clear in her mind. She kept her signs small, furtive. "Was that truly a god?"

"No, my child." His voice was soft, face fallen in sadness. "It only pretends. Do not be drawn to its temptation. It is only Chaos made manifest—a spirit who has slipped through the Veil during the Spirit Moon. We are entering tumultuous times." His gaze went distant. "I can feel it."

Sorin wondered if heartbreak ever made a sound. "It was beautiful, though."

"The ocean is beautiful, but its currents will drag you under. A fire burns. Ice freezes. The earth can crack beneath you. The dragons' elements created the world, but They care not at all if They destroy one little human who walks upon its surface. Chaos thrives only on itself." He drew Himself up, His gloved hand reaching out to her. "Our work has never been more important. Do you see?"

Sorin gave one jerk of her head. Took His hand and rose. He kept hold of hers, and the leather was so warm it nearly burned.

"The longer it stays, the more unstable the Veil will become. We must send it back to where it came from. Or all the relics we have in the world will not be enough to hold back the tide."

Sorin had let her faith waver. She had regretted her first kill. She had feared Magnes had doubted her. And yet here He was, showing her the path. She glowed with inner purpose. Pressing her palm against the seal over her heart, her five fingers were splayed wide in supplication.

"By Their claws."

15. EVEREN: LOCKPICK

My education began in earnest the following day, and I quickly wondered if agreeing to work with you was a gross mistake.

You had grudgingly made me up a bed in the top part of the lock shop the evening after we returned from the parade. First came the stack of books, the thump of their weight on the floor jolting me awake. You had already marked out the relevant chapters. History. Etiquette. A book on the rules of magic meant for much younger humans.

"I am not a—child." I had almost said hatchling. My nostrils flared.

"Then you'll make quick work of it," you said. "Or are you too stubborn to learn?"

We stared each other down, unblinking, and I suppressed a small glow of triumph when you looked away first.

I read through the morning, puzzling through the Locmyrian, but also surreptitiously watching you read your own books.

Later, you threw me a damp cloth. I stared at it wordlessly.

"I'm not cleaning your new room for you, princeling. You've likely never wielded one of these in your life, but you can today."

"I earned my keep," I groused. Yes, others maintained the warrens of Vere Celene, but I had taken down prey with my claws, my teeth. I had helped gut them on the stones and sawed flesh from the bone. I had studied in the archives, learning what I could, training for the day the future would open to me. The day that never arrived.

We cleared the dust from the surfaces and locks, unblocked the ancient fireplace. You kept correcting me, and I resisted the urge to snap at you. It was humiliating.

I had my orders from Cassia. I only had to pretend long enough to have you trust me. I could play nice for now. You were only one measly human, no different to the rest save for your strange spell that had drawn me here. You were beneath me. I scrubbed harder.

From the sound of your locks and the scent of magic whenever you went through the trapdoor, I could not sneak into the back of the shop without you being aware of it. I did not try. Not yet.

Over the next few days, we established something like a routine, but not one we reached with ease. I would read in the mornings until the words began to dance in front of my eyes. I knew it was a boon to have access to such information, but reading in a second language was exhausting.

Sometimes, you joined me and read your own tomes on the other side of the room. I suspected it was more to keep me to task. If you saw me staring off, you would berate me, and I would bite back a sharp response. You would quiz me, and if I did not know the answer, you would roll your eyes, as if it was what you expected.

"No," you said, again and again. "That's not what the book said." You saw things as very this or that. An answer was correct or it was incorrect, with little room for nuance.

You thought me a spoiled prince. I thought you an unworthy speck, a means to an end and nothing more.

"Stop . . . picking!" I exploded at you once, two days into this nonsense. "Always picking, picking, picking at the tiniest flaws."

"Then stop being flawed." You appeared unafraid of me, for you knew I could not hurt you. I was not used to such open defiance from anyone, save perhaps my sister. Other dragons were deferent to me, and I bowed my head only to my mother or Miligrist.

Cassia would admonish me for being so surly, but I could not help it. I had been yoked to a taskmaster. I was the one used to giving orders. I found I did not like being brought to heel.

A few times, you went out and left me alone, and it was a blessing of silence. I followed you, once. You went to a jewelry shop in the merchant quarter. In and out in less than a few minutes, with no purchases. Selling stolen goods, or something else?

Four days in, you sensed I was becoming agitated, cooped up in a dark store. I wanted the light, the sky. A break from your incessant lessons. You took me to the market at midday and purchased a few loaves of bread, cheese and meats, grapes and apples. A flagon of wine. I had long since run out of coin, so you paid for it.

"I'm keeping a tally, never you mind," you said each time. We assembled our meat, bread, cheese and sat on a bench near a patch of green park.

But even this was no rest. You asked me to observe the passersby and tell me what I noticed about them. Who seemed rich? Were they merchant or drakine? What guild might they be from? What jewelry did they wear, or where did they keep their coin purse? Endless, endless questions. I couldn't even enjoy my food in peace.

You'd mentioned this larger job you needed me for, but remained vague on the specifics. Any time I asked, you curtly told me I would find out soon enough. I hated that the mystery of it lured my interest.

It was stealing something important, a task you could not do on your own. That much was clear. But the Feast of Flowers grew ever closer—six sennights—and if anything, you seemed to trust me less than before.

As I observed the humans, I asked myself other questions. Which would survive the dragons returning, and which would fall? Who would believe the gods had returned, or who would reject us and fight? That grizzled soldier would fight. That youth? Perhaps they would flee.

Humans were fickle creatures. I would watch them gleefully cheat each other, or sidle up to those who were higher in status to curry favor and ignore the rest. Another might be casually cruel—cuffing their child without a second thought—or ignore someone, poor and starving, holding out their hands for alms. Dragons did not turn their backs on their brethren. My hatred for humans only grew.

When we went back to the lock shop midafternoon, my next task would begin. You started with diagrams and several locks from the back wall. Some were cleaned and oiled, but others dusty and stiff. You explained how they worked and what I must do. The first afternoon was an abject failure. I only managed to trip a couple of pins.

"Pity," you said. "I thought you'd do better than that."

I reared my head, my nostrils flaring. Your smirk did not shift. "You are doing this on purpose."

"What?" you asked, too innocently.

"Trying to drive me to violence."

"Maybe you're just particularly fetching when you look at me like you want to skin me alive."

I gave you my best glare, as if I were imagining just that, and your bravado faltered. I had moved closer to you without realizing. Your eyes went wide, and the breath hitched in your throat. Good. You needed a reminder that I was something to be feared. I pulled back.

"Look," you said, rubbing your forehead. "I know I'm being churlish. I'm trying to teach you something that should take years in a matter of weeks. If you're going to do this, we can't afford mistakes."

"It would help if I knew what I was working toward."

"You'll see, soon enough. If you learn."

With that, you disappeared down into your back room and left me be for the rest of the evening.

I stayed up late that night, and when you emerged from the trapdoor, I had all the locks lined up on the counter. Opened. The corner of your lips tugged upward before you smoothed it away again.

I worked my way up to more challenging mechanisms. Three pins, to six. Twisting the tension wrench and fiddling with the pick until I heard the satisfying click of pins hitting the sheer line. I learned how to "rake" a lock, using a hard and fast technique to help trip some of the pins, and then painstakingly picking the remaining ones. Eventually, you showed me the few master keys you had from a safe somewhere in the depths of the back room. I turned them over in my hands. They would work on certain kinds of cheaper locks, no picking required. You even taught me how to re-key a few locks, taking the machines apart and swapping the pins for ones that would fit a different pattern.

I found I liked doing intricate work with my hands. They were problems to be solved that required steady fingers. Occasionally, I would look up to find you watching me, before your eyes would dart back down to your book. But you had slowed the incessant poking at my flaws, at least. Sometimes, our long silences were almost companionable, before I remembered exactly what you were and what I must do.

Yet there were a few locks that, no matter how long I practiced, I just could not crack. I twisted one of the master keys between my fingertips, letting the light play on the tip. I had stolen a key before, of course, when I had broken into one of the few locked rooms in Vere Celene. I had found a prophecy that had proved to be another type of key, one that had let me fall between worlds.

All that was left was to pick your defenses.

◇◇◇◇◇◇◇◇◇

After we tired of wrangling locks, you began testing my magic.

This, of course, was another lesson in frustration.

You piled up little globes called saltspheres and sweetspheres on a plate before systematically working through the most common spells and counterspells with me, eating a sphere between each one. Of course, you did not teach me the spells on your door.

Human magic was rigid and strange. Whispered words, often just stating what they wished the spell to do but in a bastardized version of the dragon's language. Every time I heard echoes of Celenian on your tongue, I fought the urge to hiss. They had taken our words as well as our magic.

"*Luetakya,*" I would dutifully echo, with the emphasis on the first syllable instead of the second, trying not to grit my teeth. *Open.* The envelope between us would unfold flat on the floorboards.

"*Reukas.*" *Light.* A candlewick would burst into flame.

You could not hide your amazement that I did it without a seal of my own. One afternoon, after tiring of hovering a book a few handspans off the floor and lowering it back down again, I fought down a yawn of boredom.

"Take off your seal," I said. "Let us see if you can do magic my way."

You looked at me suspiciously, and I half-expected you to tell me to do something rude and anatomically improbable.

Yet you reached into your shirt and popped the seal from the metal setting. I peered at the stone cylinder, though you did not hand it over. You did not even know where dragonstone truly came from. Few humans did. Dragons guessed there was a large reserve hidden in the mountains, heavily guarded, which humans had poured their stolen magic into. The priests of the Order chipped off a piece, carved their seals, and gave each human one at birth, cementing it in with a closely guarded spell.

Most humans, even with a seal, only had a small spark, enough for a few minor spells, or for the authorities to locate them if they strayed too far from the law. What I found interesting was that, with enough food and study, humans' magical ability could clearly grow. Was it the dragonstone itself, or the humans adding their own power? What could you do without a seal?

"Well?" you asked, impatient.

In dragon form, we could simply think magic into being, but in preterit, we found hand gestures useful. I showed you the one for flame but told you to imagine it happening as you did so.

Your brows grew together as your fingers twisted, tracing the shape of an imaginary flame. Nothing. You stared at it harder, until I feared you would burst a blood vessel.

"Think it, bring it into being," I coaxed.

Again, you glared at the wick so intensely that I half-expected it to burst into flames from your sheer annoyance alone. Was that the faintest scent of smoke? The wick stayed black and cold.

You tried a last time, speaking the spell in mispronounced Celenian. Nothing.

You slumped back in defeat.

"Perhaps you only need more practice," I offered, but I would need to tell Cassia. This human, at least, could not do magic without a seal. That was useful information. Yet I could still feel the bond between us, despite the removal of that piece of stolen stone. Interesting.

You tilted your head at me. The frustration had fled. You seemed to be considering whether to ask something.

"What?"

You reached out a hand, fingertips hovering over the skin on the back of my hand. "I haven't forgotten what happened when we touched."

My breath hissed out.

"Does it happen every time?" you asked.

I wanted to draw my lips back from my teeth and grow my fangs. The memory of the pain of drowning in sunlight made my lungs ache. I forced myself to consider the request rationally. It might help Cassia discover more about the nature of this bond. Perhaps it would even help strengthen it.

"I do not know," I said, and I hated the note of uncertainty. It sounded too close to fear.

You shifted closer. "Can I try?" Your hand still hovered over mine. Fingernails bitten to the quick. A faint scar on the back of the thumb, long faded to white.

Before I could second-guess myself, I flipped my hand and pressed my palm to yours.

For an instant, all I felt was the warmth of skin and a pulse, deep in my chest. The chime echoed through the lock shop like a gong. Energy rushed down my arm, through my hand. Gold glowed between our palms. The color lit your features from below. You were ephemeral, like a being that belonged to neither this world nor mine.

The pain came slower, but no less intensely. My lungs ached; my eyes burned. My skin felt too tight over my skull. Cold brightness burned through my veins. I felt my handle on my human form begin to fray. My wings itched against my back, desperate to be free. My teeth sharpened.

With a gasp, I jerked back, dropping my palm. Your hand continued to glow with the same blend of gold, red, and blue as the alleyway a little over a sennight ago. You waved it slowly, eyes wide in awe. Your seal was still carefully set on its end next to the candle. Your eyes snagged on the pillar of wax.

You made the gesture. —*Fire. Burn. Reukas.*

The wick ignited.

"I—" you started, but for once, you, too, were at a loss for words. You did not seem to realize you had thought the command instead of spoken it.

I held my hand to my chest, still fighting down gasps. The glow faded from your hands. The flame flickered between us like an accusation.

"*Never*," I said, my voice shaking, "do that again." My anger burned as bright as the flame. You had taken my magic and used it. I rose, with frantic thoughts of either pushing you against the wall or backing away and fleeing to the forest, putting as much distance between us as I could. I had nearly lost my form. Even now, I felt the gap, the lessening of my magic. Because for now it was *yours*.

"I'm sorry," you said, eyes wide.

I was not quite able to meet your gaze.

"I—I knew it would hurt you, but I wanted . . . I wanted to feel it again." Out of the corner of my eyes, I caught you holding up your hands. "But I'll keep these to myself. I promise." I heard you rub your upper arms, as if you were cold. "My magic has been different since the Night of Locked Tombs," you admitted. "I thought it was your fault."

I turned my ear toward you, my gaze still on the floor.

"I—I can't keep my spells live as long. Shapeshifting was always easiest, but I can't hold it for more than a candlemark. It's all I can do to keep my charms in here going. And my magic—it—it tastes different." I glanced up at you. You shrugged, as if you had no idea how else to describe it.

"I believe our magic is fueling a half-bond," I allowed. I clenched my jaw.

"Do . . . you think if we complete or break the bond, our magic might work normally again?" you asked, voice small. That defiant facade had cracked. I had seen through it when I had caught you with your hand in my pocket at the parade. And the first night, when we had discovered we were tied to each other, I had felt your panic through the bond, even as you tried to hide it.

"Maybe." I did not tell you that any magic you took from me, I would take back from you, and more. I would take *everything*.

You nodded, running a hand through your hair. "Right. Then all we can do is keep teaching you, and I—" you broke off, forced yourself to continue. "I'll talk to my contact about setting up a meet with other people we'll need to pull it off."

"Other people?" I echoed. "Do you trust them?"

"I've worked with them before. The Marricks are the best."

That did not answer the question. My brow drew down. You had asked if the Marricks had sent me, the night we met. You thought they might want you dead. Your eyes were flat and cold—if I angled for more, you would not give it.

"Will I be ready?" I asked instead.

"You'll have to be," you said. You came closer, and I suppressed a flinch. But all you did was bend low and take the candle you had lit with my magic. Before I could say another word, you pressed your seal back into its setting beneath your shirt, slipped away, and left me in the gloom.

16. ARCADY: THE RED COAT

I was awake at first light. Sleep had largely slithered away from me, as usual. At least half a dozen times over the last sennight, I'd wondered if recruiting Everen had been a mistake. I'd been more than half-tempted to throw him out, strange magical bond or not. He was in my space, my life, and I did not want him there. I didn't want to *need* anyone, especially him. And yet, for the moment, I did.

Any remnants of dreams faded as I rubbed my face. There had been the silver beneath, the storm above. Something tall looming. A building? A bridge? I tried to sketch it in my notebook.

A faint tapping at my window.

A gray wyvern peered at me through the glass.

I pushed up the sash, and the wyvern hopped through the bars. It flapped and landed on my table, scattering a few of my drawings to the floor.

I found it a strip of jerky and, as it chewed, I unstopped the cylinder on its leg and pulled out a scroll of paper. There was Kelwyn's delicate, beautiful handwriting.

> *I know you want honeyed jobs, A, but asking me to set up a meet with L and W is inviting a whole swarm of bees. Hope you know what you're doing, Imperious Imp. One sennight. Sunset.*
>
> —*K.*

"Fuck," I whispered, and the wyvern cocked its head at me. "No turning back now," I told it. Seven more days to make my strange princeling a good enough criminal he wouldn't get us both killed. Was this my most harebrained plan yet?

I found a spare sheaf of paper and scribbled a note back, giving the wyvern another strip of dried meat while I rolled the paper and put it into the canister. In the pouch on the other leg, I added two copper suls for the delivery payment.

I gestured to the window, and the wyvern chirruped and hopped back onto the sill. It would only know to return to its roost, and Kelwyn would check for the message that afternoon. He used a postmaster that asked no questions, never opened mail, and kept no records.

I splashed my face with water, changed from my nightclothes, and climbed through the trapdoor to the front of the lock shop.

Everen was curled up on the bed, the cover thrown over his head. I still wasn't sure what to make of him. He infuriated me, but he fascinated me.

He had proved deft enough at picking locks, but he himself remained a mystery. I had decided to believe he was a prince, or something like it. He certainly acted haughty enough for it. Yet I also knew he would take any puzzle I gave him and make it a point of pride to solve it. True to our promises, he hadn't tried to kill me, nor had he run. Yet by touching his bare skin again, I worried I'd broken something between us.

I'd almost grown used to the sight of him studying in the corner of the shop, his mouth moving silently as he read, pausing now and then to ask me to define a word. I'd found myself staring at his lips and had to remind myself that attraction was a distraction. Luckily, he'd usually open his pretty mouth and act the arsehole, which helped tamp it back down.

One week until I found out if that future I wanted so badly could actually be mine.

"Up," I said, toeing what was probably his calf with my foot. A muffled groan, and he twisted beneath the blankets. He emerged, yawning, and padded toward the washroom. Did he have to sleep shirtless? I might have stolen a glance at his wide shoulders, the muscles moving beneath his skin, that narrow waist. Only a glance.

I brought the banked fire back to life and put on a kettle for tea. I'd started storing most of the food behind the counter, and we took our meals up here. After breakfast, I decided we'd skip studying that day and focus on the fine art of pickpocketing.

We cleared the lock room to give us enough space. I cracked the curtains to let in slivers of bright early-spring sun. We both slipped on gloves since we'd have to work closely. Everen was wary, and he'd been subdued since I'd stolen some of his magic. He could never know that I'd do it again, in a heartbeat, just for that moment of power again.

We began.

I flipped a copper coin and caught it, putting it in my front pocket. "Your target."

He nodded, studying me as closely as one of the locks I'd given him to break. I walked him through each step. Which pockets would be most likely to have valuables. How to open a clasp of a purse silently or cut its strings. The way to walk, how best to reach into a pocket unobserved. Though he had some natural skill and whip-quick reactions, he was clumsy and stiff.

"Again," I'd say, rapping his wrist above the shirt when I'd feel his fingertips.

"Picking, picking," he muttered, but he'd go back to his starting point without too much grumbling.

"Pickpocketing," I corrected, and he rolled his eyes.

After a candlemark, he grew frustrated and started snapping at me again. I prided myself on putting others at ease around me, and it was a skill I kept as sharp as any knife. Strangers thought me a confidant, and they'd smile even as I drained them dry of coin or information. But Everen brought out the worst in me, and I snapped right back.

"Again," I said, my voice tight. I flipped the copper coin and put it in my back pocket.

A mistake. He was staring at my backside far too intensely, and the room grew warm. He smelled annoyingly good, like smoke and spice. I cleared my throat.

"Pretend we're in a crowded square. You must bump into me so lightly I don't notice. Less than a second to grab the coin."

Everen nodded, his molten gaze still on me.

Firmly telling my heart to stop racing, I meandered across the room, pretending to pause and peer at wares in an imaginary market. I felt too aware of my body. I exaggerated to hide my unease, gawping at something. His low chuckle sent a shiver down my spine. Not helping.

He ambled closer, arms loose at his side. If I hadn't been so godsdamned attuned to his every movement, I might not have felt the faint ghosting of fingertips at the top of my pocket. I started forward, as if I'd seen another friend, waving animatedly. I caught his sound of muffled frustration.

He tried again, knocking me "accidentally." His fingers dipped and claimed the prize of that Myrian copper coin. I froze, feeling spots of color rise to my cheekbones.

I needed a firm talking-to. I'd had little experience with romance or sex. I'd flirted with a few marks, and I kissed a couple when the job called for it, though the act had left me cold. This was nothing more than a chemical reaction, a physiological response.

I was in control.

I had other reasons for my growing frustration. Though I'd never lain with anyone, I'd often found my hands down my trousers come nightfall, seeking a release to help me drift off to sleep. But I didn't know the rules of the bond. Would he sense the moment when . . . ? I'd sooner burst into flames than risk it. The past few nights, I had spent even longer wanting to crawl up the walls, staring at the scarves pinned to my ceiling, searching for shapes in the shadows.

I coughed and tossed Everen a look over my shoulder. "You're still sloppy. But that was better." I smoothed back my hair. "Again."

We practiced for another candlemark. Front pockets, back pocket. Cutting the purse I'd tied to my belt. I taught him how to loosen a bracelet clasp during a handshake. How to unfasten a necklace while hugging someone and patting them against the back, trying not to dwell on the feel of his body pressed to mine, my cheekbone resting against his collarbone for the barest second, the fabric of his shirt between our skin, or his gloved fingers at the nape of my neck.

We didn't snap at each other once.

I decided to end with the hardest challenge, putting the coin purse in my inner pocket of my jacket.

I made my same amble across the swept floorboards of the lock shop, humming tunelessly. Everen's approach this time was to subtly trip me and help me steady myself. I didn't sense him reach the pocket, but the knuckle of his smallest finger ghosted along my ribs as he pulled the purse out and tucked it up his sleeve. My breath hitched.

He stared down at his hand as if it'd burned him. We hadn't touched skin to skin. He wasn't in pain. Our eyes locked. We were still standing too close. I stepped back.

"Good." I straightened my jacket.

"Good enough?" His voice was too low, too soft.

I tilted my chin up at him. "Only one way to find out."

◇◇◇◇◇◇◇◇◇

I leaned over the edge of the Bridge of Shells, staring down at the cobbled riverwalk below. It was midmorning, and not busy. I'd chosen this bridge because it was dedicated to Kalsh, my own supposed god. Carved with nautical creatures, with the railing spiraled as a narwhal horn, it was a beautiful bit of architecture. Lovers would come and glue shells painted with their initials to the bridge like barnacles.

I stood on my toes, leaning over the railing. A steady stream of people passed beneath me. I studied the parts of their hair, the cut of their clothing. I wondered who Everen would choose as his mark.

Everen was a little further along the riverwalk, scattering birdseed for the pigeons and waterfowl. He wore one of the new sets of clothing I'd added to my tally—a crisp white shirt, dark blue trousers. That and a simple black cloak around his shoulders announced he was likely a journier-level tradesperson. His distinctive red hair was hidden by a dark hat with a bluebird feather.

I lit a smokemint cigarette as a cover for loitering, the smell reminding me of Kelwyn. I'd stub one out when it was finished and light another, pressing my lips against the sugared paper and watching the pedestrians through furls of gray smoke.

The river water came from the glacier stream up in the Fangs. This very water had flowed past Atrel, the mountain town where I'd lived with my parents. It was a ghost town these days. Nothing but rubble and bad memories. Here the water was a murky gray-brown as it made its way out to sea.

The yellow sandstone buildings rose to either side of the river, the shorter ones thatched, the tenements slated. A few small fishing boats bobbed, people shading their eyes from the sun bouncing on the water as they navigated toward the docks. An average, unremarkable morning in Vatra.

When I lit my third cigarette, I felt a thrum through the bond.

I stubbed out the smokemint. There. A person in a red coat with brown hair. Everen nodded his chin, confirming. I took a little pot from my pocket and unstopped it. I cast a quick notice-me-not charm while I grabbed a handful of chalky white stuff in my gloved hand and flung it over the stone railing of the bridge for it to splatter right on the mark below.

"Argh!"

I ducked out of sight before they could glance up at the offending "bird." Stifling a laugh, I took off the glove and wrapped it in a cloth before closing the container of ersatz bird shit. I'd perfected the recipe during my time with Larkin and the Marricks. It was a cheap trick, but effective.

I shuffled down a few steps and chanced peering over the edge of the bridge again. Red Coat was hunched in embarrassment, hands hovering over the white splashes. Everen had chosen his mark well. The gold trim and lace at the collar suggested a rich merchant.

Everen made a show of doing a double take as he approached. "My good sar!" he exclaimed. His Vatran accent had improved. "Your poor coat. At least they say it's good luck, don't they?" Everen gave the mark an easy grin, reaching into his pocket and producing a handkerchief.

Were those . . . contractions? So he simply *chose* to sound so formal and stuffy.

The mark wasn't immune to his charms. Their frantic movements slowed a tad.

"I'd rather have a little less luck today, all the same," the mark said, acerbic. They were too far and beneath for me to make out their features.

"Here, here, let me help," Everen said, coming closer and patting them down with great enthusiasm.

"Thank you, th—thank you," the mark said, trying to extricate themselves. "I'll have to go home and change before my appointment. A bother, but not a disaster." Their head turned, presumably in the direction of where they lived.

Everen gave another few swipes with his handkerchief, which only really served to spread the white around, and stepped back with a bow.

The mark looked down at the white-smeared coat in dismay. They tugged it straight and salvaged the last of their dignity. "My thanks," they said, nodding their head and backing away.

"Good day!" Everen said, brightly, and I could just make out the curl of the corner of his lips as the mark scuttled away, head ducked low as if that would make the bird shit less conspicuous.

Everen gave a last scattering of seed for the birds before tucking his hands in his pockets and making his way to the stone steps leading up to the bridge.

Everen walked toward me, looking entirely too pleased with himself. We glanced down at the distant speck of red hurrying along the riverwalk. How long before the mark realized they'd been had? Would the poor servant stuck with cleaning that coat recognize it was a mess of soured cream, chalk, black pepper, and a bit of flaked-off dried true bird shit?

"My thanks!" I said, in high-pitched imitation.

Everen laughed. It reverberated in his chest, and his shoulders shook. I'd seen him serious, and deeply annoyed, and furious. This was the first time I'd heard him laugh without reservation, as if he couldn't hold it in, and I found I liked the noise. It transformed his whole face, making him less severe. His eyes were bright, his teeth straight and white.

I tried to stop my own wheezing laugh, only to set us both off again. My cheeks soon hurt.

When our merriment finally subsided, we listened to the birds, the soft lapping of the river against the stone walls, and people speaking to each other on the riverwalk.

"So what'd you nab?" I asked.

He tossed me a velvet coin purse and a small tortoiseshell comb. I poured the coins onto my palm—about two silver suls, the same again of copper, and a gold.

"Dragon's feathers," I exclaimed. "What an idiot, to walk around with all this."

"Earned my keep?" Everen leaned against the side of the bridge, one leg crossed over the other.

"That you did."

I kept the gold and gave the rest to him. "That's about as much as working at the docks for two and a half months."

He raised his eyebrows as he tucked it away. "And how much is that yellow-gold one?"

I snorted. "Just under half a year."

He huffed a faint laugh. "Then I have already proved a sound investment, have I not?" His accent curled around the words. We started walking across the bridge toward our side of town and the lock shop. "Am I ready?" he asked. He'd taken off his cap, and his hair glinted in the sun, his eyes half-lidded against the bright.

I knocked my elbow against his. "We'll see."

17. EVEREN: LARKIN & WREN

Even meeting criminals proved to be a test.

As we left the lock shop, you tucked the sole key in your inner pocket. I was not entrusted with my own. When we reached Thistledown Street, you hung back. I had the address and my mission: arrive early and find a way to eavesdrop on the meeting without anyone the wiser. I chanced a glance back at you pretending to window shop. Your black coat was pulled tight around you, reminding me of the dark stone columns in the caves of Vere Celene.

I reached the Last Golden in good time. I had about a quarter of a candlemark. At least I had my advantage of sharper hearing and eyesight. I pulled down my hat, aiming to stay unobserved. My way forward was clear enough. There were alleyways to either side of the pawn shop, and a few small windows. I narrowed my eyes at them, calculating. I might slip through. Barely.

I glanced to either side of the abandoned alleyway, which stank of rotting rubbish. I could just reach the window. One person was already inside. Kelwyn, I presumed, the owner and "fence" for your stolen goods. You had told me a little of him, but he was probably the closest thing you had to a friend. He wore a coat of dark orange. Graying brown hair fell into his eyes as he bent over something on the counter. The next window showed a storage room. Perfect.

The window had a few wards, but I banished a few with the spells you had taught me, muttering mangled words of my own tongue. One ward was particularly difficult, and almost got away from me, but I banished it in the end.

The catch on the window was not easy to pick, especially from this angle, but I managed. Once I pushed it open, I hesitated. Stretching my awareness, I caught a ward I had missed, even trickier than the last. I spent a few more minutes chasing it away, like blowing a plume of smoke.

I will not pretend I slithered through that window with anything like grace, but I managed. Twisting my body, I jumped down silently into the dim room. I closed the window but did not lock it.

The storage area was filled with cloth-draped boxes. The bottom half of the walls were lined in a dark wood, the upper half with faded wallpaper with a stylized design of dragons. They were everywhere you looked in this blasted human realm, like a taunt.

I spied a stained-glass window that showed a rose and thorns that looked down into the shop, and I climbed onto the boxes, peering through the red-stained glass. There was Kelwyn, now marking something in a ledger. He ran a fingertip slowly along the bridge of his nose as he stared at the numbers.

The shop was full to bursting with all manner of trinkets and possessions. You had told me that some were ancient antiques—early pottery or simple coins from when Vatra was little more than a collection of huts clustered next to the sea. When dragons still roamed the lands, not that you knew that for a truth. I squinted and tried to make out any porcelain from the Eltan era, which I had been reading about earlier that week. The flowers were painted so delicately the brushes must have only had a couple of hairs each.

You had said Kelwyn was fond of little figurines that could move mechanically or with the smallest spark of magic. I spied some still ones. An acrobat suspended on a tight rope. A horse that might walk over a tabletop. A dragon—of bloody course—that hung from the ceiling. There were cabinets of jewelry. Spindly chairs tucked into a corner. It was a wonder there was any room to walk.

A minute later, the bell above the door rang.

"You're early, imp," Kelwyn said mildly, glancing at a pillar candle shaped like a spine glowing in the corner, red lines depicted at regular intervals along the vertebrae. People would light the wick at the morning bell and extinguish it at the last evening gong. Humans and their obsession with slicing time into neat little intervals.

"I'm always early," you said, and Kelwyn laughed.

Your gaze darted about the shop, and I ducked out of sight. Did you suspect where I was?

"Ooh, is that lavender shortbread?" you asked. You acted differently around Kelwyn. More at ease, far less irritated. There was a camaraderie there of long years, even if I suspected you kept him at a distance.

I chanced looking again. You had crammed a biscuit in your mouth in one bite and chewed with difficulty.

"I know they're your favorite, little imp. I figure if Larkin kills you, you'll at least go out having had one last biscuit."

"There are worse last meals," you said, your mouth full. You swallowed with effort and snatched up another. Your nerves echoed through the bond.

"Horrible manners," Kelwyn said, with genuine fondness.

"How's business?" you asked once you could speak through the crumbs.

"Fine, fine." You had told me that Kelwyn had bought as much as he could afford during the Strikes, when people were desperate to sell their possessions for coin enough for food or medicine. Now that enough time had passed since the last Strike, nobility and merchants again wanted fine things. A sound investment for this Kelwyn.

You hopped onto one of the countertops and played with the little mechanical horse until Kelwyn told you to leave it alone with your buttercrumbed hands. You grinned at him, but kept glancing at the door.

You had told me little of the people we were meeting aside from giving me first names and genders. I knew they were the criminal group you had once been part of, and that much of what they stole went to supporting the Struck communes dotted in the mountains. Something had happened before you set out on your own, and it had clearly ended on bad terms.

The bell over the door went again. Two humans entered. One was taller, with a generous figure. I knew in a world where magic could burn through reserves like kindling, fatness was something to be admired. Some gave those who were too skeletal looks out of the corner of their eye and crossed the street to avoid them. How could someone without any padding be able to resist magic's hunger? The other was of average height and build, hood pulled up, shadows obscuring the face.

"Larkin," you said, nodding warily at the taller one. Larkin gave you a full-lipped smile, lines crinkling at the corners of her brown eyes. Gray hair grew to her waist. I guessed her to be in her late fifties.

"Arcady," Larkin said, drawing out the third syllable in a singsong. But there was anger beneath the sweet tone, like burnt honey. She reached for the shortbread as you greeted the other figure. "Hello, Wren."

My eyes widened when Wren drew back his hood. If Larkin's body might appeal to many humans, Wren's would repel them. He was thoroughly average, from what I could tell of human beauty standards. Brown eyes, white hair to his shoulders and a short beard the same color. He did not look old enough for it, but the reason was readily apparent.

He was Struck.

I had seen few of them within the city walls. Mostly beggars, their striated palms held out to those who ignored them.

Wren's marks twined over every inch of exposed skin, dark enough around the eyes that it was almost as if he wore a mask. Wren signed something to you in Trade. I knew many Struck were deaf, for the illness often affected their hearing. He gave you a small smile and leaned against one of the few empty spots of wall, crossing his arms.

"So, what's this job that's good enough you'd come crawling back to me?" Larkin asked, banishing pleasantries and settling right to business. She signed concurrently, for Wren's benefit. I shifted forward, nearly pressing my nose against the red glass.

"I'm firmly planted on two feet, Larkin. It's a simple business proposition. Nothing more, nothing less." Your hands moved in Trade as well.

Larkin poured two cups of tea, passing one to Wren before taking her own. She perched on one of the antique chairs, face in profile, crossing one leg over the other.

"Hmph," you said. The back of Kelwyn's head was bouncing between the other three. Not for the first time, I wished I could sense thoughts instead of only communicating mind to mind in the way of dragons. He seemed to be enjoying watching them all puff up like creatures about to duel for a mate. The Marricks had evidently named themselves after the cats in a remote part of Myria who mimicked the sounds of their prey as they hunted at night. You were one step away from hissing and baring claws.

Larkin took you in from top to toe, and you tried not to fidget under her gaze.

"Have to admit, I almost miss you and all the trouble you caused," Larkin said finally, picking up her cup and taking a sip of tea. The candles further warmed the teak of her skin. "Kept me on my toes, at least. Life was never boring."

"Oh, you're bored now, is that all?" You pretended to be unbothered. "Please. You miss how much dosh I brought you. Nothing more, nothing less. I've an offer for you."

"Mm, I suppose that's true enough." Larkin leaned forward. "So here you are, turned up like a bad copper coin. But will this job make up for the fact you danced off with half of my fucking stash?" The last few words sharpened to a point, her signing just as angry.

Wren pressed his lips together, hands tightening on the teacup.

"Figured you were still sore about that," you said, one corner of your mouth lifting. "It wasn't half. You wouldn't be so foolish to put everything in one place. Don't insult me."

Larkin coiled back, a snake about to strike. "That money was for the Struck commune up in Anglebrook, and you damn well knew it."

Your fingertips dug into the counter. Did your eyes flicker toward the stained-glass window? This was interesting. You'd stolen money meant for the less fortunate. No honor among thieves, then. There was a story there, and I wanted to hear it.

"It was payment for what you did. It wasn't enough. Not enough by far." Your shoulders were hunched.

Wren was solemn. Were his eyes glimmering with tears? Larkin's chin was lifted in defiance.

"Look, Kel," you said in a wry aside. "We're fighting already. Did it take more or less time than you feared?"

Larkin crossed her legs in the other direction, leaning against one arm of the chair. Her signing was almost lazy. "We can dig up all these wriggling little worms of the past in good time, pet, but it doesn't change the fact you stole from the Marricks. I didn't turn over every stone and drag you out from whatever little hidey hole you've found and make you pay up with coin or a few fingers, but don't make the mistake of thinking I forgot. I didn't. Not for a day. Not for an hour."

This woman oozed power. I doubted she made idle threats, but you let the words wash over you, expression implacable.

"I can get you far more money than what I took with this job, Larkin."

Larkin clapped her hands together. "That's the only reason you're still standing. Let's hear it then, love."

You rummaged in the pack you brought, drew out a rolled scroll of parchment, and passed it to Wren.

Wren unrolled it flat on the counter, cocking his head and frowning. Larkin peered over his shoulder.

"It looks like a rotting wyvern claw," she said. "But . . . weirdly deformed. And too large." She bent closer.

It was an illustration torn from a book. Carefully sketched in black ink and painted with different shades of purple. The flesh was gray, the scales barely hanging on, a purple so dark they were almost black. It was shown in a glass vial, capped at either end with ornate silver.

"The illustration is basically to scale," you said, pleased with yourself. You pointed at a few marks in blue ink. "See? It should be just a little larger. About the size of a thumb. It's sort of the shape of one, isn't it? Strange thing. Too large for a wyvern, too small for a god. And utterly unlike any other relic."

"Jari's breath," Kelwyn swore. "That's Girazin's claw, isn't it? I heard rumors They were selling, but that comes up every few years."

You leaned forward, your smirk widening. "This time it's true. And we're going to steal it."

Coldness spread through me in a wave. It looked like a cross between a preterit thumb and a dragon's claw. The shape was humanoid, but it was topped with a curved, black claw, and it was scaled, as if it had been sliced off mid-transformation.

Was it real? Or simply a clever fake?

Your head turned in my direction, and I wondered how much of my shock had echoed its way through the bond. It took every modicum of restraint not to burst through the door and ask what they knew. My human form fell away, my preterit emerging.

Control. Control.

Your light laugh brought me back to myself. I peered through the window, breathing fast. The others' smiles had dampened.

"Where did you find the illustration?" Kelwyn asked.

"I bought it at the Night Market," you said. "It was a whole collection of relic drawings. Probably stolen off a drakine."

Larkin laughed, too loud in the small space. "Arcady, I tip my hat to your ambition, but that mansion has wards on wards on wards and about three dozen guards to boot. You don't even know if that's an accurate illustration, do you? Could just be someone's wee art project."

"Well, I know plenty about the wards on wards on wards," you said, dryly. "Because I mapped the Girazin mansion four moons ago. And I saw the real claw."

Larkin's eyebrows rose. "Truly?" She sounded impressed, despite herself. Kelwyn leaned on the counter, eyes widening.

"I was hired as a deliverer and had a little look around while they were unloading the produce." You took out another scroll and laid it flat.

"Blueprints?" Larkin breathed.

"More a rough map, as I didn't have long." You pointed, but I could see nothing from my angle. "The relic is normally held in one of the towers, but I timed my delivery to just before a soiree. It'd been taken down and put on display, and I grabbed a look when the guard went for a piss. Girazin had only invited those they thought might be after something like it. They'll be selling other relics too, but I don't have enough detail of them to be confident trying to steal any of 'em. And they wouldn't be near as valuable."

"You expect us to steal one of the best protected relics in Loc," Larkin said. But her expression was intrigued.

Kelwyn gave a low whistle. "You told me you had a job, Arc, but this is something else."

"Can you sell it?" you asked.

"Don't insult me. Of course I can sell it." He shook his head, as if to shake away his amazement. "More tea, anyone?" he asked, picking up the pot.

"Yes, thank you, sweet," Larkin said, and held out her cup for a refill. "A simple sneak and grab won't work, of course. These wards make even the most sophisticated cantrips around a bank safe look like child's play. This would be an intricate job." She tapped her lower lip with an index finger. "What's the play?"

A slow smile worked its way across your face. "We walk in and they give it to us."

You plucked a grape from the platter. You were fondest of the ones that were so dark they were almost blue-black, with thick, bitter skins. You always bought them at the market.

"Girazin always throws the grandest party for the Night of Saint Ini. But this year they said they're keeping it small."

Larkin snorted. Kelwyn shifted his position enough I could see his face better.

Wren, in the corner, silently watched your every move, trying to read you like a book.

"That's the night of the auction. Do your own research if you need confirmation."

"It's true enough," Kelwyn said, rubbing his neck. "I've heard the murmurings."

Wren signed something.

"Yes, Girazin is selling a handful of relics, including the claw."

You set your teacup down with a clatter. "And only a few drakines and the richest of merchants are allowed in, along with their guards, so you need someone who knows exactly how to act and what to say." You grinned. "And that's my role."

Larkin rubbed her chin. "You were always the jewel of any acting challenge when we were running a job."

"They won't let just anyone who has the airs of a drakine swan in," you continued. "But they also won't be fool enough to take seal impressions of attendees, in case the Order can track it. They'll be very strict. No invitation, no entry. That's when I realized the gap. Get the invitation, steal a face, and no one will know you're a fake."

"So who's the mark?" Larkin asked.

Your grin widened. "Sar Ikari Dwell."

Kelwyn was already shaking his head. Larkin sucked on her teeth as she searched her memory for the name. "Oh, talons. The merchant that trades in Jaskian goods? They walk about with a stick up Their arse and a guard wider than a mountain."

"Think on it. Most find Dwell tedious, so they never speak to them longer than strictly necessary. Dwell goes through guards like changes of socks, so we'd be able to sneak an extra person inside without too much effort. Dwell is rich enough that if they win the relic, it won't raise eyebrows. I wouldn't be surprised if Girazin hopes Dwell buys it."

Larkin pressed her lips together. "You want Wren to make a forgery."

You reached out and rang one of the bells Kelwyn had on display. "We have a winner. No one's better. Didn't you boast that half the drakines have Wren's work hanging in their parlors or displayed on plinths, with no clue they've been painted or sculpted by a Struck?"

Wren signed something.

"I agree, you are the best," you said, the smirk growing. "That's why I came to you."

"This . . . this is a big job," Larkin said. "I take it you need me to help liaise logistics."

"Got it in one."

Kelwyn snorted. "This is beyond mad, by the by. Impersonating someone that powerful to steal from one of the most powerful drakine families?

Girazin might not be the richest any longer, but that name has *standing*. That's not bold, it's suicidal. If we're caught, we won't even be offered the courtesy of a trial."

"Oh, believe me, I've thought it through." You held up a finger. "One option: we'll get our throats slit in some dark alley. Either by the Girazins or by the Dwell family. Maybe both, so let's make that two fingers." You next held up a third. "The various other gangs who would find this sort of job way too mighty for the Marricks might take a crack at killing us,"—a fourth—"the Jaskians will probably be irate if they get wind that we impersonated one of the top merchants ferrying their goods across the water, so we could well spark international tensions for an extra bit of fun." You raised your last finger to splay your palm wide. "Don't forget the Order of the Dragons and the Citadel don't want it known that people are stealing or selling relics, so we'd risk Them taking us out, too. Oh, dear, look at that, I've run out of fingers."

Wren signed something. My head was spinning with all this information.

"I'm not sure a slit throat is less painful than a hanging, Wren," you said. "They haven't exactly been able to interview the recipients on their pain levels after the fact." You looked thoughtful.

"You're not selling this, Arcady," Larkin said.

"Oh, but you haven't asked the most important question," you said, sweetly. "I've been waiting."

Larkin's expression sharpened. "How much, then, little traitor?"

"The Marricks' cut would be forty wraithwright suls, or twenty each, based on what I think it'd fetch on the black market." You watched the range of emotions play across the Marricks' faces with glee.

Larkin let out a string of invective.

This. This was why you would risk training the stranger you barely knew to help. Enough money for whatever you wanted to do with your life. The golden glow between us brightened as your emotions bled through.

If one wraithwright coin was fifty gold . . . how many months working down at the docks would forty meteorite coins be? Two thousand. The same again for you, plus whatever Kelwyn would take for the sale.

Larkin gave nothing away. She turned to Kelwyn. "Who do you think would buy it?"

Kelwyn stirred his tea carefully. "It would depend. Girazin will only invite people They know have deep enough pockets and fewer scruples with the law. But I doubt there'll be more than a score of people there. Plenty of people with deeper pockets outside of that number that Girazin would be smart not to trust and who would turn to the black market. There's also rumors that Jask is interested in relics, though that seems so strange I'm not sure how true it is. They hate our gods." He looked thoughtful. "Maybe they want to destroy them."

I hissed silently.

"How much is Arcady cheating us on this opening gambit?" Larkin pressed.

Kelwyn glanced upward. "My guess is that claw would be worth at least two hundred, and it'd sell on the black market for a little less than that. Let's call it one hundred and eighty. So aye, minus my cut, that's insulting."

You shrugged. "I came up with the plan. You'd have zero wraithwright without me."

"I want three fourths, after Kelwyn's cut."

"Sard off. Not on your life."

You glared at Larkin, and she glared right back. "Fine," you relented. "We can split it nice and even. Twenty to Kelwyn for brokering the sale, eighty or so for the Marricks, and eighty for me."

"That's lower than my current rate," Kelwyn protested.

"And you're not the one risking life and limb, are you? Don't get greedy."

"There are two of us and one of you," Larkin said.

"Ah, yes, about that." You looked right at the stained-glass window, a challenge in your gaze. I knew what that meant. I shifted back to my human shape. "You see, I'm not working alone. I've a partner."

A few beats of silence that echoed the heartbeat in my throat.

"What?" Kelwyn asked.

"You heard me." A glow through the bond. "Everen?"

There was my signal.

I opened the door.

18. ARCADY: THE RULES OF THE GAME

The looks on their faces were so perfect I couldn't help but cackle.

Everen had done brilliantly. I thought he'd eavesdrop at the alley window and come through the front door when I called. But no, he'd worked his way through the wards—tricky beasts, to be sure—and then hidden right in the heart of the pawnshop, watching it all from behind the stained glass of rose and thorns.

"Aura's blight." Kelwyn staggered back a few steps. Larkin and Wren's surprise was unmanufactured. Everen struck quite the figure. Dressed in black save for the blue laces on his shirt. A coat cut for easy movement. He'd bought better boots from his riverwalk coin, and the leather gleamed. With that sculpted face and the red hair falling into his eyes, he'd be catnip for Larkin.

"Good evening," Everen said in his attempt at a Vatran accent. He gave a passable bow and an excellent smirk.

Kelwyn darted from the room, muttering about wards and making sure nothing had been disturbed in the storeroom.

"It'll all be fine!" I called after him. I knew Everen enough by now to know he wouldn't have stolen anything without my say so.

"A *partner*, eh?" Larkin asked, the word taking on a double meaning as she gave him a slow once-over. Everen didn't squirm.

"It's a relatively new arrangement," I replied, bland as porridge, "but we work well together." So far. For the grand sum total of less than a moon. I'd let her believe the rest.

Kelwyn returned, stinking of magic from replacing the wards. He ate a biscuit with an impressive amount of sullenness.

"Everen," I said. "Meet Kelwyn, owner of the Last Golden. And this is Larkin and Wren, also known as the leaders of the Marricks." I gestured. "And this is Everen. An acquaintance."

Wren had cocked his head like his namesake, taking it all in.

Larkin's eyes narrowed. "Even if I was considering this impossible job of yours, I don't work with strangers."

"Oh, but we'll have time to get to know each other," I said, with the polite smile I knew pissed Larkin off. It worked. My heartbeat was racing, though. If she ducked out, I'd armed her with enough information that she might try to do the job on her own, cutting me out, and then I'd have her as competition. I didn't fancy my chances. Wren *was* the best art forger in the city, by yards.

Time for the hook. "You had no idea he was there," I continued. "None of you. And you're some of the best criminals in this city. So yes. He's part of the plan."

"Wherever did you find this specimen?" Larkin asked.

"Oh, you could say he just . . . fell into my lap," I deadpanned, and Everen pressed his lips together.

Wren gave a silent snicker.

"And how much experience do you have in the fine art of stealing?" Larkin asked him, eyes narrowing.

"He's got your usual skills," I answered for him. "Locks and pockets. Good fighter and climber. His handle on magic is good. Much better than yours." That wasn't saying much. I'd never seen Larkin cast so much as a charm. She left that to others. I knew her parents had been Struck—it had left her afraid to use magic. One of the many reasons I hadn't told her my secret.

"I didn't ask you," Larkin drawled.

"What else do you wish to know?" Everen asked, easily enough.

"Do I detect a hint of accent?" she asked.

Damn.

"Stormfell, but right on the border of the Myria," he said. "I am from a very small town, not open to outsiders. We do little trade and keep to ourselves."

It had been our agreed cover, and he delivered the lie well. It still captured Larkin's interest more than I liked.

"And what are Everen's disadvantages, then, if you're so keen to speak for him?" Larkin shot over her shoulder in my direction, arms crossing once she finished signing for Wren. Still not an outright denial.

I considered my answer, ignoring Everen's burning gaze. "He can be stubborn. He doesn't speak much Trade, though I'll teach him the basics. He's unfamiliar with some mainstream Lochian customs, but he catches on quick. Kelwyn, we'd probably both benefit from a couple of etiquette and dance lessons. Dragons know I probably need a refresher, it's been long enough."

"Undoubtedly, you heathen," Kelwyn agreed. He was still stress-eating biscuits. I felt a little guilty. No one had ever broken into the Last Golden, save me knocking on the window, which didn't count. He was spiraling and would likely add three more levels of security the next time I crossed the threshold.

"Do you trust him?" Larkin asked me, baldly.

I refused to look at Everen. "With my life." For now, I had no choice in the matter.

"Gods," she said in a hard exhale. "Never thought I'd see you willingly pair off with someone. Though I suppose I see the appeal." Larkin was one step away from slapping me on the back and telling me well done. I supposed I should be flattered that she thought me capable of bagging someone like him. Though I knew I wasn't ugly, compared to Everen I was plain as a dormouse. I considered telling Larkin we weren't sleeping together, but it would only raise more questions—her first would be "whyever not?" Sex was a motivator Larkin understood.

"You'd be working for *me* this time, Larkin. If that's a problem for you, you need to tell me."

Larkin's expression was hard as coffin nails. "You do have some brass balls, I have to say. Coming back to me after what you did."

"Is that many wraithwright suls enough to bury the past?" I asked, carefully. "When have you ever made a score anywhere near even five wraithwright in one go?"

She made a show of considering.

I had at least forty coins riding on her answer, too. A whole future in the university, with enough to give to Everen. He could do what he liked with his fortune. Make his own life here, or somehow find a way back to his people.

"One condition before I agree."

I groaned, suspecting what would come next.

"I want to see you both working together, first."

Everen gave me *such* a look, as if to say: *I see where you get this penchant for endless testing from.* Well. I'd learned from the best.

"What are you planning next?"

I ground my teeth. "Cinders."

Her eyes lit up. "Dwell's going, is that it?" Larkin was always whip-quick.

Everen was fairly burning with curiosity, but I ignored him.

"Aye," I said. "I still need to touch him. That's the goal, and maybe some coin."

"Marvelous," Larkin said, clapping her hands. "I'll be watching."

A muscle twitched beneath my eye, but I nodded.

"Well, I'd say this calls for a celebration, doesn't it?" Larkin beamed. "Kelwyn, break out the good stuff."

My knees went weak with relief. That's one part now.

All we had to do next was survive Cinders unscathed.

◇◇◇◇◇◇◇◇◇

"This is the third side of the holy trifecta of cheats and thieves," I said as we sat across from each other on the floor of the shop the next day. "Locks, pockets, cards."

I took out the pack of cards and showed off my shuffling skills. Everen watched me bridge them in fascination. I always found the *clack, clack, clack* so satisfying. Second only to the *clink*ing of coins. Cinders had a focus on several games: den of dragons. Snap. The bard and the blacksmith. Leaves and hearts.

I walked him through the steps, peeking at his hand when he was stuck so I could advise him on the best strategy. We bet with buttons from a jar, and I tried not to beat him too badly. Once Everen had the basics down, we played without him asking me for advice. Here, I didn't mind thoroughly trouncing him. He'd make a grand show of disgust when he lost, but some of the sharpness had leached from him.

Everen did a good job of keeping his face blank, I'd give him that. He let nothing through, and I didn't feel anything through the bond. While he did well enough, I'd still be doing the cheating on the night of the new moon.

"Tell me more about this Cinders," Everen said as I dealt again.

"Underground card den," I said. "Filled with all sorts of characters. Drakines looking for a little illicit fun. Merchants happy enough to gamble away their earnings. Sometimes people like to pretend for a night that they are more than they are in the daylight hours. They'll dress in their fanciest clothes, buy the drinks, and live a fantasy life until the sun comes up. What little coin they had is gone again, more often than not, but they have the dream that maybe they'll strike it rich and have an escape path out of their normal lives."

"That is . . . a little sad," he said, frowning at his cards.

"It is, but no more than anything else." I drew a card. Five of blue. Rubbish. "Most people are pretending, in one way or another." I discarded it. "I target those who have the most to spare. They get cocky—they think just because it's a masquerade and they've hidden their faces that they've obscured everything else about themselves. Some guests at Girazin's will be masked, too, for plausible deniability. This will be good practice."

I'd been teaching him to read people as much as count cards. The minute tells, the anxious fidgeting. The skills he'd gained to find the right mark to pickpocket would serve him well in Cinders, too. He had a knack for scenting out others' weaknesses. It was taking all my skill to keep him from discovering mine.

We played until the light fled. I yawned and stretched, my muscles cramping.

"We should come up with some signals," I said, working the tension from my jaw. One of my own tells was a tiny clench of my back molars when I was furious with my hand. I wasn't sure if he had caught it. "I'll be doing the playing, but if you find a seat with a view of a few others' hands at my table and we can communicate, we could clean out." I rubbed my cheek. "It's risky, though. If we're caught."

He drummed his fingertips on the floorboards.

"What?" I asked, narrowing my eyes.

"I believe I know the easiest way. But you will not like it."

I felt the line between my brows deepen. "Try me."

He looked at me, going strangely still. —*Arcady.*

It took me two seconds before I realized his mouth hadn't moved.

I scrabbled back, pressing against the wall. He inclined his head, a smile teasing the corners of his mouth.

—I take it you hear me.

"Oh no," I said, my fingertips digging into the old wallpaper of the lock shop. "No." I already knew the bond was mind magic, and that had been difficult enough to deal with. I felt the panic rising again. If anyone knew of this, we would both be executed. Very painfully.

I shook my head. "No. Absolutely not."

—You did it once, by accident. When you lit the candle. I wondered . . . He paused, switched to speaking aloud at my obvious growing distress. "If it was only because you'd taken a sip of my magic."

Anger surged through me, and his eyes widened when he felt it. "You're lying."

He rose. I'd struck a nerve. Anger simmered, tightening his body, echoed in my own. I didn't want to face this. I didn't want to *think*. Not at him. Not at myself. I had worked alone for a year and been reliant on no one. No one. Now, it had been weeks of this stranger, in my space, in my magic, but not in my bloody *head*. There was a ringing in my ears.

He came closer, palms out, but I shook my head. "No, no. We're not discussing this." I ran sweating palms along my trousers. "You know what? We're going to practice fighting. I've been meaning to brush up on it anyway."

—This is the best time? he asked, with a raise of the eyebrow. *Now?* Gods. I couldn't even tell if he was thinking Locmyrian at me, or if I could grasp the meaning of his native tongue.

"Stop that!" I stepped forward and shoved him. Not hard. He didn't move. But we began circling, our footsteps mirroring each other. I didn't want to talk or think. I wanted to move. "Yes. Right now." My heart beat in my throat like a hummingbird's. I needed to hit something. Him, in particular.

"Fine," he said, as if he were humoring me. "If it makes you feel better."
—But I shall win.

He struck first.

I was ready, and I ducked underneath his arm, dancing back. The night I'd met him, he'd pushed me up against a stone wall. I'd snuck from his grasp and pinned him instead. It had been so satisfying to hold that knife against his throat. I was angry enough that I wanted to do it again. Wipe that half-amused smile right off his face. He'd been driving me up the walls for weeks. This build-up felt as inevitable as a wave crashing to shore.

Everen took another swing, but he didn't get close. I let out something like a laugh. Yes. *Yes.* I darted forward and landed a light hit on his shoulder.

We weren't wearing gloves, which gave it all an extra danger. We blocked with our forearms.

"How do you do that?" he gasped, staggering after I'd nearly knocked him down.

"Do what?" I asked, panting.

"Take the power of my punch and turn it back on myself."

"Figure it out." I wasn't sure if this was a lesson any longer, or if it was an actual fight. I was not sure I cared.

Unconsciously, we mirrored each other's movements. We landed hits. Mine were harder than his, but through the bond I knew I hadn't hurt him. My fury began to settle into something steadier. We fought until my breath grew ragged, my throat burned, my hair slicked to my temples, and my shirt clung to my back. We fought until my muscles ached, until my mind finally, finally quieted.

Everen copied me, learning how to move with more delicacy and less brute strength. Eventually, he put his hands on my shoulders, and mine went up to his. We were close enough I could see the beads of sweat on his temples. How large his pupils were in the darkness. His breath ghosted across my face. We slowed, stared. My mouth opened, though I had no idea what I would say.

Everen turned, stepping away but pulling me toward him at the same time. I was lifted onto my tiptoes. Before I could get my bearings, he bent, pulled my arm forward, and my feet left the floor. He flipped me over his back, and I felt the angle of his shoulder blade against my spine. With a grunt, I landed on my feet, but only just. He let go and I fell ungracefully onto my arse. The wind rushed from my lungs.

Barely winded, he loomed over me. We had, by a miracle, not touched.

He waited for me to catch my breath. His eyes were bright, gaze too intent. I wiped my face with my sleeve. I was sure I was apple-red. Everen, of course, looked fresh as a new flower. Bastard.

"Do you feel better?" he asked, curiously.

I bowed my head. I was too tired to panic, so there was that.

He went to get me a glass of water. I gulped it down.

"Can . . . can you read my thoughts?" I asked when I could speak again.

He sat down, close, but not too close. "No, Arcady," he said, and the words were softer than I expected.

That was a relief. "How long have you been able to . . . ?"

"Always. It is how my people communicate."

"You kept this from me." I sounded like a put-out child.

He gave me a pointed look. "I had some idea of how you might react."

I sipped more water.

"There are advantages," he began.

Clearly. "What if someone hears?"

He shook his head. "Not if I direct the thought only to you."

I closed my eyes, lying back down on the floor. My arse hurt. My body was exhausted. It was dinnertime, but my appetite had fled.

"I don't like it."

"That is obvious enough." He spread his long legs in front of him, leaning back on his elbows. "But why?"

I licked my lips. "Our bodies aren't our own. Not entirely. We're liabilities to each other. I don't need more confirmation that we're connected. I know we're working together, but I don't *want* to need anyone. Or be beholden to them."

"I assure you, I like it even less." There was that simmering anger. Our mutual frustration that we were tethered to each other and had no idea how to break it. "I feel like I'm being forced to bow before you."

"You definitely haven't. Go ahead. I might be into it."

He snorted, but we stared at each other, the silence growing awkward.

"Well," I said, clearing my throat. "At least we agree this is a mountain of shit."

His low laughter filled the lock shop, breaking some of the tension. It was as nice as before, deep enough I felt it in my sternum.

He sobered. "Try to think to me."

I shook my head. "I don't want you in my head. And I don't want to be in yours." My voice went pleading.

He cocked his head at me. —*Try, Arcady. You are not one to let an advantage slip away. That is why you are bothering to teach me at all, is it not? You could have kept me tied up in here for weeks while you ran this job.* A pause. *Or, rather, you could have tried.*

He sounded more fluent in my head, with no pauses. I was right that it wasn't Locmyrian. It was pure meaning, rather than words. I shuddered.

I closed my eyes and thought his name.

"Did it work?" I asked, peeking.

He shook his head. I didn't know whether to be disappointed or not.

I tried a few more times, but he sensed nothing. Or so he said.

Defeated and exhausted, I went back to my room. I heard the pipes creak as Everen filled and heated a bowl of water to clean. He had gone to the public baths a few times but preferred to stay here. I did feel a bit rude not offering him my bath, but I wasn't about to let him into the last space that was entirely my own.

As I lay there, in the dark, I admitted a truth to myself:

Everen had already been in my head more than I'd have liked, the past few weeks, but not through magic. I didn't know how to get him out. But I'd have to. He would linger until we did this job and broke the bond, then he would leave, and I would be free.

Free to be alone again.

19. EVEREN: THE STORIES WE TELL OURSELVES

I scoffed as I turned the page.

"What?" you asked, glancing up from your own book with a frown. It was late morning, a few days before we were due to go to Cinders. We were keeping to the usual schedule: study in the morning, lunch and a walk outside, practical work in the afternoon, and playing cards in the evening. I had pickpocketed a few more times since the mark in the red coat, though none of the takings had been particularly worthwhile. There had been one clumsy attempt where I had nearly been caught. I had given them my best bemused smile at their suspicion, and since their pocket remained heavy with coin, they continued on their way.

I tapped the open book. —*I find the founding myths of all the Lumet fairly preposterous, but Jask more so than the others.*

I had started speaking to you this way when we had our more philosophical discussions, for ease of communication. You no longer flinched.

"You're supposed to be reading the den of dragons strategy book."

—*I finished. It was dry. I thought this might be more amusing. It is.*

You sighed and closed your own tome, leaning your cheek on your hand. "All myths prove silly once you try to apply logic to them. They're only stories to give a beginning to everything. Fire up loyalty to land and ruler." You paused. "Speak aloud. You'll stop improving your Locmyrian."

I flipped a page disdainfully, half-reading, half-summarizing. "A young orphan raised in the woods by a . . ." I squinted at the book. "Kind-hearted peasant. Heads off on a . . . quest to destroy a dragon with the creative name of Malice. The dragon seems very interested in charring sheep and humans in . . . small kingdoms. The young human defeats the dragon, cuts off its head, bathes in blood and becomes . . ."

You leaned over, your scent flooding my senses. "Invincible."

"Right." I leaned away. "He has the power to banish dragon demons from the land he's united and so he calls himself king."

You shrugged when I finished. "And?" Your eyes were a deep, dark blue, so different from a preterit's. I'd grown used to the sight of you. Your ears no longer seemed too round, your teeth too blunt. In some angles, I almost found you alluring, though the thought was preposterous. You were a human. All humans were hideous.

I cleared my throat. "Jask despises magic, but their founding myth is stuffed to the brim with it. The king is still seen as someone with the power to keep the demons at bay because of his kingliness. Absurd."

You rolled your eyes. "It's symbolic. An excuse as to why he and all his offspring should keep power. It's a confidence trick like any other. I almost admire the game."

I made a grudging noise of agreement. "I suppose it is no sillier than Locmyria's."

"Hm? Oh, probably. But when you grow up with it, you don't tend to notice. It's just the story you've always been told." You considered. "It's not all that different, is it? Except the first Monarch was chosen by benevolent dragon gods rather than demons from some dark realm. Opposite sides of a similar coin. A lot of superstitions and myths tend to have a little speck of truth."

Due to their shared history, Loc and Myria both believed the dragons had flown in from the cosmos to make the world. Water rushed to fill the oceans and lakes, the green of the land unfurled, mountains were raised and canyons cracked, and then it was all wrapped up in weather and seasons. Jaskians believed their one god was behind the making of the world, and that the demons had interrupted Him before He could create a perfect paradise. Dragons were therefore the cause of all earthly ills. The Lochians and Myrians had their saints, the Jaskians their martyrs.

To the Traders of the Glass Isles, dragons could be tricksters, neither wholly benevolent nor fully evil. But all lands feared chaos and the endless dark the world had come from before the god or gods had woven the stars into the sky.

I thought of that storm between the worlds. I had sensed something within, and only the bond had driven me through to the other side. Who else might have fallen through and never escaped?

"Your Chancellors do not say they were chosen by the gods," I pointed out.

"No, that was a deliberate choice after the Schism. They pretended they were more of the people. They made changes quite quickly that helped the commoners . . . to a point. They extended the vote to merchants as well as drakines, but not the poor." You were warming to the subject. "They won the re-election of their first term, but goodwill wore thin basically immediately." You fiddled with a hangnail on your index finger. "Turns out the Strike helped them out. The ultimate distraction, and they extended their term through a mandate due to the emergency. They'll do it a third time in a few years, I've no doubt, and manufacture another crisis. They've been in power long enough I suppose most of us are used to it." A shrug. "Now and again, people try to challenge them. It never sticks. Eventually, someone in their families will serve after them because they have the power, the education, and the access. They're basically monarchs but without fairy tales spun around them like sugar." You stretched your arms and legs out, tilting your head and arching your back to ease the stiffness. My eyes trailed along the lines of your body.

"Manufacture another crisis?" I echoed. "What do you mean?"

You chewed your lip. "I think . . ." You paused, then made up your mind. "I think the Consul released the Strike, somehow, and blamed the Plaguebringer for it."

I blinked, thinking it through. The dragons, of course, had heard of the human who nearly destroyed the world. I suspected Barrow Eremia came up in the writings, over and over again. "How? Why?"

A shrug. "That's the thing, isn't it? No one knows how it was released, or what proof they have it was the Plaguebringer, aside from vaguely saying that it was due to his magical experiments. They phrase it so similarly—that tends to give away a lie as well. Like it's rehearsed."

I said nothing, letting the silence urge you on. You pushed the hair from your face and hesitated, as if weighing your next words before carrying on. "I'm going to try to find that out."

I held back the laugh. "You?"

You reddened, but you looked determined. "Why do you think I want so much wraithwright, Everen? Surely, you've some guesses."

I had been wondering, but you kept so many details closed. How long you'd worked for the Marricks. What your upbringing had been like. You were like the small lizards that changed color to fit into the stone behind them on Vere Celene. You blended in so much it was hard to know your true hue.

"I am not entirely sure," I admitted. "To give you access and power to something. For security." Was that not why all humans wanted money?

You were silent so long, I thought you had changed your mind. "Yes. I'm making a whole new life for myself."

It seemed the truth, but yet again, I suspected there was more to the story. There always was, with you. My gut soured. It was a life you wouldn't be able to live.

"Anyway," you said, clearly uncomfortable with my stare. "Tell me your founding myths." The tone was playful, but I was not fooled. This was both a bald change of topic and a ploy for more information. Yet I played along. Perhaps it was homesickness. To explain it properly, I had to switch to my mind.

—*Our ancient homeland was called into being with a breath of starfire*, I sent. You stiffened, but motioned for me to carry on. *I have told you we worship celestial fire. We believe it burned a path of the way things should be. We aim to follow it. We seek visions in pools of molten metal from the depths of the earth. We trust that the center of the world and the stars above know what has happened and what will come to pass. A strong enough will can subvert it, often for ill, and while the arc may eventually return to what it should be, it causes extra pain and suffering along the way. We aim to make the arc toward justice as clear as possible.*

You twisted, lying on your stomach and pillowing your head in your hands, looking up at me.

—*That worked, for a time*, I continued. *We lived in harmony with other types of creatures. We had a partnership, fighting against . . . something, though what that was is lost to the mists of time. It was strong enough to foil the path.*

"Ah yes, an ancient evil, naturally." You picked at your nails.

"Do not interrupt," I said aloud.

You raised yourself on one elbow. "Sorry." You pretended to tie your lips closed and laid your head down again. "I still don't like you speaking in my head."

"It is the easiest way to tell it," I said. You crinkled your nose but made no further complaint.

—*Long ago, there was a war.*

You nodded, as if to say: *there is always a war.*

—*Those we worked with, who we thought loved us, betrayed us instead. They stole everything that was dear to us and cast us out. The war was lost before we realized it was being waged. My ancestors woke up adrift in a new land. An island we called Vere Celene.*

I paused. Your eyebrows drew down. "Vere Celene," you echoed aloud. "The Land of Fate?" Your tone was uncertain, yet of course you were beginning to see. How quickly I had picked up Locmyrian, and the root words between both the more modern human tongue and your "language of magic."

—*Yet this new land was a difficult place to live*, I continued. *Hot and dry, with bad hunting. A volcano erupted, staining the sky gray and red and nearly killing us. It eventually settled, but it still smokes on the horizon. We had been forcibly cast off our path. Many lost faith. The prophecies had not helped us prevent it, so why seek the true way? For centuries, we have tried to find our way back. We had thought it impossible.*

Your lips parted. The bond hummed between us.

"Your people came from here originally," you whispered. You searched my face for confirmation. "Ancient Locmyrians cast you out." A line between your brows. "When? I've read of that in no history book."

"About eight hundred years ago. You had a dark age not long after, yes? Knowledge was lost. Or the early Monarchs destroyed any record and wrote those myths instead."

You rose, sitting back on your heels. "Do you hate us, then? For what we did?"

"Of course." I leaned forward, and I let that anger always coiled within me unfurl. You felt it through the bond. I thought you might shy away, but you did not. You faced it head on. Something had cracked after I had first spoken to you mind to mind and we had sparred. You had set down some of your defenses. I only had to keep pressing.

"You have your own hatred for this place," I said, keeping my voice low. Only a handspan separated our faces. "Why?"

You licked your lips. "Because they took everything from me. And I want it back. All of it and more."

"Perhaps you burned with enough loathing to draw me here," I murmured.

Your breath caught.

"What were you really doing, that night among the bones?" I asked.

You swallowed. "I—I made a promise to someone. I was honoring it." That told me nothing.

"What was the spell, Arcady?" I was being relentless, but I had to know.

You gave a shaky exhale. "It wasn't meant to draw you. I promise."

I lowered my voice, leaned on one of my hands, closing the distance between us just a little more. "Whose bones were they, Arcady?" I whispered. "I could always go back and check." In this, too, I had a guess.

"Stop *picking*, Everen." Your voice was thick. When I looked into your eyes, I was shocked to find them shining with unshed tears.

"Just . . . stop," you whispered. "For now, stop."

The hum of the bond was louder than it had ever been. You were trusting me, to tell me this much. But did you trust me enough? Or would pushing cause you to snap shut, like the setting of your seal?

Five weeks until the Feast of Flowers.

I moved back from you, the charge between us lessening. "I apologize." The words were stiff. I was not sorry, exactly, though I had not meant to upset you.

You wiped at your eyes. "We're only working together until we do this job and we figure out how to break this bond. What I do after that is none of your business, really. But I've promised I'll do everything in my power to get you home, Everen." You pressed your palm to the seal setting at your chest. "And I keep my promises."

I could not quite meet your gaze. Something sour and tight stirred in my gut, like I had eaten bad prey. "I know."

We both went back to our respective books and pretended to read, the moment of vulnerability misting over like a scrying pool.

◇◇◇◇◇◇◇◇◇◇

"Your hair is too bright," you said five days later, on the evening before Cinders.

"Hmm?" I asked, turning the page.

You reached out and tugged a forelock. I flinched, but there was no pain.

"How many others with hair this color have you seen wandering around Vatra?"

I considered. "Maybe three in one hundred. And most of those were foreign. I see." I closed my book.

"Can you shapeshift the color?"

I shook my head. It was a half-lie. Perhaps, but I would have to return to the preterit form in the interim. It was easier to pretend I could not shape-shift at all.

You chewed your lips as you went to the water closet at the back of the shop. It was very small. I alone could barely fit in it—it would require some acrobatics for the both of us. With a sigh, you headed to the trapdoor.

"Come on, then."

My eyebrows rose in surprise. Would my fib finally grant me access to your mysterious quarters?

I followed you down the trapdoor and politely glanced away while you banished the wards and unlocked the door. We both knew it for the farce it was. I could have entered at any point since we had gone to the Last Golden. I had simply chosen not to.

You stepped aside, crossing your arms. I could feel your unblinking gaze as I took in your sanctuary. I had not been sure what to expect. Considering you usually wore black or dark hues, I had not expected the riot of color. The bed was a pile of pillows, all in burgundy, the fur cover bunched to one side, a wooden screen hemming it in. Once-bright rugs softened the floor. Artwork crowded the walls, some framed, some simply stuck up with small nails, clearly your own handiwork. A large desk, with sheets of paper half-filled with tiny script, some blotted and blurred. One wall consisted entirely of metal lockboxes, some open and showcasing glass vases, shells, crystals, and rocks, but most were locked up tight. A few empty mugs and plates with crumbs or the rinds of fruit were scattered about. Another painted screen showed mountains and clouds.

And books stacked on tables, chairs, the floor. A shelf full of notebooks. If there was ever an earthquake like the ones that sometimes shook Vere Celene, you would be buried beneath them. I realized for all my hours of reading, I had barely made a dent in your collection. A banked fire warmed the room. The place reminded me strangely of the library in Vere

Celene—though the lack of clear organization would have thrown my sister into a fit. I found myself smiling as I leaned forward and looked at your trinkets. You shifted your weight foot to foot, like a hatchling still learning the use of limbs.

This was another gesture of trust. Cassia would be pleased. My smile faded.

You cleared your throat and pulled back the painted screen, revealing a battered copper tub and a large, antique mirror with a gilded frame.

"You hid *this* from me," I said with a scoff.

"Oh, did I? Must have slipped my mind," you said, leaning over and turning on the taps. "The hot water isn't connected, since no one officially lives here or runs a business, so you'll have to use magic to heat it."

The room was not what I expected, but I found I liked it. I raised the arm of a stringed puppet hanging off a shelf, dressed in parti-colored clothing with a pointed cap on its head and diamonds drawn over the eyes.

"Yes, well." If you had been a dragon, your crest would have been half-standing in unease. You cleared your throat. "Right. Off with your shirt." Your voice was still gruff.

My eyes half-closed in surprise, a draconic reaction.

"I mean—you'd stain it—"

"I know what you meant." I tugged the plain linen over my head. Your glance snaked its way down my torso. Dragons have no shame over nakedness, in dragon or preterit, though I was mildly concerned my human illusion might not hold under scrutiny. Yet humans seemed to have more modesty. I had seen very little of you—face, neck, forearms, hands. Not even your bare feet.

Your pupils widened. You liked what you saw. Interesting. This gave a little more power on my side of the scales.

You put on old, stained leather gloves to protect your hands and me. The tub was half full, and I put my hand in the cool water and let loose a curl of magic, heating it until it was warm as the hot springs of home.

You set down a chair next to the tub and I perched on it as you mixed pigment in water until it looked like black mud.

Tentatively, you moved closer, as if afraid I would bite. I ran my tongue along the flattened teeth in my mouth, my fangs hidden. The top button of your shirt was open, showing the hollow of your throat. The light from the fire cast orange over your cheekbones, your square jaw. Your dark hair was always messy at the end of the day, since you constantly ran your hands through it. I knew so many of your mannerisms now. Yet again, I reminded myself that you were human, not preterit, not dragon. You were the enemy.

This would be our most sustained near-contact so far. When practicing pickpocketing or fighting, every touch had been fleeting, focused on our tasks. Slowly, you threaded your gloved fingers through my hair.

"I'll have to cut your hair too, at some point," you said, as I fought the strange urge to sigh at the feel of your hands on my scalp. "It's terribly uneven."

I did not relish the idea of you so close to my throat with sharp scissors.

"It's a shame to cover the color," you said, more to yourself than me. "It has all sorts of shades in it, from deep auburn to almost orange." You started applying the dye, unpleasantly cold compared to the steam from the tub, the fire in the hearth. It smelled of damp herbs and charcoal. Soon my hair would be as dark as yours.

I watched you in the mirror, your head bent in concentration. You smoothed the pigment with a brush, moving through each section meticulously. The bond between us unfurled like a morning flower, suffusing us in a mental glow. You dropped a dollop of dye onto my shoulder.

"Sorry," you muttered, dipping a rag in the tub and wiping it off. The feeling of the rough cloth across my collarbone was distracting. All of you was distracting. The smell of your soap and skin. Your fingers in my hair. The warmth of your side pressing into my back as you reached for a section behind my ear. I shivered, and felt it pass through the bond. Your hands paused. A thread of the same feeling returned.

This was not part of the plan. I tensed my back.

"The dye—" You paused, cleared your throat. "It's fast acting. Won't take long." You pulled away, taking your warmth with you. I drifted closer to the fire, staring into the flames.

You were human, not preterit. I should feel nothing. Nothing. Especially for you, who could steal my power, who had spent the last few weeks berating me. The person I had to kill, at the end of all this.

"It's growing stronger, isn't it?" you asked. "The bond."

I cleared my throat. "Perhaps, but it has not completed." We would know if it had. Our magic was still muted.

"Won't it be harder to break if that happens?"

"I don't know. Probably." —*So we should be careful.*

You pretended not to hear my added thought. I drew my fingernail across the back of my wrist, and you glanced down at the echoing welt, rubbing it. The hollow of your throat had gone pink, the color creeping up your neck.

Your current theory was that putting enough distance between us might break the connection. Once we had our bounty from selling the relic, you said I should buy a ticket on a ship heading to the Glass Isles, in the hopes of finding someone who would set sail for the horizon from there. I let you believe it was what I wanted. Was it less cruel?

One life. One little, insignificant human life for the lives of thousands of dragons. I would make it quick. Painless. I owed you that.

You gestured for me to lean over the tub. You sloshed water over my hair, your torso flush against my back again. I closed my eyes tight, against the water and against the sensation. Every nerve felt alive. It was only the proto-bond, I told myself, but I knew I lied to myself even then. I shifted, uncomfortable, all too aware of my body's traitorous reaction.

Enemy.

Adversary.

Foe.

Every time you moved against me to rinse my hair, I gritted my teeth. Your breath caught at my ear.

When you were done, you drew me upright, rubbing my hair vigorously with a towel, which startled a laugh from me and broke the strained silence. I reached up to stop your hand. Except I could not see, and my fingers found their way to the bare skin between the top of your glove and the bottom of your shirt cuff.

We froze.

The bond between us flared again. I waited for the pain, but it did not come immediately. Instead of drowning, it was like holding my breath deep in the ocean, letting the currents wash across me without fighting. That innocent touch on your wrist still felt forbidden. Warmth rushed through us both like a sigh. Your skin pebbled beneath my fingers, and my magic trickled through to you.

My back itched and I rolled my shoulders. I broke contact with a gasp before my wings could appear. It was like coming up from underwater. I worried if I went preterit and snapped back to human that the pigment just added to my hair would not follow.

You had stumbled back. "Are—are you all right?" you asked from the other side of the room.

I was still hunched over, hidden by the towel. I ran my fingertips across my features. They seemed human enough. Gingerly, I removed the cloth and glanced at the gilt mirror across the tub. I only caught a glimpse of my newly darkened hair and my non-preterit face before the reflection rippled.

The air turned sharp and cold, despite the fire.

A dragon with a crimson crest appeared, the near-mirror of my true form. It was not my sister. The swirling red jewel at the center of her forehead proclaimed that well enough, as did the look of disdainful wrath.

I jumped to my feet. The angle of the screen hid the dark-watered tub and the mirror from your view. The rents in the Veil were already healing over, the reflection growing transparent.

She said nothing. She did not need to. Her presence was enough to say: *I see you. I found you.*

"Everen?" came your voice. "Are you all right?"

—*The pool in the forest*, came my mother's fading voice, a whisper in my mind. *Now.*

I mumbled some excuse in your direction and fled, slamming the door shut behind me and scrambling up through the trapdoor and out into the dark night. I climbed onto the nearest rooftop, muscles working, my human form falling away. When my wings emerged, I launched myself toward the forest.

20. CASSIA: THE SILVER POOL

The molten pool rippled, the scent of silver and sulfur on the air. The mage lights cast a cool glow, flickering along the rough walls of the caves deep within the Lady of Vere Celene.

Cassia and her mother bent over the edge, waiting for Everen's appearance. Together, they had created a tear in the Veil looking into the pool in the woods where she had spoken to Everen. The night in the human world was clear. Points of stars, the whisper of trees in the wind.

Hurry, brother mine, she thought. They would not have long. She felt her mother's magic and her own siphoning into the rip. Soon, they would have to let it go.

They heard the distant flap of wings. Everen's preterit face appeared within the reflection, his features pinched. His feathered hair was, strangely, black.

—*Everen.* Their mother, Queen Naccara Emberclaw of Vere Celene, looked like she would happily char her son alive.

—*Mother,* he said. *You found me.*

—*Turns out you were not so impossible to find,* the Queen said with a sidelong glance at Cassia. She fought the urge to flinch.

—*It seems you made your way along the path, after all.* Her nostrils flared, her crest half-raised. Everen was right to narrow his eyes in suspicion. He and Cassia had both been on the receiving end of that anger enough to know.

—*You have known exactly where I was since the beginning.* Everen could not entirely disguise the hurt in his voice. Cassia's heart ached. They had both been raised to sift through their mother's words, searching for the true meaning. The sentiment in the sediment, they had called it.

Now she suspected he realized he would have to do it with Cassia, as well. If their relationship was a flower, she'd just watched a few more petals wither and fall from the bloom. She knew how this conversation would go. Miligrist had had the vision only this morning, and Cassia had taken the notes. She shouldn't have, considering she was within it, but Miligrist struggled to transform to preterit these days, so they had bent the rule. Cassia spoke the words she was meant to say next.

—*I am sorry*, she offered, yet they both knew that she was not. Cassia's loyalty must always be, first and foremost, to her people. She would sell her soul in a heartbeat if it meant keeping them safe. He should know that by now. She was a Queen in waiting.

You let me find the prophecy, she thought.

—*You let me find the prophecy*, he echoed, unknowingly.

The Queen only smiled.

—*I suppose I should know by now not to be surprised.* Yet his shoulders slumped. He'd thought he had deviated, taken control, and here he was discovering they had guided him once again. She could only imagine how he'd react if he knew she was reciting his words in her head in the moments before he spoke.

—*We may have nudged you to a choice, but it is still you who made it,* Cassia's next line, she knew, offered scant comfort. *Your hand found the prophecy, and you chose to fly toward the storm. We could not make you do that.*

—*You let me believe, for years, that the prophecies were dead. That I was nothing but your disappointment. So that when you laid down a chance for me to prove myself, you knew I would take it.* His words were acrid as seawater.

—*We all have our part to play, Everen. This is mine.* Their mother said the words without malice, but also without regret. The silver reflection from the pool bleached her eyes until they were nearly as pale as Miligrist's. Her mother had not read the vision. Yet she would speak the words, just the same.

Everen's head turned as he gazed toward the dark trees in the Lumet forest. His expressions were subtly different. More human. The realization chilled her.

—*So I only fly where you tell me,* he said. *Hunt what I must. Kill what I must. You are the wind and starfire and quicksilver. I am nothing but the shape you make me.*

You are everything, Everen, Cassia thought. She almost wished she could tell him, rather than their mother.

—*You are everything, Everen.* The Queen's voice quivered with emotion. *None of this happens without you. Never forget this. No matter how we follow the path. You lead the way.*

His preterit mouth opened, and he blinked. Swallowed. For a moment, he looked so like he had the first time he had entered the archives with her. Wearing a lacebark robe that swamped his smaller frame, just as hers had. Two fledglings searching for answers among old ink and scrolls and soot.

—*Have you completed the bond with the human?* the Queen asked.

—*You know the answer to that, I suspect.*

—*Finish it, Everen.*

—*And if I cannot?* His eyes were bright with defiance.

Careful, she wanted to warn her mother. *He can only be pushed so far.* But what she said would make no difference.

—*I have faith in you*, the Queen said, tilting her triangular head to one side, crest curling over her horns. *Tonight you seemed . . . close.*

Everen's jaw clenched, the muscles working beneath his skin.

—*Careful, Little Red*, she said. It was an endearment she had not called him since he was a hatchling, before she'd put up her walls and defenses. *If I did not know any better, I might wonder if you are growing soft.*

His lip curled, and his chin lifted. —*You have decided I am useful to you again, but that does not mean I fly in your wake, doing whatever is asked of me without question.*

Cassia felt a tingling along her scales. He was meant to say that he was close to bonding with the human, that he thought it would be finished soon.

—*Tread carefully, brother*, Cassia warned, deviating from her own script. Her heartbeat sped up, and her nostrils flared.

Everen's eyes gleamed. —*So must you. There are infinite futures. And in one of them, perhaps I ignore your next scry. Perhaps I cast all this off and find my own path.*

—*You cannot*, their mother said. *You will not.*

He lifted a shoulder, in a too-human gesture. —*Possibly so. But I wonder whether you truly understand what the dragons face with humans.*

There. That had been in Miligrist's vision. Cassia wanted to grab the words and draw them close to her without crushing them like butterflies.

—*We are prepared*, the Queen said, unconcerned.

He shook his head, slowly. —*There are thousands of humans for every dragon. Their magic, with their seals, can be strong. They have machines. But also . . . they do not hate us.*

—*Is that what worries you?* their mother asked with a laugh. She tossed her head and shifted down into preterit. Her transformation was always smooth and delicate. If it pained her, she gave no sign. She'd designed herself to stay a little more draconic in preterit. Sinuous, red scales clustered along her collarbone. Fingernails still black talons. Red feathered hair trailing halfway down her back. She spread her wings, wrapping them around her like a cloak. To a human, she would look fearsome and beautiful in equal measure.

—*They will worship us. They will fall to their knees and welcome us with open arms.*

—*Not all of them.*

—*Enough of them.* Her eyes were bright. Cassia felt her crest relax. All was back to what she expected to hear, to see. It had only been a brief aberration. Everen's will subsumed back into the path of what would be. For their mother spoke with conviction, and that was what was needed. Doubt and uncertainty could wither a prophecy. Fear might let others grow stronger. But belief? Belief could make them true.

Everen needed to believe.

The rip in the Veil was blurring, healing over like a scab. Her brother's reflection grew fainter in the surface of scrysilver.

—*Finish the bond by the Feast of Flowers, Everen,* their mother whispered. *Or we are lost.*

His mouth opened to ask a question, but the pool went still and blank. Her brother remained in the world they coveted. Cassia and her mother were still in their current prison as dragons had been for centuries.

Cassia's mother let herself unfurl back into her dragon form, her magic a burst of orange and red so strong Cassia felt the heat of it against her scales. Yet she could see the dullness of her mother's hide from spending too much time down in the caves. Cassia's scales were similarly poorly tended. For the three of them—Miligrist, the Queen, and Cassia—were the only ones who knew what was coming.

Her mother moved closer, rubbing an armored cheek against Cassia's own and briefly resting her head on her daughter's shoulder, their necks intertwined in an embrace.

—*Should we have told him?* Cassia asked. She knew in Miligrist's vision they had not, but a flock of worries still flapped about her mind.

—*You always were the stronger one, Cassia,* the Queen said, pulling away. *Do not lose your mettle now.* She closed her eyes in an extended blink. *He will do what he must.*

Miligrist entered the cave. She moved slowly, painfully. Cassia had no idea how old the Seer was, but she suspected it was close to a millennium. Her eyes were clouded, her teeth worn. Her once–deep blue scales were lightened from so many moultings into a dusty periwinkle. She was one of the few remaining dragons who remembered the human lands. She had been bonded to one of the humans who had broken the dragons' world. Sometimes, Cassia suspected the old dragon wanted nothing more than to rest. But she could not until she knew what would happen with the Dragon Scales Prophecies.

—*Leave us*, Queen Naccara instructed her daughter, but Cassia was already heading to the passageway. Whatever the Queen and her Seer spoke of next, Cassia would not be privy to it. She, too, knew her place.

Cassia twisted her way through the tunnels. In some places, the stone walls were so narrow her scales scraped along the rock. They were designed that way, to slow down any dragons who might be tempted to come down to the pools without express invitation.

She should go to the archives and continue one of her translations, but she wanted to see the last of the fading light. Though the worst of the heat had cooled, the air was still thick and close.

She greeted those she passed but did not linger to speak. She walked along the top of the head of the Lady of Vere Celene and sat at the tip of her nose. She tucked her four legs beneath her, her wings lying tight across her back. Her head turned toward the volcano crouched on the horizon. They called it only the Reek. It had smoked since long before Cassia and Everen had hatched, one day soon, it would erupt. Miligrist had seen it, had awoken shaking from the vision. The sky the color of fire. What little foliage on the island withering to dust. The air thick with smoke, scarring throats and lungs. A river of magma hissing its unending way into the sea. Cassia had barely been able to write the end of the Seer's warning:

Rivers of fire, wraiths of smoke,
storm, lightning, and rain.
For Vere Celene will crumble,
and only the Lumet will reign.

After that, the old Seer had dissolved into rantings. Cassia had tried to write down the snippets of imagery. Perhaps they had months. Or only days.

It was why their mother was so adamant they had to break through during the humans' Feast of Flowers, when the Veil was next at its thinnest. For who knew if they would last until the next time the Veil grew porous? When Cassia slept, she dreamt she could hear the shifting of tectonic plates growling beneath the earth. The fire at the heart of the world, the primordial beginning of everything, might also spell their end.

Starfire was sending a message, that it was past time to take back what was theirs. They had no choice. It was inevitable.

The dry wind skimmed Cassia's scales. *We will, we will.* She sent the wish out into the world. *We will take back the Lumet.* She'd fly beneath those stars she'd seen in countless scrying pools. She'd dig her claws into damp soil. Glide above green plains and dive for fat, plentiful prey.

Everen would save them all.

He had to.

PART 3: COHESION

Once upon a time, a child stumbled upon a clutch of dragon eggs. The nest was hidden in a cave in the Clouded Mountains, where the forests are bathed in mist. The dragon mother was nowhere to be found. The eggs were silver and warm to the touch.

The child had been sent to find herbs for a poultice, but instead stumbled upon unimagined potential riches. Bringing back just one egg would keep the child and their family in gold for the rest of their lives. The child tried to lift one, but it was too heavy. What if they dropped it?

As if the egg itself had heard, it trembled. And, as the child watched, it began to hatch.

The child crept closer and watched the crack widen. A small snout pushed its way through the membrane and the dragon took a first breath and gave her first cry. The child soon found themselves face to face with a dragon hatchling. She was a scrawny, ugly little thing, feathers damp and sticky.

The child was hypnotized by the swirling blue eyes. They reached out a hand, and the dragon nudged against it, like a cat marking her scent. They intertwined. Nall, the dragon; Crin, the human: two halves of a larger whole.

Crin stayed in the cloud forest. The parents, so poor they could barely feed the other three they still had, did not look very hard for their wayward child.

The dragon mother never returned. Dead, or gone, they did not know. The rest of the clutch hatched, though none of them bonded with the child. One human to one dragon—it had always been so. They took to the skies. Perhaps to find their own pairings. Perhaps not.

Time passed. The two fledglings, human and dragon, grew. Crin, now a youth, began to lose the way of their own kind. When the human and dragon shared their first kill, they grew even closer, until the bond eclipsed them.

Yet, in those days, those who were hidden could not remain so for long.

When the dragon was large enough to bear the youth's weight, they took to the skies themselves. They eventually found the grand palace at the heart of the capital city, full of other dragons and riders. They struggled to fit into their roles. Still, there were comforts. And together, they flew and fought and beat back the danger that threatened the land. It was a good life. A solid life. They lived it well.

Yet they forever missed the cloud forest. One day, they were gone. And no one looked for them very hard.

—*"NALL AND CRIN," AN OLD TALE FROM*
THE PRIOR ERA, AUTHOR UNKNOWN

21. ARCADY: CINDERS

The night of the new moon grew closer as we made our plans.

All knew the objective: steal Girazin's dragon-claw relic. I needed to touch Dwell so I could take over their form, and then on the night of the auction, we'd have to subdue both the merchant and their guard so we could take their places.

"I could simply kill Dwell and the guard," Everen had offered, and I had been disturbed he wasn't more bothered by the idea of it.

"Killing is never simple," I had responded, and he had gone very quiet.

Everyone had studied the blueprints I had made. Larkin was planning the best exit route. Wren was crafting the fake relic, as well as the jewels we'd need to secure a down payment if—when—we bought the claw. Kelwyn was sending out feelers, seeing who might be interested in exchanging wraithwright for a piece of a god.

All that was left was to make sure I could pass as a drakine and Everen my guard.

Everen was bristling at having to pose as my servant. I had started ordering him around imperiously already, to annoy him more than anything. I rather delighted in it.

We didn't speak about the night Everen fled after I'd dyed his hair. I did my best not to think of it at all. We were back to business partners who were mysteriously bonded with magic neither of us understood. Nothing more.

I had looked through my maire's notebook countless times, wondering if there was any hint that might help us break the bond. In the evenings, I'd turn the pages, reverently hovering my fingertips above her careful handwriting. The opening section was for hedge magic. The best way to light a fire. Healing-balm recipes from my paire. This was all I had left of my parents. The page edges were worn and frayed.

I bent my head over it, trying hard not to think of the color of my maire's eyes, a lighter blue than my own. The feel of her hand pushing the hair away from my face. The memory of her climbing the stunted apple trees in the orchard behind the abandoned mountain farm near our cottage, tossing down fruit for me to catch. The way she had woken me up in the morning with a specific whistle that sounded like a bird.

I thought of my paire, and the way he would sew or embroider in the evenings, making something beautiful just because he could. He would sell his creations at the local market, and they would fetch a pretty price, despite the fact everyone else was as poor as we were. I remembered the song he sang when he came back from the forest in the evenings, arms laden with firewood or foraged mushrooms and herbs.

I'd rather remember those bits, rather than what happened at the end. The familiar twist of guilt and horror settled in my gut. Flashes of the sickroom, close and hot. The sound of screaming. The red of blood and the horrible quiet after. I rubbed my eyes, trying to banish the memories. I did my best to never think of it. To never remember.

Trying to reverse-engineer the spell that had given me my new life and called Everen through was impossible. My taie had been one of the strongest magic users in the country, and both he and my maire had years of study and practice, whereas I only had what I'd gleaned from a few stolen books.

I gently returned the notebook to its lockbox.

The days passed in the usual study, practice, and planning. Time wound down and the new moon beckoned.

On the night of Cinders, I finished painting my face and made my way up to what I was, annoyingly, starting to think of as Everen's part of the shop. In an amazing feat of misdirection, my hope was to make him the peahen and me the peacock that evening.

Yet when I saw him, my breath caught a little. The planes of his face were how I imagined the fey from the stories—the eyes a tad too wide, the cheekbones high, the lips full, the tiniest dent in the chin. He wore all dark clothing, and no face paint or jewelry aside from a silver earring with a jet-black stone in one ear. His darker hair wasn't as striking as the red, but it made him look more mysterious. I'd evened it out, leaving the hair a little longer on the top and shorter at the back and sides. It had been futile to ever hope he'd escape notice.

Resolutely, I pushed away that memory of leaning against him as I'd washed the dye from his hair. The feeling of his fingers on my wrist. The way his eyes gleamed green as poison. Easier to bury the attraction down deep with all the other emotions I wasn't brave enough to face. It certainly had plenty of company.

But I felt a thrill when Everen gave a double take as I entered the shop. I hadn't shapeshifted—too risky—but I'd done the next best thing. As when I'd gone to the Lacewing Cathedral, I was aiming for sweet. A naive, rich drakine who was taking a first stab at the card tables. I wore soft, buckskin breeches. A white shirt with entirely too many frills, and a vest the same dark green as the ribbons I'd used to lace my brown boots. The shirt had a careful hole in it, showcasing my seal setting and its cover. I'd twisted every direction in the mirror I could manage, but I hadn't caught any hints of my Struck markings peeking through.

I wore a tight green cap set off with a matching wyvern feather and a false emerald pin. My mouth was a little pinker and gold shimmered at my cheekbones. I wore false eyelashes made of feathers. I'd pasted small jewels along the ring of my ears and wore a thick gold collar at my neck. More rings festooned my gloved fingers.

"It is strange to see you wear color," he said, his voice strained. "You look . . . different."

"I'm going for foppish but innocent. The hope is they'll be so gleeful over cheating me, it'll take longer for them to realize I'm draining them dry."

"I don't look innocent," Everen said, adjusting his cuffs.

"No, you look like you'd get into all sorts of delicious trouble. Act haughty and distant, as if you're above them all. Shouldn't be difficult."

"No," he agreed. "For I am."

I rolled my eyes, fastening my cloak before passing him his. "All right, Your Highness. Let's go win some coin."

The night was dark and the fog thin as we made our way across Vatra toward the merchant district, our cloaks sweeping the cobblestones.

Once a moon, Cinders appeared in the basement of the Bell and the Crown tavern. It was an average establishment, frequented by neither the richest nor the poorest. Yet the bright sounds had an edge of danger to them, as if all might break into brawling at the barest excuse.

Shoving down my nerves, I took up the mantle of a drakine with too much money and too little sense. Someone looking for a good time and almost certain to find it.

We donned our masks—green silk for me and black for Everen. I took the lead and entered first, giving the passcode of "moonstone" at the door and slipping the bodyguard three silver suls. As the guards always had Piater magic and could sense if we had weapons on us, we were both unarmed. As I waited for Everen to make his way past the door, I took in the worst-kept secret in Vatra.

Cinders always smelled of polished wood, smoke from pipes, cigarettes, and candle flames, the sharp bite of alcohol, and people's clashing perfumes. Some of the clientele wore masks as simple as ours. Some were painted wood or hardened paper. Others were ersatz priest masks, with horns of different shapes and scales made of jewels or precious metals cascading across their cheeks. A few showcased metal masks like sleek armor. I suppose many were, in a way, doing battle, and hoping for victory. I didn't spy anyone who was obviously Larkin, but she would be here. Somewhere.

My eyes snagged on Dwell immediately. Already well-settled at a card table, a smokemint cigarette hanging out of the side of their thin-lipped mouth. They wore dark green, their hair braided in a Jaskian style, and a mask of jade scales. No sign of their guard—they weren't allowed into Cinders.

Everen entered and took his place at a seat near the bar while I lingered by Dwell's den of dragons games. Everen held up a hand and ordered a drink which he barely touched, leaning against the stool. People were already stealing glances at him.

Everen had a good view of the table, but I was still nervous. What if this didn't work?

I had good timing; a couple of gamblers had had their fill and were ready to claim winnings or bemoan losses. I joined the table along with another new player and managed to sit next to Dwell. My mark tapped their cigarette into an ashtray. People stacked their coins near their elbows, and I took out my purse and did the same. Around the table were standard Lochian suls, the octagon of Myrian monarchs, and even a few Jaskian crowns carved with the profile of the past King or the current Boy King. I smiled at the people I was about to cheat.

The person across from me wore a priest's mask, and, despite the doublet and hose, I'd bet good coin that They were truly a priest when the sun came up. They were trying to hide in plain sight, but it had backfired. So many hours of prayer leave a mark in the way a person carries Themselves, like Their hands always itch to fold together, Their head to bow.

There was Dwell, of course, to my right. Their nose was perpetually creased, as if they'd smelled dog shit. The player on my left—well, they were drakine through and through. A mask of molded leather clung to their face like a second skin and they wore sumptuous clothes of deep purple, just to rub in the wealth.

The last opponent was a merchant. They were stout and older, the face beneath the fox half-mask lined as old parchment, teeth yellow, breath unpleasant. They had a splash of wine on their doublet and seemed well into their cups. They'd moved to sherry, the smell sharp. The priest wouldn't have deep pockets unless They came from a well-off family, but these other three would. Priest, Dwell, Drakine, Fox.

Everen took a sip of his drink as the dealer returned to our table, dressed in a black fabric that shimmered red and orange in the light—the uniform of those who worked at Cinders.

"Are you ready to begin?" they asked behind their full-face black mask. The Priest, Dwell, and Fox brought out their chains with their seals, and Drakine and I unsnapped the covers over ours. A little extra insurance that no one would be using magic to win. I had checked that my seal did nothing when Everen spoke to me in his mind, but I was still nervous. I could only rely on my wits, and the observations of a certain princeling I still didn't entirely trust lounging against the bar.

The dealer passed out the cards and I kept my hand tucked close to my chest. It was an average start. A pair of a ten and nine of stones. A five and a four of waves. A dragon flame and three of leaves. I'd want to try to get a hand of either three matching suits with the highest numerics or a flush.

I studied everyone over the tops of my cards, searching for the tics and tells they couldn't hide. A tightening of the eyes, a nervous clearing of the throat, or a line high on the forehead. The masks made it harder to read people, which was another reason all wore them. But even a subtle shifting in their chair could hint at excitement or dismay. Priest kept moving Their head to the right slightly. Drakine's lips twitched. Fox took a very large gulp of sherry. Dwell gave nothing away.

There was no easy way to cheat at Cinders. Decks were carefully controlled by the dealers. There was no way to cull or stack the deck on that front. There was also no opportunity for slipping in marked cards, and the gloves we all wore and pulling up our sleeves prevented anyone from being a hand mucker and swapping cards. Some of this could be subverted with casting a temporary illusion, hence the visible seals.

I stared at the skin of Dwell's wrist. I just had to find the right distraction. One tiny brush of fingertips against skin, and I could become them in a blink.

I still hadn't spotted Larkin. Cinders always made me ill at ease. It had that level of background noise that was hard for me to parse with my weakened hearing. All the voices blurred together, high and low tones blending into senseless din. I got by with the help of lipreading, but places like this put me on edge. At least people didn't speak much when they played cards.

Priest played badly the first round, losing about half of Their take. Drakine won, gathering the coins close with a smirk. Dwell's jaw tightened in annoyance. Fox grumbled and drained their glass. I'd lost a little, but not enough to be nervous, not yet. From Everen's vantage point, he could see Dwell's hand and, with luck, perhaps even the Drakine's. Fox's and Priest's I'd only be able to guess through card counting.

—*The merchant with the green mask has a near flush in waves, so watch that.* Everen's voice in my mind still made my skin prickle. *The dragon mask has at least two stones, a four and a two, but I cannot make out the rest of the hand.*

I blinked once, slowly, in an affirmative, and scratched my ear, subtly touching the jewels to indicate to him what I had in my hand.

A pause. —*Discard the dragon flame?*

Very good. I did as he suggested. When I drew my card, I fought back a triumphant grin. Better.

I won that hand and took my coins. Nowhere near enough to impress Larkin, but a fine start.

We played a few more hands and, with Everen's help, I took care not to win too obviously or largely. Drakine was, overall, making off with the most, but Fox was doing all right. Priest, meanwhile, was losing terribly, and Dwell wasn't much better.

I glanced at Everen in the middle of my next hand. Someone had come up to speak to him, but I could only see the back of their head. Larkin? The hair was long and dark, rippling down the back. A good wig. The body type was a little different, but you could do a lot with corsets and the cut of clothing. Everen frowned, his head ducking slightly as he asked the person a question.

Focus, Everen! He could not hear me, but my annoyance must have seeped through the bond, as he narrowed his eyes at the table. —*Carry on. Your hand is sound.* Yet he sounded distracted. Just what had Larkin said to him? I let myself bite my lip, so the other players might think it was me upset over my hand.

The others at my table were playing more aggressively. Was Everen still speaking to Larkin? I peeked. Yes. I fought down a scowl.

Priest barreled on, desperately chasing the copper, then silver, and then gold on the table. I wondered if They had any wraithwright hidden in Their pockets for when They became truly desperate. Wouldn't that be a boon to give to Larkin? Dwell kept betting bigger, and I wondered if they were a gambling addict. I knew they came to Cinders whenever they were in town, but I thought it was more for pleasure than a genuine need for a fix.

I placed my wager on the table. My hand was strong, though not as good as I'd prefer. I chanced a glance at the bar. Everen was alone again, watching the table without being too obvious. Yet I felt his agitation through the bond. My fingertips inched closer to Dwell's wrist.

Fox also grew antagonistic as the take in the center of the table grew larger. I was walking a tightrope—taking advantage of Everen's intelligence, playing my role, and avoiding suspicion. The other players were underestimating me, I hoped, but it was hard to tell.

There was no small talk between hands. Everyone was too centered on the promise of money. It was at the bar and at the tables where you only drank but did not gamble that people spoke amongst themselves. More coin might change hands, for high-quality smuggled smokemint, or a drug called Pollen, made from the powdered nectar of a particular flower in the Myrian rainforest that offered visions and euphoria. Sirens would be here too, enticing people to come back to their rooms in a nearby brothel once the games were finished. Cinders was about indulging in desire. The scent of perfume was strong, making my head spin. I lost and had to push most of my coins back into the center of the table.

I'd hopefully get them back in a moment.

We reached the last round of the game. I had a strong hand, but I still hesitated. Drakine bet high, their confidence rising off them in waves. Fox gave everyone suspicious looks as they refilled their wine. Dwell hesitated and then matched the wager. Priest folded.

The pile of coins in the center was large. I discarded and drew, peering down at my hand. It was good. Good enough? Bet or fold, bet or fold?

—*Call the cards, Arcady,* Everen sent. With a quick prayer, I pushed my coins into the center of the table.

Drakine had a decent enough hand. Dwell had a suit of green leaves, but it had low numbers. They let out a howl of dismay, and the dealer gave them a firm warning. Fox set down their hand next. A higher flush of stones. It was a fine hand.

But nothing compared to my near-royal flush of blue waves, more than half of them dragons. Groans broke out around the table.

"Oh, is that good?" I asked the table innocently. Internally, I wanted to jump up and down and scream. A few observers clapped. Priest looked relieved They had folded. Drakine gave me a sardonic salute. They'd lost an eyewatering amount, but this, I suspected, was little more than pocket change to them.

I reached out to draw the pile of coins to me, a grin splitting my face, but Dwell's hand struck out, grasping my sleeve. I froze.

I ripped my hands back, but I angled my wrist so the skin barely—just barely—brushed the warmth of Dwell's skin, letting the angle of my torso snap the cover of my seal shut. I fought down a triumphant grin as I felt the echoing pulse of blue in my seal, hidden from view. Done. I had them.

"They've cheated," Fox hissed.

"What proof?" I demanded of both Dwell and the Fox, my heartbeat in my throat.

"Just a feeling," the fox-masked merchant sneered.

Out of the corner of my eye, I saw Everen rise and prayed he would be smart enough to stay back.

"I have detected no cheating," the dealer said.

"I'd never be fool enough to try, not here," I said, with all the haughty drakine pomp I could summon. "It might be my first time, but I know that much." I raised my chin. My demeanor might have channeled Everen when he was being particularly insufferable.

Dwell sent me a look that could kill.

Oh, I'll enjoy ruining you, I thought savagely.

"There are more ways than magic to cheat." Fox straightened their coat, not quite steady on their feet.

"And there are plenty of ways to lose, as you've so neatly evidenced." My voice was clipped, but inside I was shaking.

The dealer stepped between us. "Your game here is finished."

Translation: *Sard off and if you're lucky, you'll be let back in on next new moon.*

Priest listed from the table, dejected at Their loss. Dwell and Fox almost snarled at the dealer but grudgingly gathered up their coins.

I dimpled at them all, safely tucking away my coins. They weren't the first to be sore to lose money to me, and they would not be the last. I tied the drawstring of the purse tight. "I've had enough beginner's luck for one night, I should think."

The drakine chuckled. "Well played," they said, and wandered off to another table. I made straight for the door, knowing Everen would follow.

It was noisy in the alley. The revelry would continue until dawn, when people would leave either elated or despondent. They'd all be back again.

I kept my wits about me. Often, the most dangerous part of the night was leaving. On the night of the new moon, plenty of chancers knew that people might be leaving with fortunes in their pockets. Blood had spilled on these cobbles. Hopefully, all our blood would stay firmly in our veins.

Of course, within a few seconds of leaving the alleyway, we heard footsteps.

22. EVEREN: THE COTE

The fox-masked merchant had followed us. They staggered, raising a hand. "Wait, wait, we're not done here!"

"Oh, but I do believe we are," you called back. I clenched my hands.

Still the merchant came toward us, weaving unsteadily. "You've my money, you bastard. Wastrel. Cad!" Were these truly the best insults they could come up with? After a few sennights with you, I had learned far more colorful ones.

—*It would barely take a tap to knock them out*, I offered, helpfully.

You turned and glared at me with a sharp shake of the head. I supposed it would hardly be a fair fight. If this drunken merchant cracked their head on the pavement, we might draw the attention of the guards.

"Sod off, oldster," you said, with all the impudence of the youth you were pretending to be.

They leered, coming closer, curling a lip to show yellowed teeth. "I want my coin." They stank of alcohol. I angled my body so I came in between you and the merchant.

"Protective, are we?" the merchant said. "Just give me my money and I'll be on my way. You cheated, I know you did, you imperious little imp."

I glanced at you. Your eyes were narrowed. And then, abruptly, you laughed.

"Fuck's sake," you said, doubling over. "You nearly had me there."

The merchant raised their fists in a pantomime of a fighting stance before grinning and standing straight and tall.

"Dragons above, Larkin," you said, still chuckling. "You look absolutely hideous." You pointed a finger. "And only Kelwyn's allowed to call me 'imp.'"

I shook my head. *That* was Larkin? My surprise echoed through the bond to you.

She cackled, raising her palms. "Too much?" she said, striking a pose.

"I have to say, Wren did an incredible job on your paint," you said. Larkin framed her face with her hands and batted her eyes at us, which looked rather horrific.

"Sherry, really?" you asked, sniffing disdainfully. "Thought you hated it."

"I do. Smells like feet." She took off the fox mask. There were gaps in the paint, but she had not changed the shade of her eyes. She had strapped down her breasts and wore trousers loose enough to hide the curve of her hips. Taking off the wig, she let her gray hair tumble down her back.

"Job done, then?" Larkin asked.

I caught the scent of sea salt and smoke. You slid off your mask, and Ikari Dwell stood next to me wearing feathered eyelashes. You gave a twirl and a curtsy before switching back.

"Easy," you said, drawing out the purse. "And a nice little bonus, to boot. Here, a peace offering." You tossed it over, and Larkin caught it neatly.

"How'd you do it?" she asked, tucking the purse into a pocket. "You couldn't have card counted easily, not with me messing with your hands. Your little helper was too far away to see or hear much, and you barely even looked at him." Her eyes flashed to me, sharp as daggers. "Even when he's so pretty. The new hair looks good on you, pet."

I said nothing.

"Saint Ini gave me a spot of luck." You kept your voice cool.

"Horseshit," she said, her eyes traveling between us. "I saw you fondling your rings and figured that was some sort of code. But I can't work out the trick to it."

You kept your face as blank as you had at the card tables. "We have our ways."

Larkin relented. "Well. It was clever, whatever it was. I'll give you that." She gave us another considering assessment. "I suppose you two do make a good team."

You preened at the praise. "Good enough you'll come work for me, then?" you asked.

Larkin's nostrils flared, cracking the paint around her mouth. "I will work *with* you."

"I'd have final word, Larkin," you pressed.

You stared each other down, shared history passing between you.

"Remember, darling, being a leader isn't always what it's cracked up to be. It all falls on your shoulders. For better, or for worse."

Another aching moment, and you nodded. "Aye. I know."

"Right, best be off." Larkin blew us both a kiss from the mouth painted to a ruin. Over her shoulder as she walked away, she called: "Looks like you've successfully hired the Marricks, pet. Have Kel set up the next meet."

Once Larkin was out of sight, you radiated satisfaction. You did a jig on the cobbles, holding your hands out wide and tilting your face up at the sky.

You looked at me with such excitement that it pained me. When I did not share your mirth, you hesitated, the smile faltering.

"What's wrong?"

I shook my head. "Nothing."

We kept our masks on as we walked through the city toward the lock shop. The faint lights of the dimmed streetlamps barely illuminated your face and its strange paint. You pulled the cap from your curls, tucking it in your coat pocket. As we took a roundabout path through the streets, you pretended nonchalance, but kept a wary eye on the dark night. Our boot heels echoed instead of being swallowed by the usual fog. Winter was well and truly passing, and each night grew a little warmer. Though to me, raised in my burning world, it was always cold.

Another night closer to the Feast of Flowers. Just under a moon left.

"Who was that you spoke to at the bar?" you asked, finally.

"No one," I said. Another lie.

For Cinders had proven strange for more reason than one.

At the bar, I had seen Mirel, the siren I had accidentally hired the night you and I met. She even wore the same green gown. She'd sat right by me and turned on the charm, clearly trying to pick me as a client again.

"Mirel?" I had asked, wary, one eye still on the card-table game.

She had paused, a line appearing between her brows. "Have we met?"

The last time she had seen me had been in my preterit form. She had been terrified.

"You do not remember?" I asked, carefully. "At the end of the Spirit Moon?"

She laughed. "If I'd had you in my rooms, I'm sure I'd remember." She ran a fingertip down my forearm, leaning forward enough to give me a glimpse of her chest.

This is wrong, this is wrong hammered in my mind. That night, she had not seemed under the influence of anything that would make her forget.

She peered at me, and an expression flickered across her face. I half-expected her to break into a smile and declare it all a jest, but instead she was troubled. "Sorry. Don't recall." Her gaze went distant, and I suppressed a shiver.

She had been spelled to forget. I knew it in my marrow. Mind magic was forbidden in this land, but that had not stopped someone. For what reason?

I folded my features into a smile. "Apologies, I must have been mistaken. May I order you a drink?"

"Depends. Will we spend the evening together?" Her tone was back to teasing.

A flash of abject annoyance through the bond. I glanced at your table, sending you a burst of useful information before turning my attention back to Mirel.

"I am sorry," I said. "I am here with someone."

"A pity," she said, easily enough. A half-smile. "I will take the drink, though."

I raised a finger and paid for her glass of red wine. She took a long sip, raised her glass to me in thanks, and wove through the crowd with that same grace she had shown the night I had seen her in the Dragon's Heart.

Alone at the bar in Cinders, I had swallowed, tapping my fingers on the polished wood of the bar. Mirel must have told someone what she had seen. And now she no longer recognized the dragon that had been right in front of her.

"Everen?" you asked, nudging me with your shoulder and startling me from my thoughts. We were on an unfamiliar wynd curling off from a larger road. "Where were you?"

I was spared from offering up a paltry excuse by a scream. My head whipped in the direction. A scuffle. The solid sound of a fist meeting flesh. "A fight."

You strained but shook your head, unable to make out the noises. I suspected that your hearing was not quite as keen as other humans. You clearly did not wish me to know, so I pretended not to notice.

"It's late on the night of the new moon. There are always fights." You shrugged.

A second scream drifted toward us, this one louder. Someone was in pain.

I went in the direction of the noise. You followed, whispering all the reasons why we should not interfere.

"We don't have any weapons," you hissed.

"I need no blades," I said.

"Oh, gods above," you muttered.

Another shriek of pain. As one, we began running. The sound cut off with a horrible gurgle. We came to a small, cobbled square. The streetlamps had been doused, the silver-white of the moon the only illumination.

Someone crouched over a splayed body wearing a dark, hooded cloak. Something about the movements were so strange, I found myself thinking again in inanimates. It glanced up at us, but I could not make out the features aside from a blood-soaked chin. Something between a hiss and a growl left its throat and it fled. I made to follow, but your hand gripped my forearm, hard. "No," you said, harsh. "Let them go."

"Why?" It would an easy enough task. Yet your attention was on the mangled victim. The body lay sprawled on the cobbles, head turned away from us.

We crept closer, the tang of iron on the air. It was clear that this was no longer a living human. The breath in the lungs had gone stale. The heart had ceased. It was fallen prey that would soon rot. The corpse had no face, only a mess of meat and blood and bone. The seal still glowed softly beneath the fabric of the shirt. In their last moments, they had tried to protect themselves.

You pressed the back of your gloved hand against your mouth, gagging. You grabbed me and we darted back to the shadows at the edge of the square.

"Let's get out of here. Now," you said, glancing up at the windows. Lights were flickering in the flats, shadows and outlines dark against the yellow-orange. "This place will be crawling with the night watch. We can't be seen." Your hand gripped my forearm in a vice and dragged me from the corpse. The fingers of your free hand ghosted to your mask. "Keep yours on."

"I do not understand," I hissed. But you would not let go of me, and the fear radiated off you in waves, echoing through the bond, until we reached the Loc & Key. You took the long way, leading us through false trails and doubling back. We went around to the courtyard and climbed into the window to the back room where you had only let me in once before.

You renewed the wards after the lock snicked shut. Leaning against the wall, your chest heaved as you caught your breath.

"What is it?" I asked.

"That person was killed by a Starveling."

I had heard about them, of course, but it was something else to be confronted firsthand with the aftermath. I knew it was why humans always kept emergency food on them. A very few even drank the blood of animals or other humans, in the belief it would protect them from magic's hunger. As if I needed any other reminder that humans were monstrous.

The incident had clearly rattled you, too. I'd seen you nearly pay a price, the first night in the tombs. You'd been smart enough to bring food with you, but if you hadn't . . .

"Was the hooded figure one of the Struck?" I asked.

"Doesn't matter whether they were or not," you said, shaking your head. "This will ignite a lot of the old fears. Any Struck left in the city should leave, or they'll risk being beaten to death by a mob. It's easier to blame those you already fear." You gave a shaking breath.

"A sour end to a celebratory night," I said as you went to the storage behind the counter and found a bottle of something dark and amber. You took a swig straight from the bottle.

"Aye." You took another long pull. "Just . . . be glad the plague didn't come to your shores. I wouldn't wish it on my worst enemy. The Struck have already been left to slip through the cracks. Since the marks don't pass onto the next generation, the Citadel is just waiting for them to die. Doing everything except flat-out rounding them up for slaughter. And now they're blamed every time someone turns into a monster, even if they never use magic at all. They merely have the curse of the marks."

You took a last drink and set down the bottle with a *thunk*. You rubbed your forehead. "Good night, Everen," you said, tilting your chin toward the door in an obvious dismissal. I rose, weaving through your room full of books, locks, and small treasures.

I paused at the threshold. "Good night, Arcady," I whispered. Your head bowed, and you turned away from me, reaching for the bottle again. I made my solitary way up the stairs.

◇◇◇◇◇◇◇◇

A few nights later, we met the Marricks on a barrow hill.

You had proposed a neutral location, but Larkin had written back and made a grand show of inviting us to "the Cote."

"Power play," you had muttered, but you'd sent back your acceptance via wyvern just the same.

Evidently, Vatra was surrounded by a ring of these ancient barrow hills. This one was at the end of an overgrown track off the main highway that headed toward Redwing Valley, where the rich, including Girazin, kept their estates. We had had to leave the city gates before curfew, and we would not be let back through until the next morning.

The low gravestones along the hill were almost obscured by tall grass. There were no dates on the few tombs I could see, but I suspected some of them had been interred even before the dragons were banished. Some of the graves could even have belonged to those who had cast us out. My lip curled.

"This place was abandoned long before the Strike," you said as you led us around the side, your footsteps sure despite the fading light. I wondered how many times you had taken this route. "The pyre didn't use to be the best way to honor the dead. But anyone who might have mourned these dusty bones is long gone."

I huffed in amusement.

You took a left turn. The hill had once been stepped, and remnants of a path twined around the rim to the half-crumbling stone edifice at the top.

"Hurry," you said. "Larkin can't stand tardiness."

The building was much larger than I had suspected. Up close, it was deceptively sound, with rounded walls and an intact roof, though it all was choked with moss and ivy.

"What is this?" I asked.

"It was a wyvern cote. See, the holes for the nests have been boarded up." You pointed out the indents. "Wyverns were once considered the guardians of the dead, rather than servants to the gods. Funerals were held here before the bodies were laid to rest."

It made a strange sort of sense as a base for a den of thieves. The Marricks were the guardians of the forgotten, and many of their stolen goods went to the Struck, the ghosts who were still living.

"This is where we hunkered down in the depths of winter when business is slow," you said. "The Marricks have plenty of dens dotted around Vatra or in a few other cities in Loc." You paused. "I almost miss this place." The words were hushed, as if you were embarrassed to admit it.

Straightening your shoulders, you strode up and knocked. The door opened, the hinges completely silent, and Wren gestured us inside.

I was not sure what to expect, but in comparison to the timeworn outer walls, the inside was immaculate. Lights glowed in the alcoves of the old wyvern roosts, and thin strips of tapestries softened the stone in between. The floorboards were new, of warm pale wood. A wooden staircase twined up the wall. The innards of the building were three stories high, though you said they had also dug down into the hill as well. This ground floor had a timber ceiling and a large table was near the far side, curved to follow the shape of the stone. Somewhere, the smell of food was tantalizing.

There was no fireplace. Warmth came from heat stones—rocks that could be touched with fire magic and kept cozy for hours. Dragons did something similar. You had none in the Loc & Key. I suspected they were dear.

"Where's Larkin?" you asked Wren.

Wren signed something and you laughed. I should have been more diligent about studying Trade.

We did not need to wait long. Larkin soon came down the staircase, resplendent in an ornate coat, long skirts, and a hoard of golden jewelry at her neck, ears, wrists, and fingers. It was a considerable improvement over the sodden merchant in a fox mask at Cinders.

"I feel underdressed," you drawled, though you had taken care with both of our appearances. The embroidery at the neck and wrists of my dark shirt itched.

"You know I do love an excuse to sparkle," Larkin said, her smile so sharp I nearly expected fangs. Her hands still moved fluidly in Trade, to save Wren from exclusively lipreading.

I was not sure what to make of these humans who had known you for years. Thieves who took from nobles for noble enough reasons in turn, but who kept plenty aside for themselves. You were the architect and had decided to hire them, but I did not trust these Marricks one bit.

You drifted over to the table and stole an olive off a plate, popping it into your mouth.

"Manners!" Larkin said, reaching over to slap your wrist. You gave her such a dirty glare I smothered a laugh.

"So . . . darling *leader*," Larkin said, the word like a swear on her tongue.

She did not like ceding control, and you clearly reveled in your newfound power over her.

"Where is Kel?" you demanded.

"He arrived hours ago. He's upstairs assessing some jewels for me. He'll be down shortly."

"No other little Marricks scurrying about, I notice," you said.

"They're off singing for their supper in the city. None would wish to see you, in any case. Except perhaps to spit on you."

"Oh, my heart," you said, resting a hand on your chest over your seal. Yet I saw the tightness around your eyes, felt the twist of guilt through the bond. My curiosity rose once again.

"Hmm, I admonish you about manners and then I forget my own. Welcome, Everen." Larkin swished closer. "Thank you for joining us this evening."

"Everen," you said. "If you were a guard, how would you greet Larkin if she were an upper drakine?"

"Gods forbid," Larkin said.

I gave a bow of the proper depth and greeted her as Sar Larkin, for I did not know her surname and she was not quick to supply it.

"Not bad," she said, approvingly. "Why don't you give it a go, Arcady?"

"I'd sooner bite the head off a wyvern than bow to you."

Wren signed a clear admonishment, which you ignored.

"Oh, pet, let's hope you're a little politer when you're pretending to be Dwell." Larkin feigned lightness.

"Dwell's a right wankstain—that was obvious enough at Cinders. I can be about as rude as I like and get away with it, most likely. What's for dinner?" you asked, changing the subject.

As if on cue, Kelwyn descended, dressed in a long tunic of green and burnt ochre.

You waved at him lazily. His smile to you was warm but strained when it saw me. He was still upset with me for breaking into his shop. He should have set better wards.

Larkin gestured for us to take our seats in the plush armchairs around a heat stone where covered dishes waited for us on the low table in the center. "Wren cooked."

"Thank goodness," Kelwyn said, mild. "It'll be edible."

Wren lifted the salvers. Over the past few months, I had enthusiastically learned more about human cuisine and recognized most of it. A soup of some sort in a grand tureen. A meat in a dark brown sauce, surrounded by roasted vegetables. Pearly flakes of white fish sprinkled with herbs. A dish of rice dotted with almonds and yellowed with saffron. Buttered green spears of another vegetable I had not yet tried. It all smelled good, and I was famished from the long walk.

"Let's not stand on ceremony," Larkin said, gesturing. "Help yourself."

We loaded our plates, balancing them on our knees as we ate. It was strangely intimate, more like we had our meals. Some of your wariness bled away as you ate. You joked with Kelwyn or signed something to Wren one-handed. You even relaxed a little more around Larkin. The shared history was obvious. This, long ago, had been your home. When Larkin recalled a story from three winters ago, you laughed so hard you nearly upended your wine. You were slipping back into an old role, whether you meant to or not.

I hunched over my food, focusing on the flavors, but feeling strangely jealous and cut off from the conversation until, when the plates were nearly empty, it circled around to the auction.

You refilled your wine glass, your cheeks a little flushed. "How is the replica of the relic coming along?" you asked.

Wren nodded enthusiastically and signed something, disappearing up the stairs and returning with a wooden box. He set it on the low table between the chairs and gestured for you to open it.

You did, revealing a velvet-lined interior. It was like the illustration I had seen in the Last Golden come partially to life. A glass vial with silver caps was nestled to one side. Next to it was something that, indeed, looked like a piece of dead dragon. I fought the urge to curl back my lip and bare my fangs.

Kelwyn leaned closer, inspecting it critically from various angles. "As ever, you're a master, Wren. What's it made of?"

A quick, sharp flutter of hands.

"Wren will never reveal his secrets," you said for my benefit.

"I stand admonished," Kelwyn said.

"May I see?" I asked, reaching for the box. At Wren's nod, I picked it up carefully.

The model was still missing some of its scales. Wren had woven the shape with wire and packed it with something white to give it form. Dried meat, cast gray, worked for the skin, and the scales were some type of fish, filed sharper and dyed dark purple. The attention to detail was perfect: the larger scales on the knuckles, the sharpness of the talon, made of an antler stained black. I had few doubts from the painting, but this only confirmed it: the real relic *was* a preterit left claw just beginning the shift back to dragon, perhaps during an attack. Had the dragon survived, or perished?

"How old do you think the original is?" I aimed for nonchalance.

I caught the odd word as Wren signed Trade, but relied on your translation. "Hard to say. This is the only one Wren or Kelwyn have heard of with flesh. They are always bones, teeth, horns, scales. He says he's still concerned about the weight. He's aiming for what a wyvern claw might weigh at the same size."

"That would likely be correct." You frowned at my stiffness.

"It only has to buy us enough time for Arcady to make the switch and disappear," Larkin said. "It's the linchpin of the whole plan, isn't it?"

You nodded. "It all hinges on this. Which is why I couldn't risk anyone else making it."

Wren beamed.

"You could make an absolute killing crafting more of these, even if you advertised them as fakes," Kelwyn said, taking out his magnifying spectacles and looking at the claw anew. "I know collectors who would give their own pinkie finger for this. Beautiful work. Gruesome, but beautiful."

Wren's smile only grew.

"What about the jewels?" you pressed. Wren flipped up the bottom of the trunk and took out a diamond necklace. It glittered in the light. The setting was an ornate gold. A larger jewel lay at the center, the chain dotted with smaller ones, like stars.

Kelwyn reached out his hand and Wren passed it over. He spent a long time looking at it from every angle.

"Well?" you asked, a hint of nerves bleeding through. "Would it pass muster?"

Kelwyn made a considering sound. "It's, as ever, excellent work of course, Wren, but . . ." He paused. "What about using real jewels, just to be sure?"

You leaned forward, steepling your hands together. "I thought about it, but it'd have to be worth at least a fourth of the overall amount, and that'd eat into the profit something awful."

"I agree," Larkin said, clicking her tongue against her teeth. "But this is good enough to work, wouldn't you say, Kelwyn dear?"

Kelwyn nodded, reluctant. "Unless they have someone who's very strong in Piater magic handling it. Always the risk."

As Larkin passed out a dessert of plum and almond cake and poured cups of tea, the group continued debating the merits of false versus true jewels, but it all faded to a distant buzzing. Whom had that claw once belonged to? A dragon with purple scales so dark they were almost black. All the dragons that shade in Vere Celene that I knew still had all ten claws. This dragon was as dead as the humans buried in the barrow hill around us. I felt a pang of unexpected grief.

I had never considered the possibility that I was not the first dragon to fall through. Cassia had never hinted at it, though I supposed I could not trust her to tell me.

To everyone else in the room, the original relic was simply something extraordinarily valuable, a rarity to exchange for their little human coins. But it was a piece of my kind. And knowing it was displayed as a mere curio by the descendants of those who had banished us . . . I swallowed bile.

I stared at the false claw until Wren closed the top of the box with a snap.

23. ARCADY: PARTITIONS

"Try not to steal the candlesticks," Larkin called after me from her arm-chair as Everen and I followed Wren up the stairs. Trust her to end the night on a little barb.

"Good night to you, too, Larkin."

"You'll leave first thing in the morning."

"Wouldn't dream of lingering." I gave her a lazy salute.

It'd been over a year since I'd last set foot in the Cote, and I never thought I'd be here again. I'd spent more time in the city-center hideouts, but this had always been my favorite. For when the Marricks were out here, we hadn't been thieves. We had been ourselves.

Larkin and Wren. Aby, Joana, Driscoll, Brev, and Lightfinger. I had memories of them in every corner of this old stone building. I'd sat at Brev's favorite seat during dinner. I'd had such a sharp vision of Joana polishing a knife by the largest heat stone. There were the dents in the stair where Lightfinger had dropped a stolen mace from the Indelin job. It all felt like a lifetime ago.

Since there were few windows in the Cote, Wren had gone up to the roof and painted the views in each direction at different times of the day and hung them up inside. The rolling fields and woods to the east were shown in sunrise. The distant spires of Vatra and the Citadel to the west were in sunset. North and south, Wren would choose the time of day depending on the room. One might be full night, the other late morning. I resisted the urge to run my fingers along the frame of my favorite one, the sunrise at the end of the short hallway on the first floor. My throat was so tight it burned.

Wren went to fetch extra bed linens. Larkin had tried to get us to share a room, but I'd insisted on two. I claimed that Everen was too warm and it was like sleeping next to a heat stone, and he'd given me one of his molten looks. Maybe it would have been easier to keep playing along, but actually lying next to Everen in the same bed would be impossible, even without the risk of an accidental touch, and making him sleep on the floor would be unkind. Wren gave us rooms right next to each other, and my footsteps slowed when I realized which ones.

"I thought you might want the familiarity. Which one?" Wren gestured. "Your old one, or . . . ?"

"I'll take Lightfinger's," I signed back. "Who sleeps in them now?"

"No one, yet. Larkin hasn't replaced either of you, you know. Everyone else stays in their old rooms."

I blinked. I thought she'd have gone and plucked up two more orphans before she'd even washed our bedclothes.

Wren followed me into Lightfinger's old room and handed me the linens while Everen settled into mine.

After I'd finished tucking in the sheets, I felt Wren's polite tap on my shoulder.

"Yes, Wren?" I gestured.

"Are you going to double-cross us again?" Wren's expression was calm, but his eyes wary. He shook his head so the white hair fell back from his face. The Struck marks were even starker in the dimly lit room.

Well. That was direct of him. I was glad we spoke in Trade. There was no way for Everen to overhear.

I swallowed, then shook my head. "I could ask if Larkin's planning to hang me out to dry again, too. Is she?"

"Not to my knowledge. As long as you don't . . ." His fingers trailed off.

"Misbehave?" I signed, archly. I paused, my fingers hovering in midair. "No, I've no plan for tricks, no catches. Just the job."

Wren searched my face. Whatever he found there, one side of his lips quirked. He raised his hands. "You could come back to the Marricks after this, you know, if you wanted. Larkin's still angry, but this job will more than make up for it. You could be a part of the family again." I always loved the way he signed. He gave these subtle extra flourishes that made his hands look so beautiful, like bird wings. Like dancing.

I smiled sadly. "Kind of you to offer, Wren." My own signs were stunted in comparison. "But I'll never fit in here again. I'm not sure I ever did." I swallowed. "This is my last brush with thieving. I'll be going on the straight and narrow. This job will let me leave it all behind and more."

"Remember what Larkin says," Wren began.

"Once a thief, always a thief," Wren signed as I said the words aloud.

"Whether you're stealing coin or no," he continued. "You'll always be looking at the world a little sideways, seeing the gaps where fingers could slip in and come out with something that shines. You'll always sense when there's something to be gained."

"Maybe so, Wren," I agreed. "Maybe so. But I think I'll need that, where I'm hoping to go next." I gave a long sigh.

"I've missed you," he said.

"And I you."

Wren stepped forward and squeezed my shoulder. I fought the urge to pull him close. But we had never been like that, and he'd think something was wrong. Was it?

My eyes were stinging. Those blasted emotions I worked so hard to bury were sending little seedlings up. I hunched my shoulders. "Thank you for the linens."

He studied my face. Not for the first time, I wondered how much he knew. If anyone might have seen through me, it would be him. He, at least, wouldn't have treated me any differently. But he'd never have been able to keep it from Larkin, and if she knew I was marked, she wouldn't let me anywhere near a spell.

"I'm fine," I reassured him. "I'm focused."

"I'll let you sleep," he signed, and patted me on the cheek. "Try not to dwell too much on the past." He left silently. Though he never came on jobs with us, he'd make a decent thief. I'd always thought so.

It felt both right and wrong, to be in Lightfinger's room instead of my own. The chambers were about as big as broom cupboards. On the wall was a looking glass that was cracked in the corner in the same shape as the Vatran river. There were the flowers embroidered by one of the Marricks when the group had been bored one especially cold winter and had decided to take up needlepoint. They were in every room. This one was violets. I think Aby had done it. I ghosted around the room, searching for little signs of Lightfinger. I found a carved "LF" on the corner of the dresser and traced it.

Whatever emotions I was sending through the bond drew Everen's darkened shape to the doorway. Very annoying—sometimes you just wanted a mope on your own.

I cleared my throat and straightened. "Is all fine with your room? You're in my old one, you know."

"Really?" he said. "Wonder what a younger Arçady used to hide in it."

"Oh, all sorts of goodies. I had a special little spot for sweets. Right next to the knives."

He chuckled, and I hated how much I liked the sound of it. He leaned against the doorjamb and crossed his arms. "Do you want to switch?"

I was half-tempted, but in the end, I shook my head. "No, you're already settled. I spent plenty of time in this room, too."

His eyes narrowed slightly as he tried to work out what that might mean. We paused, taking the other in. He'd rolled up his shirtsleeves, showing his muscled forearms. He had no hair on them, but I'd never caught him shaving. I'd drunk enough wine that the thought didn't linger. My face was warm. Hopefully I'd stumbled on the right balance of enough alcohol to help me sleep, rather than making me queasy and my ears ring as soon as I lay down.

He drifted back, closing the door behind him.

I took my time changing for bed. I'd packed a long-sleeved, long-hemmed nightgown of thick, dark material. I'd be sweat-soaked by morning, but at least if the Cote caught fire and I had to run out into the damp grass in the middle of the night, my marks would be covered.

It hadn't been easy to hide them when I lived with the Marricks. When the others went swimming, I'd read in the shade. I took quick, furtive baths on the lowest level of the Cote, locking the door tight. It was why I'd been so determined to have that tub at the Loc & Key, so I could luxuriate until the water went cold.

It was my first time sleeping away from the shop for over a year. The room seemed so barren in comparison.

I could hear Everen's movements through the wall. The sound of him brushing his teeth, a splash of water in the basin. Even the rustle of his clothes as he undressed.

Do not think of Everen undressed.

I slid beneath the covers and heard him do the same. Sleep, sure enough, would not come. I opened the tiny wyvern-roost window, letting in cool, fresh air. Our beds were both pressed against the interior wall. I remembered quietly knocking on the side of the wall where Everen was now and waiting for Lightfinger's response. Our own little codes, the stifled giggles. I turned on my side.

—You keep shifting about, Everen finally complained.

"Sorry," I murmured. "Am I keeping you awake?"

—Sleep is proving difficult to hunt tonight.

"Are you missing the pond in the woods?" He'd told me about it at some point, I was sure. I could picture it so clearly.

A low laugh. *—I miss sleeping beneath the stars. They are so bright here, compared to where I am from.*

Here, in the dark, the bond felt suspended between us. I could almost imagine it slipping through the wall and twining around his form in the bed. I was sure he was lying in mirror image to me, his hands pillowed behind his head.

"Tell me more about your land, your life." It was easier to be bolder in the dark. "Tell me a secret." I'd gathered a few little slips, hoarding them like gems. He'd told me his people worshipped starfire. I knew he had a sister. It was obvious he had a complicated relationship with his mother. He had referenced a few friends, obliquely. But I had the sense that he'd spent much of his time alone. Lonely.

Like recognized like, after all.

He was silent for a long time, but eventually his voice unfurled in my mind again. *—Vere Celene is harsh, but it is beautiful. Always dry as tinder. The sun determined to bake you where you stand. But sometimes the wind off the sea is cool.*

He shifted a little in the bed. *—Here is my secret: sometimes, I do not wish to be a prince. I do not want all the expectations that come with it.*

I couldn't help but scoff.

—I know. You want every little morsel of power, and I do not blame you for it. I thought I did, once. But it comes with so many catches. A sigh on the other side of the wall. *My kind would say fate brought me here, on the Night of Locked Tombs. If you think everything you do has already been foretold, that it is inevitable, it all feels . . . futile.*

"Then why believe it? Why not choose your own life?"

A quiet laugh. *—I tried. You have more control over your days than I ever did. Even the way you present yourself to the world, the way you move through it.*

"As a thief?"

—In part. But I also envy how fluidly you flit between genders or blend them. I

am from a world where there are . . . so many expectations put on me. I was told that, as a male, I was dangerous, on the verge of losing control.

I chose my words carefully. "Do you believe masculinity is always violent?"

—I would like not to.

I rolled onto my back, pillowing my hands behind my head. "In Jask, they tell men that nothing matters more than physical strength. Women must be gentle and protected and pretty. I'm glad Loc isn't that rigid. But we're not entirely divorced from gender roles or expectations, either. We were more like Jask, long ago. There are remnants, but they're like . . . blurred graphite marks instead of black ink."

I grew silent, mulling. Just like our conversation about founding myths, it was hard to pull back and explain our ways to someone outside of them. "But me? I was never drawn purely to femininity or masculinity. Neither felt like me." I took a moment. "It's like being at a banquet. Why would I limit myself to one food when there are so many other options on the platters? I get to consume what pleases me and my tastes, and no one else. I know what I like, and what I don't." I stared up at the ceiling. "I dunno. Gender is both so important and yet inconsequential, in the grand scheme of things. The more you think about it, the stranger it all seems. Trying to unpick what feels innate to you, and what is put upon you by others. But I'm glad that here you can live how you wish, more or less, at least in that respect." I tapped the wall, softly.

"I don't think I could live in Jask," I continued. "And it sounds like I'd find it hard in Vere Celene, too. I think I'd make myself smaller, to try and blend in. Choose a side and stick with it. But that would mean closing off a part of myself to please others, and I think that would be a shame."

I felt uncomfortable, almost embarrassed. I'd not actually spoken much about the topic, except with Lightfinger, but they were the same, so of course they'd understood.

Everen's voice went silent in my head. I didn't add that there were already so many parts of myself I had killed or pruned to survive in Loc. My name. My history. I didn't want to give up anything else. Outside, the night bugs sang.

—What keeps you awake? he asked after another half-candlemark had passed.

"Memories."

—*Why did you leave the Marricks?* If he'd asked even a few days ago, maybe I wouldn't have told him. But there, in the dark, it was easier to offer up a secret, too.

"Kelwyn introduced me to them," I began. "I worked for Larkin and Wren and the others, but I stayed for Lightfinger." I closed my eyes, letting an image of them play against my eyelids. The tilt of their nose, the wicked way their eyes lit up after a particularly cutting joke.

"They were a friend. More than that. A sibling, in all but blood. A little over a year ago, we went on a job. Nothing unusual. Snuck into a merchant's warehouse on the outskirts of town. Lightfinger was unmatched at cracking safes—hence the name. Kelwyn taught me pickpocketing, but Lightfinger is why I'm good with locks." I paused. Swallowed. Continued.

"The job went wrong, of course. Someone messed up a ward. Private guards arrived—basically mercenaries. The merchant who owned the warehouse was little more than a gang leader, they ran so many illegal goods. We should never have targeted them. Larkin and I managed to get out, but not Lightfinger."

I found myself tracing patterns along the wall with a fingertip. Swirls and loops.

"The guards beat Lightfinger. Some of the worst sounds I'd ever heard. I tried to claw my way to them, but Larkin held me back, saying we couldn't risk ourselves or the loot."

The bond moved back and forth between us, like steady breath.

"One guard eventually stopped. But the other—the other went Starveling. The first tried to drag them off but was injured. I fought my way free of Larkin just as the guard killed the Starveling. They—they let me take Lightfinger." I leaned my forehead against the wall.

"I carried them to a healer, but it was too late. A bleed in the brain, they said. Most healers can only speed up what a body does naturally. It would have taken a grand master to heal Lightfinger. I begged Larkin. Desperately. We had the coin in the vaults. I knew we did.

"She said no. She was crying, but she said no."

I pressed my eyes closed so tight, dark red spots danced along the back of my eyelids. "The healer helped with the pain, at least. I sat with Lightfinger and watched them die. And I couldn't do a damn thing."

—So you left the Marricks, Everen sent, soft.

My fingertips had stilled on the wall. I moved them again. Larger circles, growing smaller. "I realized she would have let me die if I'd been the one injured. Larkin thought of the big picture. One of us versus several Struck. We were acceptable losses. Maybe it's the only way to keep doing what she does. But it wasn't for me. I stole exactly as much as Lightfinger's healing would have cost on my way out."

—What happened to the merchant who owned the warehouses?

"They died, a few months later. From a lingering illness."

—Do you think Larkin did it?

My fingers stilled. I hadn't considered that. Larkin had lived a whole life before the Marricks. She'd mentioned, once, that her paire had been a villein healer. She could mix a sleeping draught and a few other potions. Did she know the ingredients for a long, painful death, something that left them choking on their own blood? Would she have done it?

"Maybe," I allowed. "I'm not sure it would change anything, if so. She still let Lightfinger die. And what's worst is: was she right? Is helping hundreds better than saving only one person you know and love?"

Everen shifted on the bed.

"For all Larkin's lofty ambitions and her insistence she's doing this for the good of the Struck, she steals for the thrill of it. Like me. She grew up a child of peasants. She likes luxuries. The fine clothes, the silverware. She steals to be more than society told her she could be. Money can open any door without the need to pick it."

—Why do you want all this money, Arcady? What doors will it open?

I had given him a little information, after we'd spoken of myths and legends. I was so used to wrapping all my secrets up tight.

"Because Loc stole my future, and I'm going to steal it back. I'm using that coin to go to that university up on the hill and learn everything they told me I didn't deserve to know. I aim to find proof that those at the top decided letting so many die was worth it if they could remain rulers of the rest. And that they let someone else take the fall. I'll weasel my way into the heart of that corrupted Citadel and do what I can to rip out the rot. And when I'm done, I'm leaving this place behind, and I'm never looking back."

I didn't sense much surprise.

—You are surprisingly idealistic, for a thief.

I shrugged, though he couldn't see. "I'm not going to pretend there isn't plenty of selfishness there, too. But that's the difference between politicians and thieves: only one admits they're stealing what isn't theirs."

I sensed more than heard his laughter, coiled around my ribs. —*I am sorry,* he ventured after another pause. *About your friend.*

I dropped my hand from the wall, my fingers finding their way beneath my shirt to the warm metal of the seal setting. "I learned something from it, though I should have already known, really. Anyone who cares for me winds up hurt or dead." I whispered it into the dark. A warning. For him. For me. I left the second half unsaid: *and anyone I care about, too.*

I sensed an indecision as Everen searched for the right words to say.

"Good night, Everen." It'd become our signal: *that's all you'll get for now.* —*Good night.*

I squeezed my eyes shut and turned my back to the wall. The bond between us had thinned to a thread. As the night passed, neither of us reached for it again.

24. SORIN: THE CAPTAIN

Sorin crouched in the belly of the ship.

She'd snuck in on one of the crates stored in the hold, and she'd been crammed between bolts of silk for hours. *The Iris* was docked on the far side of the harbor so it could slip out on the earliest tide. Only a skeleton crew was aboard overnight, the rest enjoying the last few hours of life and color before a moon spent sailing toward gray horizons, back to Jask and its frozen fjords.

When the moon was high enough, Sorin wriggled out from beneath the silk, weaving among the boxes of spices, fruit, dyes, and other luxury goods.

She padded through the cramped corridors as the ship shifted gently in the calm harbor, water sloshing against its hull. On deck, the crew passed around a bottle of rum as they took in the lights of Vatra on shore. Sorin smelled tar, treated wood, the remnants of meals from the mess, and the faint stink of sailors' sweat. The captain's quarters were at the back, and that was where the true treasure would be found.

The lock was tricky, but she soon found herself inside. The windows to the rear were shuttered and locked, the curtains drawn. Sorin whispered a spell and let the small flame dance above her hands long enough to light one of the lanterns. The captain's lair was sumptuous: brocade and fur on the box bed, tasseled velvet curtains, gold filigree on the lamps. A large slab of a desk was bolted to the floor, the ship's log open, a stoppered inkpot next to it along with a letter opener and a few envelopes. Sorin glanced through the papers but found nothing of note.

She explored the room systematically, yet no nook or cranny revealed what she sought. She went through the captain's clothes, running her fingers along the seams. Rifled through the jewelry box at the back of a cupboard. Found a few bottles of good alcohol, an extra cache of sweetspheres and dried fruit. She nibbled a few apricots as she continued. She searched under the mattress and through the down stuffing. Reached into the pillowcases. Checked the skirting boards, molding, and floorboards for hidden compartments. Nothing. Worry gnawed at her. She could not return empty-handed.

The captain was meticulously tidy. No dust gathered in the corners, and not even an errant splatter of ink stained the wood of the desk. Sorin sighed. She would have to wait for her target's return.

She slipped beneath the box bed, her back aching anew. Yet her luck held, and half a candlemark later, just as her feet began to fall asleep, drunken soldiers stomped up the ramp to the ship.

A few minutes later, the captain entered Their quarters. Sorin heard Them stretch, kick off Their boots and place them in the wardrobe. A burp. The soft pop of a flask and the sound of sucking down water. The whisper of cloth as They changed. The captain hummed an unfamiliar tune, breaking out into muffled, half-remembered lyrics. Even in song, the Jaskian tongue sounded ugly, harsh. They unshuttered the windows, propping one open to let in the scent of salt and distantly rotting fish.

Soon, the room fell silent. There would be a sailor or two on watch, but the rest would be catching a few hours of sleep until just before dawn. Sorin's work for the light was always done best in the dark.

When the captain's breathing slowed, Sorin unfurled from beneath the bed. She had her widow's sleep in a vial at her breast. A garrote wire, her array of blades, including the trident knife. Sorin was reminded uncomfortably of her first kill. A flash of Karys Fall's hair spread across the pillow. The phantom scent of orange oil.

Sorin must keep her mind clear, her heart open to the will of the gods. This was how she served the Order of the Dragons. How she served Magnes.

The open windows let in the faint silver of the new moon, the smudged yellow of the harbor lamps. Sorin took care not to block the light and cast a shadow over the sleeping captain's face. She had seen few Jaskians up close, and she paused to take Them in, searching for echoes of her own features.

Captain Tellreg's hair trended toward rose-blond. Their skin was milk pale, much paler than her light brown, but sparkled with freckles not unlike Sorin's own. She guessed They were in Their mid-fifties, stocky and strong.

The captain's eyes shot open, and They jackknifed upright. There was no surprise, only determination. Sorin blocked the strikes, backing up a few steps. She should have known an old sea dog slept lightly.

She dodged again, but the captain must have been a brawler or boxer in Their youth. The footwork was sound, the cuts sharp, with no extra ex- pended energy. Sorin only managed a strike or two before the second attack took her by surprise. They tackled her to the floor, her head narrowly missing the corner of the desk. The air left her lungs as she landed, the back of her skull hitting the wooden boards with a *smack*.

Tellreg hissed something at her in Jaskian. She could imagine the insults. *Demon worshipper. Half-blooded bastard.*

Sorin gritted her teeth and angled enough to use her forehead to smash Their nose. Pain blasted across her face. The captain groaned but loosened Their hold enough that Sorin could push Them off. They struggled to raise themselves, but a knee to the solar plexus brought Them down again.

Sorin grunted as she tried to pin Them, but Tellreg was slippery as a fish. Her trinity knife was in her hand, glinting in the light of the lamp. The captain caught her wrist, but she used her other forearm to press against Their throat until They wheezed and Their grip loosened. She brought the knife to Their throat before she lessened the pressure.

They knew why Sorin was here. Their eyes flicked toward the desk involuntarily. Aha.

While Sorin was distracted, the captain used the same move upon her. She ducked enough that Their forehead hit her cheekbone instead of her nose. Pain still echoed through her bones. Fire spread across her face. She let out a low grunt, but her training had held. The trinity knife remained at Their throat.

"You would kill me?" the captain asked, eyes roving over Sorin's features. Their Locmyrian was accented but fluent. "Who is your family? We could be blood."

Sorin's grip tightened on the hilt. She shook her head, once.

Their eyes flickered down toward the blade. They licked Their lips, bravado cracking. "I know what this blade means. I have heard the whispers, warrior priest."

Sorin leaned closer. Her cheek pulsed with pain in time with her heartbeat, and the iron tang of blood was sour in her mouth. The inside of her cheek had cut on her teeth. She kept the blade firm against Their jugular and risked a quick sign of "why" with her free hand before pinning Them again.

The captain grimaced. "I am incurious by nature. I take my coin. I ask no questions. This is why I am trusted."

She refused to rise to the bait. Captain Tellreg was not stupid. Before the Schism and the Strike, Jask and Locmyria had been bitter enemies. Uncountable wars, so many lives lost. Jask produced very little of its own—they always needed more, and they would rather pay for it in blood than coin. Resources, faith, belief: there were many reasons why tensions could rise again, and with so much of Magnes's efforts devoted to guarding the leylines and rips in the Veil, Loc could not afford to fight a war on two fronts. Not when so much was at stake.

Sorin kept the blade to Their neck, pressing up in a clear message: *stand.*

The captain kept Their hands raised as Sorin moved off Their torso. Slowly, the captain moved to Their feet.

"I am a dead man by week's end if you take them."

She could make Them a dead man now, if They'd rather. Magnes had given her a little more discretion for this second task: if she found the relics without issue, she could give Them a warning, like Sar Saunder Bane or the siren in the abandoned house on the hill. But if the captain gave her trouble, she was meant to kill Them quietly.

"An unremarkable death," Magnes had said. Like Karys Fall. Did this captain deserve any of her mercy?

Don't spare Them because They are the first Jaskian you've ever interacted with, she admonished herself. *They mean nothing.*

Tellreg swallowed, perhaps seeing something harden in her face. With shaking hands, They reached for the inkpot next to the ship's log and opened a hidden compartment in the base. Sorin had checked it, but there must have been a clever catch. Out scattered three teeth, about the length of a human palm. Yellowed as ancient ivory. Dragons' teeth. Gods' teeth.

Tellreg set them on the desk and backed away from the points of her trident blade, hands up. Not breaking eye contact, Sorin spirited the relics into a hidden pocket.

"Who?" she signed, one-handed.

Their lips curved into a faint smile. "You know I cannot tell you this."

She could make Them. She hadn't yet had to torture someone, but she knew the methods. Magnes had taught her how to light up every nerve of Their body, make Them think They were aflame. How to slow Their heartbeat, or force it to beat so fast it might burst.

"You're young, yet," he said. "What, eighteen, a little older? I've a daughter your age."

Sorin froze, her mind spinning, reassessing.

Tellreg set the ink pot back in its holder. "You're wondering if this is some ploy. To get you to see me as a person so you do not kill me. Maybe. I suspect you don't often converse with your victims." A pause. "Ah. They do not allow you to speak."

Sorin's hand tightened on the blade, waiting for Them to rush her.

"I thought about turning down this job," Tellreg said. "Perhaps I should have. I was due my quiet days on land, soon enough. But the money was too good." They turned to stare out the window, which showed the dark forest of masts and hulls of other ships docked and waiting for the dawn tide.

"What is your name, young one?" They asked. "When we fight our own, we always announce ourselves. It is the honorable thing."

Sorin's mouth opened, her throat clicking. She shook her head, once.

"Hmm." Tellreg pressed a palm against the polished wood framing the window. "This ship always served me well. Perhaps I might keep it. Will you let me?"

Before Sorin could work out what the captain meant, They struck like a snake, punching through the glass panes. They held a shard at Their wrist.

"No!" she said aloud, the word torn from her throat, rushing forward as Tellreg slashed his wrist once. Hard. No hesitation. She didn't know why she tried to stop Them when they both knew how this night would end. The captain had simply hurried it along.

The captain stumbled to the desk. "Let it come with me," They murmured, blood spilling onto the ship's log, staring up at her with dimming eyes. With a jolt, she understood what Tellreg was asking. Jaskians were buried at sea with Their favored possessions so They could arrive with them to the afterlife. Weapons, jewels, tools of the trade. They wanted her to scuttle the ship. It was a selfish wish—it should be left to family. But perhaps They had enough money, or the daughter had no real need of it.

"Please," They asked, voice catching. "I want to keep it."

Sorin made a pained sound in her throat, but she reached into her shirt for her seal. The dragonstone flashed silver as Piater's magic loosened the planks of the hold. She felt the moment the water rushed in.

"*Gratje*," They said. "Thank you."

Sorin leaned closer. "Sorin," she whispered. "My name is Sorin." She had no last name.

Captain Tellreg laughed weakly. Their skin was even paler, Their lips white. "I hope these three teeth are worth what they do to you," They said, Their words faint over the creaking of the ship. "But you'll never stop what's coming." A raise of the head, a curl of the lip. "I'll say hello to your demon gods for you, Sorin."

Before Sorin could ask what They meant, the captain lost consciousness. Their heartbeat chugged sluggishly. It would not be long.

She heard the cries of the crew as they realized the craft was sinking, and she locked the door to the cabin to buy a little more time. Some rushed to the hold, but they'd flee when they realized there was no way to stem the leaks. *The Iris* was already beginning to list to one side, but Sorin risked a last look at the captain. Their head had slumped forward. They were gone.

There, where no one could hear her, Sorin screamed. It hurt, glass shards in her throat. An ugly, pained sound.

Her hand shot out, lifting one of the lamps from its holder and smashing it to the floor. The flames caught on the velvet curtains of the box bed. Tellreg's funeral pyre completed.

Sorin felt the heat at her back. She crouched at the open window, mindful of the broken glass. She would not look back. Gathering herself, she jumped.

The water was shockingly cold, driving the air from her lungs. She broke the surface. Refuse bobbed on the murky surface.

The ship had caught quickly, flames already flickering from the window, jumping to the deck above. She fought the urge to sputter as she swam with strong, sure strokes, ducking beneath the docks. She shivered, clamping her jaw shut so her teeth wouldn't chatter as she heard shouting above her in panicked Jaskian. She did not need to speak the language to know the moment the crew realized the captain was going down with the ship. A poor end, to sink in the harbor rather than on the wild, open sea. But it was better than dying on land.

When Sorin could stand the cold no longer, she swam to the edge of the dock and climbed the metal rungs hammered into the stone wall. No one noticed her, Their attention drawn by the shouts and the sight of a burning, capsized ship. Sorin spent some of her green magic to fight the worst effects of the cold. Her cheekbone pulsed with pain, but she had never been good at healing herself. She needed warm, dry clothes. Still, she felt she had to stay. Tucking herself into the doorway of a closed shop, she wrapped her arms tight around her body. The end of the dock was bright yellow from the blaze, joined by the smaller spots of lamps and mage lights as port authorities, guards, and those few who had business at the docks this late at night rushed to help.

Horror painted the salt-stained crew. A few sobbed. They had all made it off the ship, save Their captain, it seemed. At least Sorin had only taken one life this night.

The masts of *The Iris* stuck out of the water, still tall and proud, the sails wrapped. The fire was dimming as the water claimed more of the ship. Silence fell over the docks as dawn peeked over the horizon. Without the ship, most had lost the only home They knew. How many would find easy passage back across the open water? When only the tip of the crow's nest was poking above the water's surface, the flames extinguished, Sorin started the long, wet walk back. She turned at the near-silent flap of wings above her. Jaculus gave a soft cry as he circled her once, twice, and landed on her shoulder, lending his warmth. The wind stung her eyes. She touched the god teeth in her pocket with frigid fingers, sensing the soft hum of its divinity. Three more weapons for three rips in the Veil. In that, her second assignment had been a success.

But Tellreg had not met an unremarkable death. While perhaps it might be explained away as an accident, it had drawn undue attention. Who else knew what cargo Tellreg had truly been ferrying?

At that, Magnes would not be pleased.

"But you'll never stop what's coming." The captain's voice taunted her.

Sorin kept the teeth clenched in her palm all the way to the Citadel, the tips digging into soft flesh.

25. ARCADY: THE QUESTION

The tinny song from the music box wound down.

"Again," I said. "I was still too stiff."

Everen stifled a sigh. We had climbed up to a flat rooftop large enough that we could practice sweeping court dances. The brick chimney wall shielded us from the worst of the wind. The top floor was abandoned, so no one would hear our footsteps save the mice. As my guard, Everen wouldn't be dancing, but I would as Dwell. We'd practiced at the Last Golden with Kelwyn watching us earlier, and once he'd recovered from laughing, he had sent us off with the firm instructions to practice until it looked like we'd fallen from the womb with dancing shoes on. What a picture.

So there we were, as afternoon shifted to sunset, dancing above the Vatran skyline.

I finished re-winding the music box and took up the beginning pose. Everen followed. The thin music twined through the air, and on my count, we started yet again. Our gloved hands hovered, palm to palm, so close I could feel the heat of Everen's skin. Focus. Focus.

Step close, turn, turn, step back, twirl apart, come together. Step forward, back, forward, back. One of us led for a refrain, then the other. We were close, only a few inches separating us. Those eyes were so damned green.

Everen kept eye contact, unblinking as we swirled again, the hems of our formal robes spinning about our legs. I could sense the bond humming in harmony with the music. We moved. We danced. Little by little, we found our own expressions in the movement. Our shoes whispered against the floor. My breath was loud in my ears. I should look away. If I were in a ballroom, staring so openly would be rude.

And yet I drank in the sight of him, despite myself.

He moved. I moved, drifting until we were nearly touching. I wanted to tear off my gloves, to have a sense of that sunlight against my skin and that brush of power that had lit up every nerve. But I still remembered his anger after I'd lit the candle with his magic. His panic after we'd touched when I'd stained his hair black.

The gestures became looser as we mirrored each other, the bond guiding us. The sunset was in full glory, staining the sky orange, pink, and red. We spun out, spun in, and with a last twirl, the music came to a close as I twisted into the final position. He was behind me, arms encircling but not touching, palms hovering over the backs of my crossed palms. He was so warm, like a banked ember in the shape of a man.

We paused in the silence. The bond was still open, the softest sound, gold as coins.

I took in a shuddering breath, my shoulder blades playing against his ribs. I'd done better, I'd thought, at cramming the attraction down. Focusing only on the next step of the job. Yet in that moment, it all came roaring back, so strongly there was no way he couldn't feel it. I wanted to hunch in embarrassment.

Everen dropped his arms.

We were silent as I rewound the music box, and it was like it wove a spell over us once again.

Maybe I only wanted to dance a little longer. Maybe I wanted a little closeness, a chance to pretend someone like me could have someone like him. Like we were people without barriers, mistrust, and fear. Like I was someone who deserved something like this.

I turned around, keeping my gaze lowered. My gloved hand snaked up and took his again for a waltz. My hand went to his waist, as his went to mine. There were two layers of fabric between us, but I could feel the hardness of his muscle. I could imagine how smooth his skin would be.

Every movement felt charged, about to spark. I finally raised my gaze and I startled. His eyes were dark, intense and unblinking. Bruised clouds and lightning, like the storm in the cave the night he arrived.

I thought it was all on my end. That I was being the mooncalf because I was lonely. He'd driven me to anger, to distraction, but underneath it all had been . . . this. I was a lowly thief. Of course I coveted a pretty prince.

His hand tightened at my waist. The warmth grew between us, and I burned.

I stepped away, but my traitorous hand tangled in his sleeve, dragging him forward. Then it was him, pushing me, step by step, until my spine pressed against the brick chimney.

Stop, a small corner of my brain thought. *Stop*. His eyes darted to my lips, hands leaving my waist to press against the brick, framing me. His chin was raised in something like a challenge. Part of me felt caged, but another part, the selfish part, had escaped right through the open door.

"Do not move," Everen said, his voice so low I could barely hear it. Or maybe he thought it at me.

He took off his gloves, slowly, deliberately, gaze unblinking. His hand reached out, his fingertips near my skin, but not touching. But I could feel the energy, the heat, the magic of it. He almost traced my eyebrows, my temples, my cheekbones. My hands bunched into fists with the effort of staying still.

His hands fell, and he drew closer, until it was his lips hovering above my cheekbone. I closed my eyes and felt the warmth move from my cheek to pause over my lips. If I tilted even a tiny bit, they would touch. We stayed like that, balanced.

"Do not move," he whispered again, and I held my breath as he shifted to my other cheek. He tracked lower, until he was just above the pulse point at my throat. My held breath hitched.

His lips barely grazed my neck. I heard him hiss with a jolt of pain, and the tiniest rush of power came through, warming me to the tips of my toes. Another brush against the angle of my jaw. He raised his head.

His expression was raw with the same need. That barrier we'd both put up had cracked open. He was asking me a question, without words, that I desperately wanted to answer.

"We shouldn't," I whispered, even as I wanted more, more. More than he would ever give.

"We should not," he agreed.

I pulled his gloved hand back to my waist. It rested against me, lax, and just as I thought he'd take it away, he squeezed, hard, and pressed his body into mine.

I moaned, and his hands tightened further, his breath harsh against my neck. My legs opened and he stepped between them. After weeks of not touching myself, of stolen glances at him as he studied, a too-constant awareness of his presence, I throbbed with need.

His hands slid lower, cupping my arse before one hand dipped to the back of my thigh. He lifted it, and we fit together. It was like dancing. A push. A pull. A hitch of breath. An exhale. The metal of my seal setting pressed against his chest.

Tentatively, I ran a fingertip down his spine, and everything in me tightened at the sound he made.

It wasn't enough.

We still hadn't touched. But it seemed we had found an interesting loophole.

"I want to learn the shape of you," he whispered, and his gloved hands trailed up my sides, down my chest. My head fell back and I raised my gloved hands to his scalp, pulling at his hair. I wanted him to kiss me, to drink his magic down.

This didn't have to be anything. But, damn it all, I would let myself enjoy it. I would take what he gave.

Everen's hips moved against mine in an aching rhythm. I'd never felt so awake, so aware, so alive. I felt him, hard against my thigh. His hand dipped between us, palming me beneath my clothes. I pressed against him, my eyes closed, urging myself closer, to let myself fall.

He pulled back, and I felt a tug at the stays of my shirt.

It was like falling into cold water. My eyes opened wide, my body stiffening.

Everen hadn't been raised to be afraid of the Struck, or to hate them. He knew the limits of my magic. But he'd seen the Starveling in the street, and it was an image he wouldn't easily chase out of his head.

The marks were ugly, and I hated everything they represented, and all the memories they brought up. The thought of baring myself to him was completely unthinkable. His attraction to me would wither, right in front of my eyes, and I wouldn't be able to take it.

I was breathing hard. The bond was still between us, open. And I cursed myself twice over. I'd promised to keep my hands to myself, and what had I gone and done? Broken it, like all my other promises.

Everen staggered back from me, expression dazed, jaw clenched tight.

"We can't," I said, raggedly, one hand clenching my shirt. Had he seen?

"No." There was a horrible note of finality in that one word. His face was angular in the orange-pink light of sunset, and his eyes flashed so green they almost glowed. I closed my eyes, digging the heels of my palms into my eye sockets, breathing hard, my body still aching.

When I took my hands away, the rooftop was empty. I hadn't even heard him leave. I ran to the edge, resting my hands on the waist-high wall. I didn't see him on the street below. Where had he gone?

The city spread out below me, and I had a clear view to the horizon. My eyes caught on the water, and I froze, the sight driving away any other thoughts or fears.

At first, I thought it was from the sunset, but the water was too red. Bright crimson, like a whale had been harpooned, life spiraling into the water. As the light of the sun continued to fade, the color grew brighter, until swirls of glowing pink traced the shape of the waves.

A red tide.

My skin prickled, cold setting in. It'd been years since we'd had one this big, and the Zama and Kalsh mages at the Citadel should have had warning and been able to divert it. I'd studied red tides. Both storms and warmer winter rains brought nutrients to the surface. What fed the crops ran into water and instead nourished the algae come spring, and so it bloomed in rivers, lakes, and oceans.

My fear choked me. I glanced at the other buildings below me. People were clustering at the windows, some of them clutching their amulets. At the Citadel, mages would be gathering, doing what they could to chase away the bloom, but it was too late. Fish would wash onto shore, pale and stinking. Shellfish were poisoned.

I stayed up there until full night, and I could feel the anxiety rising in the city, like everyone was holding a collective breath.

For the last time there had been a red tide this strong, the second Strike had followed.

26. SORIN: THE WOLF

Magnes was still angry with her.

After Sorin had left her report about Captain Tellreg—with minor omissions—in the puzzle box along with the teeth, He had ignored her for more than a week, even though he had not left the Citadel. Dread was a constant knot in her stomach. She had been slow with her chores, neglected her prayers, picked at her food. Gemiean, one of the other acolytes, had teased her by asking if she'd gone and had her heart bruised. She'd flicked an almond at him in annoyance and left the table. No one else had bothered her.

Finally, finally, the crimson flame flickered against her eyelids in the dead of night. Excitement pulsed through her as she picked up the note wrapped around the base of the candle holder.

Dress for riding.

She changed as quickly as she could, drawing on knee-high leather boots, black trousers, and a large cloak. Jaculus jumped onto her shoulder, curling around her neck as she wove through the familiar passageways, red candle-light leading the way. Magnes waited for her in the library.

"Come," he said.

An hour later, they were on horseback, following the Vatran river through the Royal Forest, searching for the rip in the Veil, Jaculus circling overhead.

Sorin should be honored. For months, she had been hoping Magnes would ask her to help mend one. She had begged Him, time and time again, but He had always demurred. Until now. She couldn't help but fear that this was somehow a punishment.

"You were reckless, child," He said, finally, glancing at Sorin out of the corner of His eye. His voice was quiet, soft. It was worse than if He had yelled. He always kept His anger coiled deep and tight.

"I am sorry," she gestured in Trade, head bowed. She offered no excuses, listening to the sound of hoofbeats on damp ground.

"Remember yourself," He commanded. "Our goal is so much more than the sum of any one of us. Our goal lies with the gods."

He paused long enough she wanted to squirm.

"This will be larger than more recent rifts," He relented, and Sorin nodded, her heart lifting. This was her chance to step back into His good graces.

Magnes paused the horses, closing his eyes. Sorin waited, hands loose on the reins of the horse. She had not ridden often, but Magnes—or one of His Eyes—had chosen a biddable gelding for her from the stables.

"This way," Magnes said, nudging his mount forward. "Not far."

Within a quarter of a candlemark, they arrived in a clearing. Magnes dismounted, and Sorin tended to the horses, tying them up a safe distance away. To her eyes, it seemed no different from any other part of the forest. A still pond, its surface unbroken. Conifers and beech trees, white as ghosts in the moonlight. But it was . . . different. The earth beneath her feet hummed. Though her green magic tended more toward animals than plants, Sorin could feel every root, every tree, every leaf. They snagged at the edge of her awareness, bright and green and bursting with life. The horses were nervous, and Jaculus circled high overhead, unwilling to come close. There were no animals—not even bugs. They had all fled what was coming.

"It has already begun," Magnes said. "Wait." He reached into His robes and passed her a long knife in a holster, bringing out a matching one for Himself. Her hand closed on the hilt reflexively. She drew it halfway and realized, with a start, that the blade was made of bone. Dragon bone. Part of a rib, she guessed. Her breath caught with reverence. Carefully, she tested the edge. It was near as sharp as any metal blade.

Some part of Sorin almost wanted to hiss.

The wind picked up, whipping her cloak about her legs. Magic crackled in the air. Sorin had never seen a proper rip in the Veil. She was about to. She remembered the Eye, ranting in the infirmary, all senses fled. Gripping the handle of her new blade, she prayed she was strong enough to withstand it.

A dark line appeared in the fabric of the world, an unearthly shrieking unraveling from within. Sorin raised the blade, determined to keep her hands steady, as Magnes watched the rip, His seal already glowing purple beneath his robes. The rip in the world called to her. She wanted to move closer, to look within and see what lay on the other side of the world.

Magnes's hand shot out, dragging her back as swirls of smoke undulated through the infinitesimal cracks in the Veil. Hissing filled the air, along with a low clicking and something like a growl.

It was *hungry*.

Magnes stalked closer, eyes intent and unblinking. The wisps of smoke coalesced into . . . something. Like a wolf, with legs too long, sharp teeth in a maw of a mouth. Its eyes glowed white-blue, like two spots of lightning. Sorin's bone knife felt too small, too useless, to ever protect her against *this*.

Magnes's mouth moved, His power crackling along His palms. The monster considered Him, the clicking growing louder. Below the creature's insubstantial paws, darkness radiated, like a shadow staining the ground.

Its head whipped to the right, and those lightning eyes met hers. Sorin shivered, ice shards of fear growing in her spine and throat. The monster darted around Magnes and made straight for her, faster than she had ever seen anything move.

It knocked her down, far too solid for smoke, and she crashed hard into the undergrowth. She caught the scent of something sulphuric and rotten, and it was on her in a flash of teeth and claws.

It was not *alive*, her magic told her that much. But it was animated by something sinister.

The dragonbone blade between them held the monster at bay, barely, though her arms were pinned to her side, and she couldn't move enough to thrust it up.

She felt herself fracturing as the monster's bright eyes trapped her in place. It wanted her. Her memory, her dreams, her emotions. Her life.

She stared up at her own death.

—*Fight.*

The command as if given by someone else. It echoed through her, breathing life back into her limbs. She yelled her fury at it, as if those black teeth did not frighten her. As if those eyes weren't ready to devour her whole.

The monster roared back, echoing through the forest. The maw of its mouth was darker than blackest night. Somewhere, their horses were screaming.

Sorin felt a burst of power hit the beast, and it shrieked, its face turning, twisting, snarling.

Toward Magnes.

It jumped from her, claws digging into her flesh through her robes, drawing blood. She grunted, but scrabbled to her feet despite the pain.

Magnes stood His ground, breathing hard, palms upraised. The monster writhed, muzzle frantically gnawing something at its torso, and screeched once more. Through the smoke, Sorin saw a white point, surrounded by purple light. A dragon's tooth.

The monster's head whipped toward the Veil, as if it heard something, calling it back. Though part of her wanted to answer that same call, Sorin took up her blade, her arms shaking.

"Strike!" Magnes yelled at her over the din.

Sorin aimed straight and true. Her knife sliced through layers of smoke before it hit something solid, before it *gave*.

The smell of rot threatened to overwhelm her, but she struck again, ignoring the monster's shrieks, as the tooth at its center grew brighter.

Magnes gathered another burst of power and hit the demon in its chest. It rose into midair, twisting, still trying to dig the tooth out of itself. With a last push, Magnes heaved the creature back through the rent as the Veil rippled, the edges of reality curling, gathering it back into the storm raging on the other side. As the rip grew smaller, Sorin heard strange whispers, words overlaid in an echoing, unfamiliar language. She couldn't help but strain toward it, as if she could understand if she tried that bit harder.

Before she could make her way toward it once more, Magnes drew out another tooth. Sweat dampened His temples, and His features were twisted into a snarl as He threw the tooth at the Veil. It exploded in a burst of power so bright it knocked Sorin to her knees.

Gradually, the howling of the wind dampened.

Sorin bent over double and vomited, bitter and acrid, before forcing herself upright and sheathing her dragonbone knife. She staggered to the sole horse—Magnes's had slipped its rope in the maelstrom—and ran her palms along his flank until she convinced the gelding to quiet.

Half-blinded with pain, Sorin rummaged in her pack for the sweetspheres in the outer pocket. Magnes had used too much magic, and His hunger would be raging.

She approached Him almost cautiously, one arm cradled over her torso, the other hand holding out the food like an offering. He took them. Ate one. A second. Sorin had always known He was strong, but she had just witnessed something she doubted even the Chancellors were capable of. He was truly gods-touched.

As the adrenaline wore off, Sorin stifled a hiss as the pain grew worse.

He knelt in the mud next to her. "Show me," He demanded. "Now."

She pulled up her shirt. Dark marks of the creature's claw punctures were already turning black against the skin of her stomach. She felt sick at the sight of them.

Magnes reached into His pocket and took out a third dragon's tooth, putting a gloved hand just below her collarbone, pinning her into the mud.

He paused, looking down at her. "You see, now, what we face," He said, His face half-silvered by the light of the moon.

Sorin writhed, clamping down on screams.

Magnes leaned forward. "Do you see why we can afford no mistakes, no distractions? There is true danger here, child."

Sorin grunted, her vision blurring with tears. The pain was pulsing, pulsing, driving out all other thought. She wanted to crawl out of her skin.

"Do you see?" He asked, again. "There is no room for weakness. Not for any of us." His eyes burned. "Say it."

"I see," she gasped aloud, barely a whisper. "I see."

"What are you to me?" He asked.

She cried out as a spike of pain stabbed her.

"Quickly, now. You do not have much time." Magnes's face was as hard, pale, and unyielding as the bone-bladed weapon.

"I am the knife." Every word was another agony. Her throat burned.

"Yes, my child," He hissed. "*You are mine.*"

He placed the tooth on the first puncture. A flash of light and magic, and the pain lessened, barely. Another. And another. When he had finished, she chanced looking at her stomach. There were scars, already white as if they were years old, rather than mere moments. The pain was gone, but the memory of it still took her breath away. She felt like a broken string on a lute, still reverberating from the snap. His hands were empty, the dragon tooth gone.

Magnes placed His bare right palm gently on her cheek. He smiled at her, beatifically. "Now you understand."

Her eyes were still wet. Gone was Magnes's intensity. Gone was the harshness. As if it had never happened. As if all were truly forgiven.

She raised herself gingerly to her feet. Her robes were sodden and heavy with muck. Her head was still spinning, and she crossed her arms and hunched over her stomach, sick with guilt and other emotions she couldn't hope to name.

She forced herself to straighten. "What was that . . . wraith?" she signed, fingertips shaking.

Magnes shook His head. "Something new. Something dangerous." He wiped at His face, and His hand shook as badly as hers. She had never, not once, seen a hint of fear in Magnes. "The Chaos that walks in our world," He whispered. "Just like the creature that escaped that we must find."

The dragon.

Magnes staggered to the remaining horse, leaning against it. His face was gray with weariness. "The relics are our defense."

And He had just wasted one on her. For her error, her weakness.

"There will be an auction in a few nights' time," He said. His lip curled. "A handful of foolish drakines plan to swap Their little bits of treasure between them, with no knowledge of their worth. We cannot risk any making their way south to Jask."

"A raid?" she signed.

"This requires a more delicate touch." He raised His head, meeting her gaze. "There is one the Order wants above all. A claw. The owner has kept it hidden for years—we did not even have a record that it had been gifted to that family—but Girazin was foolish enough to show it at a ball recently, discreetly trying to find potential buyers." His lips pulled back from His teeth. "They were not discreet enough."

A dragon's claw. Sorin's mouth was dry.

"Your next task is to obtain it," Magnes continued.

Sorin inclined her head.

His face turned contemplatively toward the forest. He whistled, and Sorin felt a tendril of power quest into the woods.

They waited in silence until the escaped horse trotted back to them, skin lathered in sweat. Magnes held out His hand, and the beast quieted. He raised Himself onto the saddle, and she followed on her own beast. She kept expecting pain when she moved, but there was nothing. As if it had never happened.

He gave a last look at the clearing. "The gods' work was done this night." He held his palm wide, up to the sky and the hidden stars. The rain fell harder as He sent His prayer to the firmament. Sorin raised her hand in an echo, letting her own silent prayer follow.

Magnes gave the horse her reins, and they headed back to the warmth and lights of the Citadel.

◇◇◇◇◇◇◇◇◇

Deep in the caverns of Vere Celene, Cassia raised her head from the scrying pool, growling low in her throat. On the silver surface, Cassia saw the elder priest's head turned back toward His charge, the horse slowing. Humans had never noticed her scrying, but then she had never been able to slip so closely into one's mind, to view the world through their eyes. She had a horrible suspicion the elder priest—this Magnes—knew she was there. With a stab of panic, she wrenched herself from the young priest's mind.

She fell to the cave floor with a thump. The rip had sealed so thoroughly she could sense nothing. Her mouth burned from scrysilver, her tongue acrid. She was sure the young priest—Sorin—had just slumped over the saddle, unconscious.

Miligrist entered the chamber, her crest raised in alarm.

—*Cassia,* the ancient dragon said. *What have you done?*

Cassia could not find the words.

—*You slipped into a human's mind,* Miligrist said, her gaze too knowing. *It will take time, to return fully to yourself.*

Cassia's lungs moved like a bellows. She had checked on the clutch of eggs in the nursery that almost certainly wouldn't hatch. Her translations held no interest, and she had been drawn instead to the pools. She was still new enough at it, and she wasn't meant to do it alone. But the scrysilver had glimmered, the molten surface still. Color shimmered on the surface, like oil mixed with water, inviting her to weave them into a vision. Before she'd known what she was doing, she had leaned over and kissed the surface, the magic settling into her skin and her eyes seeing beyond the Veil.

—*Turn preterit,* Miligrist instructed.

It took her much longer than normal. Finally, magic nearly spent, Cassia sprawled on the ground, small and humanoid. Soft and weak.

Miligrist knelt, and Cassia stared at her mentor in confusion.

—*Come, child,* Miligrist said. Cassia, bone weary, climbed onto the ancient dragon's back, gripping the spines at the base of her neck. A dragon rarely carried another this way. It was the utmost sign of tenderness.

Cassia had only the energy to hold on as Miligrist wove through the wider canals of the tunnels and brought her to her rooms. Gently, the old Seer tilted Cassia onto the furs in the corner and dimmed the mage lights.

—*I will send someone down with food and water,* she said. *You need to regain your strength.*

—*Please,* Cassia said. *We have to warn Everen the Veil is changing.*

—*Do you think I have not seen it, child?* Miligrist asked, her eyes milky with cataracts. *Do you think I do not feel the same fear as you? We cannot tell him too much. It's too delicate. Too dangerous.*

Cassia let herself unfurl back into a dragon, her preterit cry deepening to a draconic one. A wordless keen of fear.

With a last sympathetic look, Miligrist left her.

Everen had to open the rip in the Veil by the Feast of Flowers. If he didn't, he may never be able to at all.

27. EVEREN: THE HOUSE OF IKARI DWELL

"*Veir vaun pyu shu vaushast*," I swore in my own tongue. I bared my teeth in a snarl, stalking down an empty alley at the darkest part of the night. It roughly translated to "fate, with blood in her eye."

When I had panicked, I had risked flying to the chimneys above, and after you left, watched the ocean change color. I had read enough about the tide to understand the threat.

Later, I walked, my clothes drenched by the rain. Through streets and alleyways, and down the wynds of Vatra. I kept little track of where I went or what parts of town I strode through. Perhaps another group of would-be thieves would attack me. Perhaps I wanted them to.

I had almost turned preterit on that rooftop. I did not think you had caught it, but it had been a near thing. My back burned with two strips of pain; my wings had been hidden too long and ached to be free. Would you be awed or terrified if you saw the truth of me?

I paused, leaning against a stone wall and staring up at the sky, my false-black human hair slicked against my skull. The city was quiet this late, the taverns long shut, and even those rising early to the bakeries or the docks had not yet stirred. Vatra was holding its breath, waiting to discover how devastating the red tide would be.

The bond between us had been more open than ever before, but I had hesitated and the moment had clamped shut. I could barely sense the golden chime at all.

I could have had access to your magic and opened the Veil long before the Feast of Flowers. I could have ripped right through the fabric of the worlds. Dragons could have flown over this city by dawn. I would be the hero, the winner of a war. The Seer they had dreamed of, and the prince of a new world. Your world.

But not without your death.

I was risking everything, letting emotions cloud my judgment. There had been no need to let myself be drawn in. I could have made you trust me in other ways.

The truth was I had not been thinking of fate and prophecies. I had been thinking about the way you felt beneath my gloved hands, and the sounds you had made. All else had faded, even though you were human and should represent all I hated and more. And yet, if you had appeared out of the darkness before me that night, I might have simply pushed you up against a wall again.

I walked until the sun rose and the human world awoke. Eventually, I found my way back to the Loc & Key and picked the lock. You had taught me well. The shopfront was empty, the trapdoor locked up tight, but I knew you were there.

If I knocked at the door, would you let me in?

I suspected it would be like the last time I had fled. In the morning, you would emerge at the usual time. We would have breakfast and pretend nothing had happened between us.

The auction was only a couple of nights away. What mattered was the job. For me to see if that dragon claw was real, and whom it might have once belonged to.

There was still time before the Feast of Flowers.

Time to regain the strength of mind to do what I must.

◇◇◇◇◇◇◇◇◇◇

On the night of the auction, we crouched outside Dwell's Vatran residence in a shadowed alleyway. The house was tall and thin, nestled in an upscale neighborhood at the base of the Citadel hill, pale yellow stone crosshatched with dark timber.

An hour before dinner, Larkin knocked on the door, posing as a wine merchant. She was offering samples, she claimed, to share the "truly excellent vintage" from a vineyard in Redwing Valley.

The bottles were laced with a sedative. You had been watching the house for months. The Dwell residence servants were unusually close and always had wine with their evening meal, but it was cheap and often the same vintage. They would jump at the chance for something new.

It seemed Dwell was fond of a Jaskian tradition called *haldvam*, or "keep-

ing the warmth," where the household, even the servants, took a rest after
dinner while food digested.

Your face was intent as we waited. You were already wearing a scent that
Ikari Dwell favored, and I did not like it compared to your usual one. Since
the night on the rooftop, you would not meet my eyes.

When the lights dimmed, we made our move. The wards flickering
around the perimeter were strong, but your spellcraft was better.

You unpicked the lock of a servants' entrance near the stables. With another "notice-me-not" charm, you began to climb the stairs, and I followed
suit. We went to the third floor, tiptoeing down the hallway. Over half the
household should be asleep or resting. There were more wards outside Dwell's
room, and you disarmed them as I kept watch. We slipped inside. The merchant drakine slumbered on the bed, tucked up on their side, snoring softly.
To be safe, you bent over and blew a little sleep powder into their face to
keep them dreaming until morning.

You picked up the invitation on the vanity. Thick, cream paper, with
gold ink. It said "Admittance" and tonight's date. It was subtly spelled in a
way that not even Wren could have forged, you said, but since it wasn't tied
to Dwell's seal, we could use it without issue.

My head snaked to one side as I heard someone moving in the adjoining
room. My nostrils flared. It was the guard the servants called the Bulwark.
We had known the risk that the guard might not drink the night of a job.

—*Stay here*, I commanded. *Do what you need. Leave the guard to me.*

You nodded, already opening the door to Dwell's walnut wardrobe to
rifle through the fine fabrics.

I prowled back into the hallway, my nerves alight. This was a hunt, and
I was more than ready to take down my prey. I stretched my senses through
the house. All was quiet save for the shuffle of the guard in the room next
door. Downstairs, a human snored.

I knocked on the door.

"Yes?" I heard from within, impatient. I made no answer.

I heard a sigh as the guard scraped back a chair and took steady steps to
the door.

"Teff, if this is about the carriage again I—"

As soon as they cracked the door, I slammed it open as hard as I could. I
heard a cry as I swept through. The guard was stunned, hands over their

bloody nose. My lips quirked up and I drew my fist back, but the guard recovered quicker than I expected. They dodged and I took a fist to the stomach and wheezed. They opened their mouth to scream but I managed to cast a silencing charm and the sound choked off.

It was an ugly brawl. The guard focused on brute strength, and those large fists landed a few more swings. Even after weeks of pretending to be human, I was unused to fighting in this form. I pushed the guard back. They stumbled but regained their footing. I was lucky—they were not armed, but even if a preterit was stronger than most humans, this well-trained guard was not most humans. They were a bulwark indeed.

I twisted away from the worst of the blows, but with a start, I remembered every punch that landed would be hurting you, too. In the next room, you'd be doubled over with pain. White-hot rage burst through me, shattering my human shapeshift.

The guard caught sight of my preterit features and froze, their mouth going slack.

I pressed my advantage and tackled them to the floor. Rearing up, I let them get a full look at me. I pulled my lips back from my fangs. The guard's face twisted in fear, unable to speak a word.

This had not been a part of the plan. Even if I knocked them out, they would remember what they saw. My body still pinned them to the ground. My hands came up to their throat. I could end it. A quick wrench, and it would be finished.

Just one human life. I could prove to myself I had what it took.

My hands tightened, and the guard choked, face purpling. They still looked at me, unblinking, the pupils wide.

The door behind me opened, and I sensed your presence. My fingers slackened. The guard sucked in precious air. I was faced away from you, hunched over the human.

The guard was not unconscious, but they had stopped fighting, staring off into the distance blankly.

I shifted back into my human form. You crouched next to me, hauling the guard upright, or trying to. Their weight slipped back to the floor.

"What . . . what's wrong with them?" you asked. You had changed into Dwell's clothing, and it was too large on you.

I shook my head, as if I didn't know. A long, slow blink from the guard. A vagueness, like they were asleep with their eyes open.

Had I done that?

As I froze, uncertain, you had no such hesitation. You reached into your pocket.

"Hold your breath," you warned before blowing another fistful of sleep powder into the guard's face, stepping back before you could inhale any yourself.

"Put him on the bed."

You helped me, grunting with effort.

"There," you said. "It's done. Come on. Larkin will be here soon."

Without another look, you strode from the room and back to Dwell's.

"The guard's clothing won't fit you," you said. "I found some of Dwell's that are plain enough. Hurry."

I pulled the cheap black shirt over my head. Your eyes strayed to the red marks already beginning to bruise from the guard's fists.

"Are you badly hurt?" I asked.

"You know the answer," you whispered. "It's fine. We're fine." Your hand went to the place just below your ribs on your right-hand side, your gaze lingering on me a few moments more, and then you resolutely turned. Lochians and their modesty.

I pulled on the clothing quickly, and you helped me with the buckles and ties, working fast.

You glanced at the clock. "Larkin should be pulling out front any minute. What if she doesn't show?" you muttered. "I gave her too much information. She knows where it is, and she has the false claw and the jewels just now. What if she decides she doesn't need us?"

You were agitated, your movements jerky. I sensed your nerves through the bond.

I placed my palm on your back, between the shoulder blades, and you stilled. I leaned forward, whispering into your ear. "Look."

A carriage drew in front of the house, the driver pulling up the reins. The two horses shook their heads, their breath misting in the night. Dwell's coat of arms was painted on the side, courtesy of Wren, in a magicked pigment that would fade by sunrise. Larkin was dressed in Dwell livery, well hooded. Wren and Kelwyn were staying behind, though you had said you had no doubt that Kelwyn would be spending the evening wearing a track in the rug as he paced his rooms above the Last Golden.

We pulled on our own cloaks and hoods, so you would not need to shape-shift just yet, and we made our way through the sleeping home and slipped into the carriage.

Larkin clucked at the horses and snapped the reins, and we took off through the cobbled streets. It was just before the gates would close for curfew. You sat on the bench, stiffly, until we were outside of the city confines. Finally, you relaxed.

Larkin knocked on the top of the carriage and pulled over. She hopped down and leaned in through the window, her grin wide, and passed you the rosewood box. You flipped it open to reveal the false jewels glinting on velvet. Raising the false bottom, you gaped at the artificial dragon claw in all its glory. Only a little bigger than my own thumb.

"Are you ready, my doves?" Larkin asked as we settled in for the ride. "Let's go rob 'em filthy."

28. ARCADY: WIDOW GIRAZIN'S

The carriage finally turned down the long drive to Widow Girazin's manor. Everen and I had barely spoken aside from logistics, both of us sitting with our nerves. Dwell's fine clothes were itchy and too loose. I'd chosen red velvet so dark it was almost black, dotted with rubies and stitched with fine, silver thread. I'd pinned another ruby the size of a large beetle to my cravat. Like I could pass up an opportunity to steal a little extra.

I rubbed my hands together, preparing. I knew I could hold a shape for at least a candlemark, but the ball and the auction after would go on for at least two or three. I had a small sack of sweetspheres with me, and I'd eat liberally from the feast. All I'd have to do was sneak off somewhere quiet, rest for a few minutes, and build the shapeshift back up again. I'd practiced it twice, holding Dwell's form all evening with only short breaks. I'd been exhausted the next day, but it would be worth it for the promise of all those pretty coins.

The driveway was endless. It was so dark I could barely see the outlines of the trees against the sky. It smelled different this far from the city. Crisp and clear.

"You . . ." Everen began, paused, and switched to thoughts just in case Larkin was listening. —*You should take some of my magic.*

I stared at him.

—*It will make it easier for you to hold your form.* Everen's jaw worked.

"Are you sure?" I asked.

He gave a curt nod.

I swallowed but didn't argue. I couldn't dampen my thrum of excitement. I wasn't sure if it was for more power, or for the chance to touch him again.

He swung his long legs out of the way, and I settled next to him, taking off my gloves. I held my fingertips above his cheeks, as he'd done to me. I'd thought of that damned rooftop constantly. He sat very straight, very still. After a hesitation, he gave another sharp nod.

Carefully, I put my fingertips to his skin. I couldn't help myself. I traced the sharp line of his jaw like I had wanted to so many times, brushing my thumbs across his cheekbones. His skin was smooth, without even a hint of stubble.

He shivered. His breath hitched, the faint line between his eyebrows deepening with the pain.

"All right?" I asked, feeling his magic flow into me, the tips of my fingers glowing. I touched the pulse jumping at his throat. I wanted to press my lips against it, but resisted. Just.

Every part of my body sang. Any lingering aches or pains left me. I felt as though I could run for candlemarks without tiring. I was burning with magic. I tasted brimstone on my tongue.

It was bloody brilliant.

Everen's skin went gray, shadows hollowing beneath his eyes, his breathing shallow. With effort, I lifted my fingertips away, letting the last of his magic settle against my skin. I shifted into Dwell with no effort at all. It felt like my power used to be. Before him.

"Did—did I take too much?" I asked, my voice deeper. The warmth of his magic singed through my veins.

"I am fine," he said, head bowed as he adjusted his cuffs. I'd unwittingly added a delicacy to his beauty. I wanted to give the power back. And I didn't.

The carriage made a small turn, and there was Girazin's home, a beacon in the dark. It was nestled in Redwing Valley, not far from the coast, on the Ocul peninsula to the west of Vatra. The manor was impossibly large—like a whole tenement block in the city, but just for one family—and Widow Girazin was the last of their direct line. All their offspring had died in the Strike. Stringed music echoed through the warm night, melding with the sounds of singing night bugs.

It wasn't a masked ball, though some would still wear them. But I hadn't gone to all this trouble of stealing Dwell's face not to show it off.

I caught Everen looking at me as we walked up the path. I really was in full drakine splendor—the finest breeches, boots up to my knees, my broader shoulders filling out the shirt and doublet. My fingers were thicker, the silver bangles like manacles. The first few minutes after shifting the dimensions of my body was always uncomfortable. My tongue kept running along my shifted teeth, which were larger than my own. I wondered if Everen found it strange to see me looking so different. I touched the ruby at my throat self-consciously and smoothed my hair.

"All right," I said, passing him the rosewood box. "Look suitably menacing, my servant-guard. Apologies in advance for being an arsehole to you."

He grunted.

I strode up to the door with all the false bravado I could muster and passed the invitation to the person at the door with an ostentatious flourish. They peered at the paper, sensing the spells, and then at both of us.

"My guard, of course," I said with a little flutter of the hands. Everen did an excellent job of looking stone-faced and intimidating. Still, this was a pinch point. Would they make guards wait somewhere separate? I held my breath.

After a moment, the guard bowed and motioned us to enter. I exhaled. No one checked my seal, so there was no one to see it glowing blue beneath its cover. A benefit of a highly illegal gathering is that no one would be foolish enough to keep an official record.

A servant took our outer cloaks and gave us tokens to collect them later. I'd been here once before, but I'd entered through the servants' door. I tried not to gape. I'd slithered my way into some fine, fine homes in my day, but they were nothing compared to this. The grand hallway echoed. Everywhere I looked there was marble, or gilt paint, or huge framed oil paintings of members of the family. Everen was my darkened shadow behind me, and I hated how comforting I found his presence. This would have been harder without him.

If I'd thought the hallway was grand, the ballroom put it to shame. It was large enough to fit five Loc & Keys and two Last Goldens with room to spare. It was full of some of the most powerful merchants or guilders in Vatra. Jewels glittered, brocade shimmered, gold gleamed. A lot of it paid for from profiteering during the Strike.

I was looking forward to swindling them.

Musicians played stringed instruments in the corner. Security was conspicuous. People with the muscles and upright posture of guards rested easy on the balls of their feet, eyes dancing around the room and hands lingering at their belts.

"All right?" I whispered to Everen.

—*Yes.*

We made a slow circuit. We'd arrived as late as we could get away without being rude. A grand table in the corner groaned beneath a feast. I tried not to let my mouth water, the shapeshifting sharpening my hunger. Roasted peafowl glistened in orange glaze. I spied beef with peppercorn and cost-mary sauce. Grilled catfish. Steamed fern fiddleheads with salt and spices. Boiled potatoes in melted butter, honey, and chili oil. Mounds of cakes decorated with marchpane frosting twined into shapes of flowers or birds. Piles of sweet seed and honey spheres. Roasted pistachios and cob nuts. Custard-drenched apples. Anything and everything the guests could want.

I filled a gilded plate and ate the morsels with an impossibly tiny fork, letting the food ground me and feed my borrowed magic. I couldn't eat as much as I wanted—my stomach was still tender from the punches the guard had given Everen. My "faithful servant" stuck to wine. He still looked drained. A servant whisked my empty plate away.

The gathering was small—twenty people at most. Only those Girazin trusted to buy relics without selling them out to the Citadel. Magic was thick in the air.

Some had exaggerated their features until they looked like creatures from old myths, and Everen kept giving them strange looks. They pointed the tips of their ears or changed their hair to impossible colors. Others wore face paint, in a vague attempt to obscure their identity. One or two wore masks that were so fine they put the ones in Cinders to shame.

I murmured the names to Everen, who lingered close. At least four others had their own guards. There was Guilder Tiphani Grace, who was high up in the wheat guild—although whispers said they had a thriving smuggling business on the side. One or two I didn't recognize, but all were as rich or richer than drakines, and none of them minded looking the other way when it came to the law. Girazin had chosen well, it seemed.

One of the many benefits of impersonating Dwell was that they were so often away and had few close friends in Loc. Even so, my heart pattered in my chest. I could do all the observing in the world, but if someone were to reference a conversation that happened behind closed doors, I would have no way to know if I misspoke. I only had to make it through the next few candlemarks.

The few times I was spoken to, I adopted Dwell's signature gestures—the lazy way they lifted a finger to illuminate a point, and the crisp way they pronounced their Ts. The steady stream of conversation about horrifically boring things, with rarely a pause to ask the other person a question.

Plenty outright avoided me. In addition to Dwell simply being odious, many were suspicious of someone who spent so much time in the land of a former enemy, even if they would happily buy what was in the holds of Dwell's ships once they returned to harbor.

I played this up, peppering the odd Jaskian word into my conversations and watching them stiffen, make their excuses, and move on to someone else. Soon, me and my "guard" were left to our own devices, observing from the sides. Just as I wanted.

As the drinks flowed, so too did the displays of power.

Merchant Bielva, hands held above their head, raised two others on their chairs to circle around them, the partiers giggling and clutching their drinks to avoid spillage. Another merchant whose name I couldn't remember showed off their shapeshifting prowess, transforming not into other humans, but animals. I fought down a whistle. Few could change their physical form so drastically. They became a house cat, slinking out from beneath robes of delighted onlookers, and then grew to a larger cat native to Myria—a puma. They didn't even return to their human form between changes.

The shifter eventually padded from the ballroom, one of their friends taking their clothing so the drakine could reemerge with modesty intact.

The grand drakine merchant Sar Sydra created thunder and lightning inside, darkening the vaulted ceiling and chandeliers with bruise-purple clouds. Few weather mages were strong enough to shift the climate indoors. Sydra had rain fall only in one spot in the middle of the ballroom, over a grand brass basin, the lightning illuminating the water like falling beads. Everen and I exchanged a look, reminded of another storm, deep in the darkness of a cave. I thought of the dreams that slithered away from me when I woke up.

The displays left a bitter taste in my mouth. During the Strikes, how many of these merchants had been willing to help? All this magic, for spectacle and beauty and pride, but little else.

The music shifted into a waltz, and people paired off. Girazin swept over to me, and my heart rate sped up. Why Dwell? Because Girazin knew they were one of the wealthiest in attendance? Here came my true test.

I hadn't been able to observe Girazin much, only what I'd gleaned that one time I snuck in to see the claw. I hadn't thought they were overly familiar with Dwell, but they could have had dealings behind closed doors.

My mind whirred, eyes darting to guards I half-expected to drag me from the ballroom. The game up before we'd even begun.

"Dwell!" they said. "It's been an age, my dear."

I simpered. "Sar Girazin, the delight is mine." I bowed to the correct depth.

Girazin extended their gloved hand and I took it. Girazin had gimlet eyes and a wide mouth, and the top of their head came to Dwell's lips. Their robes were loose, the sleeves bursting with silk and lace. Jewels sparkled in their hair. They looked almost as regal as the paintings of older Monarchs.

The song began in earnest, and we slipped into the steps. Robes and skirts flared. At least if I messed up the steps, it could be excused as a Jaskian merchant out of practice with Lochian dances. Down there, Dwell would always have to lead, only swirling about with those wearing corsets and skirts.

"Thank you for coming to my little gathering," Girazin said, and I nodded, letting some of Dwell's usual imperiousness drain away. Girazin's eyes darted to Everen, sipping at his wine and watching the festivities from the side lines.

"I'm looking forward to the later festivities," I offered, not wanting Girazin to take too much notice of my "guard." I pitched my voice lower. "I've half a mind to buy a thing or two, of course."

Girazin's eyes glittered. "You'd have to win it, fair and square."

"Oh, I've no issue with that, never you mind. I have had a *very* good year."

Girazin exhaled and we swung around again. The chandelier lights caught on their necklace. "So I have heard." I half-expected their eyes to reflect coins as they calculated what Dwell's money could help them buy.

"Should have done this ages ago," Girazin continued. "Silly of me to hold onto them for so long, really, when they will go to homes where they will be most appreciated."

"I promise to cherish them," I said, even as I privately wondered why anyone would treasure old bones and one bit of mummified flesh.

The dance finished, and we entered the final pose. They put their hand on my arm and we left the floor as the next dance began. I made a grand show of bowing over the back of their hand, brushing Dwell's thin lips against the silk. "Thank you, Sar Girazin."

Girazin smiled, but I caught something like relief flicker across their features. For all the beauty and the glitter, it must gall them to sell off their riches to keep this grand estate running.

I caught Everen's eye and made toward him. It was time.

"Fetch me a rose lemonade," I ordered. "Don't be long. I'm parched."

Everen gave me a subtle nod, even if his eyes narrowed at the command. I tried not to watch him ring the outside of the ballroom and slip outside. He would check on Larkin and made sure she'd changed from livery to a guard uniform and taken her place at the agreed escape route.

And to make sure she wasn't deviating from the plan.

I drifted out to the gardens. The topiary had been carved into the shapes of mythical animals, and night-blooming flowers were thick on the air. The jasmine reminded me of both my paire and the Night of Locked Tombs. Mage lights strung up between the trees offered some illumination, but most came from the pools.

The red tide had made its way this far up the coast. The algae bloomed in stillwater ponds every year, but the problem was easily solved with the help of a green mage. Girazin had elected to leave it for the party, and so the pools of the fountains glowed pink with bioluminescence. The soft, flattering glow was picked up by tendrils of mist. What struck fear into any villager on the coast and poisoned their food was only a bit of decoration. I leaned my elbows on the stone banister, watching those who wandered through the grounds below.

Someone I didn't recognize strolled to my side.

"Sar Dwell," they said. "What a delight to see you returned from your travels."

Aura's sarding ballsack. I had no idea who they were. Tall, dressed in dark purple with a few flashes of orange, red, and black. Expensive boots. They were so fancy I found myself slipping into thinking of Them in the honorific despite myself. Their eyes were a warm golden-brown. Black hair that curled over Their shoulders and a thin golden circlet perched on Their brow. Pale skin, though not as pale as Everen's. A drakine, maybe, but someone too smart or too influential to be seen at parades or races. Or a merchant who was smart enough to let everyone else do the dirty work and few realized just how rich They were.

"I'm sorry, we've only met the once, and it was quite some time ago." They did not offer a name, instead taking a long drink of wine. They wore oxblood leather gloves.

"My memory is not what it used to be," I offered.

"I wanted to meet the person I expect to be my main competition this evening," They said with a smile. "Girazin let it slip you're in the market for what's on show."

They wore too much scent—like dried roses and burned paper. The lack of jewels announced Their wealth almost as much as anything else. I sensed I was right—this was probably the richest person in attendance.

"I have my eye on one," They carried on, Their tone cool.

"The scapula?" I asked, archly, even as my palms dampened.

They chuckled. "I like to collect the unusual and the rare."

"Well." I raised my wine glass. "May the best bidder win."

Their smile widened, and They raised Their glass to mine with a satisfying clink.

"Happy hunting," the stranger said, and disappeared into the thin crowd.

Everen returned. I set down my empty glass and took a sip from the new one without tasting it.

—*Who was that?* he asked.

"No idea," I murmured. "But I think 'Dwell' is going to have to pay out the nose for that claw."

There was some time before the auction, but I was loath to go back into the ballroom until I had to. We wound deeper into the gardens. Hardly anyone was out, preferring the light and the music in the manor above. I took it in, draining my glass. The lemonade was too sour and floral, and my mouth puckered.

It had been close to an hour. Once we'd ducked into a corner of a hedge maze, away from view, I sighed, letting Dwell's form fall away. Something in Everen's expression shifted when he saw my true face. As an excuse to look away, I reached into my pocket for the bag of sweetspheres. I nibbled one, and I should have eaten more, though my stomach still hurt.

"Can you imagine living somewhere like this?" I asked, dusting my palms of crumbs once I'd finished. Paused. "*Did* you live somewhere like this?"

A low laugh. "No. We live in a warren of caves, deep in the heart of Vere Celene. Nothing like this."

My eyes snagged on the tower where Girazin housed the relics. If I won the claw, I'd go up there and pass over the jewels for the chance to see it, and then I'd have to make the swap with the fake one burning a hole in the hidden pocket of my sleeve. Surreptitiously, I pressed it, feeling the comforting hardness of a glass spelled to be unbreakable.

"Fuck," I muttered. "I wish I could feel more confident this isn't about to somehow all go to shit."

"The plan is sound," Everen said.

"I feel like I've swallowed a bumblebee. I've been working toward this for so long, and now it's here, it doesn't feel real." I pressed my lips together. "Can't lose my nerve now."

Yet the panic was still lurking at the edges, my breathing growing shorter. The music drifted out into the gardens. What if that stranger won the claw? What if we walked out of this empty-handed? *Focus.*

He held out a hand. "I did all that practice," he said. "Seems a waste not to use it."

I laughed, a little nervous, but we were well-hidden by the hedges. "You're trying to distract me, aren't you?"

"Obviously." He wriggled his gloved fingertips. "Well?"

Almost hesitantly, I stepped closer.

I rested my hands on his shoulders, and we moved, slowly, softly, not even attempting all those fancy court steps.

"Stop worrying so loud," he whispered.

I closed my eyes and exhaled, trying to let out my anxiety. I thought of nothing. Not the stranger who wanted the claw for Themselves. Not Larkin, hopefully not halfway up the tower stealing the relic for herself. Not all the hundreds of ways things could still go wrong. I thought only of music and the feel of Everen's shoulders beneath my hands.

It wasn't like the last time we danced. That little jolt between us was still there, but it was diffuse. Grounding.

By the time the song finished, my breathing was steady. I felt ready to tackle anything. I shifted my features back into Dwell's.

"Thank you," I said.

"Think nothing of it," he replied, and there was that half-smile I liked so much.

A long, low call sounded through the windows. The ball was over.

The auction was about to begin.

29. SORIN: THE AUCTION

Sorin stood at attention as Girazin's guests strolled into the glitter of the auction room.

She forced her features smooth, her hands relaxed near her weapons. She recognized a few faces from the Citadel, despite the paint or masks. Drakines and merchants who were able to think of pieces of gods as nothing more than lots for sale.

Sorin had arrived at that manor that evening, another hired guard for Girazin's fete. She wore her true face, though her eyes were darkened with kohl, and a wig beneath her cap hid the harsh priest's cut.

As everyone settled, her eyes flicked to Magnes. It was strange to see Him in something other than priest or plain black robes. To see His hair long and His features shifted. He'd left His eyes the same, though He did not glance in her direction. Not once.

She should have been used to that by now.

Her palms were damp. Another task. Another test.

Each guest was given a fan with an animal painted on it to bid with. They fluttered like wings, sending faint breezes over the bidders' faces. People murmured to one another, excitement palpable.

Girazin arrived last, unhurried, the auctioneer on Their arm. The widow had changed, Their gown the gray-purple of a mourning dove. Sorin did not recognize the auctioneer but assumed They had been suitably paid for Their silence on this evening's event.

The auctioneer took Their place at the pulpit, the whispers in the audience rising to a crescendo.

"Sar Ulla Girazin's esteemed guests are welcomed tonight," They said. "We invite bids on several exclusive artifacts of divinity and antiquity. And, of course, it need not be overstated that you, my dear sars, were never here this evening. Tonight, we are all but shadows."

A low chuckle went through the crowd. They enjoyed the illicit game as much as the chance to own a piece of divinity. Sorin clenched her jaw, then forced it to relax. Why hadn't Magnes simply confiscated the relics? Why go through this farce at all?

The answer arrived immediately: because there was something else He wanted to learn. Or someone He was drawing out. Sorin's eyes narrowed, taking in the crowd.

"The first lot is the section of a rib bone of a dragon . . ." One of the other guards stepped forward, opening the case. They delicately held the long, curved bone in white-gloved hands. It was flat, thin but nearly as wide as Sorin's palm. Like the blade of her new knife. A few people murmured as the guard held it out for a better view, then took a slow walk around the stage. Necks craned. The auctioneer smiled at the interest.

"It has been carved with scenes depicting the indigo god, and so it may be of particular interest to those chosen by Zama, though we are sure it would prove a boon to any collector. I start the bidding at one wraithwright. Do I hear one wraithwright?"

Sorin blinked, stunned that they would begin with meteorite rather than gold or silver.

A drakine with a nimbus of blond hair raised Their crane-painted fan, golden bracelets clinking as They slid down Their gloved forearm. The auctioneer nodded and raised the bid to one wraithwright, ten gold. The rounds continued, the rib proving popular. Up went a fox fan, or a magpie, then a marrick cat. Eventually, it sold to a brawny merchant in the back row holding a bear fan for the sum of eight wraithwright, two gold. Sorin's lips tightened.

"Our next lot," the auctioneer continued, "is a collection of green scales." The guard stepped forward to display the glittering relics within the glass-topped box. An approving hum emanated from the crowd.

"We will start the bidding at one gold." Scales were relatively common, as far as relics went. Many sifted through the mud and dirt in the fields or along rivers in search of the telltale glimmer, knowing they could donate it to the church for extra prayers, if they were devout, or sell them on, if they were not.

After a few bids, the green scales sold for twenty gold to a plump drakine in the front row wearing dark crystal spectacles—the one with the marrick-cat fan.

Still more objects emerged. A round patella of a dragon, uncarved, sold for twelve wraithwright, ten gold to the jellyfish fan. A broken fang went for nearly the same price to the peregrine falcon. A triangular scapula, gilded, went for an eyewatering twenty wraithwright to the magpie. Sorin had trouble even imagining that much money.

The last lot was the claw. A few bidders crinkled their noses at the sight, for the mummified talon was not as beautiful as a gilded or carved bit of bone. The scales were dark, almost dull. But others sat up straighter, fans at the ready.

Magnes leaned forward, His brown-orange eyes trained on the claw.

The auctioneer gestured. "Here we have an unusual relic: a mummified dragon's claw. Experts are unable to determine its age with any certainty. Like the rib, it belonged to an avatar of the indigo god. We start the bidding at two wraithwright."

Magnes raised His gloved hand with measured precision. The auctioneer recognized this with a nod, nodding again as a merchant lifted a fan with a hare.

The bidding rose, but as the price topped three wraithwright, then five, bidders dropped like flies. Soon, only Magnes and the merchant Ikari Dwell remained.

Sorin's eyes darted between the two.

The rest of the audience watched the bidding war with interest. Twenty. Thirty. Fifty. The bids were footsteps, one gaining ground only to be followed by the other. When the price topped seventy-five, she stifled a gasp—how deeply could Magnes's hand dip into the Order's treasury?

At one hundred and ninety, a calculating look crossed Magnes's features. He closed his eyes, as if listening. His paddle lay in His lap.

"Going once . . . going twice . . ." the auctioneer paused, Their gavel raised. "Sold to the esteemed guest with the sea serpent for an incredible one hundred and ninety wraithwright." Dwell glowed with triumph, the ruby pendant at Their throat catching the light. They had bid on nothing else.

Magnes leaned back in His chair, the lion-painted fan falling from His hands, hitting the ground with a sound like the softest slap.

30. EVEREN: THE TOWER

My legs burned as we climbed the seemingly endless stairs to the top of the tower. I followed, wishing we had a moment to speak. You had won the auction. The relic was about to fall into our hands, but as your fear in the garden had shown, there was still danger.

We reached the top, two guards immediately flanking us. Another two stood to either side of one of the windows. My eyes went straight to the locked box resting on the sill. The guards bristled with weapons. I had been able to fight off four attackers on the street, but I did not fancy my chances against these. Were you as uneasy as I was? I could not feel you through the bond.

We were the last to offer our deposit and claim our prize. "Sar Girazin," you said with a low bow. "I am honored to be the new custodian of your esteemed relic."

Girazin smiled. "It was quite the back and forth, wasn't it, Sar Dwell? I am glad you emerged the victor."

"The lion made me pay dearly enough for it," you replied. "My coffers will be weeping for months."

"My apologies," They said, not sounding the least apologetic. They inclined their head at you. "The deposit, if you please," Girazin said.

You took out the rosewood box, popping it open to reveal the glittering jewels housed within.

"Lovely," Girazin sighed.

"Just valued at fifty wraithwright by the best jeweler in Vatra," you said, boastful as the real Dwell would be. "That should be more than enough to secure the sale. I can return on the morrow with the rest in coin."

Girazin leaned over to admire the sparkle. They passed it to another guard with speckles across their nose and cheeks. That guard's eyes kept flicking to me, sizing me up.

"And the claw?" you asked.

Girazin motioned to the guards with the locked box. Girazin held up a thick brass key. They made a grand show of opening the lid. I could not help but lean forward a little.

The claw looked exactly like the one Wren had made. The lines of your shoulders slackened in relief. Yet I would be able to tell the two apart immediately. The relic rippled with a magic I felt in my bones, even if none of the humans seemed to. Except you, maybe. You wrinkled your nose, as if you had smelled something foul, but it was gone in a blink.

I angled myself closer to the window and, unseen by the other guards, threw the smallest mage light from the ledge. It would barely twinkle, but if one was looking for it, they would see.

You took the box, reverently, observing it from every angle and waiting, waiting—

Boom.

Everyone's face turned as a loud firework exploded outside the window, raining sparks of red.

Girazin startled, hand to their heart. "Gods damn it, one of the servants must have sent that off early. The display isn't due until midnight."

"Gave me a fright!" you exclaimed, passing the box back, but the corners of your mouth tilted up in triumph.

Girazin clutched the box, as if they did not wish to sell the claw, not even knowing they no longer held a box with the true one. I felt a strange pulse of magic, like the deepest drum. I smelled the sharpness of petrichor.

"I promise, the relic will be well-protected," you lied smoothly. I wanted to warn you, but of what, I did not know. Dread rose within me, so thick I nearly choked.

Girazin opened their mouth to reply. Paused. Their face pinched with confusion, a line appearing between their brows.

"Sar Dwell?" Girazin asked, one hand raising to the hollow of their throat.

Your skin had darkened a shade, eyes shifting from brown to blue, Dwell's deep auburn hair rippling to near-black. You read the dismay on my face instantly.

Your illusion was fading. Either you had not eaten enough, or you taking that much magic from me earlier had left our bond uneven. Or, more likely— something in the magic of the relic itself had disrupted it. The guards reached for their weapons.

"The jewels are not diamonds," the guard said in alarm, their seal flaring silver. "Only crystal. Sar, this is an imposter." They drew their blade.

"Fuck," you swore, swiping a knife from your boot and grabbing something from your pocket and throwing it, hard, against the ceiling.

It exploded, filling the room with smoke. My preterit eyes could see through the worst of it, but most everyone else would be blind. The guards could not swing their knives around without risking injury, and in the confusion, I managed to throw two against the wall. They slid, stunned and breathless.

I used the bond to find you and dragged you to my side. You struggled until you realized who I was. Another guard tried to grab you, and the vial with the true claw fell, the glass rolling across the stone flagstones. One of the remaining guards snatched it up.

Girazin cowered against a stone wall, clutching the locked box. The magic of the true claw guided me like a lodestone. If our bond was golden, then this was a deep purple.

The guard holding it attacked, and though I darted away from the blade, I felt a blinding streak of pain in my side. Your own cry echoed in the smoking darkness.

I swiveled back to my assailant. The guard was of average height, their face bared in a snarl. The vial was in their right trouser pocket. They attacked, and I only barely blocked the blows. They were quick and lithe, and every time I tried to hit them, they spun away. My bruises from Dwell's guard and the wound on my ribs slowed me down, and smoke stung my eyes. I had given you too much of my power and left myself weak.

More pain bloomed on my—and your—thigh. My knuckles stung as you fought one of the other guards with your fists, not trusting a knife in the smoke.

We had given each other too much pain this night.

Shouting rose from further down the staircase. Once reinforcements arrived, we had no hope of escape. Had Larkin fled when she saw the smoke? I suspected we were on our own.

Perhaps fate told me what I had to do next. It seemed so obvious, so clear—I had no choice but to take it.

We were moments away from failure, and with it both our plan and my people's would crumble to dust. Who knew what these humans would do to me, if they realized what I was?

I shrugged my jacket to the floor, and for the second time that evening, I let myself unfurl into my preterit form. But this time I held nothing back.

The guard fighting me paused, mouth parting. The smoke was fading and thinning around us. My features had sharpened, my eyes glowed. A rip of fabric as my wings emerged.

It felt like stretching tall after being hunched over for hours. My wings were almost too large for the tower. The scent of my magic was on the air.

The guard's face slackened and they fell to their knees. Girazin, cowering behind a fallen guard, gaped up at me, still hugging the box to their chest.

"Chaos," the guard whispered, voice cracked and raw.

Girazin muttered prayers under their breath, voice quavering and high.

A sharp pain at the back of my head and a pressure against my neck made me gasp. I twisted. The last guard had you pressed up against the wall, a forearm crushed against your jugular. You were sputtering for breath, but you had seen me. Your eyes were wide and unbelieving.

With a cry, I grabbed the one hurting you and threw them toward the door. "Run if you value your life," I snarled, and they listened. I slammed the door shut behind them, barring it.

You had slid down the wall, head lolling to the side. While my skull was agony, I still had my wits about me. We shared wounds, but my preterit body could take them better. Or perhaps you, too, were overwhelmed by the sight of me.

I heard banging at the door. They would not be long.

I bent down and gathered you in my arms, grateful I still wore my gloves. Your head fell against my shoulder.

"Must be dreaming," you mumbled.

"Believe that, if it is easier." I climbed onto the window ledge. A scuffle behind me. I turned back to the remaining guard. They rose to their feet, shaking their head as if fighting off a spell as they found their knife and met my eyes. They crouched, muscles coiling.

I jumped.

Wind whistled along my body, but it did not drown out the *thick* of the blade being thrown. It grazed the top bone of my wing and glanced off into the night. I cried out with the pain, but instinct kicked in, despite the extra weight. I hugged you tighter to me as I gained enough momentum to spread my wings wide.

The winds caught me, and I used a last burst of magic to draw us up and swoop out into the sky.

PART 4: CONVICTION

On the Feast of Flowers
Broken promises will fall from lips
like petals.

Rivers of fire, wraiths of smoke,
storm, lightning, and rain.
For if Vere Celene will crumble,
only the Lumet will reign.

But the bond that binds can
push back the line.
So unwind the weave.
Rip the threads and all will cleave.

Do not fear: deep sutures make
the strongest scars.

—Seer Miligrist, Vere Celene Year 691, Second Month

31. ARCADY: BLOOD, FEATHER, BONE

My head hurt. My stomach swooped. Wind whipped across my face.

I clutched something. It was warm, and I turned my face to it. A band of heat behind my shoulder blades and another at the back of my knees. A strange, uneven rocking, and a sound I couldn't place. I burrowed closer, my arms tightening, and I drifted toward unconsciousness. The edges of hunger twisted my stomach.

—*Stay awake.* A voice echoed in my skull. *You have to stay awake, or we are both gone.*

I snapped back into horrible awareness.

The world dipped. The dark tops of trees swayed below me, broken by ribbons of roads or rivers. The sea and coast gleamed in the distance. I had only seen the world like this in my dreams.

I started squirming, but the arms tightened around me.

—*Stop*, said the voice, too close and yet too distant. I froze. The ground was so far below, and my head spun with vertigo, my stomach lurching and tightening. I reached for my magic, wanting it as protection, but it was nearly spent, and I couldn't risk any more. Not when my limbs were already shaking.

It all hurt—my rib, my thigh, my lip—small aches blending into larger injuries, my nerves screaming with every jostle.

There had been smoke. Fighting. The claw. *I lost the claw.* All that work, and all that planning. I swallowed down a sob.

The movement changed into a shuddering glide. I forced my eyes back open, still too afraid to look down. The stars blurred overhead.

Yet over his shoulder I saw *wings*, and that was entirely too damned much. *Stop*, I kept thinking. *I want this all to stop.* That steady rhythmic flap against the wind, every movement punctuated by a pained grunt. This was hurting him. But I didn't feel it the same way.

Because I didn't have fucking *wings*.

We landed hard on a beach.

I tumbled free, rolling in the sand, every part of my body complaining. I crouched on my hands and knees, emptying my stomach, bile sour on my tongue. The hunger only dug its claws in deeper, and I groaned.

This was as drained as I'd been on the Night of Locked Tombs. I clutched my hands to my midsection, but that only made the pain of my injuries worse. My fingers reached out, grasping for something, anything. My mouth opened, my teeth snapping against each other, hard. Anything to make the agony stop.

I sensed movement and lunged for it. A thump as I was pushed unceremoniously into the sand, something heavy at my back. I snarled, writhing, desperate to break free, my cheek against the sand.

A press at my broken lip made me hiss. I smelled honey and my mouth opened, sweetness spreading across my tongue. I lifted my head. More was pressed to my lips. I ate. I ate. My mouth grew dry and it hurt to swallow, but I ate until there was nothing left.

It wasn't enough, but I was no longer on the edge. Had my eyes turned black? My breath rasped against the back of my throat.

Gradually, the weight on my back lifted and I turned over, keeping my eyes closed.

I felt a hand on my forearm through the sleeve of my robes, and I flinched.

"I am going to touch you," he said. "You . . . you need more magic."

Even through the maelstrom in my head, I felt a sharp craving for that bright, golden power. I nodded and his hand was beneath my chin, angling my face, his ungloved fingers rough against my skin. The tiniest trickle of magic came through, like a streak of sun through clouds.

He murmured my name, his voice edged with pain.

When the pressure of his hand lifted, I tried to follow it but the pain in my ribs forced me back down. The magic was singing, and I wanted to listen a little longer.

The hunger was bearable. I was myself again.

Eventually, I opened my eyes.

I couldn't take him in all at once, so I saw him in pieces. The texture of the skin on the back of his wrist and neck. The way the hair seemed . . . lighter, like long, thin feathers of copper and scarlet. His shirt was ripped, just like the first night we'd met. The tips of his ears were pointed. Everything about him sharper, more dangerous.

And those wings. They trailed behind him, limp. Like bat wings, but topped with feathers. The tips were buried in the sand.

Fear avalanched through me. The animal part of my brain bleated at me: *danger, danger. Hunter. Run.*

I staggered to my feet. How could he be so unlike the Everen I'd known? I couldn't even think of him as that name. He looked at me, a stranger again, those green eyes luminous in the darkness, pupils slit like a cat's. Like a dragon's. Whatever he saw on my face made him flinch.

I ran.

My injuries slowed me down. Every step on my left leg sent a stab of pain to my hip, but I dragged my sorry, broken body down the beach, until I was well and truly alone.

The sobs came as soon as I fell to the ground. I've always been an ugly crier, but that night I put myself to shame.

The image of him was branded in my mind. Already, I was trying to convince myself I'd imagined it. Maybe I'd been hit too hard on the head. I'd run from the man I'd grown to trust.

But he wasn't a man.

He was something else.

A god? A monster? A spirit spat out from the realm of the dead? But I'd seen him bleed. He was bleeding, even now, a hundred steps away.

I rocked forward on my knees, the tears coming harder. I had done it. Won the auction, swapped the vial. All we'd had to do was walk down the stairs and find Larkin with the carriage at the ready. We were meant to be making our way back to the Cote, screaming out the windows, reveling in our win.

What would Larkin be thinking? That I'd betrayed her, yet again.

I'd have had my life. He'd take his money. We'd have found a way to break the bond, and then he'd have left, taking this secret with him.

My sobs slowed to hiccups. I stared out at the ocean. The red tide had made its way this far north, too, and the tips of the waves glimmered crimson, the white sand stained pink. It smelled acrid and wrong. I felt wrung out, my body meek and my mind empty.

My thoughts kept churning, my emotions dark.

Had *he* created the bond? Had *all* of this been a lie? Had I been duped from the start? What if tonight, he'd somehow set me up to fail? I'd sipped his magic just before we went into the auction.

What *was* he?

Carefully, I opened my awareness to the bond, but it so was muted I could barely sense it. My own deep, bubbling anger built. I buried my hands in the sand and clenched them, wanting to throw fistfuls like a child.

Only one person could tell me the truth. One creature.

I twisted my head back in the direction I'd come. The fury made me brave. Or dense as a rock. One of the two.

I limped back along the beach.

He was hidden from view by a large white boulder. Part of me hoped I'd see him as I knew him. As Everen. A human, not something out of myth, legend, or religion.

He was still there. But the creature was slumped over on his side, breathing shallowly. The wings were spread out behind him, layered on top of each other. They were so unbearably large. Each wing had to be longer than I was tall. They shifted subtly with each breath. I held my own, afraid to make the smallest noise. They glowed softly, like they were lit from within. Except for a dark spot, blotting out the light. As soon as I saw it, my anger snuffed out like a candle.

Blood.

I took a tentative step toward him. His half-lidded eyes were brilliant green crescents. A low groan. Through the rips in his shirt, I saw the red streak of his rib injury, and his trousers were as stained as mine. The blood had slowed for both of us, but not stopped. His right side. My left. My eye went back to the stain of blood. A gleam of white bone.

And he had flown, despite it. Girazin's manor had been at least two leagues from the sea.

"Shit," I exhaled. His eyelids twitched as he focused on my face.

The glow on his wings dimmed, as if they were burning out. Some of the pieces writhed into place. His magic was low. From giving it to me.

He wasn't Starveling, though. He was something entirely, incomprehensibly, other.

I pressed my lips together and focused on his face. He watched me warily, holding his hands over his injured thigh. I ignored the echoing stripe of pain on mine.

Somehow, I found the courage to limp a little closer, bringing his face into clearer view. I made myself take him in properly. Still, he waited, lips barely parted. Beneath the strangeness, I finally saw familiar echoes. The cheekbones weren't cut glass, they were diamond. His lips were pale, but the same shape. Split down the middle from a punch one of us had received. I suspected it was me. My fingertips went to my mirrored scab.

I still couldn't think of him as Everen. Whoever this was, he was enhanced, magnified. So ethereal I don't know how I had ever mistaken him for one of us. He winced, unable to stop a grimace of pain that I felt, too. He flashed fangs like curving, snow-white thorns.

"What are you?" I whispered.

He groaned again. If he lost consciousness, I suspected I would follow.

"Shit," I muttered again. "Shitting shit."

I had to work my way up to getting nearer to him. Keeping him in the corner of my eye, I ripped strips off the bottom of my shirt, tying them tight over my left thigh and around my ribs as best I could. Would tending one wound help heal the other? My trousers were slit by the knife but didn't gape.

I glanced down at my white silk gloves, stained with dirt and smoke. They weren't close to sterile. But I couldn't touch him skin to skin either. And even if we weren't bonded, I don't think I'd be brave enough. He still emanated so much warmth I wondered if he'd burn.

I decided to lean into impossibility. Pretend I was still asleep, back at the Loc & Key. If I died, I'd wake up in the lock shop, reaching for my charcoal and ink to draw what I'd seen. My heart rate did not listen to me.

So I stepped up to the monster.

I ripped more fabric and hesitated, my hands hovering above his thigh. Brisk as any nurse, I moved his knee and tied the bandage. He hissed, and I cringed.

Dream. Dream.

I laid another strip of cloth against his rib, and he sucked in a breath. Bracing myself, I lifted his hand to the wound.

"Press," I said, throat tight with fear. His fingertips tensed around the fabric, fingernails black against the pebbled, hairless skin of his hands.

I turned my attention, finally, to the injury I should have started with. I ran a gloved fingertip down the longest feather at the leading edge of the wing. It twitched, and I startled.

My hands hovered over the "elbow" part of the wings. Covert feathers, they'd be called on a bird.

The membrane was like warm leather, flexible and strong. The long, thin bones stretched between them from the "wrist," like elongated finger bones. Darker lines of veins ran through—a leaf seen through sunlight.

Don't lose your nerve.

A feather was twisted, its pinion jutting out from the top of the wing. I moved it back into place, and the shoulder blades of his back shifted as he exhaled.

A knife had notched the edge of the wing, near the bend and the feathers over the vestigial thumb. On a bird, they were the alula feathers. The bastard wing, they called it sometimes, and I suppressed a frantic laugh. If I started, I wouldn't be able to stop. There were many names I'd like to call this creature just now. That was definitely one.

The wound looked ugly, and I knew as soon as I touched it, it'd be agony.

"There is fresh water," he rasped. "A spring leads to the ocean. Northwest."

"You can . . . smell fresh water?"

A groan was my only answer. I limped off and found a small trickle falling down the cliff and winding its way to sea. My thirst roared back, nearly as desperate as my hunger had been, and I tilted my head back and drank my fill. Crouching on one of the flat, white stones at the base, I washed my silk gloves and tore more bandages from my overshirt. So armed and thoroughly damp and shivering, I returned to the impossible.

Nothing for it. I bit my lip and pressed the wet cloth to the wound.

He gave a muffled scream. From this angle, I caught the bump of his cheekbone, the feathered eyelashes. The point of the ear.

I forced myself to mop up the worst of the blood. He hissed, and my heart rate ratcheted up. No small part of me wanted to run again. Climb the cliffs despite the risks in the dark.

"Please," he said, the word raw and broken.

Dream, I let myself pretend. *It's all a dream.*

I exhaled hard through my nose, my nostrils flaring. Without warning, I reached up to the injury, pushed the bone back inside, and drew the two halves together.

He roared. It was not a human sound. It was so deep it reverberated in my bones. It took everything I had not to drop my hands and fall over, babbling feebly.

Magic sparked along his wings, like from flint and iron.

The blood soaked through the silk of my gloves. My skin began to tingle. With difficulty, I lifted my fingers when I felt shocks of power traveling up my arm. Even after everything, that bit more stolen magic was a balm. The wound had partially healed. It was still ugly, but the bone was hidden, the skin pulled together. It'd probably scar.

His pale skin was gray, and the shadows beneath his eyes were even darker.

With effort, he twisted toward me.

Still unable to look at him directly for too long, I gazed out at sea. The sound of the waves was constant.

"What are you?" I finally asked again.

The silence lasted long enough that I worried he'd passed out, but I heard his hitch of breath.

"I have told you much," he began. "But not all."

"Oh no. You're going to speak very plainly," I said, my jaw tightening. "No cryptic nothings. Where are you from?"

"Vere Celene is from beyond the edges of your maps. But it is . . ." He trailed off with another grimace of pain.

Maps warned of monsters. Creatures drawn at the corners, danger rising up from the waves. Serpents, kraken, mer. What kind was he?

"Because it is another world," he finished. "And I think you know what I am."

"A dragon," I whispered. The word echoed between us. Time curled around itself like melted glass.

Some part of me had known as soon as I'd seen him. I tried to let my mind hold that word, turn it around. Make it feel real. *Dragon.*

"Are . . . are you a god?"

"Your people banished us. They stole our magic, and they forgot their crime. Twisted us into something to worship." He sounded exhausted. "We may not be gods, but they should fear us."

"I do," I whispered. "Right now, I do."

I thought of that skull in Lacewing Cathedral. The scapula at the auction that was larger than my trapdoor at the Loc & Key.

"All dragons can shift to this smaller form," he said, seemingly guessing my thoughts, "though many do not. Since I fell through the Veil, I've been trapped like this. I can—I cannot turn back into a full dragon."

With effort, he shifted, drawing himself up to his elbow. I fought the urge to scramble back.

"Were you ever on my side?" I asked, and I hated how petulant I sounded. Everen's eyes closed, pain flitting across his features again.

"Look in my left pocket, Arcady." His features were lined red from the glow of his feathers.

Once, my paire and I had come across a bear in the mountains while gathering firewood. He'd made us back up very slowly before he scared it off with a burst of magic. Just before he did, I remembered making eye contact with it and feeling like prey. I felt like that now.

He did not move.

I edged closer.

The glint of silver just peeking out of the top of his pocket. My throat closed as my heart lifted in hope. I took it out, slowly.

A glass vial. Capped with silver. When I'd first seen it at that long-ago ball at Girazin's, I hadn't felt anything from it. Now the claw inside coiled with a power that moved over my skin like oil.

"You stole it back," I breathed.

"You keep saying . . . I learned to pickpocket from the best," he said, with a weak smile. His head fell back, eyes closing again, breathing labored.

I held the relic reverently in my fingertips. It was a hideous thing, really. A few scales had fallen off. The glass wasn't even cracked.

"I—" My voice failed. Hope could be just as painful as grief, I'd found. But I was suddenly sodden with it, and tears pricked at my eyes again. I thought I'd lost everything, and here he was . . . the one to give it back.

I pressed the vial against my heart, holding it close. I squeezed my eyes shut. No more tears. Not tonight.

When I finally opened my eyes, I was met again with that eerie, unblinking stare.

"What do you *want* from me?" I said, hating how it sounded more like a wail.

His mouth opened, throat clicking. "I want your trust, Arcady. From the beginning, I have needed that." He sounded haunted.

"How can I, when you lied?" My throat was burning. Memories flashed. His laugh on the Bridge of Shells. The look on his face when he finally cracked a difficult lock. The words we exchanged through the wall at the Cote. The expression on his face when he pushed me against the wall after our dance on the roof.

"Because I didn't want you to look at me like this," he said.

I could sense his secrets, lurking beneath the words. I opened my mouth to ask another question, but—

"Truce," he whispered. Like the first night, when we'd held knives to each other's throats and he'd looked at me like he wanted nothing more than to rip my heart out from behind my ribs. "Tomorrow. Tomorrow, Arcady."

I hated how I still liked the sound of my name on his lips. I held myself carefully. He was still undeniably alien. But in the dim, pink light of the glowing red tide, I finally managed to accept that this creature was truly Everen.

I clenched my teeth, drawing Dwell's tattered finery closer about myself.

"You're cold," he said, finally noticing my shivering.

"I'm fine."

Everen gave me one of his looks. We both knew what needed to happen. The night was cool, and he was nothing but warmth.

"Truce," he said again, soft.

I rubbed my face, but my fingertips were like ice. It took a few tries, but eventually, I crawled across the sand. I faced him so I wasn't lying on my injured rib. Of course, we did not touch. Eventually, my shaking slowed. I still clutched the vial in my hands, unwilling to let it go.

I knew there were so many other questions to ask, but I was afraid of the answers. He wouldn't give me anything more, and this was all I could take, for now. My bruised body ached. My head still hurt, and my eyes burned. Everen fell asleep before me from sheer exhaustion. I stared at him, memorizing every new detail, until he did not seem quite so frightening.

I hated him for lying. I hated for him for being not human. I hated him for saving me so I couldn't quite hate him enough. Even if, I knew, it was only to save himself.

When I woke, sometime in the night, I was almost too warm. Still more than half-asleep, I squinted up at soft-glowing red and orange, like frozen flame, before falling back asleep under a dragon's wing.

32. EVEREN: ENTANGLED

I was choking.

The storm hovered above me. I tried to free myself from the silver disc. I knew I had to find you, but you were hidden in a thick fog. I kept calling out, and I would hear your answering response, but we were both trapped.

In the way of dreams, it shifted. Miligrist was there, and I felt no surprise. She was in her preterit form, which I hadn't seen for years. Her feathered hair was such a pale blue it was near-white, and she wore her lacebark Seer's robe. She did not look as old as a human would—her skin was taut across her face, but still lined from centuries of movement. Those milky eyes remained ancient.

Miligrist had raised me like I was her own hatchling. She might be distant, speak in constant riddles, and seem to know too much. But she had also loved me, fiercely, in a way I was not sure my mother was capable.

—I envy you, Everen, that you can walk beneath that Lumet sky. *A sigh.* It has been so long. *With every word she spoke, petals fell from her lips, whipped away by the wind.*

—Miligrist, *I said.*

—You keep fighting, *she said, sounding so sad.* It is valiant, but in vain. You might move starfire's path a small step, but it always comes back in the end. I learned, long ago, it is better not to fight, no matter what you see in those depths.

—I see nothing, *I said, bitter even in dreaming.* I never have.

She came forward, reaching out a hand. —There is so much heartache to come for you, featherheart. I am sorry for it, but you will understand.

—I am not what you want me to be, *I said.* I do not think I ever was.

—We shall see soon enough, won't we? *She smiled, patting me on the cheek.* Come now, it is time for the thread to unspool. To find out if the scales find their balance, or if everything upends.

Far off, I heard a dragon's roar. I startled, and when I looked back, Miligrist was gone. Dark smoke swirled around me, hissing and clicking. I caught the glimpse of sharp teeth, black as obsidian. The smoke undulated over the golden bonds that kept me chained, blocking out the light.

I struggled, fear rising up my throat. I called out for you again, but you were gone. A dragon's claw emerged from the fog, violet-black, the tip wickedly sharp. It aimed straight for my heart. Just before it reached me, all froze.

—No. We are not here yet. Wake up, Everen. Wake up.

◇◇◇◇◇◇◇◇◇

I awoke with the taste of sand in my mouth. It took a moment to remember where I was and what had happened. That you knew too much. The bond was nearly as weak as the first few days in Vatra, before I had found you.

Yet in the night, you had moved closer to the warmth, your forehead a scant inch from my bare skin. My wings protected us from the wind off the sea.

I heard the crashing of the waves, caught the bracken of the red tide. Sea birds and wyverns called out to each other. Morning had broken.

I cataloged my injuries. The thigh and rib cuts and assorted bruises were ultimately superficial. The wing was more severe, but it seemed to have set straight enough I would not have to re-break it.

Some of my magic had replenished itself in the night, but fatigue still dragged at my limbs.

I shifted, raising myself on my elbow to look down at you. I had never seen you asleep. You muttered something, head moving side to side. A line deepened between your eyes. I wondered what you dreamed. You still held the vial, the glass murky from your fingerprints.

I pulled my wing back and you made a protesting noise as the dawn light hit you. I had enough magic to let my preterit form fall away, save the wings.

You blinked, your gaze foggy with sleep and confusion. A slackening of relief as you saw my human features, and a tightening at the wings. A frantic double-check that you still had the relic safely in your hands.

"Not a dream, then," you said, resigned and wary.

"No," I said, though my own nightmare still plucked at the corners of my mind. "But I thought this might be less jarring."

You peered at me, pupils bouncing as you searched my human features for echoes of the dragon beneath. You had grown easier to read, these past few weeks, but now you were a closed book. Was that hatred, fear, mistrust? Or was it resignation, or cunning?

"Your hair is back to red," was all you said, tone flat. The dawn light gilded your face. The ocean waves in the distance were the color of diluted blood. A few dead jellyfish had washed ashore, and more would follow. The eerie beauty of the night had been replaced with the poisoned starkness of day.

I sat up, moving gingerly.

We walked to the waterfall, and I drank deeply, then stood under the water, letting the cold shock me awake. I shook the water off my wings, carefully, grimacing in pain. With effort, I tucked them back out of existence, and your eyes widened. We said nothing, dancing around the obvious. Yet you were marginally more relaxed. Even if you knew my human features were a falsehood, you preferred the lie.

You had spirited the claw away in one of your many hidden pockets.

I glanced down at my torso. My rib was still sore, but not broken. The scab had softened in the water, but held. The same with the leg. "How are your wounds?" I asked.

"Fine." Your hand covered the bandages on your thigh protectively.

Climbing the cliffs took well over a candlemark. We were both slow, breathing heavily. You stumbled, once, and I grabbed your clothed forearm to steady you. You flinched at my speed.

"How had I never noticed?" you asked, pulling away as soon as you caught your bearings. "It was all right there from the bloody beginning, wasn't it?"

I said nothing, for you were speaking more to yourself.

Fear and regret swirled between us, but at least I could sense it, at least a little, through the bond. You were frowning so furiously I imagined the angry scrawl of your thoughts floating above your head. Giving you the vial had been the right choice. It proved to you that I was still on your side.

Even if I was not. And I could never be.

Each step of silence made it all the harder to break. The morning was cold and clear. We trudged through the forest in the direction of the coastal high road to Vatra. My body ached, and I knew that you would be hungry soon, and so would I. It was still leagues back to the city.

"I should hunt," I said. "Will you make a fire?"

You hesitated but nodded.

I slipped off into the undergrowth. It took little time to catch a few hares. The few moments out there in the greenery helped me center myself, reminding me of right after I had arrived in the Lumet. In many ways, those few days had been simpler: just me, the trees, the soil, and the hunt.

I returned to the clearing. The small fire was smoky. You had foraged berries, along with greens I did not know the name of. Your lips were already stained purple.

I gutted and skinned the animals, and you turned them on a green sapling spit over the fire.

We sat on moss-strewn rocks as we ate. The sharp greens gave a little more flavor to the meat. The trees rose around us, choked with creeping vines. It smelled green and vibrant. Mushrooms bloomed on a fallen tree in flat, orange-yellow shelves, the gills a deeper red. We did not have those in Vere Celene. The dead tree was decaying, gradually breaking down to join the forest once again. Eventually, you fractured the silence.

"What is the bond? Why does it exist?" you asked before taking another bite, tearing the meat from the bone.

I turned the hare's leg bone between my fingers, giving myself time to think. "It is the ancient connection between dragon and rider." I pre-empted your next question. "We used to work in tandem, against whatever darkness we fought. Details are long lost to us."

You swallowed, wiping your mouth with the back of your hand. "Do you actually know how to break it?"

"No. Human children and hatchlings half-bonded until they were close enough to complete it. Even if it did, I have no idea how to break it." *Other than killing you*, I added in the privacy of my head.

You grimaced. "How is it different, then? Once it's finished?" You bit a berry with a little more viciousness than required. I tried not to remember you writhing on the sand, ruled only by hunger. It was easy to forget that humans had twisted our stolen magic.

"If it happened . . ." I began. "It would be stronger, less mercurial. Your magic would be reliable again, as would mine. I would be able to become my true form." I paused.

You ran a hand through your hair.

Above us, birds sang, morning making its way toward noon.

Why even tell you this much? Our time was winding down. The Feast of Flowers was all too soon. If fate decided this would pass, I would be your enemy once again.

Soon, this land would belong to dragons. This forest. The ocean. My mother on the throne, my sister to follow, with me at her side. If humans bent the knee, they might survive. But any who attempted to rise up would be slaughtered. Thousands, hundred of thousands would die.

And it would all start with you. The first among many.

We were two small beings caught in something so much larger than either of us. And it felt like giving up, to surrender to what fate had written for us.

The fire had nearly burned down. I extinguished the rest with a thought, and we set off once more.

By midmorning, we reached the main road. Eventually, a cart and horse came into view. We paid the forester for the ride with the ruby at your neck, and we sat in the back among fiddlehead ferns and morels, wrapped in scratchy blankets. Hopefully the jewel was worth enough to keep the forager's silence as well.

At the stone gates, we joined the crowds heading into the city.

"I'll go to the Last Golden." Your voice was flat.

I opened my mouth, but you shook your head, cutting me off. Of course. You wanted a break from me, from all I represented. You reached into your pocket and gave me the key to the shop. I stared at it. You had never let me have it before.

"To save you picking it like last time. Will you still be there when I'm back?" you asked.

"I will," I said. "You have my word."

Another searching look, a small nod, and you hunched your shoulders and disappeared into the crowd.

33. CASSIA: HOLD FAST

Cassia felt a tug behind her ribs. Everen was searching for her through the Veil. She shifted into preterit and threw on her robe, running to the archives, hoping to intercept it before Miligrist sensed it and fetched the Queen.

She reached the mirror just in time, throwing out a rope of her magic into the infinitesimal gaps.

There he was. She still hated the sight of his false human features. He seemed no longer her brother, but a stranger. His time in the human world was changing him. She could only hope that soon he would be among his kind again. That he would not lose his way.

—*The Feast of Flowers is but a few days away,* she said, a little breathless. *We have made our preparations. But the bond is still not complete.*

—*No,* he said. *It is not.*

Cassia clenched her hands together. —*Miligrist says you are close. That the little human knows the truth of you.*

—*Are you sure this is the only way?* he asked, almost pleading. *That you cannot amass enough power on your side of the Veil to break through?*

Cassia glanced away from the mirror, taking in the careful stacks of scrolls, the leather spines of ancient books. She looked back to him, her heart aching at his obvious distress. —*I know you care for the human, Everen. It was obvious to all. To Miligrist, who was sympathetic. To their mother, who was not. Sometimes I wish you could see what is so clearly in front of you. The longer you delay, the more it will hurt.*

He grew wary. —*I am not weak.*

—*Did I say you were?* She tried to keep her tone gentle. *I've looked through the Veil enough to know for myself that humans come in many forms. Mother does not want to see their softness, or their kindness. Because it makes it harder to do what she must.*

Her brother bowed his head, his feathered crest hiding his face. When he looked up, his eyes were shimmering. —*I do not know if I can do it, Cassia. His* thoughts were so pained, her own heart wanted to crack for him. *I thought I could. It is too heavy.*

—*The Reek will burst,* she said, ignoring Miligrist's advice. *We might have days. We might have moons. But we suspect we do not have years.*

His face crumpled.

—*Hold fast, Everen,* she said. *I know you have the strength. It has not happened, yet, but it was written, and so it shall be. Do not judge yourself too harshly for what you'll do.*

The last thing she saw was Everen hiding his face in his hands.

34. SORIN: BELIEFS

Sorin's footsteps were heavy, dragging along the stones as she made her way down to the dungeons.

She stared at the back of Magnes's head, wishing she had His power to read minds, if only for a moment. To find out how she could best please Him, how to convince Him that all the time he had spent training her was not wasted.

Sorin had never been down to the dungeons. They were in another part of the same cave system that housed the Locked Tombs. Just after the Schism, they had been filled to the brim with dissidents.

These days, criminals were instead kept at the newer, larger prison on the edges of the city. That was where some of the other guests from Girazin's auction had been held for a night. If They had not bought anything, They were let go and fined heavily for attending. If They had, Their relic was confiscated, and They were fined double. Those in guilds would likely find Themselves relieved of Their positions. Drakines would lose Their standing in court.

Magnes always found a way to make people pay.

The dungeon smelled of wet stone, green mold, and despair. Sorin's hood was pulled up to obscure her face. The guard posted outside Girazin's cell opened the bolt with an echoing *clunk*.

Girazin's head was bowed when Sorin entered the dungeons. They looked up belatedly, face streaked with dirt, hair greasy and matted. Drakine prisoners were still afforded certain luxuries. A desk, paper and parchment, books. No fireplace, so They were swaddled in blankets against the chill of the stone walls.

"Girazin," Magnes began, omitting Their title.

Girazin drew Themselves up and lifted Their chin. "I demand to be released at once."

Magnes cut an imposing figure. The anger still simmered under the surface, making His eyes look more orange than brown.

"Did you truly think you would get away with it, Girazin? Or have you become so comfortable, so arrogant, you thought the Order of the Dragons would not know or care you betrayed your gods and country?"

Girazin suppressed a wince, a sliver of fear shining through.

"Was it worth the risk, Girazin?" Magnes asked.

Girazin stifled a sob but kept Their head high. Sorin would give Them that. "I had no choice. The taxes were raised again this year. It was sell or lose my ancestral home."

"You could have given the relics to us and been welcomed into rooms in the Citadel. You could have kept your standing, and we would have found a way to ease your burden." His voice was so smooth but undercut with sharpness. "Your aim was profit, and nothing more."

It would send a message, to strip one of the oldest families of Their title. Sorin suspected the Order was preparing to confiscate or convince the drakines to offer up more relics to keep them safe within the confines of the Citadel. Magnes and His Eyes would need all they could find, and more, to hold back rips in the Veil.

"But you are a smaller piece in this game, Ulla," Magnes continued. "I am here for what else you know."

"I know nothing!" They said. "I have already told you who I invited. Surely that must count for some clemency?" Their voice was wheedling.

A flick of the gaze toward me. "Child, kindly hold Ulla's arms."

Girazin rose, the blanket falling, revealing the gray robes They had worn to the auction. They struggled, but Sorin made quick work of it. Girazin was older, and even Jari healers could not slow the frailty that came for everyone in the end. Sorin held Them hard enough They could not escape, but not hard enough to hurt.

Magnes took off His right glove and spread His bare hand on the top of Girazin's skull. Sorin watched, her heart rate quickening as she realized what He meant to do. Magnes delved into Their mind, and Sorin's viewpoint wrenched as she saw the memory of the night in the tower from Their point of view. As with Mirel's memory, it was scrambled, some parts clear, others blurred. Conversation was muffled or echoed strangely. The tower room came into view. The burst of the firework, the blur of smoke.

The image froze, like actors on a stage taking direction. Through the ghostly smoke, Sorin took a better look at the interloper. Dark hair. A wider mouth, straight brows, and blue eyes. She committed the details to memory.

"Do you recognize them?" Magnes asked.

"No," Girazin said. "Never seen them in my life."

Magnes's fingers tightened imperceptibly on Girazin's head, and the memory continued.

Sorin held her breath as she watched the strange echo of herself fighting the bodyguard who, too, was an imposter of a different sort.

They moved impossibly fast. Sorin watched herself punch the bodyguard. Girazin had covered Their eyes in places, hunching over the box that contained the false relic. She heard echoes of the drakine's sobbing in the dungeon.

Here was the moment that had haunted Sorin these past few nights, seen from Girazin's vantage point. The creature's hair brightening to flame, the face sharpening, and above all, those great, magnificent wings bursting into existence, lighting both the echo of the tower room and the dungeon cell.

Even the memory of it smarted Sorin's eyes.

Magnes looked so solid compared to the wisps of memory. At the sight of the creature, His molten eyes sharpened.

Girazin was gasping, Their own magic fueling the memory. Hunger took its hold, but Magnes made no move to stop the memory.

Sorin's hands tightened on Girazin's arms as the chaos god stared down at Sorin's ghost. Sorin wanted to beg Him to stop, that He had seen enough. Magnes now knew that Sorin had been dazed by the sight of it all. Fallen to her knees, face as slack as one of His Eyes when they were taken by cracks in the Veil. The god, the demon, picked up the dark-haired interloper and climbed onto the windowsill, and Sorin watched her ghost rise, reaching for her knife. Here, she had done what Magnes would have wished. She had thrown the blade. All was as it should have been.

But would He realize that, at the last moment, her own hand had betrayed her? That she had missed on purpose?

Magnes finally banished the vision.

Girazin was making horrible noises. Recognizing the risk, Sorin let go of Them and darted back, reaching for her new metal knife. It still did not feel as correct in her hands as the old one did, but that was lost somewhere on the grounds of Girazin's estate. Her bone blade was still hidden in the alcove behind the hidden wall of her room.

The drakine was slowly losing Themselves: the eyes darkened, the features hollowed. Their mouth opened, with a keening howl, before their teeth clicked shut.

Sorin crouched in front of Magnes, shielding him.

Magnes gave a wave of His hands and Girazin slammed against the stone wall, arms and legs pinned by magic. Girazin snarled, hissed, straining against the invisible bonds. Their eyes were entirely black, the veins on Their face darkening.

"Have you seen a Starveling properly take hold before, child?" Magnes asked, almost conversationally.

Mutely, Sorin shook her head. Horror unfurled within her. Girazin thrashed so hard Sorin feared that They would break Their own bones in the struggle.

"The dragon gods did not make humans into perfect beings," Magnes said. "Every creature is flawed. This is the worshippers' punishment. Their magic has turned against them. They sickened, and all pay the price. It is easy to forget. To succumb. As Ulla Girazin did."

Magnes had spared the siren. Sorin had helped Them home, even tucked Them beneath the covers. Girazin would have no such mercy.

Girazin snarled again. They twisted, and bit at Their own shoulder, drawing blood. Sorin wanted to be sick.

"You have a choice, child," Magnes said. "You can put them out of their misery."

Sorin's gaze whipped up to His. Magnes's expression was implacable.

"You see, again, the cost of hesitation."

Sorin's blood went cold. She felt an answering twinge in the injuries at her torso. *He knew.* He knew she'd missed when she could have struck true.

Girazin screamed, and there was a horrible crunching sound as Their bones broke.

"Which is the kinder option, child? A quick, clean kill, or letting nature take its course? You could do nothing and say your hands are clean. Would it be a lie?"

Another scream. Sorin forced herself to look. Girazin's limbs were bent in unnatural angles. Their right shoulder was a mess, like a fox chewing off its own paw to escape from a trap.

Sorin gave a sharp inhale, more of a sob, and threw her knife. It landed true, right in the chest. Girazin gave a sharp inhale, a last screech that wheezed out as Their lung collapsed. Magnes released the bonds, and the body crumpled like a doll.

Silence fell upon the dungeon cell.

"Yes," Magnes breathed. "Yes, my child."

All Sorin could do was stare down at the empty corpse of Girazin. Bloodstained, dark-marked. Gone to the gods, for Their soul to be weighed and judged.

"I know that creature you saw that night was convincing," Magnes said. "I, too, might have once thought it a dragon." A shake of the head. "But it is as false to say that as it would be to say the wraith we fought in the forest was an animal. And the longer that monster stays on this side of the Veil, instead of within the storm where it belongs, the more at risk we are. No amount of relics will save us."

She saw the exhaustion tugging at Him. The burden He bore. And, lurking deep below, she realized He was afraid. That scared her more than anything.

He held out His arms. She stared.

"You are with me, aren't you, Sorin?"

She couldn't remember the last time He'd said her name. She took a shaking breath and stepped into His arms. She felt them close around her, safe and soft and warm. She hadn't hugged Him since she was a child.

She clung to Him, trying to draw strength from His nearness, and He clung to her. As Head Priest, He was the closest thing to the gods among Their believers.

She only had to believe.

35. ARCADY: LAY DOWN YOUR WEAPONS

Kelwyn looked up at the sound of the bell tinkling over his door, mouth falling open when he saw it was my dirty, bedraggled arse.

The two customers in the shop glanced curiously at my expensive clothes, sand-dusted and ripped to shreds, as Kelwyn hurried them through their purchases.

"Costume party!" I said to them amiably, even as I swayed on my feet with exhaustion. "I'm going as the shipwrecked Sar Farlane Marvel. From that adventure novel, you know."

"*The Marvel of the Glass Isles!*" one exclaimed, clapping their hands. "I loved those books as a child."

I'd forgotten it was a series. I'd only stolen the one volume. I'd read it over and over in the Cote, until the binding broke. "Didn't we all?" I said with a grin. It was almost a relief, to pretend to be someone who went to parties for fun rather than nearly dying at one the night before.

As soon as the door shut behind them, my smile fell and Kelwyn pulled the curtains tight.

"What the spirits happened?" he hissed.

"We were made, and we had to escape. No way to contact you until now. Only just got back to the city."

Kelwyn shook his head. "Gods above, I guess your lucky god does look out for you." He gave me a considering look. "So. Are you fleeing the city for your life? Larkin won't let you get away with insulting her twice. I mean it. She *will* kill you. Creatively."

I took the vial out of my pocket and set it on the counter between us. "Might not."

Kelwyn's mouth fell open as he took in the claw. "You did it," he breathed. "You actually pulled it off."

"Nice to see you had such faith in my plan."

He picked the vial up, turning it over in his hands. "Then it looks like you have a choice to make," he said. "Are you telling Larkin, or aren't you?"

I stared at him. "You'd sell it without telling her?"

A shrug. "For the right price."

I won't pretend I didn't consider it. I could take that coin and leave Loc and all of this behind. I'd be rich beyond belief. With enough distance, maybe the bond between Everen and me would break, and I'd be free. But would I be able to live with myself?

I'd have money, but I'd still have all that guilt.

A long sigh. "Write her, gods help me."

"Soft as a pudding, you are," Kelwyn chided, but a corner of his mouth lifted.

"Sard off," I said. "And for the love of all the gods in the sky, please put on the fucking kettle."

He laughed and dashed off a hasty note to give to a wyvern. While the water boiled, I made use of his commode, changing out of Dwell's ruined clothes and wiping off the worst of the dirt, sand, and blood with a damp cloth. I applied some ointment to my wounds and wrapped them in fresh bandages. The gash at my ribs had closed neatly, but the one on my thigh was angry. I shrugged into a change of Kelwyn's clothes.

By the time I emerged, Kelwyn had made tea and a spread of food. I clutched the mug, letting it warm my hands. Lashings of cream and sugar. Tasted gorgeous. I drank half before falling upon the food. Bannocks and sharp cheese and a thick, dried plum jam. I had a third with butter and honey, and my stomach finally settled. My magic was still weak, and it'd take at least a day to go back to its more recent wavering half-strength.

It didn't take long for the two heads of the Marricks to arrive. The bell dinged far too merrily.

Larkin took me in. Her eyes were shadowed—she hadn't slept. Wren hovered behind her.

"Well," Larkin said finally, signing for Wren as usual. "Have to admit this is quite the godsdamned surprise." She was trying for nonchalance but failing. "I've spent the last twelve candlemarks wanting to gut you and wear your innards as a necklace."

Kelwyn held up the vial, wordless. Larkin strode to it in two steps.

"This is the real one?" she signed before passing it to Wren.

He nodded an immediate affirmation.

"Thought you'd be halfway to Jask on a ship with the tide," Larkin said, and all the anger had bled out from her voice. I even caught a hint of a tremor. "I really did."

"Well. Here I am." The words felt inadequate. Kelwyn was giving me a too-knowing look.

"Where's Everen?" she asked.

"He's safe."

Wren was admiring the vial, looking at it from all angles.

"You did a good job with the fake one," I signed at him when he looked up at me with overflowing eyes.

I felt a pang of guilt for my earlier impulse but shrugged it off. *It doesn't matter what you almost do*, my taie had always said. *It matters what you do.* And here I was, spending everything I had to prove what he hadn't done.

"What happened?" Larkin asked. "I saw the smoke and heard the guards swarming the place. I waited, but when you didn't show . . ."

"You ran," I finished. If she'd stayed, she would have seen something very unusual falling from that tower, and she wouldn't be able to pretend she hadn't. She was a good liar, but she wasn't that good.

"Don't pretend you wouldn't have done the exact same. When a job goes south—"

"You get out. I know."

"And how'd you manage to get out, then?" Her Trade was sharp and punctuated.

Wren and Kelwyn chewed on bannocks while I gave a heavily edited version of events. I pretended we'd fought our way through the guards but made it to the servants' staircase. I claimed Everen and I had had to escape through a different route in the woods, chased by a guard. By the time we shook them, we were lost in the dark and so spent the night before coming back the next day.

Kelwyn's eyes were too sharp. He'd seen the sand on my clothes. I met his gaze with a challenge, and he took a deliberate sip of his tea. He would keep my secret, for now. Until it suited him to spill it.

Larkin still appeared skeptical, but I'd done my best. She looked at the claw again, shaking her head. "You brilliant, infuriating bastard, Arcady." A slow smile was spreading over her face. "Do you know how many Struck hamlets I'll be able to set up now that I have *wraithwright* to play with?"

"So all is forgiven?" I asked, wary.

Larkin laughed, incredulous. "Dunno about that, pet, but your debt to the Marricks is well and truly cleared."

She looked at me, and it felt like she saw me for the first time since the night Lightfinger died. No animosity. No derision. No pretend lighthearted barbs that were actually thorns. And in that moment, I saw the Larkin I used to know. The one who had watched out for me, in her hard, scrappy way. She'd never been a parental figure; she'd been an employer. But she'd been there as I grew from a scrawny twelve-year-old to a slightly less scrawny twenty-year-old. She'd dragged me across that threshold from child to adult by the scruff of my neck. Larkin gave me a small nod, and I found it suddenly hard to speak.

"Kelwyn," Larkin called out. "More of your good stuff, if you please."

We raised our glasses of rum in a toast. "To new beginnings," Larkin said.

"To new beginnings," I echoed, and threw it back.

◇◇◇◇◇◇◇◇◇◇

I was jaunty with success and rum as I made my way back to the Loc & Key. Kelwyn was sending out feelers and setting up a meeting for a buyer. He'd laid the groundwork, so it shouldn't take more than a few days.

The closer I came to the lock shop, though, the more my footsteps slowed. What would be waiting for me in there? The man or the monster? Or would he even be there at all? I had briefly considered leaving him and everything behind. Had he done the same?

I peeked my head through the front door. He was sitting in a shadowed corner of the shop, elbows resting on his knees. He still wore the ripped clothes we'd stolen from Dwell. He glanced up at me, and I tried not to gasp.

He hadn't bothered trying to look human for my sake. The vertical pupils shone yellow as a cat's in the low, reflected light. The scab on his lip almost looked like a deliberate mark. He was all hard angles and coiled muscle.

My earlier excitement had fled, my nerves tingling.

"Why are you sitting in the dark?" I asked. I realized, with a lurch, that he could probably see perfectly in the dim light.

He blinked in a way that was decidedly reptilian.

"I was just . . . thinking," he said, after a silence. "Lost track of the time." He didn't elaborate. "Is all settled?"

"Yes. Kel's setting it all up. Nothing to do but wait. Come on," I said, moving to the trapdoor. "I'm sure you'd like to clean up."

He rose, too quick and too smooth. Again, I tried not to jump. He was still Everen. I knew that by now. But he was also something more.

I hadn't let him into the back room often, for it still left me feeling exposed. Though I'd washed my face, I rubbed the back of my neck and my fingers came away streaked with dirt. Grime clung to me, and I had the desperate urge to wash away the night before.

I ran the bath, and Everen heated it for me. I watched his fingers skim across the surface, steam soon following. I'd known since the beginning he didn't need a seal to do magic. I kept wanting to berate myself for not putting everything together, but how could I have ever arrived at *dragon*?

"You first," he said, with a little incline of his head, like a bow. "Should I leave?"

"No," I said impulsively. "Stay. Over there." I gestured to the chaise longue, and he settled while I adjusted the screen, making sure I was hidden. The mirror showed me as I was. As ever, I tasted something sour on my tongue at the sight of my marks.

I almost groaned when I slid into the hot water, all the aches and pains making themselves known. My cuts stung, and Everen hissed on the other side of the screen.

A few minutes later, I heard him turning the pages of one of my books. This felt strangely intimate, almost domestic. I had never let anyone be in the same room as me when I washed, screen or not. Through the bond, I knew he found it comforting too. Neither of us wanted to be alone.

I ducked my head under the water and lathered the soap, working the last of the sand from my hair. It felt like I was washing off my persistent fear, my anger. I was back to feeling dangerously close to optimistic.

Because any problem could be fixed with enough wraithwright. We could hire a master mage with some of that money and see if they could break the bond. Someone, somewhere, would know how. I had to believe that.

I didn't linger, much as I wanted to luxuriate in the water. I stood, dripping and warmed through. The wound on my thigh still hurt.

I pulled on my thickest, softest robe. Finally, I stepped out from behind the screen. He glanced up from an illustrated book of saints—one of my priciest ones, stolen one afternoon on a whim from a drakine who had been foolish enough to leave their carriage doors unlocked. His eyes traveled from my wet hair down to my bare feet.

"You'll have to cast the spell to clean the water," I said, acutely shy. "I can't risk it."

He nodded, rising and moving past me, so close his arm brushed my sleeve. He hadn't bothered with another shirt and I took in the sight of the muscles playing beneath the skin of his back. There were two faint lines on either side of his spine, like seams.

I laid back on the seat, tucking my legs under the robe and staring at the prints on the wall. I heard Everen take off his trousers and lower into the water. I gritted my teeth at the sting on my injuries. When I peeped back at the screen, I could just see his silhouette, and blushed when I realized that meant he had likely seen mine. The sound of his splashing was soothing.

"How are your . . . wings?" I managed to ask.

"Better. I tended to them. Earlier."

We lapsed back into silence. I glanced at the book of saints. It was open to Saint Ini, and Their cup of blood. Lips red-stained. Waves swelling in the background. It was an illustration style popular a hundred or so years ago. Bold lines and bright colors.

"There's something I think I've guessed," he said.

I stiffened. "Oh?"

"Who the Plaguebringer was to you, and how you knew that spell."

I sucked in a breath, staring up at the ceiling. Past time for this hand to be laid down on the table, I supposed.

"Barrow Eremia was my grandsire. He began developing the spell. My maire finished it. I spoke the words and rewrote his seal into my own. With the name of someone dead, so I could take their life." This time I wasn't as afraid to spill more secrets.

He exhaled, slowly, but I sensed little surprise. "The light and the dark," he said. "Fire and water. For one is chosen, the other cursed."

"What?" I asked, though something about the words were familiar.

"There's a strange sort of elegance to it, isn't there? I was fated to save my kind, and you're the scion of the person who nearly destroyed this one."

"He didn't do it," I burst out. "He wouldn't." I almost spat the words. "They made him take the fall."

A soft splash of water. "Remember when I told you that my kind equated being male with violence?" he asked.

It was always easier to speak to him when we weren't looking at each other. "Aye."

"What I did not say was that I am the first male dragon to hatch in three hundred years."

I made a choking noise.

"The one before me was also meant to be a great Seer," he continued. "Ammil. He saw vision after vision. Filled scrolls and tomes with them. Magic was returning to dragons faster than in the centuries before. We had hope, for the first time in so long, that he was going to save us all." He lapsed back into silence as he leaned forward to wash his feathered hair.

"And then . . . ?" I prompted when he came back to the surface.

"We think he read through the oldest archives and found ones written about his life by an earlier Seer. He ranted, saying that it was only another method of control. That there were too many paths, but that trying to un-pick them would make fate twist into itself. He thought dragons were better off not knowing." Another long pause. "He set fire to the library, with him-self inside, and we lost most of our history. If they had not put the fire out in time, he might have destroyed Vere Celene entirely." A long sigh. "Some-times, dragons or humans do what we do not expect. Even those we trust to do the right thing might do the opposite, and the rest pay the price. Dragons learned that well enough." He stared into the distance.

"My taie did not release the plague," I said through my teeth. "And I aim to prove it."

More silence. "With time, I have no doubt you would." He sounded so very tired.

I gave an indignant noise, finding his response condescending. I would find out the truth. Rummaging in my collection of spare clothes, I found a pair of trousers that might fit him, tossing them over the divider. He slipped them on and came out, cautious.

We stared each other down. Me, seething. Him, weary.

"Apologies," he said. "I did not mean to upset you."

"You didn't," I lied. I shifted on the chaise, wincing as the motion pulled at the wound on my thigh.

His brows drew down. "Is your wound still paining you? It is nearly healed on me."

That stopped us both.

"Shouldn't we heal at roughly the same speed?" I asked.

He shook his head. "I am not sure." He seemed disturbed. "Let me see."

"No," I snapped, pulling the robe down enough to cover my feet. I felt the wound, hot and stinging.

He paused, and then, slowly, he perched next to me. "Arcady."

I froze, staring hard at a tassel on a pillow.

"You helped me," he said. "Let me help you."

"It's not that," I said, my voice rough. "It's not only that." My throat ached. "You already know too much. You know more than anyone. I don't want you—or anyone—to know everything."

Those hands, with those long fingers, rested lightly on his knees. We stayed there, suspended, both breathing silently. The last of my anger leached away as quickly as it'd come. Gold pealed between and around us.

I was tired. Of always carrying my burdens alone. Always being convinced everyone was working against my best interests. Hadn't I just seen the benefit of trusting Larkin instead of being selfish? Hadn't Kelwyn helped me fit my seal setting? Maybe it was time to admit that sharing myself, even the parts I thought were ugly, dark, and broken, wasn't going to send everyone off running.

"All right," I whispered.

He nodded, once, and went for the medicines. My whole body was shaking. He pulled on a new pair of gloves.

"Just . . . be gentle." I hated the way my voice cracked.

Slowly, achingly slowly, he pushed up the hem of my robe. He hesitated when the beginnings of the marks appeared on my upper calf. He paused, taking them in.

He pushed the robe up to where the markings darkened at my knee. A little higher, and the knife slash appeared. It followed the curve of my thigh muscle. He leaned closer, focusing on the injury rather than the marks. My heartbeat hammered in my ears and I wanted to flee. The bond was open, but still muted. Was he horrified? I couldn't tell.

"I can give you a little magic," he said, his voice quiet, as if afraid he'd startle me. "It might help the healing."

I let out a shaking breath. "Up to you."

He took off one glove and hovered his fingers above my skin. I focused on the ceiling, blinking fast. I felt his fingertips, the spark of magic falling into my skin. I jerked, and his fingertips raised. When I glanced down, his head was bent, and I only saw the top of his head.

Everen put the glove back on and smeared the paste that smelled of mint and medicine onto the wound, which already hurt less. He raised my knee so he could wrap the bandages around my leg, and the robe fell further up my thigh. I held my breath, but I couldn't help but gasp when his gloved fingertip grazed the inside of my thigh. His other hand rested just above the knee to hold me in place. I was acutely aware of how exposed I was.

"When?" he asked when he was finished. His gloved hand stayed on my knee, and I was too aware of it, and how my body responded to nothing more than a few, simple touches.

I cleared my throat. "At the tail end of the last Strike, when I was twelve. We thought we'd missed it." I toyed with a pillow tassel. "I'd been playing with some children while my parents were at the market. One of them looked fevered, but they insisted it was just the cold. I sickened a few days later."

I stared into the distance, feeling his eyes on me. "I can still remember the smell of that sickroom. My paire banked the room with coals and burned herbs, hoping to sweat the fever out, but the smoke couldn't hide the scent of illness. I hallucinated so many things. I . . . dreamed of dragons that night, strangely enough. They seemed so real." A low laugh. "Little did I know."

Everen said nothing, but his eyes sharpened.

"When—when it was all over, and I was the only one left alive, I came back to Vatra." He sensed I had skipped a large part of the story, I was sure, but also knew not to push. I was giving him all I could. "I found Kelwyn, eventually, and he sent me to Larkin."

"Do they know?"

"The Marricks don't. Kelwyn knows about the marks, but he only found out the night I met you. He was the one to set my seal." My hands drifted up to my setting. Everen still had the barest trace of the triangle in his skin. I wanted to touch it. My fingers curled against my palms.

The chime grew louder.

Everen's gloved fingertip traced one of the markings on my thigh. My breath caught.

"They're hideous, I know," I said, and made to pull away. His hand tightened on my knee, and I stilled.

"They look like smoke caught beneath skin." His fingertip kept moving, following another line. He would stop if I asked him to, and yet again whatever fragile thing we had between us would snap.

This time, I didn't want to break the spell.

His fingertips inched a little higher. Paused. His pupils were so wide they almost looked human. Almost. I gave the tiniest nod.

He made a low noise in his throat and shifted, some of his weight settling on my legs. My injury no longer hurt. His gloved hand slid up my skin. The other went to the opening of my robe.

"Do you wish me to stop?" His voice was a breath against my skin.

He was making me admit it out loud, the bastard. "No," I said in an exhale. "Don't you dare."

He pushed down the robe, exposing my collarbones, my marked and scarred shoulders, my setting and its seal. He flipped open the cover and touched a fingertip to the seal itself, which made me shiver. Traced the triangular outside of the setting. I hovered my bare hands over his skin.

"Why does it hurt when I touch you?" I whispered.

"A limit of the half-bond. Dragons are physically much stronger. It gave the human some protection, I'd guess." He paused. "I always pulled away when I started to lose hold on my human form."

My fingertips danced over his skin, not touching. He shivered, as if I had. I felt his hand on my side through the robe like a brand. My entire body felt lit up, alive.

My lips hovered closer to his. "A kiss would cause you pain. Is it awful of me, that I still want to?"

"Maybe I want you to hurt me." His voice was a rumble.

We stayed like that, the bond crackling between us like lightning. My hands hovered on either side of his shoulders, my muscles straining. I'm sure my expression was as challenging as when I'd held that knife against his throat. This felt just as dangerous. Were we laying down our weapons, or were we picking up different ones?

"I shouldn't want you," he whispered.

"But you do." It felt bold to say it. He wanted a human. A thief. A little nothing, in the grand scheme of things.

"Fates help me, I do."

He was the one to grab my jaw and drag my lips to his.

The spark ignited. His tongue ran along the seam of my lips and I opened for him. He gasped as the pain took hold. The cuts in our lips broke, and I tasted iron and salt. I drew him closer.

His magic was a flame running through me, pooling in my chest, down my belly, lower still. I felt the wounds at my ribs and thigh heal, all at once. My bruises and hurts chased away by the sheer power between us. His hand on my jaw tightened. I gripped the nape of his neck, hard. We glowed together, gold between our lips. Threads of blue and red wove around us, tying us tight.

He paused long enough to tear off his gloves, and then finally, finally, his hands were on me. His magic continued to flow, but he made no move to pull away. He traced the circular scar on the meat of my shoulder, as if he could smooth away the memory of past pain. A fingertip down my sternum. A hand splayed across my uninjured rib, a brush of a thumb against a nipple. A squeeze of my waist. Lips still on mine, he pushed me down onto the chaise longue, crushing me into the green silk.

We wouldn't have long before the pain overwhelmed him, so I savored every moment. Soon, we'd come to our senses. Until then, I let myself take leave of them, wrapping my legs around him, arching up. How much would he give? And how much would I take? I wanted all of him.

The gold grew so bright I had to close my eyes, the back of my eyelids turning red. There was little finesse. Little gentleness. Hard squeezes. The rake of fingernails. It was a claiming. His mouth moved to my neck, and I almost wondered if he'd bite me, and if I wanted him to. His teeth scraped lightly over my collarbone before he glanced up at me.

He looked as desperate as I must. I hadn't fully realized until I couldn't touch him that I had spent so much of my life being afraid to touch *anyone*. My skin hungered for close contact. I hadn't known how starved I was.

Though his desire was obvious as mine, he forced himself to slow down

He leaned back, outlining the marks on my lower stomach. I ran my hands along his sides, marveling at him. He shouldn't be real. He shouldn't be here. And he was. With me.

He kissed me again, deep and searching. I slid my tongue into his mouth, and he took it with a groan before giving his back. It was warm, and wonderful, and I never wanted it to end.

The gold around us grew brighter, brighter still. The chime was so loud, ringing so clearly, it drove out all other thought.

Gradually, it faded, though the ringing lingered in our minds and souls. Everen pulled back.

We stared at each other, lips swollen, cheeks flushed. The blue and red threads were still just visible on my palms, dancing up my forearms like my markings had spread and changed shade. As we watched, they disappeared.

My own magic, which had been flighty and temperamental ever since I'd switched seals was . . . back. It had filled all those gaps. The glow where we touched faded. I didn't need him to tell me it no longer hurt.

Everen's eyes were wide.

My body was still clamoring. For him, or his magic? The entire front of my robe was open, leaving me bare. He was half lying on me, still wearing his trousers. The horror dawned on us, our emotions echoing each other's easier than ever before.

"What have we done?" Everen whispered.

We both knew.

The bond had completed.

36. EVEREN: HALF-REMEMBERED DREAMS

I had known what we risked, but I persisted in being the featherbrain—as I would for the rest of the night, and far longer.

Silence hung between us in an accusation.

You pulled your robe tight around yourself, your eyes wide. It was undeniable. My body vibrated with my returned magic.

All because I had stopped thinking and let myself be swept away.

Do not judge yourself too harshly for doing what fate has already decreed, Cassia had said.

My eyes fell on the book of illustrations of the saints. The cup of blood. Laid open like a sign. Perhaps it was. Fate pointing it out clearly enough I could no longer miss it.

Starvelings craved any energy, including blood, to help bring them back to themselves.

What had you said, when we were talking about founding myths? Superstitions often had a kernel of truth.

My hand went to the scab at my lip. While our other injuries had healed, that wound was still tender. My fingertips came away blushed red.

"Blood," I said, dazed. "There was mention of a ritual to cement the bond, but it was lost to time and flame. We thought it only symbolic." Had the trust been needed, or was it truly as easy as this, all along?

Your fingers echoed my movement, touching your own cut. I no longer only heard the chime in my mind—we embodied it. Magic moved beneath your skin, concentrating into a point at your seal. You glowed gold around the edges, but I suspected only I would see you that way. At your wide-eyed gaze, I suspect it was the same for you. A mutual illumination.

You reached down to your discarded boot and took out a knife, the silver flashing between us. You placed the blade to the back of your forearm and dragged the blade across your skin, your hiss echoing between us.

There was no answering injury on me.

"Now what?" you asked, and there was real fear beneath the question, even if it was tinged with wonder.

Before this, I could claim it was not up to me. The bond had not completed, so I could not take next steps.

Now?

My mother would be wondering why I hesitated. They must have sensed it happening in Vere Celene if they were watching the pools. Even now, I could imagine Miligrist raising her head, calling out for my mother.

I had run out of excuses. I had run out of time.

I shook my head. "I am sorry." I rose, stumbling back, my mind a swirl.

Something closed in your features. "You're running again."

"No. This is a retreat. I—I need to think." I was babbling. My hand was already on the doorknob. I could not take your eyes on me. The taste and scent of your skin. The memory of you beneath my hands.

—*A retreat is running!* you called after me. A pause as we both realized you had not spoken aloud. You raised your head in triumph, but you could not disguise the hurt. It thrummed through the bond like a plucked string. I pulled back from it as much as I could. This was almost humorous. I had spent weeks trying to gain your trust to complete the bond, and as soon as I had, I did not want it.

Your expression closed and you turned, curling up on the seat. Dismissing me.

I paced the storefront for hours. For you, beneath the current uncertainty, there was a sense of everything falling into place. For me, all was unraveling. How had everything changed so completely in so little time?

It took all I had to keep everything tucked in tight, or else you would know what I meant to do. What I had to do. A human versus all dragons. Dragonkind versus one human.

My eyes darted to the mirror behind the commode door, but I did not want my sister, my mother, or Miligrist's voice in my head.

"*Veirkuetaun*," I swore. Dark fate, it translated to. Always said as a curse word. I was fire, you were water. Frustration was all prophecies were good for. I could almost understand Ammil letting them burn. If fate was to happen anyway, what was the use of torturing ourselves with it? Why not simply let it fall?

I walked myself to exhaustion before I finally collapsed on the bed. By that time, it was deep into the night. I sensed when you drifted off to sleep. I wished I was brave enough to go down and lie next to you on the bed of blankets. Slip an arm around you and draw you close. There was a surge of protectiveness, of possessiveness. A knowledge that, for better or worse, you were meant to be mine.

No. No. I should not want that. I should never have wanted that. When it was only you and me, with nothing of the outside world, it seemed so easy. As soon as everything else came into play, it was anything but. Step by step, moment by moment, I had become far too tangled up in you.

◇◇◇◇◇◇◇◇◇◇

I awoke from another nightmare. The storm was there, as it was each time I closed my eyes, but now I knew what the silver discs were.

They were opposing sides of scales. A dark purple dragon perched on the fulcrum, orange eyes blazing. All hung in a delicate balance.

"*Kjetim-lei ak ar-dźakain*," the dragon had said, staring down at us.

I call the storm.

This time, too, I knew that you had dreamed the same thing.

I threw open the trapdoor, for there were no longer any wards between us.

You sat in the bed, a notebook in your lap, drawing quick, angry lines across the page. You were hunched, so intent you had not yet noticed me. Your hands moved fast, as if you were possessed.

"Arcady."

You looked up with a gasp, slamming the notebook shut.

Suspicion flared. "What are you doing?"

You hesitated, your hand resting on the cover. "I never remember my dreams unless I sketch them. It's silly, really."

"Let me see," I said, my voice low and dangerous.

You stiffened at whatever expression was on my face. You smiled: a deflection that did not reach your eyes. "No, they're rubbish."

I stalked closer and snatched it from your hands.

"Give it back, Everen." You reached for it, but I stepped back, dark certainty spreading through me.

I opened the notebook to the last page. The ink hadn't dried, so it had smeared. Even so, it was an obvious echo of my dream. The scales, with a figure on either disc. The dragon perched at the top. Swirls that denoted the storm in a jagged line across the sky: a rip in the Veil between worlds. You had left deliberate spots, the white of the paper showing through. Petals, like when I had dreamed of Miligrist.

You held out your hand. "Give it back, Everen."

I flipped to the previous page. Words overlaid on top of each other, difficult to read, but I gradually picked them apart. Phrases Cassia had said to me. Other fragments. One jumped out: *On the Feast of Flowers, broken promises will fall from lips like petals.* My hands clenched around the edges. How many dreams had we shared? Each one since the night I fell?

"Everen?" You rose. There was a smear of charcoal on your cheekbone.

"Stop," I snapped. You froze. I flipped the pages backward. The lines were often scribbles, only suggestive of a form. Others were thick swaths of ink that rippled the page. Certain elements of the foreground might be more detailed. There was a hand, sketched dark in charcoal, painted carefully with golden ink, like your markings, reaching up toward the top of the page.

There was the clearing in the forest. A sketch of the masts of the ships at the docks, with one ship half-sunk in the harbor. I stopped at the page that showed the Lady of Vere Celene, with the distinctive chip on one of her teeth, the angle of her stony jaw. The crevice down her neck toward the jagged rocks and the foam of crashing waves. There were daubs of ink suggesting flying dragons—red, purple, blue, green. The date at the bottom was over two years ago, long before the Night of Locked Tombs. I felt cold.

Your hand rested against your collarbone, your fear meeting my growing anger through the bond.

I kept turning pages. There was the hunt where I caught a stringy stag. A page that was black save for the gray of a scrying pool. A red dragon curled up, nose to tail. Me, or another red dragon from Vere Celene?

My eyes landed on one of your bookshelves. More bindings of a similar make. I dragged them out and they toppled onto the ground.

"Stop it!" you cried.

I rifled through them, careless of your privacy, opening at random. A dragon's eye, the background a maelstrom of a storm. A snake, curled around itself, biting its own tail. You had glued thin yellow thread to the page, the strings cut and dangling. Over five years ago. Hundreds of drawings. Hundreds of dreams.

My dreams. My visions.

"How long?" I asked, and you took a few steps back.

You said nothing.

The anger grew. For years, I had searched in scrysilver pools for the past, for the future, and found nothing. When you had nearly died of the Strike, you had said you had dreamed of dragons.

"Did you bring me here on purpose?" I asked. "Did you know exactly what that spell would do?"

You shook your head, mutely, but the proof seemed unshakable.

Sometimes I wish you could see what's right in front of you, my sister had said, the last time we spoke. Had she meant this?

I'd sensed your avarice for magic, your hunger for power. You were the one to say the spell. Your magic, the Plaguebringer's magic, had drawn me through. The prophecy had only told me where to fly and when. We had finished bonding. I could steal your magic, but you could also steal mine, if you knew how.

You were the one who planned everything—who always thought three steps ahead.

I threw the notebook across the room, and it hit the wall with a smack. You flinched, drawing back.

In that moment, all the sourness of my failure rose within me, so thick and bitter I choked on it. I did not know what to do with a decade of frustration, of guilt, of anger, and so, I made one of the largest mistakes of my life: I threw all of it straight at you.

37. ARCADY: THE BARROW HILL

Everen rushed toward me, magic rippling over his skin.

I shuffled away, my back pressing against the wall by my desk. I'd seen him turn into his dragonish form before, but this—this was different. Fear clawed its way up my throat.

His wings burst into existence, knocking over books and scattering a jar of paintbrushes. A pot of ink crashed to the floor, breaking and spilling over my scattered sketches.

His eyes brightened to green fire, and his skin darkened, turning red, erupting in scales. His fangs curled over his lips. The air smelled of brimstone. Something at the base of his throat glowed like an ember. He was still shaped like a man, just, but he'd grown. I raised my hands, as if that would stop him.

He crowded me into the corner. A wind whipped through the room, scattering torn pages, more books crashing to the ground.

The tips of his fingers had sharpened into talons, and scales armored the backs of his knuckles.

Like the relic.

He reached out a hand and grasped my chin.

His expression was murderous. The talons didn't break the skin, but I felt the sharpness of them.

A tug, somewhere behind my ribs, and I gasped. In a reversal, my magic trickled into *him*. Everen felt it, a shudder moving through his body. I tasted sea salt and cinder on my tongue.

At his touch, images and impressions flashed in my eyes. Things he didn't want me to see. A red dragon, reflected in a pool.

—*Make your little human love you. Do what you must. And then kill it.*

Understanding was wrenched into me, my mind struggling to sort it out. But an obvious pattern emerged: Everen had planned to kill me since the beginning.

My magic was still flowing into him. He now knew exactly why I'd craved his power, because he hungered for mine. His wings grew even brighter, though his eyes were blank, like he didn't even see me. He'd take my magic. More, and more. More than I could give. Enough to do what he wanted: to open a door for dragons to return to the world.

My knees sagged, his scaled hand the only thing holding me up. I inched my hand to the right, fingertips searching for anything that could help. The air in the room grew hotter, sweat breaking out along my skin, pooling at the small of my back. I smelled something burning, and bits of ash floated through the air.

I whimpered, despite myself. —*Stop*. One word, one plea.

Everen froze. His eyes snapped back to me, the vertical pupils thinning into slits.

Everen's claws left my jaw and I slid down the wall. My magic slammed back into me, all at once, as overwhelming as the stream of information. I bent over, clutching a hand to my chest, my throat making a strange wheezing as I heaved in frantic breaths, my vision darkening around the edges. My searching fingertips found something metal.

Once my sight cleared, I saw Everen stumble back. His fangs dulled, and he stared down in horror at his hands. The talons retreated, the skin paling back to white. The overbearing heat in the room lowered, until the sweat on my skin chilled. Ash still danced in the air, coating everything in gray, darkening the bright red of Everen's hair.

"I—" he began. "I—did not mean—"

I staggered to my feet, brandishing the small knife I used as a letter opener. A piddly little thing, dull and nearly useless, but it was something. His eyes were unblinking, mouth slack. His palms were up, as if he didn't have so many other ways to hurt me.

"Since the beginning." I was proud my voice didn't shake.

I stumbled toward him, my unsteady footsteps kicking up more ash from the ruins of my drawings. "You manufactured all of this to finish the bond, and then *kill* me." He had accused me of dragging him through on purpose, but what if it was the opposite? What if he'd just been waiting for me to use my taie's spell as an excuse? Or I'd sent out just enough magic for him to bring himself through? I wasn't anything special. I was an annoying obstacle. A hindrance until he got what he really wanted.

I pressed the dull knife against his throat. It was blunt, but if I pressed hard enough, I could hurt him. It was another echo of that first night, except this time, if either of us drew blood, the other would not bleed.

He'd dared accuse me of keeping things from him. It'd all been a confidence trick, and I'd been the witless mark.

"Do it, then," I said. "Kill me."

It was a bluff. Or if it wasn't, I at least wanted to know I went down fighting. That I stood up to him, right up to the end. I searched his face. The anger was gone and his anguish reverberated through this awful bond I wanted nothing to do with. What if it was only more manipulation? He could send through whatever he wanted, to make me believe him. Or even if it was true and he regretted it now, what did that matter? It didn't undo any of it.

His hands stayed still. I searched his face, and I found him lacking. Now, when all the chips were down, he'd gone and lost his mettle.

"Thought so." I raised my chin. "Get out."

He opened his mouth, but I didn't want to hear another word of a lie.

"Get. Out," I said, a press of the dull knife with each word for emphasis. With all the effort I could, I wrenched myself back from the bond, rejecting every mote of that golden light. "Fuck you and fuck your fate." A ripple of his pain came through the bond that I ignored as best I could. "I want nothing more to do with you."

My eyes narrowed. "Nothing."

His expression shuttered. For a moment, he was still, then he pulled away, physically and magically, leaving so quickly he nearly blurred in my sight.

I fell to the floor, ash clouds dancing around me.

I wouldn't let myself shed a tear over him. I wouldn't be that weak.

◇◇◇◇◇◇◇◇◇

I spent the night clearing up singed paper, my fingers stained with ink and soot. Years of drawings and dreams, lost.

My mind kept whirring like the pinwheel my maire had once bought me at the market, a lifetime ago. *Had* I unwittingly stolen Everen's dreams?

I picked up a fragment of paper that wasn't entirely burned. There was a green smear of a dragon's wing. Even after drawing them, my memories of those dreams were fuzzy. I had sometimes flipped through the pages and found stories and threads, but I'd only ever thought of it as a fleeting fancy. I'd *liked* dreaming of dragons. They'd been an escape.

Every memory I had of Everen was just as ash-stained. He'd played me like a fiddle, and I'd sung just what he'd wanted. Most of my magic was back, but what he'd stolen was still missing. I dragged myself to the wall of lock boxes and opened one, taking out sweetspheres. I chewed them grudgingly, and they tasted of ash.

He didn't kill me though, did he? a little corner of my mind whispered.

I locked away every emotion. I could still sense Everen, no matter how much I pulled away from the bond. It was different, now it was complete. It was like every time I turned my head, I expected to catch him out of the corner of my eye.

The arsehole was somewhere in the Royal Forest. What would he do now? I couldn't expect this was over. From the jumbled information I'd taken from him, something was meant to happen soon, but I didn't know exactly what, or how to stop it. So I did what I always did: focused on what steps I'd take to reach my goals. Getting that wraithwright, and staying alive.

At dawn, Kelwyn sent a wyvern with word that he had already set up a meet with a buyer for that night. Hadn't taken long. Part of me was tempted to hold out for another who might pay more, but there was no real need now that I'd keep Everen's cut for myself. I wasn't giving him a damned copper.

The day dripped by like a leaky tap. Every muscle was tight. I kept waiting for Everen to leave the woods and come back to finish what he'd started. When the scab at my lip pulled, I refused to think about our kisses, his hands on my body. It had meant nothing. It never had.

Still, I felt him, the golden threads tied around my mind, through my muscles, right down to my bones. I was afraid, but it was still power, right? There was always a way to play it. There had to be.

Eventually, I scrubbed the worst of the ash from my face and hands and changed into dark clothing. I slid knives into my boots, another at the small of my back. Still more on my forearms beneath my sleeves. I was properly bristling with blades, but I still felt weak and exposed.

On the way to Kelwyn's, I dropped off the last payment at the jewelry shop for my seal setting. The shopkeeper smiled at me and tried to make small talk but gave up at my stoic expression and monotone responses. A completely different person had taken out that loan compared to the person who settled the debt. I'd been so hopeful. So godsdamned naive.

The city was blooming for the Feast of Flowers. People hung garlands of real or silk flowers on the lintels. Bouquets were in the windows. Tomorrow, petals would dance through the wind along with the sound of the flutes and the hum of honeybees. Jari magicians would be the focal point of the floats, buds bursting into blossom. It was one of my favorite parades. I wondered if I'd be alive to see it.

Kelwyn was shining silverware, the smell of polish strong enough to make my nose smart.

His welcoming smile shifted to a frown as he peered at me. "Are you all right?"

"Never better," I lied with forced cheer. "I mean, I'm about to be filthy rich."

"Where's Everen?" he asked.

"Who's the buyer?" I made no attempt at subtlety, but Kelwyn let me wrench the conversation away.

An elegant shrug. "You know as well as I do it's all anonymous. But it's someone with deep pockets, and They seem very keen."

I picked up the vial with the claw, turning it over in my hands, the loose purple scales skittering from end to end. I wondered what the buyer would do with it. Lock it away in some dark cupboard? Use it for something else? I felt some power emanating from it, sharp and vaguely sinister. I put it down, the glass clinking against wood. It didn't matter who bought it. Only that they paid.

"Hideous thing, really. I'll be glad to see the back of it," Kelwyn said.

"Aye. Wraithwright sure is easier on the eyes." The longer we kept it, the more we put ourselves at risk. I wanted my coin, and my future, and to get on with my new life.

I was always so quick to usher myself into the next bit of trouble.

Larkin arrived in the late afternoon. Wren was back at the Cote. He was an artist, not a fighter, though I hoped it wouldn't come to that. Hand over claw. Receive coin. That was all it had to be. Everen was still in the forest, and he'd pulled back from me, too. Unease had hung over me all day, like I was waiting for a trap to snap shut.

"No Everen?" Larkin asked, with a tilt of the head.

"No, not tonight," I said, and didn't elaborate. My jaw tightened—a tell that Larkin picked up immediately.

"Hm," she said, the single sound layered with meaning.

We walked through the north gate of the Vatran walls before nightfall. We had chosen another burial mound for the meeting place, similar to the Cote but much closer to the city. It was the golden hour, and all was beautiful. Spring was on the air, the new trees budding with growth. I filled my lungs with it, hoping the scent would ground me.

The sun was kissing the horizon by the time we reached the barrow hill. The sky had turned a blend of gray, blue, and purple, the undersides of the clouds a pretty pink. All was silent—not even the birds called. As the sun went, the full moon rose, half-obscured by clouds, and it grew colder.

No one arrived. I felt too exposed. We were closer to Everen, but I skittered away from the bond as best I could, even though I was sure he knew exactly where I was. What was he doing? What was he planning?

Just when I'd thought the buyer had left us to twist in the wind, Kelwyn straightened. "Look, someone's coming." He couldn't hide his nerves. He was usually the one doing the deals through intermediaries. He was spindly and had never fought a day in his life, and it'd be up to me and Larkin to keep him safe. My stomach clenched, and it seemed a foolish idea to meet somewhere so remote and quiet. But back when we'd chosen it, I thought I'd have a dragon at my side.

We pulled up our hoods, clustering together and reaching for our respective weapons. Differences discarded, we waited to see who would buy this rotten claw we'd risked so much to steal.

I swallowed down a laugh when the figures came into view. This person, too, was wearing a mask, but I recognized them immediately, because I had worn their skin.

It was Ikari Dwell, flanked by two Jaskian bodyguards, judging by their flaxen hair and ice-blue eyes. Dwell held a small chest. Large enough for a nice, wee pile of wraithwright coins. It was a tidy enough twist.

"Good evening," Kelwyn said, with his best courtier's bow. "Thank you for agreeing to meet."

Dwell inclined their head. Some of the haughtiness was gone. I supposed a night in a prison cell might do that.

My intuition was buzzing uneasily. The claw burned a hole in my inner chest pocket, its magic cold.

"I'll admit to being astonished to see it on offer, and so soon," Dwell said. "Anyone who was at that auction had a rather severe warning that relics were off limits."

"And here you are, just the same," Kelwyn said, with the same blandness. "Seems the message didn't stick."

Dwell's expression was cool. "The Order confiscated all the relics at Girazin's. Why should I believe that you have the one They covet the most?"

"Because we're the ones that stole it," I said, drawing out the vial. Their eyes snagged on it immediately. I wondered if they sensed its . . . oddness. The taste like sour metal on the tongue. A feeling like when you look down and notice a wasp on your skin and wait for the sting.

Their expression hardened. "Which of you stole my face, then?"

None of us said a word. Dwell scoffed and focused on the claw again.

"Sar Girazin was killed for selling that," they said, voice hushed.

Something twisted in my stomach. I hadn't known Girazin was dead. The drakine had broken the law by holding the auction in the first place, but if we hadn't run the job, they might still be alive. I had known the risks. They weren't the first to be caught in the crossfire of my schemes, and they wouldn't be the last. It was still hard to shrug off the guilt.

"You want it," I said. "Because you know exactly who to sell it to."

It was obvious. Dwell was a merchant, through and through. The claw would go across the water to Jask. Why were our former enemies willing to part with a fortune for it?

Our greed, feeding Dwell's, feeding Jask's. It was greed all the way down. Some tiny part of me desperate for self-preservation knew I should call this all off; selling it might create more problems than it'd solve. But without the wraithwright, I had nothing.

Larkin, as if sensing me wavering, stepped forward and plucked the vial from my numb fingers. "The payment, if you please."

Dwell smirked and opened the small box.

"One hundred and eighty, as promised. A steep price, but . . ." There they all were. Wraithwright coins, stamped with the three prongs of the Council. Each piece of glittering dark blue-green metal representing fifty gold. Bits of stars. Enough for a university education and all the trappings of life at court for years, with leftover funds to help me once I was done. I might have stolen a new life when I took the seal from those bones, but this was how I'd really live it.

It was one thing to think of the wealth, and another thing to be confronted with it. I wanted to run my hands along the metal. To clutch the box tight and never let go. Was I responsible for what might be done with the claw as a result? Or could I explain it away?

I was a good thief, but I still did not like being reminded I was not always a good person. Still, I hesitated at this inconvenient, persistent prick of conscience.

Dwell snapped the box closed and stepped back.

"Do we have a deal?" Larkin asked, voice sickly sweet.

Dwell opened their mouth, but no sound emerged except for a dull thud.

Everything slowed down. I blinked, uncomprehendingly, as something emerged from their sternum. It took me too long to recognize it as a crossbolt. Blood stained the front of their shirt.

We froze. Dwell choked, mouth opening and closing uselessly. Their face went blank, skin paling as they lost more blood. They fell to their knees, and then facedown into the dirt with a muffled thump. I swallowed down a scream, my throat making a hoarse whine.

Larkin's mouth was slack, and Kelwyn ducked and sheltered his head with his hands, as if that would do anything against a crossbolt.

The Jaskian guards brandished their weapons at us. "*Færædai!*" one called in Jaskian. I knew that word well enough. Treachery. It was the last word they spoke. More bolts rained down, neatly taking down the two guards.

Distantly, I felt a deep strum of alarm through the bond, but I pushed it away. I didn't need him. I didn't want him. I'd solve my own problems.

Larkin grabbed my arm and started dragging me away. I held my paltry knife, waiting for my own crossbolt.

A figure emerged from the trees, clad in black, the cloak catching the wind. A mask covered their face and a hood hid their hair. Above them, a dark green wyvern circled and gave one sharp cry.

I glanced at Larkin. She still held the claw in its glass vial and gave me one half-panicked, half-apologetic look before racing off into the forest, leaving me to face whoever had just killed three people alone. Kelwyn had already darted off into the trees, but the hooded person seemed to have no interest in him.

Fucking deserters, I thought savagely, though Larkin got the brunt of my anger. I gripped the knife, hard.

The figure paused, taking me in. Even with my hood, I had the sense they recognized me.

"Where is your chaos god?" they signed in Trade.

"My dragon will come," I said. For I'd felt him—a bright spot of gold, growing closer. Part of me sang with it, despite everything. "You'd be wise to leave." Inside, I was panicking. How did they know about Everen? What deeper plot had we stumbled into?

"Remember this: chaos cannot be trusted." They spoke aloud, their voice hoarse.

A flare in the bond. He was here. I lifted my head, seeing the red-orange glow of his wings in the distance. When I twisted back, the hooded figure was gone. Farther off, I just caught the hunting cry of a green wyvern, the sound nearly drowned by the flapping of much larger wings. The figure was after Larkin and the vial.

She didn't stand a chance.

I stood there, shaking, surrounded by three corpses, waiting to find out if a dragon was here to save or kill me.

He landed, wings spread out behind him. He wore the trousers I had given him yesterday, and his chest was bare. The expression on his face froze me in place—he was more afraid than I had ever seen him. Terror emanated off him in waves, so strong any barriers in the bond were swept away by them, taking some of my anger with it.

"Everen?" I asked, hesitantly.

His eyes blazed green. "I cannot stop it. Even though I didn't do it, I didn't kill you, it's still coming." He leaned into the bond and the sheer amount of anguish nearly knocked me down. His voice broke. "Can you feel it?"

I did. A charge on the air, a sharp smell like lightning. Like a storm. I sucked in a breath, my face lifting to a particular point in the sky.

"Yes," he said.

He sent me a few flashes through the bond. A rip in the Veil between worlds. Dragons streaming through, destroying everything.

"They did not trust me to do it. It will be harder, but they must have planned another way. In case I failed." His voice was pained. "If I don't let them through, they could die. But if I do . . ."

Flashes of my—our—dreams. That dragon scale tipping, fire burning all to the ground.

I opened my mouth to reply, but a lurch caused me to fall to my knees. Everen hunched over as well. Even though we weren't touching, I felt some of my magic begin to trickle into him again. Was he doing this? No. I knew that much at least.

I cried out with the pain of it, and Everen's head fell back.

And he *changed*.

All thought fled from me, and every muscle locked into place.

Magic, his and mine, twined together. His pale skin turned scaled and red once more. He crouched, and his whole body grew, grew. The dirt beneath him shifted, and he dug his claws into it. His neck lengthened, until the head was the same size as the one in the Lacewing Cathedral, but it seemed even larger, with eyes in the sockets, with flesh and scales filling it out. A crest of feathers sprouted from the top of the head. Spines along his back. The sheer power in the muscles at the shoulders and legs. A long tail, feather-tipped, lashed. And those wings. They made his smaller ones seem like a child's toy in comparison. The glow alone was enough to turn the night bright as day.

The creature opened his mouth and roared up at the sky. The teeth were long and sharp, and flame emerged from the nostrils. There was a glowing ember at the hollow of the throat. The plume of fire rose to the sky, the heat of it dancing against my skin.

The head came down and I was met with the full force of those glowing eyes.

There was nothing of Everen. I saw only what was absolutely, undeniably a dragon. I understood, with an overwhelming certainty, why people might consider Them gods. How could you look at one and feel anything other than fear and awe? Like you were nothing more than a bug staring up at a snake.

I scrambled back, but there was nothing I could do. My magic was still leaving me, and I wouldn't have long before I lost myself. Impossibly large claws closed around my torso, holding me tight, pinning my arms to my side. I scrambled, beating my fists uselessly against scales as hard as armored plates.

"Let me go," I screamed up at him, my voice breaking.

—*We cannot run from it*, he replied, his mental voice echoing and sonorous. *And I am not going to let you die. Not for dragons. Not for me.*

And with that, he launched up into the sky, taking me with him.

38. CASSIA: A VEILED STORM

Cassia flew through the sky, tracing the path Everen had taken on the Night of Locked Tombs. She could feel it building. The storm in the Veil, the convergence of fate.

Her mother was just ahead of her, but Cassia saw nothing of her parent in those regal lines. She was Queen Naccara, through and through, waiting for the worlds to open for them.

Behind were the five strongest dragons of the pryde. The rip would only potentially let a small number through—for now. But the other dragons were ready and awaiting word, ancient armor strapped to their bodies like silver carapaces. The Lady of Vere Celene grew smaller with every wingbeat, and Cassia could just make out Miligrist, a pale blue dot in stark contrast to the scorched brown-gray of the island.

They had not been able to contact Everen, not properly, but the bond had completed. She had caught a few glimpses of him. His eyes had been dim, like a light behind them had extinguished. She had to believe that, when it came down to it, he would not falter. That he would save them.

Cassia spied a dark glimmer in the air before them, and she wished she could be among the first. She wanted to smell the fresh air, to see stars unspoiled by the endless smoke of the Reek.

Cassia wore no armor. Fate—and her mother—had decreed she must stay behind. They could not risk Queen and Heir in one fell swoop. Once the way was clear, Cassia would follow. Briefly, she would be the last dragon in Vere Celene. They would leave none behind.

—*Today, we take back what is ours,* Queen Naccara sent to her dragons. They roared in agreement, hovering above the waves. Red, green, blue, purple, gray, all wrapped in silver. Cassia was overcome by the sight of them. After so many years scrabbling for survival, now they had a chance for more. The chance to right a centuries-old wrong.

The rip in the Veil was growing. The dragons circled it, inching closer until they were caught by the current.

—*To our new world!* Queen Naccara cried, and the dragons dove. One by one, Cassia watched them blink out. Her mother gave her a last look before she went, inclining her head. Equal to equal.

Cassia let out a cry as she watched her mother disappear. The rip stayed open, and for a moment, she was so tempted to follow. Instead, she forced her wings to work hard and bring her back from the brink. She banked, making for home, ready to join Miligrist and watch the events unfold in scrysilver.

Her faith must remain unshakable, but, no matter how much they had planned, a small part of her feared that something might yet upset the Dragon Scales.

39. EVEREN: GOLDEN BONDS

I tried to block out your screams.

No matter how I plucked at the bond, I could not stop what was happening. I felt as though I had been hollowed out into a shell, our combined magic as bright as starfire. I was doing what I must and there was no way to fight back.

You twisted in my claws. I took care not to hurt you in the short flight back to the clearing in the Royal Forest, my foot tucked up tight against my body to shield you from harm.

Your magic was sweet and cool as water from a stream. I still wanted more, and it was all I could do to hold back the thirst. Scant weeks ago, this was what I had desired. I had been so desperate to prove I could be all the dragons wanted and more. But even finding the prophecy had been a trick.

Everyone used me for their own gain.

By the time the sun rose, it would be over. One way or another. If dragons took over the world, with no regard for its human boundaries and lines, it would never be the same. Whether they worshipped or fought us, they would bow in the end. There would be no cooperation, no bonds. This was my mother's dream: humans beneath us, and dragons to rule above them all.

Her dream gave me no pleasure.

I flew too close to the city. The sky was clear. I stretched my wings wide. Let them see. What would they think me? A portent, or a sign? I heard guards cry at the outer wall, raising the alarm. Perhaps they would amass enough bodies to follow me. Though even if they arrived in time, how would they stop dragons?

The rift was appearing above the same clearing I had made my home. Had I been drawn to it that first night because of that? I landed carefully. You had quieted, too exhausted to fight me.

We were tethered even tighter than before. I must have already taken at least a third of your magic. You stumbled.

—*Hold on,* I sent. *Hold fast.*

I shook my head, trying to keep my focus. The magic still trickled toward me, and it'd be easy enough to make it flow in my direction. To turn it into a stream, a torrent. I wanted it. I did not want it.

You wriggled free from my claws, falling to the ground. I tried to push the magic back to you, but it would not slow. I raised my head toward the sky, roaring at it in frustration.

—*It is time, Everen*, I heard, far away, on the other side of the Veil. The barrier between worlds was thin enough that I did not even need to look through the pool to hear my sister's voice. *We are coming. Finish it, Everen.*

Above us, the rip widened, black stripe drawn across the gray cloud sky, edged in lightning. Already, I could hear that unnatural storm: a deep, strange wind, the whispers of a language none could understand. And, even further in the background: a dragon's roar.

It would be simpler to pay the price and save my kind.

Our magic came to me unbidden, like I wound it around a claw. Gold, blue, red. Your hand went to your heart, skin paling. Your face twisted into a grimace. Your expression haunted me: lingering betrayal, confusion, and hurt. You still feared I was causing this.

The dragon roars grew louder. I raised my head again, and the magic arced up toward the sky, as if calling to them. The rip tore larger. I was their lodestone, guiding the way. Guiding them home.

And despite what I wanted, what I willed, the sky opened for me.

40. SORIN: COLD METAL

Sorin ran through the woods, following Jaculus in pursuit of their quarry. Magnes had instructed her to retrieve the claw and kill everyone except the dark-haired interloper who had been in the tower. Sorin was not sure why They should be spared, but she had her instructions.

The gray-haired thief was fast, but Sorin was faster. Little by little, she gained. Her breath was loud in the darkness, the forest quiet enough she could hear the thief crashing through the undergrowth.

Sorin sped up and caught a corner of the thief's cloak, pulling hard. The thief choked, and Sorin tackled Them to the ground.

The thief screamed, wriggling. They freed one hand and scratched at Sorin's face, and she barely avoided a fingernail in the eye. Ducking, she pressed Their arm back into the mulch. The vial was clutched tight in Their other hand, the glass slippery with sweat.

"It's not my time," They said, voice urgent. "I swear it's not my time."

They wriggled again, but Sorin only pushed harder, until They grunted in pain.

This should be easy. It should be simple. Sorin always knew exactly what to do, where to press. She had the trident knife in her hand. One quick stab, and it would be done. Another life taken, another offering to the gods.

But the thief was fighting so very hard to live.

"Not my time," They panted, over and over. "Please. I know it. It's not my time."

Sorin held on grimly. She had another flash of Karys, dying afraid in Their own bed. The fear in Sar Saunder Bane's eyes. Captain Tellreg going down with Their ship. Girazin's limbs bent backward, wrong. The three people she had just killed. One bolt after another. Each death had left Sorin's soul a little more tattered.

Six deaths. This was merely one more. So why was she hesitating? She was meant to be a knife. Cold, unfeeling metal. Magnes had made her that. Hadn't He?

"I've saved Struck," her target said. "Hundreds of them by now. Your Citadel would let them starve in the streets."

Sorin's hands tightened on the thief's wrists.

"I'm here," the thief spat. "Picking up the slack. I'm trying to do good." Their breath was harsh and fast, brown eyes imploring. They had a faint scar to the side of Their nose. "I might not always manage, I'll be first to admit that. But I'm trying. I'm—I'm trying. And I want to keep trying. Let me."

Sorin's eyes flicked down to the vial clasped in Their hand.

"It would save so many," the thief said. "Do you know how much it could help?"

Sorin pressed her knee into Their stomach.

Anyone who would sell a relic deserved death. Fall. Tellreg. Dwell. Their names hung heavy around her neck as her seal. She did not even know the names of the bodyguards she had killed. Hadn't Tellreg stressed the importance of names for Jaskians?

Sorin was so tired of death. Was this it—was this all she would ever be?

Jaculus gave a cry and settled on a branch, watching them both with beetle-black eyes.

The thief's head turned toward the vial. With effort, They opened Their hand, letting the vial fall onto the loamy soil.

They met her eyes. There was fear, unshed tears, but also a deep conviction. What did Sorin know of this stranger beneath her, other than They wished to live?

Sorin moved, fast, and her trident knife was above the thief's heart. They reached up, grasping her wrist.

"If I let you live," Sorin said, each word as painful as a slash to her throat, "you and anyone who works for you must leave Vatra. Never to return."

The thief inhaled, the three points of the knife digging into Their shirt.

"Do you agree?" Sorin pressed a little harder.

"I agree. I swear it. I swear." The composure dropped, tears leaving tracks down Their cheeks.

Sorin kept her knee on the thief and used the trident knife to draw out the chain around Their neck. She ran her fingertips over the indents, reading them with a touch.

She let the seal fall. She could not make Them sign a promise, but she had the next best thing: she had Their name. Sorin snatched up the vial from the forest floor and rose, backing away.

"Save more lives, Larkin Nash, so I feel it was worth it to spare yours." Sorin had made her choice. Magnes had wanted the claw above all. That was her success.

"Thank you," Larkin Nash whispered.

Sorin gestured for her to go, and watched the thief run into the dark.

She turned back toward the barrow hill, yet before she had taken a score of steps, she felt a twist of pain at her torso. For a second, she wondered if she had made a terrible mistake and the thief had attacked her.

But the pain was in five familiar blazing points. Sorin tasted the memory of wraithlike smoke. She grunted, steadying herself on the trunk of the nearest tree. Her head twisted deeper into the forest. The Vatran river was close— the leyline that ran from the capital to the monastery in the mountains. She could feel it, even from here, and as she looked up at the sky, it rippled, the sky turning a shade of purple she had only seen once before: in the gap between worlds.

—*Run, child.* Magnes's voice boomed in her mind. *Bring the claw and hold back the tide until I arrive. Do it, or we are lost.*

Sorin held the vial close to her chest and sprinted toward the rip in the Veil.

41. ARCADY: THE MONSTER

My body shuddered, more magic leaving me.

The dragon sat on its haunches, wings outstretched, neck craned up toward the sky. A warm spot like a star beneath the skin at his throat. He was glorious.

He was killing me.

Whether he willed it or not, I was fading. I tried to stop the flow, but it was like trying to escape a whirlpool. I could rage at it all I wanted, but it'd get me nowhere. I smelled the sharp ozone of the storm and I arched, arms flung back, mouth open in a silent scream as I lost more of myself.

The first dragon emerged, all shined scales and sharp teeth and blazing eyes. It was red, with a jewel at the forehead. An echo of Everen. His mother? I sensed I'd dreamed of her before.

Everen snarled, launching himself from the ground and rising to meet her, the wind from his wing buffeting me.

The storm pulled the dragon back into the rift, unwilling to let her go. Another dragon's head emerged again, this one green. Half of her neck was visible before, she, too, was dragged back.

The dragons would eventually break through, and they'd burn everything in their path. I'd wanted to take down the Citadel, but not like this. If my magic was what let them through, I'd be just as hated as my grandsire.

It would be my fault.

My hunger roared to life, demanding to be fed. My body twisted with it, hollowing against my ribs and spine. Every mark on my body burned, like red-hot iron stabbed beneath my skin, and even as I watched, they expanded, darkening the backs of my hands. I screamed again, my eyes rolling up in my skull. I hadn't lost myself like this since the night I'd nearly died of the Strike. The distant roar of dragons quieted. I tried to claw my magic back, any of it, but it wouldn't come.

I was weak. I'd always been weak.

I poisoned everything, and everyone I loved died. I'd only stayed alive by dumb luck, and it'd just run out.

Traces of black thread through the blue and gold. My marks burned hotter. Everen wheeled, flying toward the storm but unwilling to attack his own kind. I was still being drained, the hunger now past the point of pain.

For a moment, the storm and chaos overhead blinked out. I was no longer lying in the dirt. I was back in my nightmares, the ones I never put down to ink and paper. The ones so intense it felt like I lived them, again and again.

The too-hot room of the mountain cottage in Atrel. The scent of death and incense and medicinal herbs. I am twelve years old, swamped beneath sweltering covers. Drenched in sweat. Mouth dry. The seal at my chest is a bone shard stabbed into my sternum, and I am about to die. I hear the rustle of wings, the dragons' call. It's almost a relief.

My paire's hands are on me, green magic like the scent of spring. Some burrows into my body, trying to drag out the darkness. I scream and beg for him to stop.

"That won't do it," my maire whispers. "Don't you see, Thand? Their soul is already crossing the barrier."

My paire's voice is thick. "He must have come up with a way. Do something!"

My maire's hands tighten on mine. Every touch hurts. My body does not feel like mine. I hear a sound, somewhere far away, like a chime calling me home.

They argue, but I'm too far gone to care.

I drift through the gaps in the world. I am in a storm, but everything is silent except for a call. I follow. Dragons circle an island with steep cliffs. I think I've died, and I am not afraid.

Another jolt and I'm somewhere dark. A dragon bends over a pool, desperately seeking something.

I hear my maire speaking, far away, unfamiliar words echoing through the gaps. It's telling me to come back, come home.

The god looks up. I reach out and I barely brush against them. I hear another chime.

*I'm dragged back into my own dying, plague-ridden body. I don't
want to go.*

In the clearing, I screamed again. Behind my eyelids, I was still twelve
years old, broken and dying. Somewhere, far off, I felt shock, guilt, panic. It
wasn't mine. Whose was it? It seemed like I should know.

Everything fractured. It was the present and it was the past. The memories, now unleashed, wouldn't stop. No matter how much I wanted it all to
stay where I'd locked it away.

*She leans over me, but she is no longer my mother. Black eyes, dark marks
scribbled on skin. Her magic is wrong, wrong, all wrong.*

*"Maire," I croak, but she is gone. Only her body remains. Only her
hunger. Her hands are on my throat, squeezing. Her teeth dig into my
shoulder. I scream.*

*There's a horrible sound, and the pressure and pain lessens. My
paire, his face broken with grief, hauls her back and jumps between us.
He raises his hands—*

*I have forced myself to forget the rest. The fever burns everything
away, and I lean into it. I don't expect to wake up.*

I hovered both in the clearing and the mountain.

*A long time later, my swollen eyes open. The fever has broken, and I'm
on soaked sheets. My paire's body is hidden beneath a blood-stained sheet.
My maire, next to him, is still breathing, barely. I crawl to her, weak as a
kitten. She whispers the words to me. Tells me the secret of the Plaguebringer's seal. I don't listen to her for many years.*

My paire sacrificed himself, and my maire became a monster.

To save me.

I will never think I was worth it.

Scattered flashes of my life back in Vatra. Stealing alone. Stealing for
Kelwyn. Stealing for the Marricks. Always keeping everyone at a distance,

save Lightfinger. I spent eight years waiting for the past to repeat itself, and eventually it did.

In the clearing, beneath that broken sky, I gave up and waited for death.

—*No.*

I caught a drop of magic. It settled into me, like a snowflake melting on skin.

A dragon crouched over me. Everen had been that dragon by the pool, searching, searching, reaching out with everything he had.

And he had found me.

We hadn't become connected the Night of Locked Tombs. He had, deep down, been with me for years.

Above us, the dragons fought their way through, but they weren't alone. Storm clouds emerged from the rip. No, darker than that. Thick, black smoke transformed into shapes. Teeth, too many eyes, bristles of fur and claws.

They were attacking the dragons, dragging them back into the storm. A few of the smoke creatures had slipped through, curling around tree branches, sucking the life from them. My hunger was almost forgotten as I watched the impossible battle above. It was like those ancient founding myths, of gods fighting chaos. It would be visible for leagues. What would people think of this?

It didn't matter. I lost the thread of reality again, and I thankfully remembered nothing that happened next.

42. SORIN: GODS IN FLAME

Sorin reached the clearing just before the god fell.

A dragon, blue and bright, appeared through the rift in the firmament. Wraiths flitted through, snapping at scales, the air filling with the same clicking that sent shivers down her spine.

A red dragon swooped, swiping one of the monsters in Their jaws, biting down until it disappeared before gaining altitude once more. But there were too many. The wraiths converged on the first god, until the blue scales were nearly lost in the black.

And so They dropped, crashing to earth with a horrible, final sound. The body lay broken, wraiths circling the corpse. Sorin shrieked and threw herself into the fray, unsheathing her bone knife and slashing the god killers to wisps.

Jaculus cried, swooping on the smaller wraiths. Sorin feared for him until he flew through one, jaws snapping, and it turned to wisps. Her small, fierce guardian.

They fought together, and above them the sky raged. The red dragon destroyed the larger ones, but for every one that disappeared, another took its place. It was an unending wave of darkness.

Where was Magnes?

She had the claw, but she did not have His magic.

She could only fight. She became nothing but a swipe, a stab, a slash of a white blade. She killed wraiths that looked like malformed boar, or cats, or lizards. Some looked like no creature she had seen before, with curling tusks or spiraling horns. They all had those black teeth, those purple eyes.

She fought until something grabbed her from behind and dragged her back into the entrance of the cave.

She twisted, ducking from a desperate swipe of a hand, sweeping out a foot to try to trip her assailant.

Sorin backed away, holding out her dragonbone blade.

The Starveling rushed her, snarling, the magic burning through Them giving the Starveling preternatural reflexes. Sorin stabbed, but the Starveling swerved out of the way and hit her hard on the forearm.

Sorin forced herself to keep her breath steady, to move as lightly on the balls of her feet as the Citadel arms keeper and Magnes had taught her. *You have to be careful when fighting a Starveling*, Magnes had told her, long ago. *Because they don't have anything to lose.*

All Sorin could do was beat them back. She might have gotten a slash with the dragonbone blade, but the Starveling knocked it from her hand. It clattered along the stone. If the Starveling felt any pain, They gave no sign.

The Starveling attacked again, and Their face was caught by a sliver of silver moonlight from the entrance of the cave. With the black eyes and deeply marked face, it took Sorin a moment to recognize the interloper from the tower, the person from the forest who had tried to sell Dwell the claw in Their pocket. It was a shock to see someone so utterly transformed. Girazin's face flashed in her mind again. The sound of the snapping of bone.

She lost her concentration for only a moment. That was all it took.

The Starveling knocked her to the floor, a fist landing squarely on Sorin's nose. The crunch meant it was broken. Before Sorin could even register the pain, the Starveling sank Their teeth into her forearm, as hard as They could. Sorin screamed, her silence forgotten. She battered at the Starveling with her free hand, trying not to move too much so They didn't tear a chunk of flesh from her arm. Blood streamed down Sorin's face, over her lips, and the scent of the blood was only making the Starveling more feral.

A blast of magic would have knocked Sorin down if she hadn't already been splayed out, looking up into the entirely black eyes of the Starveling. She was sobbing, babbling, saying anything to try and convince Them to let go.

—*Stop*, came a voice in her head, so loud it chased out all other thought. The Starveling above her froze.

Sorin wanted to cry. Magnes had called for her, and now He had come. His silhouette was against the cave entrance, holding His own dragonbone blade.

The Starveling grunted, but the agony on Sorin's arm lessened as They loosened Their jaw. As soon as she was free, Sorin rolled over and away, cradling her arm and hissing with the throbbing pain. She pressed her palm onto the wound to give it pressure but couldn't bear to look at it.

Magnes knelt in front of her. The Starveling was in the corner of the cave, crouched on Their haunches, watching with those horrible eyes. The mouth was smeared with Sorin's blood. Sorin fought down a wave of revulsion. Magnes's seal flared purple, keeping the Starveling at bay.

"The talon." His voice quivered in its intensity.

"Inner pocket," she rasped, and she moved her aching arm down enough that He could reach in and take out the vial. It glowed as purple as His seal and the storm above. "Bless you, child." He tucked it away.

"I have some Eyes with me, but not enough," He said. "Are you well enough to fight?"

Sorin gritted her teeth and forced herself to look down. Two crescents of bloody red on the outer edge of her left forearm. It hurt like chaos. Her right—her weapons arm—was fine.

"Yes," Sorin said. Magnes disappeared for a moment and returned with her blade, closing her fingers around the hilt. The Starveling snarled again, but with another burst of magic, They quieted.

He took off His glove and ran a fingertip down her broken nose. Another stab of agony, and then it muted. A touch quieted the throbbing of her arm.

"It isn't healed. Be careful," He instructed. "I'll join you soon. There is something I must do." His eyes glittered as they focused on the Starveling.

He leaned forward, pressing His forehead to hers for the barest moment. "Fight well, Sorin."

Sorin forced herself to her feet. She could smell nothing, and her nose was entirely numb, which was almost more disconcerting than the pain would be. But she gripped her blade tighter and staggered back out into the clearing in the woods.

43. EVEREN: STARFIRE

The Veil was an ugly wound against the sky.

I had not stolen enough of your magic to fully open the Veil, but neither could I close it. The smoke wraiths came fast, their screeching and hissing so loud it hurt my ears.

Rivers of fire, wraiths of smoke,
storm, lightning, and rain.

Rain lashed at my wings as I flew as close to the rift as I dared, the rain burning my face with cold. The air was charged with lightning. I slashed at wraiths with my teeth, satisfied by their shriek of pain before they wisped into nothing. My mother, still half-trapped, snapped at another, and it exploded in a burst of black smoke.

My mother was injured, bleeding from dozens of cuts. Other dragons—Mace, Feith, and others I had known my whole life. Dragons who had loved me, feared me, ignored me, revered me.

I could let them all through, but the price would be your death. There had to be another way. We only needed time.

—You have to go back, I sent to my mother, slashing at more wraiths. *This will not work.* Everything was out of balance. Everything was *wrong*.

—No, she snarled. *This world* will *be ours.*

Dragons had not expected resistance. Yet the wraiths were defending the storm, and humans had arrived below—dressed in black and working for the Order, I would guess. They loosened arrows from the ground, and I swerved to avoid one.

—I am not your enemy, I sent them, and several fell to their knees from the force of my magic.

More wraiths emerged. More arrows left bowstrings. Far off came a klaxon call, and I sent a thread of awareness in that direction. Soldiers from Vatra, moving at speed on horseback.

Another bolt whisked by my head, barely missing me. I veered, watching in horror as it landed in the meat of my mother's shoulder instead. She roared in pain, head jerking to one side, the crossbolt embedded in her scales through a gap in her armor. The storm dragged her back in its embrace.

—*Mother!*

I flapped my wings frantically, grabbing another creature in my claws and hurling it through the rip. Would she emerge again?

The whispers of the storm grew louder, echoing in my mind. Neither Locmyrian nor Celenian, or any tongue I could recognize. It was something ancient and primordial. Was it giving me a warning, or a promise?

In that moment, pure understanding sizzled through me like lightning. I realized, with perfect clarity, exactly what was coming.

The dragon scales will be upended, set aflame as if made of coal.

I saw different versions, different paths—that web I had searched for in scrysilver and glass. Your magic, combined with mine, was enough to unlock it all. It was all I could do to keep myself in the sky as I was overwhelmed with dozens of futures at once.

One way: I let them through, and you pay the ultimate price. The Lumet falls in flame.

Another: I close the Veil and remain on this side. You are saved, but Vere Celene falls in flame.

Or: I do nothing, and both worlds burn.

I rifled through more paths, searching for what might do the least damage. I could only see what might happen in the immediate future. After more than half a candlemark, the options diverged and forked until it was nothing but nonsense. I saw dragons burn alive. Humans crumple to the ground. I saw two worlds, both sick. Both doomed.

One, unchanging constant: the Veil had to close. And I alone could do it.

I almost wanted to laugh. For all my mother's machinations, this was doomed from the start. She and Miligrist had been too desperate for that sliver of a chance of victory. The dragons swirled in the storm between worlds, a film keeping them back. More wraiths darkened all, until I could barely see the forest floor below. My wing was still injured, and each beat sent another pulse of pain.

Everything was falling into place. I only had to let go. My heart broke at the thought, but this was what I deserved.

I saw you turn Starveling moments before it happened. Time was going strange, the present and the future running concurrently. Either way, you did not have long.

More wraiths converged on me, one slashing the membrane of my wing. The pain seared me back into the present and I flapped frantically, unable to focus on anything but destroying them before they could destroy me. The creatures were both heavy and insubstantial. When they snarled, there was no real force behind it. These were not alive—they were only pretending.

My mother reemerged, and I felt her pain as keenly as if it were my own.

—*End this*, my mother called, her thought thick with agony. *Kill the human and bring us through.*

—*I cannot*, I sent, anguished. *There is no future where dragons come through, right here, right now, without both worlds falling.*

—*Lies!* She roared, flashing her teeth. *I should have known you wouldn't have what it takes.* She eviscerated another wraith, still pushing to free herself from the space between worlds.

Mace took a slash to the snout. Another dragon cried out in pain. There had been at least five dragons fighting, but I only saw three. Glisten's body lay broken below.

—*I am trying to save you.* I knew what words to say, and how my mother would reply. I shaped them, all the same. *We will find another way. For years, you believed me your Seer. Believe me now.*

—*No!* She demolished another wraith. I was so bloated with magic, I could pluck her thoughts from her skull: she wished she had killed me as soon as I had hatched. Miligrist had told her not to, and only that had stopped her.

The knowledge hurt, even though I saw it coming.

—*I am doing what I must, Mother*, I said. *I hope one day you will see I made the right choice.*

You were still hidden from view in the cave. I knew what happened within, as I knew it must.

I flew higher, destroying another wraith above the rip, waiting. This next step would be harder. I knew all the pain you were about to go through, since I would share it. I wanted to shield you from it, but I could not. Not if this was to work. The bond between us was as dampened as the first night I had arrived in the Lumet. You had to do this part alone.

I kept fighting, killing as many of the monsters as I could with my teeth, my claws, the tips of my wings. I gathered more scratches and teeth marks. They barely dented my scales.

The records had said dragons and humans had fought a shared enemy together. With fate rushing through me in a torrent, I knew they had fought these creatures together. The Veil had existed long before humans had twisted it to their own ends.

The dragons let loose more roars. My handle on past, present, and future was slipping. Our shared magic was fraying, and you were only holding on by a thread. If I was to do it, I had to do it now.

The bond that binds can push back the line.

I could almost hear my sister whispering in my ear. Maybe she did, from the other side of the Veil. Had she, too, seen all of this, and done what she could to bring it true?

So unwind the weave. Rip the threads and all will cleave.

There you were, returned to yourself, but still on the brink. You stumbled from the mouth of the cave. With this new understanding, I unspooled magic from me, back into you. I beat my injured wings, flying higher, higher, as far above the rip as I could manage. Your face was a small, white oval below.

—*Everen!* you screamed. I felt your fury, your hatred once more. Did you see what I meant to do? Was this, too, shared?

I gave you all your magic back, and a little of mine. You staggered with it, leaning against the rocky overhang.

—*Do it,* I sent. *Do it.*

Your mouth opened, and you began to mutter the spell.

—*I am sorry.* I wish I had been brave enough to say something more. That what I felt for you was the opposite of hate.

A spear of pain hit my stomach that I had only felt once before. My first fall.

The second time, I dove. My wings tucked tight against my side. The Veil used more of my magic to heal the rent between worlds. The golden threads would tie it tight. I let myself fall into the web of fate, and the storm was waiting to catch me.

In that instant, I was almost at peace. I felt the moment the bond between us snapped. A ripped thread. A last whisper, from somewhere deep within the storm:

Do not fear: deep sutures make the strongest scars.

44. ARCADY: PROMISES BROKEN

I returned to myself in pieces.

The taste of blood.

The smell of something animal or human.

Something sweet at my mouth, on my tongue. Someone held me, tilting my head back. Part of me thought time had broken, or that a spirit had slipped through the Veil to help usher me off to death for good. I imagined my maire or paire pushing my hair back. Or maybe it was my taie, come to tell me that sometimes it's better to let the past go.

I drank down the ambrosia, like a babe suckling at a breast. With every gulp, I felt more of myself coming back. My magic was almost empty, but what little I had, I kept. Eventually, the warmth moved away, and I heard the shuffle of footsteps. I tried to open my eyes, but I only caught the outline as they moved away. Tall and broad.

"Taie?" I whispered in the dark, just like I had on the Night of Locked Tombs. The figure did not answer.

The last parts of me snapped together all at once. My eyes opened and I heaved in a gasp like I was coming up for air. I was alone in the cave in the clearing. And I remembered everything.

Everything.

All my rage reignited. Perhaps it was what had pulled me back. It wouldn't have been the first time I'd survived out of pure spite. I crawled to the edge of the cave on all fours. Every movement hurt. I was no longer starving, but I was hollow. I wiped the back of my mouth and my hand came away with blood, and I shuddered. I had no memory of however long I'd been Starveling. No idea whose blood I wore. That's the way of it. You lose yourself, and you *become* hunger. That's all that's left.

Many who went Starveling and survived couldn't face their actions, or not being able to remember. I couldn't wonder what I might or might not have done. If I did, I'd stay there, trapped in the dark, unable to move.

There was something I hadn't finished.

I kept crawling forward, more memories flicking into place. My knuckles were bloody and swollen. I let out broken shards of laughter. Everen had set out to steal my magic, and even if he'd changed his mind, he'd still almost succeeded. Larkin had been conflicted, too, but she'd still gone and let Lightfinger die.

Emotions don't matter one whit compared to actions.

I reached the flat stones outside the small cave.

—*Everen!* I howled.

For a moment, all I could do was look up at the scene above. That dark rip in the Veil surging across the sky. Dragons fighting to break through, each charge more and more desperate. One breathed flame and it came through the Veil, burning something made of smoke. There was more than one kind of monster.

I noticed the people last. They wore all black, swinging knives or strange white swords. They took no notice of me, too intent on the monsters. The sounds of fighting disappeared behind the rushing in my ears.

As Everen had pushed a little more magic into me, trying too late to fix what he'd broken, a bit of knowledge had come with it—I knew exactly what he meant to do. And what I had to do. We both had our parts to play.

My gaze snagged on him.

He flew, destroying more of the creatures. Despite injuries, he still moved so gracefully. Words couldn't capture even the edges of what I felt, seeing him fly. Everything was all tangled up.

Not for long.

Trust evidently completed that bond, along with blood, so perhaps betrayal might *break* it. The spell that began all this affected the Veil. Both when I was dying of the Strike, and when I drew him through.

I fumbled with my seal setting before it finally clicked open. I took out the stone with shaking hands.

—*Do it*, he sent. *Do it.*

"*Kjetim-lei ak ar-dźakain,*" I began. "*Lei-turei, iév-turo.*"

This was deeply untested magic—an experimental spell partly created by the man who they said almost destroyed the known world. I had been a fool to use that spell on the Night of Locked Tombs, and I was even more a fool to try it a second time. Through the bond, I understood the words. *I call the storm. Within you, within me.*

My seal began to glow gold and blue through my fingertips.

"Ar-réal vanok vaugain, śajak val jain reno." My tongue stumbled over the unfamiliar words. *The dragon scales are upended. Two halves of a larger whole.*

Intent mattered most. I imagined my grandsire in the courtyard of our grand house in Vatra. Sitting beneath trees, always with a book in hand. He'd shown me spells: made my toys dance, or woven water around my head like a crown.

Hoping wherever he was, my taie was guiding me, I imagined that Veil above us shrinking, folding back in on itself. Some of the wraiths around us began to scream, like they were in pain. *Good*, I thought with a twist of satisfaction. *Good.* I wanted them to hurt. I wanted them destroyed, whatever they were. Spirits, chaos, monsters, magic.

My power was hard to control, and my body shook, barely able to hold it. I had some of Everen's magic, too. I could tell by the taste of brimstone and soot on my tongue, the flashes of red at my seal.

The black-clad fighters, after a moment of shock, renewed their efforts against the wraiths. More fell, and no more came through the Veil. The edges were closing.

"Dźo eje loj el-dźakain," I snarled up at the sky. *And if we are the storm . . .*

More magic funneled through me, and I wondered if I'd actually survive this. I decided it was worth it. If this was the way I went out, at least I was the one choosing it.

"Fanas arfan lo."

It must rage for us.

A burst of magic shot through the clearing, as I kept what I wanted at the forefront of my mind. The remaining smoke wraiths on this side of the Veil fell to the ground as one. Up above, there was Everen. He wasn't angry at me. He understood. That was worse.

The bond between us grew thicker. For an instant, we were joined again, as closely as we'd been for those few minutes right before we realized the bond had completed. Like we were one being split into two bodies. I saw through his eyes, up in the sky. For an instant, I was the dragon, and he was human.

Every nerve in my battered body was screaming. The Veil continued closing, and the wraiths were dead. There was only one more thing to do.

I hooked my magic into Everen, and I *pulled*.

The dragon above me roared. He had flown high, to attack the creatures that had streamed upward from the rip. He went entirely boneless.

He fell. Slower than the laws of nature decreed. Light glimmered around him, the same purple-dark as the storm.

I almost lost my grit. Even after everything he'd done, I didn't want to discount all the good parts of the last two months and, on some level, the last nine years. Some of what we had seemed so real. Part of me had come close to loving him.

My instinct was, as ever, right. He was never meant for me. Not really.

The storm reached out for him, and I felt the moment the dragons were pulled into it. I didn't even know if they'd be able to find their way home, or if I was dooming them to death. The rip healed over. A last burst of wind, and the sky above was utterly silent.

The bond broke.

It was an absolute severing.

There was no other way to explain it. More magic ricocheted back into me, and I collapsed. Everything was too loud, too much. My mind was desperately trying to reach out, to reconnect to someone who was no longer there.

Too slowly, I raised my head. The black-clad fighters started toward me. They were part of the Order of the Dragons, I guessed that much. Far off, I sensed the soldiers, too late to be any use.

I still had that stubborn sense of self-preservation that had gotten me this far. With a whip of this overflow of strength, I pushed everyone else back. The one nearest me cradled their arm close to their chest, and let out a grunt of pain as they were half-thrown against a tree trunk. I backed away, and when I reached the edge of the clearing, I turned and ran into the forest.

The magic settling into my skin kept me running longer than should have been possible considering how close to death I'd come. Finally, I slowed, my ears straining, heart a too-fast drum, but no one chased me.

The bond was nothing but tatters. Loneliness threatened to swallow me. I was a ragged, half-formed thing, feral and wild. A wave of emotion rose so strong, so overwhelming, I almost wanted to lie down and die.

My stubborn heart kept beating. My lungs kept breathing. And magic still moved its way through me, strong and sure.

How many people had seen dragons flying across the sky? Did they think the gods had returned? Things would be in upheaval. Nothing would be the same. One way or the other.

I let myself linger and put off whatever was waiting for me in the city. It was deep in the night. Everything was quiet in the forest. Everything still hurt so badly. I wandered, letting instinct guide me, and found myself back at the barrow hill.

The bodies were still there. I don't know why I'd half-expected them to have disappeared. Facedown and unmoving, blood soaking into the grass and soil. I knelt next to them. I'd never really believed in the gods. Now I didn't know who to pray to, so I simply apologized to them in silence, head bowed. I hadn't killed them, but they wouldn't have been here if it wasn't for me.

Then, because I was still, at heart, a thief, I searched for the money. The chest of wraithwright was gone. I found nothing but a few scattered silver coins in Dwell's pockets, and copper Jaskian crowns in the guards'. I slid the aquamarine ring from Dwell's inert finger and slipped it on my own. I'd keep it as another remembrance of my guilt.

Claw and money. Gone.

Who had taken it? The assassin who had chased Larkin into the woods? Somewhere back in the trees, was Larkin facedown in the soil too? I poked at the idea of her being dead. I wasn't sure if I should mourn her or not, and the fact I had that indecision made me feel even worse.

Maybe Kelwyn had come back for it. He had disappeared right when things went sideways. A little lift of hope punctured the numbness, but not much. Most of me was . . . somewhere else. I moved through a fog, and I was grateful for it. If my emotions came back, I knew I'd scream, and scream, and maybe never stop.

I retreated into the shelter of trees, and found a soft patch of moss. I had more than enough magic to keep myself warm. I lay down, and finally, finally, I let go.

45. ARCADY: PROMISES KEPT

I knocked at the door of the Last Golden. It opened almost immediately, Kelwyn's face pinched with worry.

"You're alive," he breathed. "What happened? Where's Larkin? I went to the Vatran hideouts, but no one was at any of them, not even Wren. I was about to head out to the Cote." The words stumbled over each other.

Seeing him undid all my false calm. My body broke out in a sweat, and my breathing came short and fast as fear re-flooded my system. I stumbled inside and grabbed the front of his shirt. "Do you have the wraithwright?"

His face crumpled. "I went back for it, when it seemed safe, but it was gone."

My hope cracked, falling around me in pieces. Only anger remained. Anger was simple. Uncomplicated.

I pushed him a few steps until his back reached the counter. I brought my face closer, my eyes searching for signs he was lying. "Are you and Larkin working against me? If you hide even one wraithwright coin from me, I swear . . ."

Something in my expression scared him. He paled, and I finally took in how awful he looked. His hair scraped back into uneven tufts, his face drawn.

"I swear, Arcady. I'd never cheat you like that, not after all we risked," he said, palms up. "This was *your* job, *your* plan."

A few moons ago, I had taken him at his word. I wouldn't now. "Prove it," I said, and my voice was so harsh I didn't recognize it. "Sign for it."

Kelwyn took in a shaking breath. His eyes shuttered at my demand. After an aching pause, he took out a plain sheaf of parchment. He penned the letters carefully. I watched the words form.

I, Kelwyn Crowl, hereby swear that last night, on the Feast of Flowers, I did not take or find any money from anyone at the barrow hill and have no knowledge of what became of the wraithwright coins for the illegal sale of Girazin's claw relic.

I blinked at the words. This was a bold confession. No way to hide. If he signed it and gave it to me, it would be dead easy to have him sent to prison for the rest of his earthly life, if he was lucky enough to escape the noose or blade.

He went to roll his seal, but I shook my head. We weren't done.

"Did you know?" I demanded, still merciless. "That it was Dwell who was going to buy the claw?"

A furtive half-shrug. He bent his head again, and the scratch of pen nib against paper was loud in the silence of the shop.

> *I freely admit that I suspected Sar Ikari Dwell might be the prospective buyer for the claw relic, as it would be an easy matter for a Jaskian merchant to smuggle it on one of Their ships.*

He glanced up. "But I didn't know for sure. Didn't think They'd bring actual Jaskian guards and didn't expect to see someone murdered right in front of me."

He looked a little green. In many ways, Kelwyn was sheltered from the uglier parts of our job. It was cushy being a fence compared to being the thief. He exchanged money for goods, but usually within the confines of his shop or in clandestine but relatively safe handover locations. He had a good reputation for keeping sales private. He'd almost come to blows and had received death threats, but nothing serious. I doubted he'd ever seen someone die so violently. From plague, maybe, which was its own horror, well I knew, but not violence. The image of Dwell's chest darkening with blood flashed in my mind's eye. It was branded there for good. No one should ever see something like that.

"And where's Larkin?" I asked.

"Not a sarding clue." He held up the pen. "Want me to write that down too?"

I believed him there. His face had gone grim, his jaw set. Some of my anger leached from me. "Finish the promise, Kelwyn."

He picked up the pen, but hesitated. "What's your surname? You've never actually told me."

"Dalca," I said, the lie that was not technically a lie falling easily from my lips.

I swear that this is all true to you, Arcady Dalca. This is my vow, and I will suffer the pain if it is broken.

He took his seal off its chain and rolled it carefully in ink. He gave me a pointed look before he set it onto the parchment.

Once he finished, I took out my seal and bathed it in the ink. Rolled it carefully along the bottom. There was my false identity. I held the seal I'd fished from the old bones of someone I'd loved. The seal that had drawn Everen to me, and the one that had banished and maybe killed him.

"*Naustje,*" Kelwyn said aloud in the dragon's tongue. Everen was gone, but his knowledge of the Old Tongue remained within me. The spell was simply the word for "truth." But the etymology was a compound—a literal translation was "sharp teeth." Truth was something that could be rent out, or dug in. Truth was a wound that could bite.

As soon as he spoke, there was a burst of magic. Kelwyn was Aura-touched too, but his magic tasted different from Everen's. More like incense than soot.

Stop thinking of Everen.

He was gone. He wouldn't be back.

The ink on the parchment shone before settling back into black. Kelwyn showed no sign of pain. If he'd written a falsehood, he'd be writhing on the ground, screaming until I smeared the ink.

"Are you satisfied?" Kelwyn bit out.

I picked up the scrap of parchment. He stiffened. If I walked out with this, would he try to stop me? I held his life in my hands. I kept it there. Let him feel me with it. I held the power to end him with one little sheaf of paper.

In a swift movement, I threw it onto the fire. The edges curled, then caught. The spell was ruined. Only the person signed to had the power to break it. I'd set him free of his promise.

Kelwyn's shoulders shook a little with relief.

We were silent, the flames in the grate crackling.

"I ran," Kelwyn said, eventually. "At the first sign of trouble, I ran. I thought I was braver than that."

I stared at the flames. "None of us really know what we're made of until it comes down to it. And running isn't always so bad. It's better than being dead."

"I suppose." He lapsed back into stillness. I should have been full of aches and pains. But all that magic going through me had healed everything, just as it had when Everen and I kissed. It was unnatural, to feel hale and hearty when my mind and soul were so damned battered.

"Arcady. Where is Everen?" Kelwyn finally asked, voice quiet. I stared at him. Had he crouched in the forest and seen Everen come on wings like flame, and then turn into a god and tear me away? He had to have. The light alone would have drawn his eye, and his dragon's roar could have been heard back in Vatra.

"He's gone." The two words felt so heavy.

He knew better than to ask any more, much as he clearly wanted to.

"Come on," Kelwyn said eventually. "I'll make you tea."

But I shook my head. "I have to get back to the shop. I have to think." At the door, I paused, my palm on the handle. "I'm sorry. For making you sign for it." I wasn't sure if that was true.

His gaze was unblinking. "Don't fret yourself. I'd have done the same, Arc. I'd have done just the same."

◇◇◇◇◇◇◇◇◇

I let myself in through the front door, too tired to check if anyone was on the street to see me. I stared at the upper floor of the lock shop. The pile of pillows of Everen's bed. I reached out, cautiously, for the bond, and jerked back. It was like a missing tooth, an open sore, a bleeding wound. I edged past his bed, his pile of books. A lock he'd been working on, just for the fun of it and to quiet his mind before he went to sleep. It was still so hard to marry the Everen I thought I'd known with the dragon that had snatched me up in his claws. Or the serene creature that hadn't fought when I'd pushed him back into the storm. What had his last words meant?

I didn't know if he was still stuck in that space between worlds, or if he was dead. I hoped he and the other dragons had made their way back to Vere Celene. Even if they had, he'd told me that world was dying. Wouldn't that mean they were as good as dead?

Imagine. The grandchild of the Plaguebringer, also the killer of gods.

I sobbed, once, and hauled up the trapdoor, climbing down into the dark. I paused halfway down the ladder. There weren't any wards. The hairs on the back of my neck stood up, intuition clamoring.

I scrabbled down and took out my knife from my boot. It'd served me well, the last day. I threw open the door to the back room. It wasn't locked.

And froze.

The room remained a tip, every surface covered in ash and soot. But each door of the safes along the wall stood wide open. I stared at them, uncomprehending. Everything had been rifled through, upended, but not trashed. I went straight to the lock that had housed my university funds.

It wasn't empty. My heart started beating again at the sight of my jewelry, my coins of copper, silver, and gold. My one wraithwright coin.

Why would someone break in and go to the effort of opening all those locks, only to leave the coin?

My eye caught on what had been added, right at the front, neatly stacked. A pile of five wraithwright coins. Far, far less than the eighty I was owed.

It was a statement. *Look*, Larkin was saying. *You were probably wondering what happened to the wraithwright. The Marricks have it, and here's me rubbing your nose in what you lost.*

I picked up the coins, watching the green-blue play across the metal's surface in the morning light through the barred window. I picked up a note hidden beneath the coins and unfolded the single sheaf of paper.

> *Sorry, darling. You won't find this fair, but it's more than you deserve. I helped myself to a little extra insurance.*

How many times had I seen that little drawing of a lark? She'd signed all her missives with it, even though a marrick cat would have made more sense. She'd doodled it on pieces of paper, idly, when she was scheming. The same bird, posed the same way. I'd seen it hundreds of times.

It took me too long to realize what her last sentence meant. My eyes scoured the open lock, and my heart jumped in my chest when I realized what was missing.

Larkin had taken my old seal.

She'd have read the carvings, but she'd seen I'd had my other seal at the barrow hill. Larkin was many things, and clever was foremost amongst them. Had she already figured out I had a seal with the name Eremia because it was my own, and that I, impossibly, wore someone else's? If she knew someone who could cast the right spell, it could perhaps be magically traced back to me. She would always know exactly where I was.

I should have ground it to dust.

"Fuck!" I hit another safe, slamming the metal door shut with a reverberating bang.

I scrunched the note with my hands, smearing the drawing of the lark with my fingertips. In her mind, this was fair. More than fair. She'd left the money I'd taken from her vaults. She'd given me a tiny share of the payout. She'd never known what I planned to do with it, that I had needed at least forty to get through university. Even with the extra wraithwright, I had just enough for a year of tuition, and maybe the same of room and board, if I was more miserly than a drakine should be. How would I even hope to steal three times that amount while also studying and trying to discover the truth?

I searched through the locks and the back room systematically, even though it was obvious the seal was long gone. She wouldn't have moved it somewhere else just to mess with me. It was, as she said, insurance.

I yelled, throwing my pillows across the room, banging more of the lock doors. I tangled my fingers in my hair, pulling until it hurt.

I never, ever learned.

Larkin had betrayed me. Everen had betrayed me. Maybe he was dead, maybe he wasn't, but no matter what, the bond was snapped. We'd had one moment, here, in this room, where everything had been perfect. And that was all I'd ever get.

I looked around at the ruin of my haven. My books. At least they hadn't burned, though they were soot-stained. My drawings, the crystals dangling in front of the window, catching and scattering the light. I caught sight of my reflection in the mirror, haggard, pale, dirty.

I shucked off my bloodstained clothes and paused again. The black marks had extended over my collarbone instead of stopping beneath. I stared at them dispassionately in the mirror. I'd have to wear higher collars now or develop a penchant for scarves. The marks stretched further down my legs and arms too. I wouldn't be able to expose my forearms anymore. I should be glad it wasn't worse, I supposed.

My heart was breaking. I couldn't stay here. It was no longer home. It had been desecrated. Everywhere I looked, there were echoes of memories with Everen. And now I'd always know that Larkin could get through the wards. Who had she gotten to undo them for her? Brev, maybe. He'd always been good with them. Joana was a dab hand with charms, too. Maybe they'd both stood right here, realizing that one of their own had never been that far. What lies had Larkin fed them, or what truths had she shared? Didn't matter. Shouldn't matter. I hadn't seen them during this job, and I'd never see them again. They were only more ghosts.

I choked back tears as I grabbed my rucksack and started packing a few belongings. I put the money in a few different purses and tied them up tight, casting protection charms on them. I folded up my nicest clothes, ones a drakine might get away with wearing. Another bag housed my rarest volumes and the two dream journals that were only lightly singed.

Everything else I left. Maybe I'd be able to come back for them, and maybe my hard-won possessions would still be there when I did. I sniffed again, wiping my nose with the back of my hand, and took a last look at this place I'd made my own little corner of the world. It'd go back to being as silent and dust-covered as I found it.

I set the wards, just in case. They'd last a few months before they faded, since I wouldn't be entering them each day.

"Thank you," I whispered to the door after I locked it with the key, resting my forehead briefly against the wood. It felt silly, but I won't pretend I don't have a sentimental streak. This place had kept me safe.

I hiked the rucksack higher up my back and headed off into the night, keeping my eyes sharp for any would-be thieves.

I tried to think of the future. I had my magic back and more. I had some money. It was enough to make a go of it. It would be harder, much harder. I needed somewhere to lie low until entrance exams, and then, with luck, I'd still be up on top of that hill by the time the leaves started to turn. That was what I'd always wanted, wasn't it? Even if I only had one year, maybe that would be enough time to find out what really happened during the first Strike.

I knocked on Kelwyn's door for the second time that night.

He opened the door immediately. He took in the bags weighing me down. My grim face. He reached into his pocket and took out one wraithwright coin.

"This was left on my windowsill. With a drawing of a lark."

"Yeah." A long moment passed between us.

"I think I'll take that cup of tea after all," I said.

He gave me a sad half-smile and held the door open.

46. SORIN: UTTERANCES

A moon after the storm, Sorin stared at the crimson flame and wondered what would happen if she simply blew out the candle and went back to sleep. Would Magnes drag her from the sheets, or would He simply never call her again?

In the end, Sorin swung her legs off the bed and changed into the dark robes hidden in the alcove behind the false wall. Clasping the crimson-flamed candle by its holder, she took the familiar bends to the hidden room in the library, every step breaking cobwebs.

Magnes was waiting for her. She came to the center of the room, slowly, not sure what would happen next. Not long ago, she might have been afraid. Part of her still was. But there was an iron in her spine that had not been there before. She stood tall.

They had saved the world, Magnes and His Eyes. She'd glowed with the knowledge of that when she couldn't sleep. Together, they had sent the bits of chaos, both the wraiths and the dragons, back behind the Veil. She still didn't know if the dragons were gods or monsters. She kept praying at the altars, but she was no longer sure whom she was praying to, or if anyone was listening. She'd lie there in the dark, listening to the soft rustle as Jaculus preened his feathers or the steady sound of his breathing in his sleep. He had a few scars from his run-ins with the wraiths that night. But, since he was dragon-like, the wounds hadn't given him lasting harm like they almost had her.

"Are you angry with me?" Sorin signed.

"No." He shifted, His gloves creaking as He folded His arms and took her in. "You needed to rest, to recover. And now, I must decide what to do with you."

The smallest pause left her cold, for the words that would fill it were loud: *because you know too much*. Sorin swallowed, cocking her head to the side in a silent question.

"There are various paths." His tone was that bland pleasantness that she knew could spell trouble. "You could stay at the Citadel, living the life you've created. I would not call you again, but you would live a safe, if unremarkable, life. Is that what you wish?"

Sorin tried to picture it. Continuing to train at the grounds. Praying at altars. Reading religious texts. Being helpful, but with no ambition. Even if she were to take hold of Order life—join the university, or brick herself up in some monastery—her days would be full of silence whether she had taken the Vow or not. Was that really what she wanted?

"No," she whispered, aloud. She wanted something more. She wanted something extraordinary.

His eyes glimmered. "I thought not. You can also continue as you were. Kill for me under the cover of night. Whom I choose. Where I choose. How I choose. That work still needs doing, now more than ever."

Sorin's throat closed with panic. She tried to imagine sneaking into another manor, tiptoeing down the hall, and dripping a little bit of poison into another glass. Watching someone else fight so hard to live only to face death.

Magnes watched her closely. "I suspect, perhaps, this has also lost its appeal. I think I have tried to force you into a mold you do not fit." He paused. "And that it is not fair to either of us to insist you continue, at least for a time."

"You think me weak." Sorin forced the words past atrophied vocal cords.

"No," He said, shaking His head. "I have seen the strength of you. It should never be easy. If killing doesn't cut deep, that is a sign you have lost your way."

Sorin couldn't look at him. "Even Girazin?"

"Ulla Girazin was not evil. Nothing is—perhaps not even chaos. The drakine took a wrong turn. I pray for them, as I pray for all the others. What we do is not for pleasure, or for a sense of personal vindication. It is a means to an end, in service of a Holy Order."

Sorin's throat ached. "I don't want to kill anymore." A confession.

Magnes did not look surprised. There was no anger, either. Sorin felt herself uncoil a little. "Then what do you want, child?"

He was unpredictable. Was this another test? Her head spun, spiraling out in different directions. She had no clear, hidden desire, no goal she'd secretly harbored. She had only ever wanted to be what He wanted of her.

He made a considering noise. "I have a suggestion, then. I lost Eyes that night," He began. "It will take time to replace them. Though we have been lucky and there have been no large rips in the Veil since, I don't expect it to last."

Sorin said nothing. Had the claw been that powerful?

"You, child, could monitor the leylines for the next few moons. We'll say you're doing an exchange with Nalore Monastery. It will not even be a lie. Many Eyes rest there between their treks."

She said nothing. Not yes, not no. She stared at her feet.

"And then there is one more option," Magnes said. "You could leave the Order. Go wherever you wish. A fresh start."

Her head shot up. This felt a trick, and yet it didn't. His eyes were unblinking, boring into her. This was her chance for an out. He might not even send another assassin after her.

She tried to imagine a life outside the Order. She had no money. No family. No friends. Her only skill was fighting, or perhaps basic scribe work, and that'd pay a pittance. She'd likely end up working as a mercenary and killing again anyway. Magnes watched her, either guessing her train of thought or plucking it from her skull.

"Those are your options," He said, steepling His hands. "What is your choice?"

She was still half-caught in that daydream of the world outside. Even if it was hard, she could almost imagine it, and she was tempted. The door of her cage was cracked open. She'd have Jaculus. They could become hunters, or trackers. Surely, she had other skills, or she could retrain. There was a whole life out there to live.

"I would keep you," Magnes said, His voice soft. "For you are mine."

He came closer, His gloved hand touching her cheek like how she'd imagined a parent would comfort a child. She leaned into that touch. They were the same words He'd said in the clearing, when she was pinned to the mud with agony and He held the tool to heal her in her hand and made her wait. Why, why would she consider staying?

Because He was also all she had, in so many ways. He was the only one who truly saw her. She didn't know how to give Him up, any more than He did her. That other life faded from view. The door of her cage did not slam closed—she pulled it shut and locked it herself, and with her next words, she handed Him the key.

"I am still yours," she said. "And I will become your Eye."

47. MAGNES: RELIC OF THE PAST

Magnes stared out of the window of the South Tower of the Citadel. It was one of the oldest parts of the building. The glass was bubbled and warped, diamonded with leaden panes. The window was too large for the size of the tower and impossible to keep warm in the winter, so it was considered long out of commission. Not even cleaners ever climbed the steep, curving steps. There was nothing in the room but a mirror turned toward the wall, the wooden back painted with a blue sky dotted with flying wyverns.

Magnes came here when he wished to be alone. He knew there were no hidden corridors behind the stone wall. No chance of wandering eyes or ears.

He opened the window wide. Many would be afraid to sit this close to the edge this high up, where one wrong move, one moment of unbalance, could spell the end of everything.

Below him spread the pale gold stone and gray-slated buildings of Vatra leading toward the harbor and the glittering expanse of the sea. This high up, all was quiet. Magnes stared at the horizon. The early evening light cast the room in red-orange gold. He had been in this land for so long, but sometimes the beauty of it still stunned him.

He brought the goblet to his lips, the wine dark and heady against his tongue. The wind played against his skin. He flexed the fingers of his left hand, watching the dark-red leather move. Taking another sip from the wineglass, he set it down on the windowsill.

He let himself savor this moment of victory. His adversaries had been beaten back, and the dark tendrils of the smoke wraiths were pinned behind the Veil for now. Magnes had his reprieve. Still. It had been close, closer than he had liked. He'd almost had to sacrifice something too precious.

He took the claw from his robes, twisting the glass vial idly. He'd delayed taking the next step. Fear, perhaps. Speaking to Sorin had reminded him it was better not to leave open endings.

Sometimes, his first home seemed more like a dream. He'd lived his share of lives, most of them in shadow. He had been called many names. Taken many faces. He had been consort and advisor to Monarchs. He'd left Loc for the first time after the Schism, after the axe had cut through Laen the Ignited's white neck, the blood running down the executioner's block as red as she'd painted her lips. He had wandered, poorer than any tinker, lost in more ways than one. He had raved in madness.

He had not always been a priest, and much of what he had done in his past none would consider holy. He had built, and he had destroyed. He wondered how much longer he'd keep this current life. He had come back to Vatra near twenty years ago, not long before the first Strike. Much had changed in the time he'd been away, but it had been easy enough to work his way to the top of the Order. A role where he could whisper in the ears of Chancellors. Send a thread of magic into their minds and push their decisions into the directions he chose. He'd learned it was best to hold onto power sideways. Hold it, wield it, but make it less obvious to those outside that he was the one who had it. When things inevitably went wrong—for all empires fall—it was much easier to simply walk away and pick up the power slantwise again wherever he landed next. He finished his wine. It wasn't often the past plagued him, but he let himself indulge in the nostalgia.

He had delayed long enough. The dragons would keep trying to find a way through, and he had to be ready.

Change was coming to Loc. The dragons' appearance had left all in an uproar. So many had seen—some thought they were fake, but enough believed. Some thought them a sign of the gods, and others wondered if it meant the Strike would return.

And at the center of it all: the human and the dragon, bonded though they should not be. Arcady Eremia and Everen Emberclaw. He'd known those names before they were even born. They had separated, for now, but would they find their way to each other again?

In careful, meticulous steps, Magnes took off his robes, setting aside the ornate, dragon-scaled embroidered cloth and piling the rest of his garments carefully on the windowsill. He removed his gloves last.

Standing in the center of the tower, he held his arms wide. The wind picked up, swirling through the small tower room. Without the clever little articulated mechanism in his glove, his left hand showed his shame. Four fingers, the thumb missing.

With a sigh, he let the magic ripple across his skin. His fangs pointed along with the tops of his ears. His skin texture shifted, going pale, almost gray. His features rearranged themselves—cheekbones widening, chin narrowing, lips thinning. He opened his eyes, brightened from tawny brown to the color of molten magma, with slitted, vertical pupils.

The wings burst behind him, as purple-black as twilight on the cusp of true night, illuminated with his power. He took the useless, decorative seal around his neck and cast it aside.

He picked up the claw, carefully unscrewing the cap. With a low growl, Magnes slid the relic out of the glass and onto his left palm. With a shaking hand, he held the claw against the stump of his left thumb.

A bright burst of magic illuminated the tower. Perhaps a guard, milling the walls, might have caught the light out of the corner of their eye. It wouldn't be the first time. There were rumors that the tower was haunted, that perhaps Laen the Ignited's spirit had wandered from the tomb in the cavern beneath the city and lingered still. The guard would pay it no mind, thinking idly of their own concerns.

Naked, wings stretched, Magnes watched night fall across Loc. He flexed and closed his left hand and all five fingers. His missing power settled back into himself. He was stronger than he'd been in centuries. Here, in this form, he thought of himself as his earliest name, his true name.

When it was dark enough, the moon and stars shrouded by cloud cover, he stepped onto the windowsill. He coiled the power in his legs and, with no hesitation, dove from the tower. He opened his wings wide, gliding over the peaks and gables of the grand drakine houses on the slope of the long-dead volcano of the Citadel. He flew out over the ocean, the wind wrapping him in its embrace. When he was far enough from the shore, he shed his preterit form and became his full self once more.

When he was sure no human ears would hear, Ammil, the former last male dragon, opened his jaws and roared.

48. EVEREN: LEFT IN THE DARK

My prison cave has two small holes in the ceiling, like a pair of eyes. I lie in the twin patches of sunlight during the day, desperate for the warmth that will flee with the fading light. At night, I crane my neck. When the moon is in the center of one of the holes, it is white and luminous as one of Miligrist's eyes.

Cassia or one of the other dragons drop wrapped parcels of stringy meat or lower pails of water at regular intervals. I stay in preterit both to conserve my energy and because the space is too small for my full form. None of the dragons are allowed to speak to me, but my sister took pity on me. A cheap ream of pounded reed paper, a quill and ink, lowered when no one else would see. It is a paltry apology, but I am not too proud to resist it.

I spend my days writing to you. Though I have kept my script as small as possible and in a cipher my sister hopefully would not break in moments were she to read it, I will soon run out. With only my own thoughts for company, I wonder how long it will take me to grow mad. Yet time does heal, as much as I might not wish it to. Parts of me are less torn. The bond is still a black, bleeding scab where once it was pure, golden light. Will it eventually become a knotted scar?

My fingers have bled from trying to climb the walls toward those eyes. The cavern is too narrow to even stretch my wings in preterit properly. When I fell and bruised my side, the fight fled me. Now, I sit. I write. I wait. Already, I am not sure how long I have been down here. One moon? Two? Three?

At night, I stare into the darkness, hoping for a vision. Just before I fell for the second time, all had made sense. I had felt the rightness of it. I had seen the past, present, and future intertwined. Everything my kind had wanted for me. I had been one with all of creation. In that moment, I had truly felt a god.

It had lingered when I'd fallen through the storm. It had been tempting to stay in between. The storm was outside of time. The wraiths had fled—or been called back. That larger presence I'd sensed was gone. There was only silence. Only peace.

Fate had told me I was not yet done, though, so I had guided the dragons through that liminal space and back home. Even my mother had swallowed her pride and, wing beat by wing beat, she and the surviving dragons had come back with me—Boreal emerged first, then my mother, badly injured. Glisten had died back in the human world, and Feith never emerged from the storm.

I was back where I had begun. Vere Celene had lain below me, unchanged. I'd felt the smothering heat on my scales, the unrelenting sun. I had flown back to the cliffs, flanked by dragons. When I had landed, I had not resisted. My mother was whisked away so the healers could pull the crossbolt from her shoulder. She had not even given me a backward look.

I had let them throw me into my prison. I had barely registered my surroundings, for I had been torn in two. What tatters remained had been somewhere else, yearning for two things. For you, and for that moment of perfect understanding. For that unshakable belief that everything was happening just as it should.

Fate, meanwhile, faded once more. There were no further visions. Even the details of what I had seen had dwindled. I was again only one person, one speck of such a larger understanding. Instead, there was—there is—only the pain of loneliness.

The Reek still smokes on the horizon, and every breath tastes of ash. At night the orange-red glow is almost like a second sun. It has not erupted.

Not yet.

I do not know what to do next. Stay here, letting solitude sink its hooks deeper into me? I wonder if I will die down here, and if I do, whether you will feel it.

This breaking needed to happen, though I cannot remember why, exactly. It does not make it hurt any less, but I must believe that starfire will guide us true.

You dreamed of me for years, and now, I dream of you.

I am not sure if they are real or only a comfort. I watch you, hunched over books and studying. You stare into the fire often, holding a cup of tea, while Kelwyn speaks to you. You look thin, and wan, but also determined.

I write this now because I awoke from another dream. You had put on your best robes and pinned jewels in your ears and made your way to the Citadel. It was summer there, and obviously sweltering, though nothing compared to here. You waited with other hopeful students with pinched faces as, one by one, you were called forward to prove your worth to a panel of stone-faced professors. I watched you reach for your magic, effortless in a way I had never seen. First, you cycled through various faces, as quickly as you could—strangers that you must have touched at a marketplace. The professors made Their notes. I thought of them as you would—with respect. Next, you had asked permission to touch Them, promising to immediately perform the spell to forget Their forms once you finished. They nodded, interest piqued. Few would be so bold.

You touched the backs of Their hands, one by one. The shifting began: you took an eye each. Another's nose. The last's mouth. A chimera of different features. You held it for a few seconds before you let the form go. You gasped and immediately ate a sweetsphere, sweat dampening your brow. But it had worked. You had caught Their attention.

You ate another and spoke the spell to forget their shapes, and then the interview began. You answered every question without pause, with confidence. You said you wished to learn how to hone your Kalsh magic. That you wanted to have at least a rudimentary handle on all five types of magic. And I had no doubt you could. You had some of a dragon's power, after all. Had you tried to light a candle without your seal and found you could?

My magic is diminished, though with time, it might return. For magic is everywhere, in everything, even in Vere Celene. In blades of grass, in the movements of the waves, or within sun-warmed stone. Magic is everywhere, and if there was one thing I remember from my strike of fate, it is that it longs for balance.

◇◇◇◇◇◇◇◇◇

It is a few hours later. My hands are shaking so badly I can barely write the words. I woke up, my belly hollow with hunger. I tried to will myself back to sleep, but as I drifted, I heard the most welcome sound in the world. So soft, I worried I imagined it. A chime.

I heard it again. I hear it now.

A fleck of gold sparks in my chest. I am still trapped, deep underground, hated by my people, and I will probably be killed when they can no longer spare the meat to keep me fed. And yet I am smiling.

I have written all of this, thinking you never would, never could read it. That we would spend the rest of our days separated, with you hating me, and me missing you and hating myself.

Some tiny part of you is still with me, Arcady. It cannot be dampened, not through time, or distance, or even worlds.

Even the tiniest cinder can be nursed back into a flame.

I make my promise, here and now, on this last sheaf of paper: I will find my way back to you, my one human, and I will do whatever it takes for you to forgive me.

Our story is not yet finished.

ACKNOWLEDGMENTS

There are always so many people to thank for helping bring a book into the world. This might be my ninth published work (what?), but it feels like every time, you're learning how to write again for the first time.

I wrote the bulk of *Dragonfall* in lockdown and wanted an escape, but I have had bits of the book idea bouncing around my head since 2018. While I love it, I also whined about it . . . a lot. So, here are the people who put up with said whining very well, with my thanks:

Craig, who had to listen to many a plot wobble whether he wanted to or not and helped me solve more than few. My mom, Sally Baxter. Other people who read bits or offered moral support: Hannah Kaner, Erica Harney, P.M. Freestone, Noelle Harrison, Becky Sweeney, Ally Kersel, David Bishop, L.D. Lapinski, Brittany Kokaya, Riley Klabunde, Elizabeth May, Julia Ember, Jay Martin, and Eris Young. To the red wizard, Seumas MacDonald, linguist extraordinaire, who created the Celenian in the book and did an excellent job. Thanks to the Cymera crew who were most excellent wingmen hyping up "sexy dragons": Kate Dylan, C.L. Clark, Saara El-Arifi, Kat Dunn, Samantha Shannon, and Tasha Suri. To all the author friends who met me in cafes and the students at Napier who listened to me share my progress with them. I'm probably forgetting someone obvious and will remember later, mortified, so if I do I'll buy you a drink.

To Adam and everyone at Argonaut Books, especially, for all their support, coffees, and guarding my phone if I needed freedom from distractions. Dougal helped me with an early version of the map. To Nick and Hideout Café, for the same, and those at Artisan Roast in Leith and Bruntsfield.

A huge thank you to my publishing team: my agent Juliet Mushens and Mushens Entertainment's Kiya Evans and Liza DeBlock. To my editors: Leah Spann, who saw promise in what in retrospect was a very ropey draft, and Katie Hoffman who ushered it to the world. To Molly Powell, who snapped it up right quick in the UK and was incredibly thorough in edits, and the book is all the stronger for it. The rest of the Hodderscape team: Natasha Qureshi, Kate Keehan, Sophie Judge, and the rest of the DAW team: Betsy Wollheim, Joshua Starr, Sarah Christensen Fu, Jordan Snowden, and everyone else who worked on *Dragonfall*. Another burst of gratitude to Micaela Alcaino for such a beyond gorgeous cover. To Deven Rue for the beautiful map that was a total author bucket list item. A map! Of a world I made up in my head!

As my dedication states, I'd again like to thank the fantasy authors I read growing up, for providing such a wonderful threshold to others worlds. Some of the influences for Dragonfall came from Robin Hobb's Realm of the Elderlings, Anne McCaffrey's Pern, Mercedes Lackey's Valdemar, N.K. Jemisin's The Broken Earth (particularly for giving me the confidence to try and be a little more experimental with narrative position), Rachel Hartman's *Seraphina*, Samantha Shannon's Roots of Chaos, and many more. Also a shoutout to the Russian film *I Am Dragon*, which is one of my top comfort movies. It has a lot of parallels to *Dragonfall*, but at least half of them were coincidental!

And, lastly, thank you to everyone who enjoys falling for Arcady, Everen, Sorin, and Cassia. I hoped you enjoyed your time in the Lumet and will follow them on their next adventure.